check this out."
—Publishers Weekly

"Packed full of fiery exchanges and passionate embraces, this is for those who prefer their Regencies on the scandalous side."
—Library Journal

INFAMOUS

"Realistically transforming the Regency equivalent of a mean girl into a relatable, all-too-human heroine is no easy feat, but Spencer (Outrageous, 2021) succeeds on every level.
Lightly dusted with wintery holiday charm, graced with an absolutely endearing, beetle-obsessed hero and a fully rendered cast of supporting characters and spiked with smoldering sensuality and wry wit, the latest in Spencer's Rebels of the Ton series is sublimely satisfying."
—Booklist STARRED review

"Perfect for fans of Bridgerton, Infamous is also a charming story for Christmas. In fact, I enjoyed Infamous so much that when I was halfway through it, I ordered the author's first novel, Dangerous. I look forward to reading much more of Minerva Spencer's work."
—THE HISTORICAL NOVEL SOCIETY

Praise for Minerva Spencer's *Outcasts* series:

"Minerva Spencer's writing is sophisticated and wickedly witty. Dangerous is a delight from start to finish with swashbuckling action, scorching love scenes, and a coolly arrogant hero to die for. Spencer is my new auto-buy!"
-NYT Bestselling Author **Elizabeth Hoyt**

"[SCANDALOUS] *is] A standout....Spencer's brilliant and original tale of the high seas bursts with wonderfully real protagonists, plenty of action, and passionate romance."*
★*Publishers Weekly STARRED REVIEW*

"Fans of Amanda Quick's early historicals will find much to savor."
★*Booklist STARRED REVIEW*

The Language of Love

Minerva Spencer
writing as S.M. LAVIOLETTE

Crooked
Sixpence
**CS
P**
Press

CROOKED SIXPENCE BOOKS are published by
CROOKED SIXPENCE PRESS

2 State Road 230
El Prado, NM 87529

First printing December 2021

10 9 8 7 6 5 4 3 2 1

Photo stock by Period Images
Printed in the United States of America

Prologue

Henry hurried as fast as he could down the freezing, gloomy corridor.

Well, as fast as a man with an almost painful erection *could* hurry.

Man? Ha!

He gritted his teeth and ignored the scoffing laughter of his companion. His *imaginary* companion.

Nobody else will be your friend, so I'd watch my tone if I were you, my boy …

Henry wasn't crazy; he knew the voice in his head that abused him every day wasn't a friend—imaginary or otherwise. It was worse than that: it was his own mind that hurled constant invective and undermined what little self-confidence he managed to generate.

One would hope that if one had to endure a mental companion that it would at least be convivial and supportive.

He snorted softly at the foolish thought, his eyes darting curiously about the corridor as he made his way through the night. This was a part of Stoke Castle that he'd only visited once before, when he'd been a mere lad of seven and had wandered by mistake into the *family* wing.

The beating he'd received as soon as he'd been apprehended had ensured that Henry avoided this section of the building for nine long years.

But this time was different. This time, he wasn't wandering into a place where he wasn't welcome. This time he'd been… *invited.*

By Julia.

Merely thinking her name made Henry's already hard cock twitch.

You'd best calm yourself or your exciting evening will be over before it gets started.

1

Henry scowled but refused to be drawn into a pointless argument. Not only did he always lose, but he was too close to Julia's room to even think straight.

Ahead was the last turn on his long journey from the servants' quarters to his uncle's ward's bedchambers.

When Henry reached the door handle marked by a pink ribbon, he paused.

His heart was pounding so loudly that it was astounding the entire house couldn't hear it. He needed to calm down. If he went to her now, he'd go off all over himself just looking at her.

This was his chance. His *one* opportunity to prove that he was worthy of her. Lady Julia was not only the daughter of a duke, she was also the most beautiful girl in the history of Britain.

And she wanted *him*, Henry Singleton—the bastard get of a disgraced younger son and a chambermaid.

He took several deep breaths and then let himself into the room just as she'd instructed.

Henry paused on the threshold and squinted into the chamber beyond, which was even darker than the corridor.

"Come in and shut the door—hurry."

Henry startled at the loud whisper and did as she bade him, the action cutting off the bit of light from the sconces in the hallway.

"I can't see anything," he whispered, even that sound unnaturally loud in the quiet room.

"Take two steps forward and then turn right and keep walking until you encounter my b-bed."

Henry smiled to himself when she stammered on the word *bed*. Until then, he'd been feeling like the only one who was nervous about what they were doing.

"Did you see anyone on your way up?" she asked as he carefully paced out her directions.

"No." He barked his shin on something hard and gave a muffled yelp.

"Shhh."

Henry frowned into the darkness. "It's not like I wanted to hit my leg."

"Where are you?" she hissed.

"I'm at the foot of your bed, I think."

He heard the rustling of bedding, and then a warm, soft hand touched his. "Remove your clothes."

"Wh-what?" It was his turn to stammer.

"We can hardly do it if you are clothed." She paused and then added, "You *have* done this before, I hope?"

Her mocking tone made his face scald. "Of course, I have."

"Well, take them off."

"All of them?" he asked, still hesitating. He hadn't taken anything off when he'd *done it* before, and he'd *done it* plenty. Albeit with other servants and not a noble lady.

"Henry…" she whispered, her soft voice making every hair on his body stand up. "Don't you want to feel my bare skin on yours?"

"*Gunph.*" The inarticulate sound slipped from his mouth before he could catch it. His cock, which had already been leaking, went off like a fountain in his breeches.

Henry groaned and clutched the footboard of the bed while his climax boiled from his aching bollocks.

"*Shhhhhh!*"

He was in no condition to argue.

"What are you doing, Henry?"

Henry somehow doubted she'd appreciate the answer to that question, so he gritted his teeth and willed away the mind-numbing pleasure as his fingers fumbled with the catches and buttons of his placket, toeing off his boots with leaden, clumsy feet. It was embarrassing and unfortunate, but it was so dark that she would never know what happened.

Hopefully.

By the time Henry tossed his shirt onto the floor, he'd nearly regained control of his extremities. His cock, ever willing, was almost up to full mast again.

"Henry, if you don't get in here now, you'll need—"

He climbed up onto the bed, and Julia gave a startled grunt. Henry patted the bedding. "Where are you? I can't—"

Her ear-splitting scream was all the more shocking for the leaden quiet that suffused the darkness.

Henry gave a mortifying yelp and flung himself backward, like a shrimp scooting away from a predator. He was so close to the foot of the bed that he toppled off the end and landed flat on his back.

Julia screamed again and this time he had no breath left in his lungs to either squawk or demand what the hell was wrong.

The door flew open and the light from the corridor—which had seemed crepuscular when he'd made his way up—now blazed like the sun at midday.

"*What* is going on in here?" his cousin's voice bellowed.

Henry was vaguely aware of Julia's weeping, cloth-shrouded figure darting from the bed toward the door. "I woke up to find him on t-t-top of me, Charles! And he's n-naked!"

By that point, Henry was actually grateful that he couldn't speak.

I told you, the voice in his head gleefully crowed. *I told you it was some sort of trick.*

Henry couldn't argue—even if he'd been capable of it.

"Get dressed you—you—*disgusting* swine!" Charles flung Henry's scattered boots and garments at him.

"What's going on?" a new voice demanded.

Ah yes, his cousin Edmund.

Henry laughed, although it came out a choked, garbled sound.

"Henry sneaked into Julia's room and—well, you can see what the degenerate pig had in mind. I said get dressed," Charles shouted again.

Finally able to draw a breath, Henry pushed himself up until he was sitting, ignoring the shouting and accusations coming from the doorway, which was now at his back.

He fished his shirt out of the tangled pile and pulled it on first.

The farce was almost finished, lacking only one actor to make Henry's humiliation complete.

As if on cue, his Uncle Robert's—the Earl of Rotherhithe—voice came from out in the corridor, "What the devil is this commotion?"

"Henry sneaked into Julia's room and tried to force himself on her." Charles's voice was almost as deep and commanding as his father's, even though he was only a year older than Henry—whose own voice was still prone to squawks and squeaks.

Julia sobbed louder and gave a little shriek when Henry stood, his bare arse pointed in her direction while he struggled into his breeches.

"Take her out of here, you fool," Uncle Robert said.

Julia's sobbing and his cousins' soothing voices faded, along with their footsteps.

"Hurry up," his uncle ordered.

Henry shrugged into his vest and coat. When he sat to pull on his stockings and boots his uncle said, "Carry those and follow me."

Out into the corridor he saw the steel gray hair of his Great Aunt Millicent in one doorway, her cap askew as she stared wide-eyed at the activity.

"Rotherhithe, what is—"

"Go back to bed, Millicent," the earl barked.

The door shut immediately, as did the others that had opened—all rooms occupied by various aged relatives who lived off the bounty of the head of their family, the Earl of Rotherhithe. All *Henry's* aunts and uncles, although not even one of them had ever acknowledged him in twelve years.

As they passed from the family wing into the part of the house where his uncle kept his study, other heads appeared—servant heads.

Henry's people.

He ground his teeth when he saw Mrs. Jenkins, the housekeeper and also the woman who had raised him, although he would never have called her *mother*.

"My lord?" she asked, pulling a fleecy gray shawl around her heavy flannel dressing gown. "Is aught amiss."

"Go pack the boy's possessions," the earl snapped, not stopping to look at her. "Get cook to put together a bag of food and rouse Falkirk and tell him to prepare the gig. He will go to the village in one hour."

Mrs. Jenkins cut Henry a terrified glance but spun on her heel to obey her master's bidding.

The earl flung open the brass-strapped door to his study and stalked over to his massive desk.

Henry dropped into a chair and put on his stockings and boots, his mind numb, his body going through the motions.

He heard the jingle of keys and absently identified the sound of a drawer opening, the distinctive clang of his uncle's strong box, and then the squeak of his uncle's chair when it took his weight.

And then he heard the thud and dull *clink* of coins.

"This is all you will ever get from me."

Henry finished pulling on his second boot before looking up.

The earl scowled across at him. "You are a disgrace. I knew that, but I never suspected you were a rapist in the making."

Henry felt his lips curling into a mocking smirk but was helpless to stop them.

"You think that's amusing, do you?"

Henry didn't say a word.

"You'll take this," he nudged the small leather purse across his desk, "and you'll take the ride to the village I'm offering. There is enough to buy passage to just about anywhere in the world and money to feed you for a month or two when you get there. What you do is up to you—starve if you like. But you will never, ever return to these shores. If you do, I will have you arrested and thrown into the deepest darkest cell in the worst prison I can find. I will see you charged with rape and you will *hang*. Don't think I fear shaming the Singleton name too much to do it, boy. Now, get the hell out of my sight. You sicken me."

Henry stood, turned, and strode toward the door.

"Boy! You've forgotten your money."

Henry stopped and turned back to his uncle—a man who'd never once acknowledged him as blood or given him a kind look or friendly word in over a decade.

"You keep it, Uncle. From the way you've been hitting the tables this past year, I'm guessing you'll need it more than I will."

"*Insolent bastard of a whore!*" the earl thundered, surging to his feet.

Henry swallowed down the pain and fury at this familiar accusation—although in the past it had always come from his cousins, rather than his uncle—and then he turned and strode out of his uncle's study.

He didn't go to the kitchen as ordered and he didn't wait for the gig to be ready. And he didn't say goodbye to a single soul.

All he did before leaving was make a quick stop in the cell-like room he'd inhabited for over a decade. He shrugged on his heavy coat, lifted the mattress to collect the money he'd earned over the past few years doing odd jobs, and pocketed the battered locket with miniatures of his dead parents.

Rather than leave through the front or servant entrance, he used the door hidden in the armory, so he wouldn't have to encounter anyone else on his way out of the house.

It was still pitch dark when he left Stoke ten minutes later fueled by a profound sense of misuse and a seething determination to never, ever, return to this place or these people who'd done nothing but reject and shame him.

Henry walked toward his unknown—and terrifying—future without so much as a backward glance.

Chapter 1

Twenty Years Later
The Village of Cocklesham

Annis kept reading and re-reading the letter from Mr. Pears, Grandmamma's man of business, as if repeated readings might magically alter its contents.

"Annis, darling? *Annis?*"

She looked up. "Hmm?"

"What is it, my dear?" Lady Cecily reached out a thin, bone-white hand to feel the air around her.

"Um…" For a woman who'd taught languages at a young ladies' academy for five years, Annis could not seem to string two words together in her native tongue.

Her grandmother's cloudy eyes—once a vivid, periwinkle blue like Annis's—blinked up at her, both blind and blindly trusting. She had trusted Annis to decipher this letter for her just as she had trusted Annis to manage the rest of her business since gradually losing her vision over the last eight years.

Annis had repaid her trust by bringing Richard Leech into their lives and giving him access to their house and everything they owned, not to mention her own person.

"Are you unwell, my dear?"

Annis gracelessly dropped onto the ottoman, no longer able to stand. "I am well," she lied. "Just a little fatigued."

"You sound breathless." Lady Cecily rang the bell she kept beside her chair. A bell that probably even now belonged to the creditors referenced in the letter Annis was holding.

The door opened so swiftly that Mary, her grandmother's maid, must have been listening on the other side.

And why not? Annis thought, *I've destroyed her life as well.* After all, what work could a servant nearing seventy find?

"You rang, my lady?" Mary asked.

"Please fetch the hartshorn for my granddaughter."

Annis shook herself out of her daze. "No hartshorn, Grandmamma, really." She smiled at Mary. "But tea would be lovely."

Lady Cecily squinted her sightless eyes at Annis for a long moment before nodding. "Very well. It seems tea will suffice, Mary."

"Very good, my lady."

The door closed, and her grandmother turned to her again. "What does Mr. Pears have to say in his letter, my dear?"

Annis opened her mouth to tell her grandmother the truth, but, as so often happened in her life, something entirely different came out.

"It seems there have been more losses than he expected, but he says not to worry as such Exchange fluctuations are common now that the war is over." She bit her lip as she considered her next untruth. "He asks that I go to London at my earliest convenience to sign some papers as your proxy."

And so I can fall to my knees and beg for mercy.

Her grandmother's smile illuminated her delicate features. "Oh, you are so good to me, Annis," she said, her words like knives. "I know how tiresome a journey to town can be, but you will see your friends—Lady Sedgwick, Honoria Keyes, and that clever woman who works with stone—what was her name, again?"

"Serena Lombard," she answered woodenly. "But she no longer lives with Freddie—she is married and lives with her husband. So is Honoria, who is now Lady Saybrook."

"Oh yes! That's right. So many lovely weddings in such a short time."

Annis could only imagine how the friends her grandmother was referring to would react if she were to confess how she'd been charmed by a scheming thief who'd forged her name on financial documents and robbed her grandmother's friends.

Using Annis as his unwitting accomplice.

Annis squeezed her eyes shut, ashamed of how nightmarish and damning it sounded when she laid it all out like that.

Don't forget to mention the fact that he robbed <u>you</u> of your virginity.

As if she *could* forget.

"Annis? *Annis?*"

9

She looked up to find her grandmother frowning in confusion. "I beg your pardon, Grandmamma, what was that?"

"I said you should pay a call on that son of mine while you are in London."

Annis was grateful her grandmother couldn't see her grimace. Lady Cecily's only living child was Thomas Bowman, a man as different from Annis's dear deceased papa as the proverbial chalk from cheese.

The idiom caught her attention like a briar snagging clothing: *As different as chalk from cheese.*

She *knew* this idiom.

Annis's fingers drummed on the faded blue muslin that covered her knee as she dredged her memory for the expression's origin. It was Middle English—of that she was certain—

"Annis, dear? Are you there?" Her grandmother was turning her head to-and-fro, as if she could actually see the tiny parlor around her.

"I'm sorry, Grandmamma, I was just thinking about the journey," she lied—yet again. "I'm afraid I didn't catch the last thing you said."

"I said you should accept your uncle's offer to frank you this Season." Lady Cecily frowned, deepening the grooves that bracketed her mouth. "Your aunt is not always an agreeable woman, but she will be frantic to marry off those girls and will drag them about madly this Season."

All the more reason that Aunt Agnes wouldn't want an impoverished niece trailing along. But Annis didn't point that out.

"I will call on them, Grandmamma." She shuddered at the thought of subjecting herself to a frosty half hour with her aunt and her unmarried daughters—Susanna and Miriam—and the horrid, spoiled heir, Percy.

Lady Cecily sighed. "I know I shouldn't mention it, but I'd had such hopes for Mr. Leech. He was such a *nice* young man, and I thought you were rather taken with him. Oh, not that I would have liked losing you to him, my dear. And it would have grieved me if you'd had to move to Yorkshire once you married, but…" The old lady let the thought fade away.

The Language of Love

Yes, Annis, too, had liked kind, handsome Mr. Leech. She'd like him so much that she'd entrusted him with *everything* they had

She was *such* a fool!

It was all Annis could do not to fling herself at her grandmother's feet and confess all. But that would spread her misery to a person who had done nothing to earn it, even though she'd suffered the most damage.

Annis swallowed back her tears, shame, and rage. What point was there in wishing she'd behaved differently? Wallowing in pity, that is what that would be. She needed to fix things, not wallow.

And to fix things, she'd need money: £11,072.

Annis bit her lip hard enough to draw blood just *thinking* about the amount.

There was only one way for a woman of gentle birth to get that much money quickly: she must marry a rich man. And she'd need to do so quickly. It was the only way to ensure that her grandmother did not end up in some wretched home for the blind or insane—which is where her aunt would likely try to put poor Lady Cecily.

If anyone could find a husband for Annis, it would be her Aunt Agnes—a woman who was as pragmatic and ruthless as an army general. The type of man her aunt would find for her was not to be thought about. After all, beggars couldn't be choosers.

She almost smiled at the idiom—of mid-sixteenth century origin.

"I have decided I will accept my uncle's offer," Annis announced—making it sound as if she'd been giving it a great deal of thought and had not just decided thirty seconds ago.

Her grandmother's smile illuminated the room. "I *am* glad to hear you say that. You are a beautiful, accomplished young woman with a loving nature. I know my son and his family can be trying, but Agnes will help you find the husband you deserve, my dear."

Annis folded the letter, her grandmother's words ringing in her ears: *you will find the man you deserve.*

She shivered at the thought of what kind of man she deserved. Her—a woman so foolish that she'd given the nest egg of the person she loved most in the world to a vile, thieving imposter?

No, if there was one thing Annis knew for certain, it was that she *never* wanted to meet the man she deserved.

Two Weeks Later, London, The Clarendon Hotel

Henry Singleton, the seventh Earl of Rotherhithe, sipped fine claret and surveyed the opulent hotel dining room.

Even though the Clarendon held the same white faces that you'd see at any Company gathering in Calcutta or Dacca, the people here looked untried and delicate.

But Henry knew that was an illusion. There was no creature on earth more resilient and minacious than a member of the English upper class, especially when it came to hounding and harrying those people they believed did not deserve to be among their number.

People like Henry, in other words.

Colin Parker raised his glass, as if eager to match Henry sip for sip. "This sounds like a jolly good lark you've come up with," Colin said. "But I should think you'll be lucky to have even half a Season before the jig is up, my lord."

Henry leaned across the table, the sudden movement making his nitwit of an employee recoil. "I shall be exposed before this bloody meal is over if you do not remember to call me Parker, *my lord.*"

Color flamed in the real Colin Parker's miraculously pale cheeks. How the devil the man had stayed so unmarked by the brutal Indian sun after living in Dacca for almost four years was a mystery to Henry.

"But—" Colin bit his lower lip, eying Henry like a rodent eyed a cobra.

"Yes, my lord?" Henry asked in as gentle and patient a tone as he could muster after seven solid hours in the other man's company.

"Er, why must I address you as Parker even when we are alone, um, Parker?"

"Because you never know who might be listening, my lord," Henry said. *Not to mention you have less sense than a leg of mutton and need all the bloody practice you can get.*

The raven-haired, blue-eyed Adonis across from him grinned in sudden comprehension and gave Henry an exaggerated wink. "Ah, yes, my—erm, Parker. Quite so, quite so. Could be lurkers everywhere." He whipped his head from side to side, surveying the room through slitted, suspicious eyes before turning back to Henry and leaning over the table, his right sleeve grazing the butter dish in the process. "But, my—er, Parker, aren't you worried somebody you knew in India might recognize you here?"

"I've not socialized outside Dacca in almost seven years," Henry reminded him as calmly as he could—which took some effort since they'd discussed this same topic only the day before. And the day before that.

He continued, "And I haven't been to Calcutta above twice in the past ten years and then only for business. I *rarely* attended Company functions if I could help it. Nobody there knew who my father was, and I told no one I was in line to inherit an earldom. Indeed, I never even mentioned my relationship to the Earl of Rotherhithe. So, no—I don't believe there is much to worry about, my lord."

Colin's brow cleared. "Er, yes. Quite so." He coughed and added in a low voice, "Parker."

Henry couldn't help being amused at the man's attempt to imitate Henry's lower and slightly raspy voice; it put him in mind of a puppy trying to imitate a wolf. Still, Colin Parker was trying.

In all senses of the word.

"By my lor—er, Parker," Colin whispered loudly, "What if somebody who knew you *before* you left England sees and remembers you? Surely your family would recognize you?"

"No."

Colin flinched like a scolded spaniel at the harsh monosyllabic answer.

Henry relented. "My *family*"—he said the word as if it left a foul taste in his mouth. Because it did—"live in Yorkshire. Even before I left for India, none of them came to London."

Not because they hadn't wanted to, but because they were all too bloody skint.

But Colin didn't need to know that. His brain was already cluttered enough.

Henry saw Colin was still staring at him, confusion marring his perfect features.

"Besides," Henry added. "It's been twenty years since I last saw any of them. They all knew of me, of course, but I doubt more than one or two of them would recognize me."

One of them being Julia, the duplicitous bitch who'd married his cousin Charles—the late earl—and the other being Edmund, Henry's slimy heir presumptive.

Thinking about his least favorite people in the world caused Henry's lips to curl into a smile that made poor Colin recoil.

Julia was the reason that Henry had sworn never to marry, and Edmund—ironically—was the reason that Henry would put aside his twenty-year vow and actually consider taking a wife.

Because he'd be goddamned if he died and left the earldom— no matter how impoverished—to bloody Edmund.

Henry looked up from his vengeful musing to find Colin regarding him with a pensive stare. "Not only has it been twenty years, my lord, but you need to understand just how it was for me in my uncle's household." He leaned toward Colin. "I would like to explain this only once, my lord. Are you listening?"

Colin's eyes widened, and his Adam's apple bobbed.

"I was the orphaned son of my uncle's disgraced, dead younger brother. The earl cast my father out of the house—out of the family— and told him never to return." He smiled unpleasantly. "So, I'm sure you can imagine how thrilled his lordship was to have me dropped on his doorstep a mere five years later, after my father died. Are you following me, my lord?"

"Yes, P-Parker."

"The earl didn't send me to school like he did his son, Charles, or my other cousin Edmund. In fact, I didn't step foot out of bloody Yorkshire from the day I arrived there at barely five until I left it at sixteen. For the entire eleven years, 8 months, three weeks, and two days that I lived with my uncle he never introduced me to anyone outside the *family*," again he spat the word. "Indeed, he never publicly acknowledged me as his nephew. I spent the entirety of my childhood living in the servant hall, under the care of Mrs. Jenkins, his housekeeper."

In retrospect, that might have been the only kind thing his uncle ever did for him. While Mrs. Jenkins had never loved him, she had never been cruel to him. She had merely treated Henry as another of her duties rather than a child requiring love and affection. His treatment at her hands had been *far* kinder than anything he'd received from his uncles and aunts, his cousins, or his uncle's lovely ward, Lady Julia Tybald.

Lady Julia. Henry snorted. He'd met back-alley robbers who behaved in a more *lady*like fashion than the former love of his life.

Thoughts of the duke's daughter who'd once broken his heart, ground it under her dainty foot, and then driven a stake through it made Henry more determined than ever to enjoy a little entertainment at the expense of the *ton*.

Henry continued his pitiful tale, "I grew up in the servants' quarters, played with servants' children, and associated only with servants and farm laborers until the day I left. So, *my lord,* unless some lads from the stables—or perhaps the kitchen wench who relieved me of my troublesome virginity when I was fourteen—pop up in a London ballroom, I doubt I'll have to worry about running into anyone I know."

Colin looked like he might weep and Henry cursed himself for terrifying the poor man, who'd be a useless, nervous wreck if Henry could not curb his temper when he spoke to him.

"Take a deep breath, my lord—take several."

Colin obeyed. Once he'd finished, he opened his mouth, but then closed it again.

"Ask me questions if you need to," Henry encouraged. "Now is the time."

"So… you're doing all this just for a lark?"

"I'm not engaging in this deception *solely* for amusement." Although that motivation—as immature as it was—was certainly a big part of it.

"Oh?"

Henry ground his teeth, hating that he had to admit this next part. "I'm also doing it because I wish—no," he corrected, "because I *need* to marry."

"But… er, wouldn't more women want to marry you if they knew you were a downy lord?"

For once, poor Colin made sense.

15

"While that is certainly true, it is also true that many would want to marry me *only* because I'm a rich peer. I'm being forced to marry, but at least I'd like to marry a woman who isn't a fortune hunter."

Colin nodded, but Henry could see that he still didn't understand.

"I'm engaging in this farce because nobody pays attention to servants or what they say in front of them." Something Henry knew well from personal experience. "I will learn more about the ladies and gentlemen of the *ton* as a servant—from other servants and from listening in on masters and mistresses—than I ever would as a feted and petted wealthy lord." He briefly showed his teeth. "I don't have high hopes of finding a wife in this aristocratic snake pit, but if there *is* a decent woman lurking in the *ton,* this deception is the best way to ferret her out."

Henry took a deep drink of wine, set down his glass, and continued, "Stop worrying about whether anyone recognizes me, my lord. Remember, whether or not I am discovered, you'll get your money for the entire time *and* a position at Leadenhall Street."

A posting in the Company's home office was something a man like Colin could never hope to acquire without the proper patronage—especially after being sacked from his clerk position in India. With Henry's name and money behind him, it wouldn't matter that Colin Parker had the wits of a turnip and the social skills of a warthog: Henry's influence would get him a job.

Whether he could keep it would be up to him.

"Won't these people hate you when they eventually discover how you've fooled them all?" Colin asked.

Henry laughed. "I sure as hell hope they do."

"But… but why would you want such a thing?"

He didn't bother answering the question because Colin would never understand. Instead, he said, "Yes, they will hate me, but my immense wealth will ensure they get over their revulsion quickly enough—or at least learn to hide it." The best part of this whole escapade would be watching the exalted members of the *ton* swallow their distaste and toad-eat him, even after he'd made fools of them all.

The Language of Love

Henry regarded Colin's baffled expression and wished, yet again, that there'd been *any* other man he could have engaged for this unusual position. But his choices had been extremely limited. Not only had Colin been desperately in need of a job, but he was returning to England—where he was unknown in *ton* circles; he was thirty-three—four years Henry's junior, but close enough; he was unattached; and he was exceedingly handsome.

That last quality wasn't a necessity, but the man's heroic good looks would make what Henry thought of as *The Great Earl Lottery* a hell of a lot more entertaining.

At first, it had amused Henry to think of releasing this handsome but clownish man upon the *ton* and watching their members scramble to curry his favor.

But his amusement had faded as he'd comprehended the sheer magnitude of Colin Parker's ignorance: the man had spent four years in India and couldn't identify Dacca on a map! Not only was he as thick as a plank, but he was also willfully ignorant and casually bigoted. Of course, one could say the same of at least half the men currently working for the Company and living in India.

Parker had also turned out to be the worst sailor in the history of humankind.

So, instead of spending their journey rehearsing for the approaching deception, Colin had spent every moment moaning in misery or puking into a basin. Henry hadn't been sure the man would actually make it to England alive.

They'd exchanged hardly a word during the long journey and barely knew each other. While that was certainly a godsend when it came to preserving Henry's sanity, it meant that Colin knew next to nothing about the man he was supposed to be impersonating: Henry, the *real* Earl of Rotherhithe.

Henry sighed and forced himself to smile at Colin. "Let's practice a bit before our next course arrives, my lord." Henry was as sick of the topic as the other man probably was, but it was the minimum Colin should know for the meeting they were to have later that day.

"How did you come to be in Dacca, my lord?" Henry asked for the fifth or sixth time that week.

"Erm, I went there by ship."

It took extreme self-control not to lash out.

Whatever Colin saw on Henry's face—insane rage? Despair?—seemed to jolt his memory. "Oh, yes, I remember now!" Colin snapped his fingers and the sharp crack caused several diners to turn and frown. "I received a letter from my father's business partner in Dacca."

Henry nodded and Colin visibly warmed to his subject and continued, "I was living in Yorkshire with my uncle—the Earl of Rotherhithe—and his five daughters." He grinned triumphantly.

Henry narrowed his eyes.

"Er, three daughters?"

"I thought your uncle had only the one son, Charles—"

Colin raised his hand in an obnoxious, halting gesture, an expression of intense concentration compressing his handsome features. "Wait, wait—I know this one. Yes, my cousin Charles, who was the last earl. He, er, died—about two years ago, now." He cut Henry a quick, hopeful look.

"I can't quite recall *how* he died. Do you, my lord?"

Colin worried his lower lip. "He got hit on the bone-box during a cricket match?"

"Close, my lord. He died ramming his mount into a rock wall while hunting."

Colin's eyes widened, as if he'd never heard the story before—rather than hearing it earlier in the day.

Fortunately, before Henry resorted to violence, the waiter arrived with more food.

"Oh! Yorkshire puddings—my favorite." Colin's grin stretched from ear to ear as he bounced up and down in his chair, his innocent enthusiasm causing Henry to feel churlish about being so short-tempered with him.

As he watched Colin enthuse over his meal, it boggled the mind to think what sort of work the man might have done for the Company. The only thing Colin seemed to have any expertise at—based on his boastful jabbering—was billiards and whoring.

Henry had witnessed Colin's unimpressive performance in the billiards room at Rotherhithe House last night.

The Language of Love

As to his whoring? Well, Henry thankfully had no personal knowledge of that, although he'd certainly had several opportunities. Instead, he'd twice vetoed Colin's request to visit a London brothel that *some mate* in Dacca had told him about. According to Colin, the brothel in question was the sort of place where a man could get up to *all sorts of bobbery.*

Henry shuddered to imagine.

"Do you suppose we might go see that waxwork thing today?" Colin asked. "I mean, after we've finished our cramming?" Parker chewed with his mouth open, *wide* open and quite full.

Henry's temperature rose.

You'd better take a damper, Henry. After all, it was your idea to engage in this deception.

Yes, it was his stupid idea; he clamped his jaws shut.

"You know the one I mean?" Parker persisted, undeterred by Henry's silence. "A mate of mine in Dacca saw her statues at the Lyceum."

If Henry had to hear the words, *a mate of mine* one more time, he would—

Colin waved his gravy-smeared knife in the air. "Damn name's *just* on the tip of my tongue."

Actually, it was roast beef that was on the tip of his tongue, along with a sizeable chunk of Yorkshire pudding.

"You *must* know who I mean, my lo—er, Parker. It's that old French crone who makes all those wax people—some bloody gory ones, I've heard." He paused to shove the better part of another pudding into his mouth.

"That would be Madam Tussaud, my lord. She is currently touring the country and not in London. And referring to her—or any woman—as a *crone* will not be well-received."

Parker guffawed, an action that sent a soggy chunk of pudding hurtling into his half-full wineglass.

Henry sighed and gestured for the waiter. "A fresh glass for his lordship," he told the gaping man, and then turned his attention to his untouched plate before he lost his temper.

He was bloody hungry. Since arriving in London they'd stayed at Rotherhithe House, but the cook Henry had hired via letter had scarpered upon seeing the state of the kitchen, so they'd been eating in various restaurants. He sawed off a chunk of rare roast beef and popped it into his mouth, smiling as he chewed; this was the first food he'd had in England that didn't taste like a packing crate.

Henry decided they would eat most of their meals at the hotel from now on. Hell, he'd *live* in the bloody hotel and leave Rotherhithe house to rot if such an action wouldn't appear so—

Colin snapped his fingers. *"I remember now! The factory my father and his partner owned made cloth of some sort."* He smiled at Henry, triumphant but wary.

Henry finished chewing and then swallowed his food before speaking, hoping to lead by example. "Interesting. So, my lord, why did you sell your interests?"

"Er …."

"Is it because the textile industry in India has quite fallen off in recent years?"

Colin gulped several times, sweat beading on his pale brow. "Er, yes, quite so. But then—" He stopped, a terrorized expression distorting his handsome features. "Wait—wait—I've got it." Yet again Colin snapped his fingers, forgetting he was holding his fork and sending the implement sailing over a nearby table, narrowly missing the ear of the elderly gentleman whose back was to them. The fork kept going and landed with a clatter on an unoccupied table.

"Oh, damn and blast," Colin muttered. His eyes darted back and forth between the empty table and several full ones, where diners had paused their eating to turn and stare.

His worried blue gaze finally slid to Henry. "Do you think they know it was me?"

Their waiter scurried over with a clean fork and laid it on the table beside Colin without a word.

Henry sighed and gestured to the nearly empty bottle on their table. "We're going to need another one of those."

Once the waiter departed, Henry turned to Colin. "We can resume this conversation later, my lord. After you've finished your dessert."

Colin had ordered a floating island and Henry trembled to think of the damage he could do with a spoon and custard.

Colin heaved a sigh of relief. "Oh, jolly good! My brain's gone a bit mushy. I say, can we look in on Whites today? A mate of mine—"

"We shan't have time." Not to mention Henry had no intention of putting his name up for membership at such a bastion of Toryism.

"Why not?" Colin demanded.

"Recall that you scheduled an appointment with Lady Winifred Sedgwick this afternoon."

"I did?" Colin's brow knitted. "Erm, who is she, again?"

"The Countess of Sedgwick is the woman you've hired to help you navigate the treacherous waters of the *ton*."

"Ah, yes, the marriage bawd."

Henry dropped his head into his hands. *Good. God.*

Colin's laughter made Henry look up.

The other man was grinning. "I was just having you on a bit, Parker. I know they are really called matchmakers, what?"

Henry sighed. "I'm sure she'll caution against plunging into things too quickly," he assured Colin—or was that more for himself? "We can wait a week before we enter the fray."

"I'd rather not wait a week—my, um, Parker. I'm better at learning on the job—hands-on, so to speak—and I'm not keen too keen on cramming. Studying ain't my strong suit."

Yes, I know.

"We could dive in today as far as I'm concerned," Colin declared with a frighteningly mindless smile. "I'm as fit as a fiddle and ready for frolics."

Henry bit his tongue. Hard.

"In fact," Colin went on, "this morning I was reading some of those invitations piled up in the library—"

Henry forbore to point out that it was *his* mail that Colin had opened and read.

"—and I found one for a whosy-whatsit—a party where you get to wear a costume."

"A masquerade," Henry supplied, dread blooming inside him.

"That's the one! Anyhow, I only got to wear a costume once— the Nativity, you know. I was an ass, along with my elder brother, Tommy."

21

"Is that so?" Henry asked, amused despite himself.

Colin nodded enthusiastically. "It was rather a cunning costume, two parts. But, erm, Tommy made me be the hind end, and I didn't see much for most of the evening."

"Ah."

"I thought maybe you and I could find a costume like that?"

Henry clamped his jaws shut. *Not. Bloody. Likely.*

Colin's eyes narrowed in thought. "Maybe a horse instead of an ass? And this time I'd get to be the front of the horse because, you know, I'm the earl." He grinned. When Henry didn't respond, Colin added, "Sounds rather a jolly lark, doesn't it, Parker?"

It sounded like a brand-new circle in Dante's Hell.

"So, what do you say?" Colin prodded. "Can we go? Can we, please?"

"I believe you are referring to the Palmer masquerade, which is tonight, my lord, and I doubt we shall be ready for that—even if we could locate a horse costume," Henry added placatingly.

Colin's eyebrows descended and his expression became downright mulish. "I *am* ready and I should *like* to go, Parker. Perhaps this Lady Sludgewit can—"

"Lady Sedgwick, my lord. And there will be *no masquerade* tonight."

Or ever.

Colin flinched at Henry's menacing hiss, swallowing a few times before nodding. "Er, yes, just so. I daresay she'll tell me I need a bit of spit and polish, what?"

"I daresay."

Colin's expression lightened. "But there will be other frisks with costumes—plenty of balls, routs, and the like?"

Henry nodded, an ache beginning in his head at the thought of such *frisks*.

Perhaps it was not too late to change his mind about this farce and flee back to Dacca as fast as his ship could carry him.

Chapter 2

Henry chose Lady Winifred Sedgwick as his matchmaker because he'd heard she was extraordinary when it came to finding suitable mates for the wealthy cits who were proliferating in a way that horrified the *ton*. He liked the idea of employing a woman who helped the merchant class penetrate the sacred inner circle of the beau monde.

The house the countess received them in was modest, but impeccably decorated. It was also a very feminine abode with no masculine imprint.

Colin was doing a fine job appearing the empty-headed charmer he was. He'd just finished mouthing some bosh about a new style of cravat while Lady Sedgwick regarded him with puzzlement. Henry could almost hear her thoughts: *how on earth had such a lackwit accumulated a substantial fortune?*

The door to the sitting room burst opened, and a girl entered, her attention fixed on her bonnet ribbon, which appeared to be wadded in a knot beneath her right ear. "This wretched thing," she muttered without looking up. "Will you help me, Freddie?" It wasn't a girl's voice at all, but that of a woman.

Colin, who'd been saying nothing of any importance, stopped talking and both men shot to their feet.

The motion snagged the newcomer's attention, and she glanced up, her blue eyes widening with mortification. "Oh, dear—I *am* sorry, Freddie, I didn't know you were with anyone." She turned as if to leave. "I shall just—"

Lady Sedgwick—or Freddie, an incongruous name for such an elegant woman—was already moving toward her. "Please, do come in, Annis." She turned to Colin, "Lord Rotherhithe, this is my dear friend, Miss Annis Bowman."

Colin bowed, his handsome face splitting into a fatuous grin. The way the younger man behaved around women—as if they were rare mythical beasts—made Henry doubt the veracity of Colin's boasts about his prodigious experience with prostitutes. Henry thought it more likely that he was England's oldest male virgin.

"I say, jolly good to meet you, er, Miss Bowman." Colin jerked her hand up and down like he was working a pump handle.

Lady Sedgwick's eyes flickered at Colin's gushing welcome, and Henry made a note to school his protégé in the art of exhibiting aristocratic ennui.

The countess turned to Henry, "This is Mr. Colin Parker, Lord Rotherhithe's—" A notch formed between her unusual slate-colored eyes.

"I am his lordship's temporary secretary." Henry could see his words surprised her. And well they should—what lord paid calls with his secretary in tow?

This was Colin's cue, and, for once, he hit his mark. "Parker is more than a secretary. He's also my good mate."

Henry shuddered at being included in that loathsome group.

"We met at school in—" Colin glanced at Henry, grimaced, and blundered on. "Well, it hardly signifies where the school was—and probably still is, I'm sure. What matters is that we go everywhere together. Positively joined at the hip, you might say. Ha ha, that's us, veritable twins." He chortled and everyone else stared.

"His lordship is very kind to me," Henry murmured, taking Miss Bowman's hand, which was as slight and delicate as spun glass. "Pleased to make your acquaintance, Miss Bowman."

She dropped an elegant curtsey and Henry looked down into huge blue eyes fringed with long but nearly invisible blonde lashes that gave her a startled aspect. She was, he realized, much older than she initially appeared, perhaps somewhere in her mid-twenties.

Her gown was well made but threadbare and out-of-fashion, the hem so heavy with dirt that she must have walked a great distance.

She wasn't exactly pretty, but striking in her own way. Henry had never seen such huge, limpid eyes. He felt like he was falling into them.

He shook himself, unnerved by the uncharacteristically fanciful thought.

A gentle tug on his fingers reminded him he'd not yet released her hand. When he did so, she took a step back.

"I was just going to ring for tea," Lady Sedgwick said, turning an inquiring eye on Colin. "If that would be agreeable to you, my lord?"

Miss Bowman removed the battered bonnet, exposing a poorly restrained mass of corn-silk colored hair.

Colin was staring at the fairy creature with his grin intact and did not appear to have heard the countess's question.

"Thank you, my lady," Henry said to Lady Sedgwick. "Tea would be most welcome."

If the countess thought it odd for an earl's secretary to make his lord's decisions for him, she gave no sign of it.

While Lady Sedgwick rang for a servant, Miss Bowman said to Colin, "You are new to your title, I understand?"

Colin nodded vigorously, a lock of glossy dark hair flopping on his forehead. "Indeed, so new I still squeak with it. *Squeak, squeak!*" He chuckled.

Miss Bowman's brow furrowed.

"The last earl died almost two years ago, Miss Bowman." Henry cut Colin a narrow-eyed look. *And the new one might not make it home tonight.*

"The Rotherhithe name is both ancient and revered," she said.

Colin's brows plunged like two ferrets diving off a cliff. "Er, is it?" He slid Henry a frantic look. "Fancy you knowing such a thing."

Henry smiled at the woman, but she was staring fixedly at Colin. "It's not so unusual, my lord. After all, everyone has heard of the Stoke Relics."

Colin's jaw sagged. For once, the other man's ignorance was Henry's fault. He'd not mentioned the damned relics because he had no intention of ever bothering to see the blasted things.

The silence stretched.

"You are correct, Miss Bowman," Henry said. "The Stoke Relics are a national treasure. And yes, the title is ancient. I was refreshing my memory with a copy of the peerage in his lordship's library and it seems the first Baron Rotherhithe was created during Henry VIII's reign. The family became well known for their ships, and, of course, their dockland."

Miss Bowman's frown eased, and she gave Henry a nod of approval.

He couldn't help preening, just a little.

"Rotherhithe is an Anglo-Saxon word," she said.

It was Henry's turn to be baffled. "Er, is it? How interesting. I did not know."

"Do *you* know the meaning of your new name, my lord?" she asked Colin.

Colin leaned back, as if she'd poked him in the chest with something sharp. "Uh. I just thought it had to do with the docks and such."

"Yes, of course, that is true. But all names have an origin, you know."

"They do?" Colin stared apprehensively at the slight, but persistent, female, as if he were about to be quizzed by a housemaster.

"Rotherhithe means, *landing place for cattle*."

Colin's mouth opened, but nothing came out.

Henry was impressed that Miss Bowman had reduced the normally garrulous man to stupefaction.

But he decided it was time to rescue his employee. "Anglo-Saxon? What an interesting piece of information. Tell me, Miss Bowman, do you speak, er, Anglo-Saxon?"

Before she could answer, Lady Sedgwick rejoined them. "Lord Rotherhithe and Mr. Parker have only just arrived from India, Annis," the countess told her friend as she sat beside Miss Bowman, gracefully settling her lavender skirt, which was—Henry couldn't help noticing—elegantly cut but made of cheap muslin.

Miss Bowman's eyes opened wider, which Henry hadn't thought possible.

"Oh, India, how wonderful." She smiled, which made Henry notice the rest of her face, and not just those eyes. A small, coral-pink mouth curled up at the corners and above it was a straight little nose that was perfectly in proportion to her heart-shaped face. But both features were utterly cast in the shade by the enormous blue orbs above them.

"I should love to go to India," she said, annihilating Henry's usually razor-sharp wits with her cerulean gaze before she aimed it at Colin.

Henry felt dazzled, as if he'd just smacked his head on a low lintel.

"Er, you would?" Colin asked, visibly betwattled

"Oh, yes! What a fascinating collection of dialects and languages." A slight flush crept across her pale cheeks as she leaned toward Colin, her posture one of barely contained excitement. "Languages are something of a passion for me, my lord. Tell me, do you speak Urdu, Sanskrit, Telugu, or any of the other languages?"

Colin's jaw sagged. "*Me*? Lord no, I can barely speak English!" He chortled and then stopped when he saw nobody else was laughing with him. He pressed his lips into a straight, serious line. "Ah, yes, languages," he said, his voice dropping at least an octave. "Hmm, well, I *do* know a few words in some language or other—I can't quite recall which one—at least enough to say, 'this tea is bloody strong,' and 'what the devil is that dreadful stench?'"

Henry looked from his chuckling employee to his aghast audience. "His lordship is jesting," he assured them. "He is quite conversant with several dialects and speaks fluent Urdu after almost *two decades* of living and doing business in India."

Colin blinked, and Henry knew the handsome sapskull had once again forgotten who he was supposed to be.

This bloody charade would be over before it even began.

As if Colin heard him, he straightened his posture and donned what Henry thought of as his *lordly* look—a lofty, smug, condescending sneer that was so convincingly *ton* it made Henry want to plant him a facer.

"Heh heh. Mr. Parker is quite correct. Just a little Company humor, you know."

Henry ground his teeth at that comment but kept his mouth shut.

"You'll have to forgive me, my lady, Miss Bowman, savage manners and all that," Colin said. "But what can you expect when I've spent most of my time with blokes these past twenty years?" He chortled for no apparent reason. "But you're going to see to those rough edges, aren't you, my lady?" Colin asked Lady Sedgwick. "Buff 'em all to a shine, what?" He looked from woman to woman, his expression eager, like a hunting spaniel that has returned to its master with the requisite fowl between its jaws. "I daresay you'll have me up to snuff, er, ship-shape, bang up to the knocker, all the crack, and so forth, in no time."

It was up to Henry to break the stunned silence. "You seem to have some knowledge of India, Miss Bowman. Do you have a connection to that country?"

She turned away from Colin, whom she'd been studying with a wrinkled brow.

Lord, those eyes. Henry felt as though he was caught in the beam of a lighthouse searchlight.

"I do not, Mr. Parker. But I am interested in all languages."

"Is that so?" Henry decided he liked the sound of her soft, precise voice almost as much as he enjoyed being the subject of her unnerving gaze. She was just a slip of a thing—not at all like the women who generally caught his interest—but there was just something about her fairy-like face and person that made it difficult for him to look away.

"Miss Bowman and I used to teach together at a lady's academy," the countess explained. "She was the languages mistress."

"Ah, how interesting. And what languages did you teach?"

"French and Italian."

"But Miss Bowman is also fluent in German, Spanish, Latin, and Greek."

Henry was impressed. "How did you learn so many languages?"

"Yes, how?" Colin chimed in, apparently deciding he was not only shirking his lordly duty but also losing all the female attention.

"My father was a language scholar at Oxford. When I was growing up, he taught me German, Latin, and Greek. The others I learned at school."

The door opened.

"Ah, here is the tea," the countess said.

Was that relief Henry heard in her voice?

"You say the prior Earl of Rotherhithe died almost two years ago?" Miss Bowman asked.

Colin looked at Henry before nodding cautiously. "Yes, that is true."

"Why are you only returning home now?" She blushed when she realized how forward the question was. "If you don't mind telling me, that is."

Colin goggled.

"His lordship could not leave his business concerns in India right away," Henry explained when it became clear that Colin had no recollection of their earlier conversations. "And then, of course, the journey itself took a little over three months."

"Three months at sea! Was it lovely?"

Both Henry and Colin spoke at the same time.

"No."

"Yes."

Miss Bowman chuckled. "There seems to be a difference of opinion. You said *no*, my lord. Is that because you suffered from seasickness?"

Colin paled at the mere word. "Every single day."

"Oh, how dreadful." She turned to Henry. "But you did not?"

"I was fortunate on this journey, but I have been sick in the past," Henry admitted.

"How do you take your tea, my lord?" the countess asked.

"Very light with three sugars, please."

Henry cringed, even though he already knew about the disgustingly sweet, milky brew Colin preferred.

"Mr. Parker?"

"Black for me, please."

"And will you be engaging in all the bobbery this Season, Miss Bowman?" Colin asked, taking his cup and saucer from Lady Sedgwick.

Miss Bowman flushed under the other man's attention and Henry had to suppress a twinge of irritation; she had not looked so flustered when *he* spoke to her.

He chastised himself for the foolish thought. Why wouldn't a young woman find the attention of a handsome, wealthy lord more gratifying than that of an impoverished, not especially attractive, secretary-slash-poor-friend?

Besides, what did he care whether some stranger preferred Colin over him? This was exactly the sort of reaction he'd anticipated, so he'd better get accustomed to it.

Miss Bowman crumbled the corner of a scone before answering Colin's question. "I have come to London to be a companion to my cousins, Lord Rotherhithe, not to take part in the Season."

She was a hired companion? Ah, so perhaps she wasn't blushing because of Parker's attention, but because of her circumstances?

Lady Winifred stepped into the uncomfortable silence the other woman's confession had created. "Miss Bowman has only recently returned to London. Until a week ago she lived with her grandmamma, Lady Cecily Bowman, in a small village north of London."

So, Miss Bowman was some sort of poor relation, passed from household to household, a fate worse than death, in Henry's opinion.

It amused him that Lady Sedgwick had mentioned the grandmother's title, just to let them both know that Miss Bowman was a woman of birth and connections, if not money.

"And who are the cousins fortunate enough to have your companionship?" Henry asked, his question drawing a rather sharp look from Lady Freddie.

Well, the sooner she became accustomed to the earl's *good friend* and his pushing ways, the better.

"My uncle is Mr. Thomas Bowman."

And not a pleasant character, judging by the tightening of Miss Bowman's kissable pink lips.

Henry sipped his tea—a paltry, tepid beverage that was a pale facsimile of the tea he'd enjoyed for the past twenty years—and hastily set down his cup and saucer.

"Lord Rotherhithe has opened up his London house," the countess said, moving the conversation away from her friend's diminished circumstances.

Miss Bowman perked up and turned back to Colin. "That is on Berkeley Square and has a rather lovely frieze above the entrance, does it not?"

All three of them looked at Colin, who'd dipped his shirt cuff in his tea and had raised it to his open mouth, as if to suck the fine linen dry.

When he noticed that he'd become the center of attention, he dropped his arm. "Freeze, you say? Isn't it rather late in the year for that?"

A brief silence followed before Henry stepped in. "Yes, Miss Bowman, you are correct. The frieze is quite old and was installed almost three hundred years ago to commemorate the family's connection to shipping."

If the women thought it odd that Lord Rotherhithe's secretary knew more about the man's house and lineage than he did, they were both too well bred to show it.

Lady Sedgwick turned her attention to Colin. "I thought we might discuss the next few weeks—perhaps arrange some meetings so that we can organize what will certainly be a busy schedule."

Colin set down his teacup and saucer with a clatter and shot to his feet, striding to the window that looked out over a small garden. "I say! That's the largest chicken I've ever seen."

The countess's lips parted, but nothing came out.

Miss Bowman bit her lower lip and made a choking sound.

Henry stood to look out the window. A turkey was strutting back and forth in the small back garden, its plumage in full display for a mild-looking turkey hen a fraction of the tom's size.

"That is a *turkey*, my lord," Henry said through clenched teeth.

Good God. Colin had *sworn* to him he didn't need the spectacles Henry had seen him wear—and then furtively hide—on more than one occasion. Clearly, he'd lied if he couldn't tell the difference between a bloody turkey and a chicken.

"No… is it?" Colin squinted and leaned close enough that his nose bumped the glass. "Ow!" He rubbed his nose. "I believe you're correct, Parker." He turned away from the fowl in question. "Hmm, interesting. I thought the only birds in London were pigeons." He gave a loud bark of laughter. "Lord, we're lucky turkeys can't fly. A pigeon overhead is bad enough, what?"

A strangled laugh burst from Miss Bowman.

"The owner of the house has always kept a pair of turkeys in residence," Lady Sedgwick explained, her speculative stare heavily tinged with… *something* as she studied Colin.

"Good eating, I s'pose," Colin said.

The countess's gray eyes turned positively frosty. "They are pets, my lord."

"We call them Mr. and Mrs. Vickers." Miss Bowman said in a more conciliating tone, her eyes still shining with mirth.

"Married, are they?" Colin guffawed at his own jest. "Jolly good, jolly good," he said, nodding enthusiastically, a vapid grin on his face as his eyes moved from the two women to Henry, and then froze, his smile draining away.

Henry gave Colin a glare that should have set his hair on fire, silently commanding him to shut his mouth and keep it closed.

The other man's eyes widened, and his lips snapped shut.

Henry reckoned he had perhaps three minutes to finish their business and get the hell out of Lady Sedgwick's sitting room before the effect of his glare wore off, and Colin did something that would force Henry to throttle him on the carriage ride home. He extracted an appointment book from the satchel at his feet and pasted a smile on his face before turning to the countess.

31

"I've brought along the earl's appointment book, my lady. Perhaps you might offer a few dates and I could jot them down for his lordship?"

Chapter 3

Annis waited a moment after the sitting-room door closed behind the two men before releasing the laughter she'd been suppressing for the past quarter of an hour. "Well, *what* an interesting pair."

An expression of wondrous disbelief flickered across Freddie's beautiful features. "That is putting it mildly."

"Lord Rotherhithe did not seem to know much about his family history or even his new house," Annis observed.

"Nor about domesticated fowl."

Annis chortled. "What kind of person doesn't know a chicken from a turkey?"

Freddie's expression turned grim. "I suppose I shall soon find out."

"Perhaps he needs spectacles but is too vain to wear them?" Annis suggested.

Freddie came as close to grunting as Annis had ever heard.

"Are you worried about launching him into society, Freddie?"

"I'm not exactly worried. Such a man—handsome and rich and titled—will always be a success. But it will be…" Her mouth flexed into a frown, and she gave a slight shake of her head. "I am not worried," she insisted.

It sounded like Freddie was trying to reassure herself more than Annis.

Annis could not blame Freddie; it was difficult to imagine turning such a gormless man loose in a London ballroom.

"He does not seem like the sort to have made a fortune from his wits."

Freddie laughed; the rare musical sound as beautiful as its owner. "No, he does not."

"In fact, he reminded me of a brainless young buck in his first season."

"Yes, although he is about fifteen years too old."

"It quite surprised me that he knew so little about his lineage."

"That doesn't concern me as much as some of his other comments." She gave Annis an amused look. "Not everyone is as inquisitive about such matters as we might be, my dear."

"You mean as inquisitive as *I* might be. Was I terribly quizzy?"

"You were being charming, as always."

Annis knew her friend was only being kind. It was true she could be awkward in company and often went off on tangents that led to confused silences or embarrassed glances.

"So, we are the first people in London to have made the acquaintance of the mysterious Earl of Rotherhithe. Why didn't you tell me you were meeting him today, Freddie?"

"His note asked that the meeting take place in confidence."

"And then *I* came blundering into the middle of it. I'm so sorry, Freddie."

Freddie smiled. "I am glad you joined us." Behind the Countess of Sedgwick's ice-queen façade was a very warm heart. "I think your presence actually made the meeting proceed more smoothly." She gave Annis a speculative look. "I thought they were both rather taken by you."

Annis felt her face heat. "Oh, pooh. They were just being polite. Even if his lordship *were* interested in me, Freddie, it would be difficult to return his interest. I thought him decorative but I don't think he is very smart."

Freddie choked on a mouthful of tea. "Oh, *Annis*," she said, laughing and daubing her mouth with her napkin.

"I did not mean that cruelly," Annis assured her. "That combination of dark hair and bright blue eyes is stunning. He is remarkably handsome, is he not?"

"Remarkably."

"His friend is quite attractive in his own, er, *savage* way."

"Savage?" Freddie repeated, musing over the description. "Yes, I suppose he looks as though he'd be more at home wielding a broadsword than dancing in a ballroom."

"And yet as huge as he is, he moved with grace and elegance."

"Which is more than I can say for his employer."

Annis snorted. "Yes, how many times did Lord Rotherhithe dip his cuff in his tea?"

They both laughed.

"Although Mr. Parker isn't as pretty as his employer, I found him far more attractive," Annis said. "His jaw looks to be hewn from stone and his deep-set eyes are uncomfortably… penetrating, but he has the loveliest eyelashes, although they didn't soften his appearance even a whit."

"They are the sort of lashes that are quite wasted on men."

Annis chuckled. "I agree." Her own eyelashes were thick and long but so fair as to be invisible. She sipped her tea, her mind drifting again to Mr. Parker's towering body and powerful build. Her hand had all but disappeared in his, yet he'd held it with surprising gentleness.

"Perhaps savage wasn't the right word," Annis amended. "Dangerous might be better, although I couldn't say *why*."

"Perhaps you found him dangerous because of the murderous looks he kept giving his employer."

Annis laughed. "He *did* look appalled, didn't he?"

"Mm-mm," Freddie hummed. "And angry."

"Mr. Parker's manners were far better than the earl's."

"Yes, Mr. Parker appeared quite distinguished and intelligent. If not for his hulking body and inexpensive clothing, he would make a far more polished aristocrat than his companion."

Annis *liked* his hulking body. She liked his thick, glossy brown hair, square, chiseled jaw, firm lips, and prominent high-bridged nose, too.

And then there were his eyes…

Although the warm hazel color wasn't especially exceptional, there was an expression in them that had made her feel almost… naked.

Annis shivered.

"Are you cold, dear?" Freddie asked.

"No, I'm fine," Annis replied, wrenching her mind off the enigmatic Mr. Parker.

Freddie caught her lip with her teeth, the pensive expression unusual in a woman who was normally so cool and reserved. "It does not make me happy to think of the reception Mr. Parker will receive when he accompanies the earl. I hope his lordship understands what he is doing."

Annis raised her brows. "Mr. Parker wishes to attend social functions *with* his employer?"

"I don't know what *his* preference might be, but the earl made it very clear in his letter that his friend will accompany him, going so far as to say that if Mr. Parker wasn't welcome, then he wouldn't consider himself welcome, either. And you just heard his lordship—they are joined at the hip."

They both snickered at the memory of the earl's ridiculous pronouncement.

"I think his loyalty to his friend speaks well of him," Annis said.

"Perhaps. But it does not speak well of his intelligence."

Privately, Annis thought Freddie would have her hands full with the thick-headed peer.

As if she'd spoken aloud, Freddie said, "I know I claimed I was not worried about launching the earl, but I am relieved there is barely half the Season left."

Annis had no comforting words to offer.

"So," Freddy said, "Enough of the earl and his enigmatic friend. By the sound of it, I will lose *your* company soon."

Annis did not wish to think about her unpleasant morning, but she could hardly avoid it.

"Yes," she admitted, "I presented myself for my aunt and uncle's inspection after my visit to Grandmamma's man of business. I'm afraid my finances are all to pieces."

"Oh, Annis, are matters really so bad that you must go live with the Bowmans?"

Annis hadn't been able to bear telling Freddie how foolish she'd been with Leech. Instead, she'd lied, telling her she'd made poor decisions with the little nest egg her father had left her.

"My situation is not dire," Annis lied, again. "But I do not wish to be a burden on my grandmother."

"Yes, I understand."

Freddie was yet another woman whose life had been wrecked by a man, not that she had ever spoken about her marriage or dead husband.

"Are you quite sure you don't want to stay with me, Annis? You could look for some other position? Something that won't place you under the thumb of your relatives. Relatives who—and I hope you will excuse me for saying this—I would not wish a dog to live with."

"It won't be so bad." At least not half as bad as it would be for poor Grandmamma if she were forced to live under the roof of her hen-pecked son and his harpy of a wife.

Not that her Aunt Agnes would ever allow that to happen. No, her aunt was the sort of woman who'd see that her mother-in-law was sent to live in an asylum for the blind. Somewhere wretched and horrible where her grandmother would be miserable. And her uncle, unfortunately, was too weak-willed to stop his domineering wife.

"Annis?"

She looked up to find Freddie's lovely eyes, which were currently clouded with concern.

"It is actually rather providential, Freddie. I need employment and my cousins need a companion. Besides, accompanying my cousins to parties and routs—and even a ball or two, might put me in the way of some eligible man."

Freddie's elegant eyebrows arched. "You would consider marrying?"

Her surprise was justified, as Annis had never mentioned marriage in the past. She had been on the verge of telling Freddie about Mr. Leech when he'd absconded with all her money.

So, thank heaven for small mercies.

"I am not averse to marriage," Annis lied. "But I am skeptical that I will meet a man who has been dreaming of finding a wife who can read and write multiple languages and plague him with linguistic questions over supper."

"Oh, Annis. I wish you would not say such things—even in jest. You have so much to offer—not only your clever brain, pretty face, and sweet nature, but you are a *good* person. Promise me you will not allow your wretched aunt to force you into some unfortunate marriage only so that she may have done with you? I want you to come to me before you agree to anything. Please. You know I care for you like a sister."

Annis's face flared with heat. "There, see what you have done?" She raised her cool hands to her hot cheeks.

"You look charming with roses in your cheeks. Now," Freddie said with an exasperated sigh. "Tell me when you are leaving me?"

"They will send a carriage for me and my things in three days."

"Well, that is quicker than I would like, but at least you shall still be here when Miles returns from the country."

"You've had a letter from Miles?"

"A letter?" Freddie laughed gently. "Well, if you would call his two sentences of scrawl a letter. He has been at Avington Park but is returning tomorrow."

"Are matters at his estate as bad as he thought?" Miles had unexpectedly inherited the earldom after his older brother died late last year.

"It is worse, I'm afraid. I daresay he is returning to take part in what remains of the Season."

"Surely Miles won't have to marry so soon?"

"He needs a wealthy wife. And quickly." Pain flashed in Freddie's eyes and Annis ached for her friend. Although Freddie had said nothing, it was clear to those who knew her that she was in love with Miles, and the feeling was mutual.

Freddie became brisk. "Tomorrow night we shall have a celebration—you, me, and Miles. And today I have a letter to share from Serena."

Annis clapped her hands. "It is like Christmas—I'm only sad the others cannot be here."

The others being the four teachers that Annis, Freddie, and Miles had once worked with at the Stefani Academy for Young Ladies.

Three of the four teachers—Portia Stefani, Honoria Keyes, and Serena Lombard had recently married. The fourth was Lorelei Fontenot. Lorie had taught English literature and composition but now lived with her brother at his vicarage all the way down in Cornwall.

"I shall save Serena's letter until after dinner," Freddie said. "But right now, you could help me draw up my plan of attack for the Earl of Rotherhithe. I have promised to have a list for him by midweek."

"I would be glad to help," Annis said, pleased to keep busy and forget about her morning for at least a few hours more.

But later that night, when Annis lay awake in her room staring at the ceiling, she could no longer keep away the dreadful events of that morning.

First had been the visit to Mr. Pears, where she'd seen the mortgage paperwork on her grandmother's cottage.

"But neither Grandmamma nor I ever signed such a thing."

Mr. Pears put the signature in question next to a document Annis had just signed that day.

Annis had gasped when she stared down at identical signatures.

"I would have contacted you when Mr. Leech brought me the paperwork, Miss Bowman, but he brought the proxy letter and knew so much about you. I thought since you were engaged—"

"*What?*"

The Language of Love

Pears had winced and then got that look on his face that said he was preparing to deal with an emotional female.

"He *forged* my name."

"If that is true, then you must contact the authorities about Leech, Miss Bowman."

"Oh, please, Mr. Pears. That would ruin Lady Cecily." If anyone would be ruined, it would be Annis if Leech ever told a magistrate what she had done. "Please—say nothing."

"I shan't say anything if you'd rather not. But what will you do? The best I can arrange is a grace period of perhaps two or three months. But if your grandmother cannot come up with the money, she will need to vacate her cottage."

Three months.

Annis had wanted to weep.

Instead, she'd said, "I understand, Mr. Pears."

Yes, she understood that Richard Leech was pond scum in human form, a vile, verminous man gifted with a handsome face and a charming manner.

And you are the fool who believed him.

She whimpered at the painful truth. It was all her fault. And no surprise, either.

Her mother's last words to her, before she'd died, once again rang in her head, "You are a henwit, Annis, you've inherited that quality—along with your freakish eyes and scrawny figure—from your father's mother."

Lucy Bowman had given Annis the half-affectionate, half-derisive look she seemed to reserve for her only child. "In fact, I can't see one thing you inherited from me."

No, Annis had nothing in common with her shrewd, russet-haired, green-eyed siren of a mother—a woman who'd been so lushly beautiful she'd even attracted the attention of a bookworm like Annis's father, although she hadn't held on to Thomas Bowman's attention for long, a fact that had turned her bitter and shrewish.

"You'd better leave your father's dratted books alone and cultivate a biddable nature, my girl, because your looks won't be enough to catch a man."

Annis's eyes burned at the memory, which only infuriated her more. She *was* a henwit. She knew that her friends—Freddie, Miles, and the others—loved her, but she also knew they considered her a dreamer who needed somebody to take care of her.

Well, she'd proven their belief by allowing a man like Richard Leech—a name which suited him—to take complete advantage of her.

Leech had come to stay at a small house close to her grandmother's cottage, a man of the cloth enjoying a brief respite in the country before moving north to assume his curacy in Yorkshire.

His charm and angelic good looks had swept away Annis and all the others. It hadn't taken him long to worm his way into all their lives and convince Annis that he loved her.

Because she was a henwit.

And then there was that horrible, horrible night. Every time she thought about it—and his mocking laughter—she felt physically ill.

And now she would pay for her idiocy by indenturing herself to her uncle and aunt and cousins, and all in the far-flung hope that she could catch a rich husband and keep her poor grandmother from ending her life in some horrid asylum.

In only three months!

Her mother had been right: dowdy, desperate, and hen-witted—that was Annis Bowman.

Chapter 4

A fan rapped Annis sharply on the shoulder and she jolted and turned to find her cousin Miriam glaring down at her.

"Susanna has been waiting for you in the retiring room *forever*. Whatever is keeping you?" She shot a narrow, dismissive look at Freddie, whom Annis had been talking to, and then spun on her heel without waiting for an answer.

Freddie shook her head. "What an appalling woman."

Annis smiled. "I had better go, Freddie."

"Yes, do. But make sure you *come back*."

Annis gave a noncommittal nod and then moved as quickly and politely as she could toward the retiring room. There was no point promising Freddie things that weren't hers to give. It was likely that she'd spend the rest of the evening dancing attendance on her cousins and aunt.

Miriam and Susanna were ready to pounce the moment she entered the retiring room.

"Your behavior is inexcusable," Miriam, the elder and more short-tempered of her cousins, snapped. Her voice carried, and several of the other occupants of the room turned to stare. "Susanna missed the second set because of you."

Annis felt like pointing out that *she* had not been the one who'd trod on Susanna's skirt, but she had learned it was better not to argue.

"Show me the tear, Cousin." She opened her reticule and extracted a card of pins.

Susanna, who was often kind to Annis when her sister was not around, lifted the hem. "It's right—"

"Can't you do anything without help?" Miriam demanded.

Susanna dropped the skirt as if it had stung her fingers, which forced Annis to kneel and go over the fabric, inch by painstaking inch.

The gown was a lovely shade of pale green that perfectly set off her cousin's dark-haired beauty.

"I cannot find a rip," she said.

"Look again," Susanna said. "It's there."

"Do you think she is inept on purpose?" Miriam asked her sister, tapping her toe.Susanna clucked her tongue. "Remember your manners, sister. Don't let her willful behavior reduce you to her level."

"I found it," Annis said.

"Get on with fixing it," Miriam ordered.

The almost invisible tear was not in the hem itself, but in the lace two inches above it. Annis removed a pin, wove it through the rip, and used the stiff card rather than her only pair of evening gloves to bend the end. Satisfied, she stood.

Miriam squinted down at the repair. "A pin? You did not have enough wit to bring a needle and thread?"

"Come, come," Susanna said, grabbing her sister's arm. "We shall miss the entire ball if we stand here expecting any sense from her."

They turned and headed for the door, and Annis let out a sigh of relief.

"Oh, Annis?"

Her head jerked up at the sound of Miriam's voice.

"Mama wishes to see you immediately. She is with Mrs. Neece and Mrs. Howell." She gave Annis a spiteful little smile and flounced out of the room.

Annis turned to regard her reflection in the mirror, frowning at what she saw: a skinny old maid wearing an old ball gown that was far too loose on her slight frame.

It was one of Miriam's from two Seasons past. Although delicate primrose was a pretty enough color, it did nothing for her pale complexion and colorless hair. And it had been so laden with bows, ribbons, and lace that a dull gown remained after she'd stripped away all the furbelows. She'd planned to embroider flowers along the hem, but her cousins had hardly left her with a moment to eat or sleep.

Even though the Season was more than half over, the Duchess of Tinley's ball was the first *haute ton* affair the Bowman women had ever attended.

Her aunt had nearly fainted when she'd received the much-prized invitation to the exclusive event, which bore Miriam's, Susanna's, *and* Annis's names.

"Annis?" Miriam had demanded. "Why is her name on the invitation?"

"Somebody must have misinformed the duchess," her aunt said.

The Language of Love

Miriam had shuddered. "Oh, Mama! What if Her Grace believes Annis is one of us? With her odd looks and even odder ways?"

"Don't fret my darling, nobody would ever mistake your cousin for one of *my* daughters."

Not only was her aunt's statement correct, but it was also one that Annis was grateful for. Although nature had favored her young cousins well above Annis in looks, she'd never met such fractious, back-biting, jealous women as Miriam, Susanna, and their mama.

If one judged her cousins on appearance alone, they would have found husbands in their first seasons. But even men lured by their beauty and generous dowries balked at the hardness around their full mouths and the acquisitive glints in their gem-like green eyes.

The invitation to the Tinley ball had been cause for glorious celebration for her cousins, but it had been the death knell for Annis's peace of mind. The past six days had been a relentless orgy of shopping for her cousins and an orgy of fetching, carrying, and stitching for Annis.

"This lounging about will not serve," her aunt had declared when she'd discovered Annis in her uncle's library, where she had—of all things—a primer on Mandarin Chinese for an Englishman visiting China.

Annis knew her uncle hadn't gone any farther than Shropshire, so the book must have belonged to one of her aunt's relations, who'd made their money from—*shhhhh*—trade, although nobody ever mentioned that, of course.

Upon hearing her aunt's voice, Annis had quickly closed the book. "You needed me, Aunt?"

"Yes, it is time we had a little talk, my dear."

Annis experienced a bolt of fear at her ominous words. "Yes, Aunt?"

"Your uncle may have given you the mistaken impression that he will pay for your Season."

Annis opened her mouth to demur, but her aunt raised a staying hand. "We will house you, feed you, and clothe you." Her eyes were critical as they swept Annis's pale green morning gown, which was out of fashion, but flattering. "In return for this kindness, you will help where we need you. Do you understand?"

"Yes, Aunt."

"I have some rather good news for you."

Annis had a sinking feeling. "Yes, Aunt?"

43

"Mr. Norburg has expressed an interest in you."

"Mr. Norburg?"

"Don't be such a dunce, girl! He is the gentleman who came to dinner two nights ago. While he is a man of business, it is banking, and therefore unexceptionable for a girl in your position."

A girl in my position? You mean a girl who is a blood relative of your husband?

Of course, she said no such thing.

"Mr. Norburg," Annis repeated. "Is he the white-haired gentleman?"

Her aunt's mouth puckered so tightly that it reminded Annis of the back end of her grandmother's pug, an observation she did not share.

"He is not yet fifty, Annis—that is hardly in his dotage."

Annis did not point out that made him twenty years her senior, but her aunt's next words made her wonder if she might have spoken aloud.

"You are in no position to quibble, miss. He is a very wealthy gentleman and appears to be taken with you, for some inconceivable reason." She brushed her hands against each other, as if she'd just completed a dirty and unpleasant task. "Now, onto more important matters. The seamstress has made a terrible muddle of Miriam's dress and needs a second pair of hands to assist her." Her aunt's gimlet eyes rested on the book in Annis's lap. "You may return your uncle's book to the shelf and join Mrs. Finch in the attic."

And then she had swept from the library without waiting for an answer.

Annis *had* carried out one minor rebellion; instead of returning the book to the shelf, she'd hidden it under the window seat cushion. But beyond that, she'd obeyed her aunt and had stitched and pressed and run errands, even though her uncle's house held dozens of servants who could have done the same work.

Fortunately, the subject of Mr. Norburg had not come up again, which was not unusual, as Annis was hardly the most important subject on the days leading up to the ball.

***

Henry surveyed the densely packed ballroom and wished, yet again, that he'd stayed home. But this was their first ball—although they'd attended a dozen other, smaller, functions—and he could hardly escape it since it had all been his idea.

The Language of Love

Beside him, Colin bounced on his heels, so excited that Henry was afraid he might break into a triple *huzzah* at any moment.

Henry cleared his throat, but that failed to attract his attention. "My lord."

"Hmm?" Colin surveyed the room with the wide eyes of a child confronted with a tempting array of sweets.

"*Lord Rotherhithe.*"

Colin flicked him a glance from distracted blue eyes. "Eh?" And then he looked again; whatever he saw on Henry's face made him stop bouncing. "Ah, yes, Parker?"

"Do you recall what we spoke about in the library?"

"Uh. The library?"

"Yes, you know, the room with all the books."

Colin blinked, visibly scouring his memory for what Henry was talking about.

"My lord?" Henry prodded.

Thanks to the ludicrously high shirt points Colin had insisted on wearing, he couldn't turn his head. Instead, he had to shift his entire torso to look directly at Henry.

"Er, yes, the conversation. In the library." He chewed over Henry's question as if it were the Riddle of the Sphinx. "You mean that thing about the tea?"

Henry told himself to remain calm, reminding himself, for the ten thousandth time, that he had brought this *all* on himself.

"No, my lord, not the *thing about the tea.* I meant the discussion about deportment."

Colin's unblinking, stunned rabbit stare told Henry the word was not familiar to him.

Henry leaned closer and hissed through a smile, "Don't look so damned excited to be here. A real aristocratic male would be *bored to tears.*"

Colin nodded several times. "Yes, of course. *That* thing." He beetled his brows and frowned, sweeping the room with a look meant to be haughty, but more closely resembling that of a man straining on a chamber pot.

Henry sighed.

"Oh, look! There's Lady Freddie." Colin's arm shot up to wave, but Henry grabbed his elbow to arrest its progress.

Colin looked hurt. "Don't you believe me? I *told* you I could see well enough without my spectacles, and there she is."

Ah yes, the glasses discussion. For the first time in his dealings with Colin, the other man had stood firm: Colin *refused* to wear his spectacles. What could Henry do? Wrestle him to the ground and nail them onto his head?

The idea was not without merit.

"I believe you, my lord. But no *waving*. And I doubt she'd appreciate being called Lady Freddie."

"See, it's her, Parker. Look." Colin waved with the hand that Henry wasn't restraining.

Henry gave up. After all, this sort of thing occurred All. Day. Long. He needed to choose his battles, or he would go stark raving mad.

As Lady Sedgwick approached them, he saw that her gown of mauve silk was of exquisite design, but again, the material was of an inferior quality.

What happened to the money she earned from her matchmaking activities? Her fee had been quite high, yet everything about her person was modest. She did not own the house she lived in, so where did she spend her money? Certainly not on clothes.

She curtsied with impeccable grace when she approached them; she was a lovely woman, but far too cool and reserved for Henry's taste.

"Good evening my lord, Mr. Parker."

They exchanged greetings and bows before the countess turned to Colin, her eyes widening slightly when she took in his salmon pink waistcoat, which was embroidered with small black dogs.

Henry had accompanied Colin to Bond Street to purchase appropriate clothing—far nicer garments than Henry was currently sporting—so he did not know where Colin had purchased the waistcoat, but the result was... startling, to say the least.

"What an unusual waistcoat, my lord," Lady Sedgwick said.

Colin grinned. "Isn't it?" He stepped so close to the countess that she had to step back to avoid having her slippers crushed. "See here," he said, plucking at the skin-tight garment as if he could pull it closer to her. "It's dogs—little black dogs! Is that terribly cunning?"

The countess opened her mouth to answer, but Colin was caught up in the excitement of the moment.

"I used to have a dog who looked *just* like these. A fine little terrier. Sniffer, we called him because he liked to sniff things. He was a bang-up ratter and once almost won a ratting contest, but when he got excited, he had the unfortunate habit of pis—" His eyes slewed to Henry.

Henry frowned and gave an imperceptible shake of his head to indicate that a pissing, rat-killing dog was not an appropriate topic for ballroom conversation.

Colin, in a show of willful independence, plowed ahead. "Er, that's to say Sniffer would *urinate* all over himself, and anything else that might be around him. He urinated on the judge's boot and was disqualified. Unfairly, I thought, as he had over forty rats chalked up." He rocked on his heels, visibly pleased with himself for finishing his story.

The countess stared.

Henry cleared his throat. "You look lovely this evening, my lady."

Lady Sedgwick wrenched her gaze from Colin. "Thank you, Mr. Parker."

"Yes, lovely, and stunning," Colin chimed in. "Spiffing! Bang up to the nines. Like a—"

"Thank you for your tailor recommendation, my lady," Henry hastily cut in.

The countess stared pointedly at Colin's waistcoat as if to say, *Too bad you didn't take my recommendation.* And then she swept Henry's person with her piercing gray gaze. Once again, he could almost hear her thoughts: Lord Rotherhithe must like his friend and secretary a great deal to be seen with him in such humble finery.

In keeping with his menial status, Henry—who had worn only the best clothing for years—was currently dressed like the clerk/secretary he was supposed to be.

Lady Sedgwick appeared to collect herself and recall why she was standing beside a buffoon and his servant. "There is a great deal of curiosity about you, my lord."

Indeed, Henry could feel dozens of eyes upon them—or on Colin, rather.

Colin did not appear to have heard her, his attention seized by a voluptuous auburn-haired woman whose low-cut bodice must surely skim her nipples.

"I *say*," Colin murmured in a tone thick with awe. "Those are quite the largest—"

"His lordship is all agog to meet everyone. Isn't that right, my lord?" Henry asked in an overly loud voice.

But Colin was leaning over to catch a glimpse down the woman's bodice and had no attention to spare on anything else.

Henry could have tipped him over with one finger and was seriously tempted to do so.

The countess's lips twitched. Ah, so even she was not impervious to the ridiculous man.

She turned her attention to Henry. "And how are you finding things at Berkley Square, Mr. Parker?"

"Drafty, cavernous, inconvenient, freezing, moldy."

If his critical assessment of his employer's abode surprised her, she did not show it. "I believe it has been some time since anyone occupied the house," she said. "I understand the late earl—not his lordship's cousin, but his uncle—never came to town and chose not to lease the house."

No, his uncle had been quite the muttonhead in matters of business—and proud of his ignorance, too. Uncle Robert would have viewed leasing the house a shameful admission of poverty. And so he had neither occupied nor rented it, and the house had fallen into disrepair. His son, Charles, had been just as foolishly proud, and even poorer.

"Yes," Henry agreed, "it has stood vacant for over nearly four decades. Isn't that right, my lord?"

Colin's head whipped around, his collar scraping his chin with an audible *scritch*.

Henry and Lady Sedgwick winced.

"I say, Lady Freddie, can you introduce me to *any* of these girls?" As if pulled by a winch, Colin's eyes slid to the clutch of females who were ogling him, thus missing Lady Sedgwick's priceless expression at either his question or the nickname, or both.

Henry had to admit the nickname was his fault. He should have known that saying anything in front of Colin—even in jest—meant the man was likely to blurt it out at any time, just like a child.

Henry crossed his hands behind his back to keep from throttling Colin.

He leaned toward the countess. "As you may have noticed, my lord is *very* excited about attending his first ball and I'm afraid it might have made him forget his manners."

The countess fixed him with a shrewd, suspicious look, and Henry wondered if she smelled something rotten in Denmark. Not that it was unusual for aristocrats to be raving idiots, of course, but Henry could see she thought his management of Colin was a bit too masterful for a mere friend/servant.

"Tell me, Mr. Parker, what part of England do you hail from? Your accent is difficult to place."

Ah, did she suspect something?

"I'm from Kent, my lady, but I've been away for almost five years, so I expect I've lost much of my regional accent."

Her smile was a slight, feline expression that caused Henry to feel more than a little like a colorful piece of fluff that she was considering batting about.

"And yet how odd that his lordship seems to have lost none of his accent."

Henry's smile became strained.

"Not only that," she added, "but he sounds like *he's* from Kent. Yet I know he hails from Yorkshire."

Yes, she definitely suspected something.

Henry was struggling for something intelligent to say when a flash of pale blond hair in his peripheral vision snagged his attention.

It was Miss Annis Bowman, and she was hovering near a raft of old biddies, leaning over one of them, her narrow shoulders visibly clenched with tension.

"I think that would be an excellent question to ask Miss Bowman."

Lady Sedgwick raised her eyebrows. "I beg your pardon?"

"She was a language teacher and seems quite knowledgeable about language-related subjects. I daresay she'd know something about regional accents, too."

Her gray eyes bored into him.

"Ah," he said, "Speak of the lady and there she is."

"Yes, she is here, along with her cousins, Miss Bowman and Miss Susannah. They all received a last-minute invitation to this ball. It was kind of the earl to use his influence on their behalf."

"Did he?" Henry asked, hiding his smirk with some effort

"Indeed. I let the Duchess of Tinley know that Lord Rotherhithe wished for the Bowman ladies to attend and the duchess was most accommodating."

Henry looked away from her too-probing gaze. "Yes, the earl is quite taken with Miss Annis Bowman."

They both turned to his lordship, who was still goggling at the buxom lass a few feet away; Colin would need to wipe drool from his highly polished dancing shoes if he wasn't careful.

Henry gave him a subtle jab in the ribs. "Miss Annis Bowman is here, Rotherhithe."

"Say what?" Colin gave him an irritable look, which quickly drained away when he realized whom he'd just snapped at. "Er, I'm sorry. What's that you say, Parker?"

"Miss Annis Bowman is here."

Colin wore the expression of a man who'd just been asked an unsolvable calculus problem. "Annis Bowman?"

"We met her at Lady Sedgwick's house. The young lady with an interest in India." When Colin's vapid expression persisted, Henry tried again. "You were quite taken with her, my lord."

"Was I?" Comprehension dawned like a weak winter sunrise. "Ah, yes! The girl who teaches Anglo-Saxons or some such." His blue eyes darted around the room. "Which one is she again?"

Henry felt an arctic chill emanating from Lady Sedgwick's direction.

"She came with her aunt and cousins." The countess inserted a significant pause before adding, "All of whom owe you a debt of gratitude, my lord."

"They do?" Colin's attention had already drifted back to the bouquet of young ladies who appeared to be inching ever closer to him.

"Perhaps you would like me to perform some introductions, Lord Rotherhithe."

Henry could have chipped ice from the countess's words.

"Smashing!" Colin exclaimed, his eyes never leaving the young ladies. "I'd especially like to meet that one with the big—"

"His lordship would be honored to meet anyone you deign to introduce him to, my lady," Henry cut in, his skull throbbing with an ache that radiated all the way down to his toes.

Lord, it was going to be a long evening.

Chapter 5

Annis had just finished delivering orgeat to her aunt—who'd sent her back for it after declining the lemonade she'd already requested—and was lurking near the entrance to the hall, where she was least likely be hailed by any of her family and sent on errands.

"Are you hiding from somebody?"

Annis squeaked and spun around to find Mr. Parker on the other side of the shallow alcove.

Her pulse quickened at the sight of him. "Oh. Why, hello, Mr. Parker."

His brows—dramatic black slashes that were far darker than his sun-kissed brown hair—jumped. "You recall my name."

"Why wouldn't I?"

"Few young ladies would recall an impoverished clerk-slash-secretary when they'd been introduced to a rich, handsome peer at the same time."

Annis did not think Lord Rotherhithe was as bewitching as Mr. Parker seemed to believe, but even she knew it would be rude to point out such a thing.

"Fortunately, I have ample mental capacity to remember the names of *two* new acquaintances, Mr. Parker."

His grin seemed to suck all the air from the room. Had she thought he was merely attractive? He was *breathtaking* when he smiled like that, his teeth a flash of white in his deeply tanned face, a tiny dimple to the right of his mouth.

"Touché, Miss Bowman."

"Do you speak French?"

"You've just heard the extent of it." He smiled again, and she found it difficult to focus; he was so intensely, suffocatingly… *male.*

He cocked his head at her and for one horrified instant she feared she'd said that out loud.

But he only asked, "Were you hiding from somebody?"

"Not really," she lied. "What about you?"

"Oh, yes."

51

His dry retort startled a laugh out of her. "Who are you hiding from?"

He jerked his chin toward a woman with a cluster of young men around her. "The lady in the red gown—I can't recall her name just now."

Annis glanced at the woman in question. "Oh. That is Lady Keating." The gorgeous young widow was spilling out of her dress as usual, but Annis kept that observation to herself. "You are avoiding her?"

"You sound surprised?" he asked, his confident smirk making her want to slap him.

Or kiss him.

Annis blinked at the astonishing thought, which had bounced through her mind like a rogue cricket ball before bouncing back out again.

"Miss Bowman?"

Annis looked into Mr. Parker's too penetrating eyes. "Er, yes?"

"I said you sound surprised that I would avoid her."

"I am."

"Why is that?"

"She is exquisite and I understand she is also very, er…"

"She's very *er*?" Mr. Parker asked, his voice teasing. "How does one go about being *er*, I wonder?"

"You know exactly what I mean," she shot back tartly, mortified at how flushed her face felt.

Mr. Parker laughed, the sound low and disturbingly sensual. "Yes, I know what you mean: libidinous."

The shocking word made her feel woozy.

"She certainly made no bones about what she wanted from me," he confessed.

They both looked at the woman in question.

The wealthy, lovely widow kept a string of lovers, which she jokingly referred to as her *hunters.* "*It's always best to keep a stable full of mounts if one is a slapping rider,*" Lady Keating was fond of saying.

The men surrounding Lady Keating laughed at something she said, and she leaned in close enough to rub her prodigious bosom against one handsome young man.

The man in question preened. Those around him scowled jealously.

The Language of Love

Annis's own bosom was anything *but* prodigious. She chewed her lip as she studied her unfashionably high neckline. She'd considered altering the garment to give it more of a *à la mode* bodice, but she hadn't had the time.

When she looked up, she discovered that Mr. Parker was staring at her, a faint smile curving his lips.

"You aren't interested in what Lady Keating has to offer?" she asked, stunning herself with the daring question.

He gave another of his sensual chuckles. "Not at the moment." His eyelids lowered, his darkened gaze moving over her like a physical touch. "I have other… interests."

Annis stared, unable to look away.

"You're staring, Miss Bowman. Do I have something on my face?"

She jerked her gaze away until she faced the crowded dance floor. He was an unnerving man, but she couldn't make herself walk away from him.

When he was content to smirk in silence, Annis asked, "How are you finding England after so long in India? Does the weather feel chilly? It must have been vastly different where you lived. Do you have family here? Will you be visiting them?"

His hazel eyes glinted with amusement. "Hmm, let's see—that was a lot of questions. Here are your answers, in order: Interesting. Yes. Yes. Yes. And no."

Annis laughed. "I deserved that. I'll only ask them one at a time from now on."

"*From now on,*" he repeated, flashing her another devastating smile. "I like the sound of that."

"You do?"

"Yes, it implies we shall further our acquaintance." His warm look made heat pool low in her belly.

"Are you flirting with me, Mr. Parker?"

"If you have to ask, then I must not be doing a good job, Miss Bowman."

"You are doing well enough," she assured him. She cast a glance in her aunt's direction to make certain she wasn't needed.

"Does your family keep you busy?" he asked.
So, he was observant as well as clever.

The last thing Annis wanted to talk about with this fascinating man was her family. "Will you tell me about India?"

"Of course. What do you wish to know?"

"Whatever you wish to tell me."

"Hmm." He propped a broad shoulder against the wall and crossed his arms. "The earl's plantation, Sheesham Bagana, is north of the city of Dacca, tucked at the edge of the jungle."

"Sheesham Bagana," she repeated. "What a wonderful sounding word." She looked up into eyes that were a dizzying kaleidoscope of greens, golds, and browns. "Tell me, what does it mean?"

"It means, in the shade of the sheesham tree."

"Sheesham Bagana." Annis savored the taste and texture of the musical word. She knew that her love of words baffled most people. Only her father had ever understood the appeal of languages, both English and foreign.

"I've never heard of a sheesham tree before."

"They are a type of rosewood the Indians use for furniture. It has beautiful pink and white flowers."

"It sounds lovely. And you say they grow around the earl's house?"

"Yes, not his town house, but the one in the country. It is far away from the noise and bustle of the city, where the air is thick with perfume from sheesham and dozens of other flowers, a banquet for the senses. At night there are an untold number of insects which provide a deceptively beautiful symphony, a pleasing background to velvet nights filled with stars."

Annis realized her mouth was open and hastily closed it. "You are a poet, Mr. Parker. That was lyrical."

His mouth pulled into a mocking smile, and his eyes flickered toward the dancefloor. "You do not care to dance, Miss Bowman?"

"I love dancing."

"Then why are you standing here listening kindly while I bore on about nothing?"

"You are not boring me. I asked you to talk about India. As for why I am here with you, instead of dancing, that's because nobody asked me to dance." She felt flustered by the time she reached the last word. His gaze was intense, yet it did not show what he was thinking. Probably that she was babbling imbecile.

"Will you dance a set with me—the next waltz, perhaps? I believe they dance it in London?"

"But…" She bit her lip. "That is the supper set."

"Oh?"

"Perhaps you did not know, as you are new, but you would have to eat supper with me afterward."

"I have no objection to eating supper with you, Miss Bowman." He paused and his mouth hardened, the humor draining away from his mesmerizing eyes. "Unless you'd rather not eat with a mere servant?"

He was a rather prickly man. Doubtless he'd been the recipient of untold snubs these past weeks as he'd accompanied his friend; the beau monde guarded jealously against allowing commoners into its midst.

"I would be delighted to eat supper with you, Mr. Parker."

Her words appeared to smooth his ruffled feathers. "How are you enjoying the Season so far, Miss Bowman?"

"I am glad I've had the chance to join in, but I can't say it has been entirely enjoyable."

"Oh? You do not care for the social whirl?"

"Perhaps not quite so much of it. My cousins keep a rather hectic pace."

He pulled a face. "Indeed. Lady Sedgwick has set a brutal schedule for his lordship, too. Although this is the first ball of this size that we've attended, we've been burning the candle at both ends." His eyes narrowed, and he gave her a sly smile. "I wonder where that saying originated?"

Annis chuckled. "What makes you think I would know?"

He merely grinned.

"You are shameless, Mr. Parker—has anyone ever told you that?"

"I can be," he admitted. "When I'm in pursuit of something I want."

Annis pursed her lips at his flirtatious words. No doubt her cheeks were a mortifying shade of red. Again.

"Did you get your love of language from your father?" he asked.

"Yes. But how did you know?"

"At Lady Sedgwick's you mentioned that he'd taught you several languages."

"Oh. Yes, my father is the one who taught me to love words of all languages. I know it sounds silly, but we used to quiz each other about idioms."

"It doesn't sound silly," he said. "But it *does* sound like a game you will always win whenever we play it."

His words were innocent, but the look that accompanied them was slyly wicked.

"Well?" he prodded.

"Hmm?"

"Burning the candle at both ends?"

"As it happens, I *do* know that one. It is French—**Brusler la chandelle par les deux bouts. It initially meant to be wasteful or spendthrift but has gradually come to mean engaging in exhausting activity, or—**"

A familiar face appeared over Mr. Parker's shoulder.

"*Miles!*"

Mr. Parker jolted at her unladylike outburst and turned to see who she was looking at.

"*Annis!*" Miles teased as he stretched his hands toward her.

As usual, every woman in the vicinity followed Miles with their eyes. And then darted envious looks in Annis's direction to see who had captured his attention.

He pulled her close enough for a kiss on the cheek. "Hallo, darling. You're looking beautiful this evening."

Annis flushed at his kind lie. "And you look every inch an earl, Miles." That, too, was a fib. Her friend still wore the same suit of evening clothes he'd used when he'd been a dancing master. Not that clothing mattered with a man as perfect as Miles.

Annis turned to Mr. Parker, whose face had taken on a sullen cast. "Mr. Parker, I would like to introduce you to my dear friend, the Earl of Avington. Miles, this is Mr. Parker, a good friend to the Earl of Rotherhithe."

Miles gave the scowling man an affable smile. "Ah, yes, you've just arrived from India. I'll wager you are wishing the miserable English drizzle of the past few days to the devil."

Mr. Parker thawed a little under Miles's friendly manner. "The gray skies are daunting but at least you don't have poisonous reptiles or insects."

"True, but we do have some other creatures that have quite a nasty sting." He nodded at the dense cluster of mamas not far away, all of whom were casting appraising glances in his direction.

Mr. Parker grinned at Miles's not-so-subtle comment. "Nothing fatal, I hope?"

The Language of Love

"I wouldn't be so sure," Miles murmured, pulling his gaze away from the clutch of watchful women. "So, will you be staying in England long, Mr. Parker?"

"Indefinitely."

"The earl, too?"

"Yes, his lordship sold his textile business to his partner and has no plans to return."

"Ah, well, that was probably wise. I understand the Charter Act of 1813 made things tough on anyone not in the tea or opium trade."

Mr. Parker looked startled. "Yes—yes, it caused some problems."

Annis smiled at the gleam of respect in his eyes. Like most people, Mr. Parker had probably underestimated Miles, believing that such a beautiful man must be empty-headed and decorative.

"Well, you are both intrepid to plunge into the Season when it is in full clip," Miles said, glancing around him with a look of mild distaste.

"His lordship is eager to embrace his new life," Mr. Parker said.

"And I'd wager there are plenty eager to assist him," Miles said, cutting the same group of mamas a significant look.

Mr. Parker chuckled.

Miles turned to Annis. "I need to have a word with Fred. Have you seen her?"

Only Miles used that nickname for Freddie.

Before Annis could answer, Mr. Parker said, "Lady Sedgwick was busy making introductions for Lord Rotherhithe when I last saw her."

Miles gave a grimace of mock horror. "Lord, I don't envy the poor man. He'll be feeling like a fox at the five-mile point before the night is through." He grinned at Annis, his eyes sparkling. "Save the supper dance for me, Annie?"

"Mr. Parker has spoken for that one. Perhaps the first one after supper?"

Miles smiled at Mr. Parker, who'd again become tense and watchful, as if he expected Miles to object to him dancing with her. "Hasn't taken *you* long to find one of England's finest gems, has it, Parker?"

Annis blushed at his teasing and, once again, Mr. Parker thawed under Miles's infectious good humor.

"We poor mortals can't allow you to soak up *all* the female attention, my lord. Someone has to give a bloke like you a decent run."

Miles laughed. "I consider myself well-warned, sir. Now, if you'll both excuse me. I need to see if Freddie has a moment to spare."

They watched him weave his way through the crowd, female heads swiveling almost comically in his wake.

"He seems a nice sort," Mr. Parker commented, a bit grudgingly, Annis thought.

"Oh, Miles is the *best* sort."

"You two know each other well."

"We taught together for several years."

"*He* worked at your young ladies' school?"

"Yes, he was our dancing master."

"An *earl* working as a dancing master?" he repeated.

"Well, he wasn't an earl then, only the younger brother of an earl. His brother died unexpectedly last year." She chewed her lip, her eyes on Miles's golden head as he stopped in front of Freddie. "Besides losing a brother he loved, he's inherited a mountain of debts and dependents."

Now Freddie and Miles would never be together since he would have to marry an heiress if he wanted to save his family.

Her eyes teared up at the thought and she blinked rapidly and looked away to find Mr. Parker gazing down at her.

"Ah, I see." Parker's eyes had turned shrewd. "He needs to sell himself for money, does he? Well, a man who looks like him will have no problem landing any heiress in London."

Annis flinched at his cynical tone. It didn't matter that it was true; it was cruel to state it so bluntly—especially since Annis was also hoping to *sell* herself for money. The crucial difference was that there was no clamoring horde of rich suitors seeking her hand. Not even the elderly Mr. Norburg seemed especially eager.

"*Here* you are." Miriam appeared beside her as if she'd sprung up from the parquet floor, her voice sharp enough to carry even in the noisy ballroom.

Mr. Parker turned, his mouth open, as if in greeting, but Miriam deliberately turned her back on him. "Susanna has been looking for you."

The Language of Love

"Yes, of course." Annis smiled at Mr. Parker, but he was staring at her cousin, arrested. No doubt he was comparing Miriam's tall, shapely beauty to Annis's short, boy-like figure.

Annis knew perfectly well how she'd come out of such a comparison.

"Please excuse me, Mr. Parker."

He turned away from Miriam—who was ignoring him in such a pointed way that it made Annis squirm—and caught Annis's hand, his eyes suddenly very green. Even with two layers of gloves between them, she experienced a frisson of excitement at his touch.

"I look forward to our dance," he said.

Her pulse pounded in her ears at the heat in his gaze, and she felt a fatuous smile take possession of her features.

"Thank you, I—"

"Susanna is *waiting*, Annis." Her cousin yanked Annis's hand from Mr. Parker's and marched her away.

"And just who is *he* I should like to know?" Miriam hissed before they were out of earshot.

Annis had to trot to keep up with her taller cousin's brisk walk. "He is a friend of Lord Rotherhithe."

Miriam stopped abruptly, and Annis bumped into her. "You clumsy fool!"

"I'm sorry, Cousin."

Miriam grabbed Annis's upper arm in a grip so tight she winced. "Come over here, out of the way." Miriam led her into a doorway close to the retiring room before releasing her. "How did you come to know a friend of the new earl?"

Annis rubbed her arm. "I met them both at Lady Sedgwick's."

"You've already *met* Lord Rotherhithe?" Miriam shrieked, startling snickers from a pair of passing young bucks.

"Yes, he came to the countess seeking introductions."

"When was this?"

"Not long after he arrived."

"Why didn't you tell us?" Miriam demanded, although it sounded more like an accusation.

"I didn't think it was important."

"*You didn't think it was important.*" Miriam closed her eyes and tipped her face ceiling ward, addressing the chandelier over their heads as if seeking divine commiseration. "She didn't think it was important."

Annis had to bite her lip to keep from laughing at her cousin's melodramatic behavior.

Susanna rushed up to them, red-faced and breathless. "Miriam! You must come with me immediately. Lord Rotherhithe is even *now* speaking with Mama."

Miriam instantly forgot about Annis and the sisters fled at an unseemly speed.

Annis sighed and sagged against the wall, grateful for her reprieve, no matter how brief.

Without her permission, her eyes slid to where she'd been talking to Mr. Parker.

But he was no longer there.

Chapter 6

Henry watched Colin dance with one of the Bowman cousins, although not the one who had snubbed him and chided Annis as if she were a recalcitrant servant.

The sisters were undoubtedly beautiful, but he saw through them as clearly as a pane of glass. They were after a title rather than a fortune since their mother had come from the merchant class and was well-larded.

Because Henry was bored—and also a little intrigued by Miss Annis Bowman—he had engaged a private inquiry agent to investigate the Bowman family.

He'd learned that Annis's grandmother, Lady Cecily, was the daughter of an earl who'd married a commoner and had two sons. Annis was the daughter of the elder son, who'd died several years back. The second son, Thomas Bowman, had married Agnes Lewis, an heiress whose social status was blighted by her overly forthright manner and proximity to trade.

Thanks to her background, the Bowmans wouldn't have stepped so much as a toe into the Duke of Tinley's house tonight if not for Henry's influence.

When Colin had solicited one of the Bowman sisters to partner him in this set, Henry had been tempted to ask the other one for a dance, just to elicit a scandalized reaction.

But he'd decided it wasn't worth it. They were naked social climbers who'd already made their disdain of a mere clerk obvious. They were exactly the type of chits he'd hoped to weed out with this little charade.

Henry couldn't help chuckling at the sight of Colin gawking down Miss Bowman's decolletage—which was impressive—like a slavering hound. Any minute now he'd start humping the woman's leg.

Well, at least one of them was enjoying himself.

Henry wondered if he should have given in to Colin's incessant demands to visit a brothel. Perhaps that might have calmed the other man's amorous behavior. If Henry wasn't careful, Colin could end up engaged under false pretenses.

61

Increasingly, Henry feared that his little deception was ill-conceived.

Just like his pursuit of Annis Bowman was ill-conceived.

It was as obvious as the enormous nose on Henry's face that the woman was in love with the impoverished, godlike Earl of Avington. Her expression as she'd watched Avington walk away had been like a kick in the crotch.

Hell, he couldn't blame her for falling for the man. The earl was so bloody handsome it was ridiculous. On top of that, he'd seemed a friendly, amusing bloke; the sort of man Henry would like as a friend.

Henry snorted. He was behaving as if he were sixteen years old again and smitten by a woman who was in love with another man. Would he never learn?

Not that he was smitten—or anywhere near it. But he genuinely *liked* Annis Bowman and enjoyed talking with her, something he couldn't recall happening with a female in quite some time.

He'd had plenty of women over the years and, of course, he had enjoyed their company, but he couldn't remember laughing or joking with any. Laughing and joking were activities he reserved for his male friends. The women in his life were for sex; wanting to talk to one was something new.

Not that his interest in Miss Bowman was entirely platonic, of course. Indeed, he found her attractive, even though he had always preferred voluptuous women. He also liked his mistresses to be sexually confident and experienced, and Annis Bowman had turned ten shades of red at a little harmless flirtation.

Or maybe it hadn't been harmless. Had he been too aggressive with her? Hell, he had no idea how to flirt with a virgin. All he'd ever done was engage a mistress, put her in a house with servants, fine clothing, and other luxuries to keep her happy, and then visit her when he'd needed sexual release.

Obviously, he needed release right now if he was interested in a female who was clearly in love with another man.

Henry rolled his eyes; this uncustomary uncertainty was bloody annoying. It was because of this sort of emotional turmoil that he'd avoided romantic entanglements for the past two decades. All love ever led to—in his experience—was pain and confusion.

Henry set his glass of warm champagne on a passing footman's tray and made his way to the card room. Perhaps a bit of mindless gambling could help him forget Miss Annis Bowman.

The Language of Love

The room was busy, but he spied a free spot at a table with four men playing *vingt-et-un*.

"Mind if I sit in?" he asked.

They glanced up, their cool gazes sliding over him appraisingly. For a moment, he thought they'd tell him to sod off, but one of them gave an abrupt nod.

The play was brisk, with little chatter initially. When they realized Henry knew what he was about, they warmed up.

"You came with Rotherhithe from India?" the oldest man at the table asked. He wore clothing that hadn't been in fashion for at least half a century.

So, they knew he was a servant, and yet still invited him to play. Interesting.

"Yes, that is correct," Henry said. "I worked for the Company in Dacca."

"Swimmin' in lard, ain't he—Rotherhithe?" A tall, stringy fellow asked while another gent mixed the cards for a new game.

"You could say that."

"And you?"

"I'm afraid not. It's been my experience that only bad things flow downhill."

The men broke into raucous laughter at that.

"What's this, then? Playing with the help?" The drawling voice came from behind Henry's shoulder and would have been enough to set his back up even without the words.

"Back for more are you, Bowman?" the oldest man asked, his tone discouraging.

Henry jolted at the name and turned to find a young buck sneering down at him through narrowed eyes. Yes, Henry saw the resemblance between this man and his sisters, especially the one who'd given Henry such a scathing once-over earlier.

"Why not, Kingsley? It seems you'll let anyone play." He dropped into a chair two spaces away from Henry, whom he eyed with contempt.

The other players grumbled quietly but made no open remarks.

Over the next half hour, Bowman kept up a stream of insulting comments about how *ton* standards had lowered, his comments becoming less subtle with each hand he lost.

Henry found the lad amusing. He'd been baited by far cleverer men, and this stripling couldn't even come close. Especially as he was one hell of a poor card player who had more money than brains. But his incessant talk rattled the other players and, one after another, they drifted away, leaving only Henry and Bowman sitting at the table.

The younger man scraped up the cards from the last hand and tossed them to Henry.

"Maybe now we can play for something other than chicken stakes. I say we switch to piquet. A shilling a point and ten pounds a rubber."

The last man to leave the table turned back at those words. "I don't think Her Grace would approve of such a thing, Bowman. This isn't a gambling hell, you know."

"Why don't you run and tell her like a good little boy, Rivers?"

Rivers' face reddened, and he stalked away without responding.

So, Henry wasn't the only person the boy talked down to.

Henry stacked the cards neatly and put them aside before standing. He nodded to the three men who'd just left and reformed their group at a nearby table. "It was a pleasure, gentleman," he said, and then headed toward the door.

"Where are you running off to? Got some boots to shine?"

Henry stopped and turned; the rest of the room had gone quiet.

He looked into the blazing eyes of the boy still slouched at the table. "If it is a game of cards you want, tell me where and when. But I will not insult my hostess by turning her house into a gambling den."

Bowman pushed to his feet. "I'll tell you—"

"Ah, Parker, old chap," a bored voice called from behind Henry. "I hope you haven't thrown away all your blunt. I wanted to borrow a pony."

Henry turned to find the Earl of Avington smiling at him.

A few chuckles greeted the earl's words, and Avington nodded to the other men. "Rivers, Kingsley, good to see you both." His eyes settled on Bowman, and his smile grew condescending. "Bowman, your Mama has been turning the house upside down searching for you. You'd better run along and see what she wants before she sends your old nurse to fetch you."

Avington turned back to Henry, seemingly oblivious of Bowman's hate-filled glare and the snickers his words had triggered. "Come get a drink with me, old chap."

Henry followed him outside the room. "What a lucky coincidence, my lord—you popping in just then."

The Language of Love

The earl flashed his blinding grin. "Wasn't it, though?"

"I suppose I should thank you for saving me from doing something foolish."

"I don't believe you are capable of stupid behavior, Parker. Unless you meant being late for the supper dance with Annis. I last saw her with that dragon aunt of hers. I've snagged Freddie for the waltz, so we'll save two seats for you at our supper table." He strode off without waiting for an answer.

Henry didn't know what the other man was up to by stepping into the fray.

Why in the world should Avington give a toss whether Henry ended up facing young Bowman on Hampstead Heath in the morning?

***

The last time Annis had danced a waltz, it had been with Miles and they had been demonstrating the steps for a room full of giggling students.

This occasion was far, far different.

First, the room was crowded not with scrubby schoolgirls, but with the *ton*'s finest.

Second, Mr. Parker's body was making her skin tingle, which had never happened with Miles.

His enormous hands were light on her person and his face was close enough that she could see his eyes were a complex constellation of greens and browns with an outer ring the color of melted butter.

His lips curled at the corners and Annis knew that she'd been staring—a bad habit of hers, according to her cousins and aunt. She dropped her gaze to her feet, frowning at the scuffed slippers peeping out from beneath her skirt.

They glided across the dancefloor in silence, his arms strong but gentle as they guided her.

"Are you enjoying yourself, Miss Bowman?"

This close to his massive chest, his voice was a deep rumble. And he smelled delicious.

"What is that scent you are wearing?"

"Is that your way of saying you like the way I smell, Miss Bowman?"

She looked up into eyes that had lightened with amusement.

"You *do* smell good," she admitted. "But I cannot place it."

"It is oil extracted from bergamot oranges grown in the boot of Europe. A gentleman I knew in India discovered it complemented black tea."

"Tea? How remarkable. I should like to taste it."

He smiled down at her. "I believe that could be arranged."

"Oh, dear—now you will think I was begging you for tea."

He dexterously guided them around a very young man and his giggling dance partner. "I was thinking of the other ways in which you could taste it."

At least that was what Annis thought he'd said. "I beg your pardon?"

"I ran into a relative of yours in the card room," Mr. Parker said, ignoring her question.

Annis frowned, momentarily perplexed by the change in topics. "Oh. You mean my cousin Percy?"

"So that is his name."

"Was he rude to you?"

"Now why would you ask that, I wonder?" One of his eyebrows quirked in a way that arrested her attention. He had such a powerful face—sharp, hard angles, yet his eyes could turn liquid when he was pleased or amused. His jaw was especially intriguing, like something chiseled from stone. She would like to touch his jaw, and his nose, too, which was big and arched and very regal. His lashes—dark brown with blond tips the same shade as the highlights in his sun-streaked hair—were as long, thick, and curly as those on her childhood pony, Pepper.

Pepper.

Annis frowned; she hadn't thought about Pepper in years. What had happened to—

"Why do you look so sad, Miss Bowman?"

"I was just thinking about my pony. I'm sorry, but you asked me something, didn't you?"

He cocked his head. "You have a *pony?*"

"Not anymore. What was it you asked me, Mr. Parker?"

He hesitated slightly before he answered. "I asked why you assumed your cousin was rude to me?"

"Because Percy is rude to everyone."

His hand tightened on her waist. "Is he rude to you?"

"I am so far beneath his notice I doubt he's even aware of my existence."

"What in the world has given him such an elevated opinion of himself?"

The Language of Love

"His mother and sisters; they dote on him excessively. What did he say to you?"

"It doesn't signify, Miss Bowman."

"I wish you would call me Annis."

"You do?" Both his dark brows shot up this time. "But wouldn't that be rather forward?"

"Perhaps, but it would be far simpler."

"Simpler?"

"There are three Miss Bowmans currently inhabiting this one room. Besides, I daresay we might be seeing a great deal of you, if his lordship's interest in Susanna is anything to go by." She looked pointedly toward where the earl was dancing with her cousin. "That is their second set tonight."

Parker followed her gaze, his eyes narrowing in a way that made him look fierce. In fact, he looked very much like a portrait of Alexander the Great she'd come across in a Greek history book.

"*Ο κατακτητής του κόσμου*," she murmured, studying Mr. Parker's striking profile.

"Pardon?"

"It means the Conqueror of the World. That is what people called Alexander the Great."

"Is that right? And what about him?"

"I was just thinking of him. Not that I know him, of course." Annis bit her lip; how much more dimwitted could she sound?

His hard mouth curled into a slow smile. "I should hope not. He's been dead for a while."

"Two-thousand-one-hundred-and-forty years."

"So, you've been reading about ancient Greece today?" There was an amused twinkle in his eyes.

"No, today I was reading about the year 1666."

"You have eclectic tastes," he said. "Interesting year—the Great Plague, wasn't it?"

"And also the Great Fire of London."

"So, a year for *greats,* in other words."

"Don't you think it must have been an exciting time to live?"

He laughed and the rich, deep sound drew glances from other dancers and observers alike. "*Exciting,* perhaps, but not very comfortable."

"Although we call it the Great Plague, the Black Death was actually far more catastrophic for Europe's population."

"Is that so? I thought they were one and the same."

"No, three centuries separated them."

"Indeed? You are a veritable treasure trove of interesting information… Annis."

Annis flushed at the intimacy of hearing her name on his tongue. "Am I boring you? I tend to spout random, strange information. I expect you think I am rather foolish."

"I do not think you are foolish. Nor are you boring. Not at all," he added, giving her a look that sent distracting sensations to her female parts. "This discussion all began with a long-dead Greek emperor—why is that?"

"He was actually a king."

Rather than get annoyed at being corrected by a mere female—as most men did—he grinned. "Very well. Why did you mention a long-dead Greek king?"

"I think you resemble him."

He looked arrested. "Indeed?" His falcon-like eyes bored into her.

"Yes, when you were looking so fierce about Susanna dancing with Lord Rotherhithe."

"Fierce, was I?"

"You look the same way now."

"Fierce like King Alexander. Hmm." He was smiling again, and it was a teasing, lovely expression on his naturally stern face.

"I'm sorry. My mother always said I was hen-witted the way I hop from subject to subject."

"Hen-witted? No, I don't think you are that. Besides, wouldn't hopping be more in line with a rabbit? Shouldn't it be *bunny*-witted?"

She gave a delighted laugh. "Excellent point, Mr. Parker."

"You must call me Henry if I am to call you Annis."

"But I thought that was his lordship's Christian name. Didn't Freddie introduce you as Colin?"

He looked momentarily nonplussed. "Ah, yes, *that*. Colin is my middle name, which I use because his lordship's first name is also Henry. It can get quite confusing, so I agreed to go by my middle name."

She studied his face, accustoming herself to the change of name. He didn't look much like a Colin. "It doesn't seem fair."

The Language of Love

"What doesn't seem fair?" he asked as he deftly avoided a collision with a man who was spinning his partner so fast that she must be dizzy.

"That you should have to give up your name just because it is the same as his lordship. Names are important."

"Ah."

Annis did not think he sounded convinced, but that would not be unusual. In her experience, people were very careless about language and words.

"Henry."

"Yes, Annis?"

"Your name is Germanic and means *he who rules his household*. I was just thinking it suits you better than Colin. I don't think you look like a Colin at all."

His body was shaking.

Annis gave him a stern look. "Are you laughing at me, Henry?"

"No, not at all. I'm amused because you think I look like a man who rules his household. How so?"

"Well… you have a very determined jaw and chin."

"Ah, I see. Why don't I look like a Colin—what does the name mean?"

She chewed her lower lip. "I must admit I don't know what Colin means."

He clucked his tongue. "I'm very disappointed to hear that."

"You are mocking me now."

He smiled. "Just a little."

"Do you have any siblings?"

"You are hopping again, Annis."

Slow down, she told herself, and then looked up to see him watching her, wearing an odd smile.

"There is only me."

"I beg your pardon?" Annis asked. "Only you?"

"I have no siblings."

"Oh, yes."

"What about you?"

"I am an only, too." And that was probably a good thing, given how much trouble only one of her had managed to cause.

"Lady Sedgwick said you lived with your grandmother before moving to London?"

"Yes, that is true." She swallowed and looked away.

Thinking about her grandmother brought all the guilt she felt to the surface, and she hated that reaction. She should enjoy thinking about the person she loved most in the world. But Mr. Leech had robbed her of that.

"What brought you to town this year?" he asked.

"Hmm? What was that?"

"You lived with your grandmother, but you've moved to London. I asked why."

"Oh, no reason in particular," she lied.

He gracefully guided her past a bottleneck of unskilled dancers. "You are an excellent dancer. Did you dance a lot in India?"

"Rarely. Lord Rotherhithe engaged a master for us and we practiced in the ballroom at Rotherhithe House for the past week."

"You've only been dancing a week? Then you're a *superb* dancer."

"I have an superb partner."

Annis stumbled a bit.

"Steady on," he murmured, his face serious but his eyes smiling.

"What are your plans now that you've returned to England… Henry?"

His powerful shoulder shrugged slightly under her hand. "I'm only temporarily serving as his lordship's secretary. I have a letter of introduction to a gentleman at the Company headquarters."

"You will stay in London?"

"I might."

"You said you had family here, but you won't be visiting them?"

Something unreadable flickered across his face. "They are distant relatives."

"Ah." They danced for a moment in silence, Annis unable to pull her gaze away from their feet. They were moving in such perfect harmony; it was quite mesmerizing.

"What about you, Annis? Will you be vising your grandmother anytime soon?"

"No, probably not until after—" Annis bit her lip, catching the words *I get betrothed or married.*

"After?"

"What is it you will do for the Company?" she asked, ignoring his question.

"Move piles of paper from one side of a desk to the other."

Annis looked up at his words.

"There, I knew that would get you to look at me, rather than my feet."

Her face heated, and she knew her pale skin would be splotchy and red.

"What were you thinking about, Annis?"

"I was wishing this dance wouldn't end."

Bother and blast! Now why did I say that?

His eyes widened, and his hand tightened.

"I just meant that I love the waltz and dance it so infrequently," she clarified.

He nodded, a faint smile on his lips.

And then the music swelled, and the loveliest waltz Annis had ever danced was over.

***

Henry's face hurt; he'd not smiled so much in years. His odd little dance partner was utterly enchanting, her bunny hopping manner of conversation adorable and invigorating. A man would never know what Annis Bowman might say next.

He was still smiling as he led Annis into the room where tables were set up for supper, a massive banquet along one wall groaning beneath enough food to feed a village for a month.

Henry led Annis toward the table where Avington and Lady Sedgwick sat.

The earl stood as they approached. "You ladies relax; Parker and I will be your servants."

"The duchess is not stinting, is she?" Avington asked beneath his breath as he and Henry took their places in front of the crowded buffet, where liveried footmen loaded plates at the guests' direction.

"Not all balls are like this one?" Henry asked, gesturing to the opulent excess of rich food, thousands of candles, huge potted plants, and almost suffocating floral displays.

"I don't recall anything quite this luxurious," Avington admitted. He nodded at the footman who approached them and said to Henry. "What do you think, Parker? A sampling of all the dishes?"

"Sounds perfect," Henry agreed, smiling at the footman.

Avington turned back to Henry as the servant fixed their plates. "The last *ton* ball I attended was years ago, before I joined the army."

71

Henry couldn't help noticing the earl's evening coat—although exquisitely cut and of fine material—was shiny from frequent pressing. There was a story there, but Henry could tell from the man's reserved tone he was in no hurry to share it.

Colin pushed up between them. "I say, my—er, Parker, this is dashed good fun, isn't it?" His pale cheeks were flushed and his eyes sparkled.

"I'm glad you are enjoying yourself, my lord."

"Who wouldn't after being stuck in Dacca with all those dry sticks at the Company dances?" Colin waved vigorously at the nearest footman, who was already busy with somebody else. "You there!" He snapped his fingers when the footman continued serving his guests. "I want two plates and don't be stinting."

Henry sighed.

"You didn't care for India, Rotherhithe?" Avington asked. "I shouldn't have thought you would have remained there for twenty years."

Henry could almost hear the puzzle pieces clunking into place in Colin's head as he recalled who he was supposed to be.

"Oh, er, yes, quite so. But not Dacca, so much. I preferred to be at Sheesham Bagana, my grand property in the country." Colin gave Henry one of his eager spaniel smiles and then leaned closer. "Have you met Miss Bowman's cousins?" he asked in a whisper loud enough to be heard down at the East India docks. "The younger one—can't recall her name right now—anyhow, have you seen the shelf of goods she's—"

Henry gestured toward the footman, who was holding two plates toward Henry

"Please, take my plates, my lord."

"Oh, jolly good." Colin eyed the well-laden plates and grinned. "I'd better hoof it," he told a transfixed Avington. "I'm hoping to hit the trough at least once more before we're back to the mummery." And then he was off.

"Seems to be enjoying himself," Avington commented mildly.

"His lordship has a gregarious nature," Henry said, his understatement earning a booming laugh from the other man.

"Well, it's nice to see somebody enjoying all this," Avington said.

"You do not, my lord?"

"No, but I'd better learn to. Quickly."

The Language of Love

Before Henry could inquire more deeply, the footman returned with their plates of food.

Henry's heart sank when he saw that Colin had found his way to their table and brought one of the Bowman harpies with him—the younger one, he thought. Still, he supposed it was good to keep his employee close at hand since he was proving to be not only an ill-mannered twit, but something of a social menace to boot.

Henry placed a plate in front of Annis and took the seat beside her, with Avington on her other side. Miss Susanna Bowman's eye darted between Annis and Henry, an unpleasant smirk forming on her lovely mouth.

Lady Sedgwick, a woman with vast reserves of patience, steered the table's conversation along lines that gave Colin no chance to say anything too shocking or inane. Between the countess and Avington, the conversation flowed, which left Henry free to observe Annis.

She ate her lobster patties first and picked at the rest of her food. She was such a dainty little thing. He did not think she looked very strong or hearty.

Henry nudged his plate toward her.

Annis turned away from Avington, who'd just said something to make the others laugh.

"Take my lobster patties," he said.

Her ridiculously beautiful eyes lowered to his plate before bouncing back up. "You don't want them?"

He shook his head.

She removed them one by one with her fork. "Thank you."

Henry realized he was staring at her mouth and imagining it doing things other than eating lobster patties.

Lord, but he was a dog! The woman was clearly an innocent.

He pulled his gaze from her mouth and fixed it on her eyes—not a hardship. "Tell me, Annis, are you ever at liberty?"

She daubed her lips with the heavy damask napkin and then cut a quick glance at her cousin—as if to see whether she was listening. "Rarely. And what about you? Do your duties for the earl keep you occupied?"

It took Henry a moment to recall he was a secretary, not a wealthy, independent peer. Sometimes he was as mutton headed as Colin. "I get the occasional afternoon to myself. Perhaps we might go for a ride in the park sometime?"

She looked as surprised by the words as Henry felt uttering them. "Do you mean in your carriage? Or do you hack?"

"Which do you prefer?"

"Oh, I—"

"Annis."

Both their heads jerked up at the nasal, unpleasant voice.

Miss Bowman's pretty eyes glinted with spite as she looked from Annis to Henry. "I left my fan in the retiring room. Run and fetch it for me."

The entire table went silent.

A wave of anger flooded Henry; what a bloody shrew.

He was about to turn to Annis and tell her—well; he didn't know what, exactly—but she stood before he could speak.

"Of course, Cousin Susanna."

Lady Sedgwick stood with her. "I'll go with you, Annis. I'm afraid I've trod on my flounce and require a few of your pins."

That was a fib if Henry had ever heard one; the countess was the most graceful woman he'd ever known. Clearly, Lady Sedgwick had a heart of gold behind her icy exterior.

The men resumed their seats after the two women left the table.

Colin, oblivious to the tensions swirling around him, turned back to Susanna Bowman.

Avington leaned toward Henry and said in a low voice, "You can't let it bother you, Parker."

Oddly, Henry was not surprised that the other man knew what he was feeling. The earl looked like a handsome, brainless doll—like Colin, in fact—but Avington was interested in those around him.

"It's a wretched way to live, being a poor dependent," Henry finally said, something he knew from first-hand experience. "Isn't there anything somebody could do?"

What Henry really meant was: *why don't you marry her—since she's obviously in love with you?*

Avington's merry eyes were grim as they followed the receding backs of the two women. "A man with money could do plenty." He gave Henry a self-deprecating smile. "But that's what we lack, isn't it, Parker—money?"

He didn't wait for Henry to answer, which was just as well, since Henry was feeling rather like a sneaking rat since he had plenty of money.

The Language of Love

"I'd do anything to save her," the earl said, his voice pulsing with emotion. "To save both of them," he amended with a quick look at Henry. "But I can't."

The flash of pain in the other man's eyes confirmed Henry's suspicions: Avington loved Annis as much as she appeared to love him.

Bitterness and pity swirled in his belly as he studied the impoverished peer. He'd only met the man a few hours ago but knew instinctively that he was honorable and kind. He would make Annis an excellent husband, but first he would have to give up his goal of a rich wife.

"Not everyone will sacrifice themselves for money," Henry said.

It was the most he was willing to say. If the other man didn't understand what a treasure he was giving up to marry a rich woman, then Henry wasn't so sure Avington deserved Annis Bowman.

Avington turned his startlingly blue eyes on Henry, an anguished expression in them. "No, not everyone will sacrifice themselves for money, Parker. But I will."

Chapter 7

Henry's days and nights passed in a blur of vapid frivolity that wore on him more and more with every hour.

Not only was each function more tedious than the last, but Henry suspected that Annis Bowman—the only person who could have made the shallow *ton* whirl bearable—was purposely being kept away from him.

On one hand, it was probably best that Annis wasn't around. After all, she was in love with another man. But, on the other hand, she amused him and he liked her. Henry so rarely met people he liked that he simply couldn't forget about her, even if all she would ever be was an acquaintance.

For years now—ever since Henry had made far more money than he could spend in five lifetimes—he'd become accustomed to getting everything he wanted. Not surprisingly, he didn't like being denied anything. Specifically, he didn't like being denied Annis's company.

In the two weeks since the Tinley ball, he'd seen Annis only twice, and both times only briefly, before one of her unpleasant family members had found some use for her and whisked her away.

And that was another thing.

Of all the women Colin could have formed an attachment to, he'd picked one of the Bowman witches. Or, rather, *they* had chosen *him*, hooking Colin as effortlessly as they would a starving carp.

Susanna Bowman—with the help of her mother and sister— was setting her hook as deeply as possible in Colin's unwitting jaw while also cutting out the competition.

And it *was* a competition; Roman gladiators had nothing on the fight-to-the-death spirit that pervaded *ton* functions. Colin was that rare beast: a wealthy, eligible, *and* handsome aristocrat. That he was an imbecile only made him more attractive to women like Susanna Bowman, because they could bend and shape him to their will.

To be honest, he wouldn't have been able to spend much time with Annis if she *had* come to the various functions because Colin kept

The Language of Love

Henry busy making sure the idiot didn't inadvertently get himself engaged.

But Henry had had enough.

If Annis wasn't at this bloody ball tonight, he was going to arrange for Lady Sedgwick to apply some unpleasant pressure on Mrs. Agnes Bowman. If he didn't get to see Annis soon, her aunt wouldn't receive so much as an invitation to the street sweepers' annual ball—if there were such a thing.

Indeed, if Annis wasn't at the Penistone ball tonight, Henry wouldn't wait to send a message via Colin; he would speak to the countess then and there.

Ideally, it was Colin who should make such requests of Lady Sedgwick, but the man was such a nitwit that he couldn't frig his own hand without making a hash of it, so Henry would *relay* his employer's requests.

The Penistone ball was one of the largest of the Season, and Henry and Colin had received a coveted dinner invitation. However— thanks to an unfortunate incident with an oyster fork and a dowager duchess's turban at their last dinner party—they'd sent their regrets and would eat at home tonight.

Honestly, monitoring Colin's behavior across a dinner table was more than Henry could bear at this point.

Indeed, Henry felt as if he'd been watching Colin all his life. He was having serious doubts that he could last the Season. And really, was there any point? He'd already proven to himself what he'd always suspected: these people despised him, just like he'd known they would.

Although he'd danced occasionally—usually because men were sorely in demand—he had not engaged in a conversation worth remembering since that one waltz with Annis.

A few weeks in London had done plenty to reaffirm his belief that the beau monde only respected money and status. Nothing else existed for these people and he'd begun to believe it would be better to just head to the Continent and find a place to live.

He certainly had no intention of visiting the family estate in Yorkshire. Why would he? He had nothing but terrible memories of Stoke.

And then there was the fact that Julia lived there.

Henry had received a steady stream of begging—or demanding, really—letters from dear Julia even before he'd left India. His cousin's widow had decided that Henry was the same smitten, slavish dunce that he'd been twenty years ago, but now he was also Julia's personal milch cow.

Every letter from the countess had included two things: Henry needed to come to Yorkshire *immediately,* as important matters could not be resolved without his presence; and Henry needed to instruct the steward at Stoke Castle to release ample funds to Julia *immediately.*

Henry hadn't bothered to write and tell her he had no intention of ever stepping foot in Stoke—or Yorkshire—for as long as he lived. Nor had he dispensed any money.

He'd written to his steward about Julia, his instructions clear: the only monies Milner was to disperse to Lady Rotherhithe was the quarterly sum from her jointure. She could occupy the Dower House *as it was.*

The Dower House was a pokey, draughty little cottage, so Henry knew Julia would never want to live in such a place. She was welcome to continue living at Stoke, but he doubted she wanted to live there, either. What she wanted—what she'd *always* wanted since she'd been a girl—was to live in London.

As far as Henry knew, she'd never even paid a visit to the city. It didn't surprise Henry that his cousin Charles hadn't given Julia what she'd dreamed of. His uncle had already sold or mortgaged everything of value before his cousin had assumed the earldom. Charles would have had to choose between taking his wife to London *or* hunting. That Charles had died while hunting with the Quorn told Henry what his choice had been.

He scowled at his reflection as he gave his cravat a final tweak. Why the devil was he thinking about Charles and Julia? There was no subject guaranteed to put him in a foul mood more quickly.

Henry flicked a speck of dust off his dancing slippers and gave his tidy, but frugally attired, body a last look.

That was another thing he was sick of: dressing in the clothing of a clerk. He'd worked damned hard to afford the finest, and he was tired of wearing cheap rags.

And whose fault is that?

Henry rolled his eyes at his imaginary friend, refusing to be baited.

He left his moldering chambers behind and made his way to the dining room, where he found Colin examining himself in the mirror over the fireplace.

The Language of Love

When Colin turned to him, Henry goggled. "Good Lord! What is *that?*"

Colin tried to look down at himself without spoiling the confection around his neck—which looked like it was made from twenty yards of linen. "You mean my waistcoat?"

Henry wouldn't have called it that; he wasn't sure *what* he would have called it other than an abomination. It was patterned with puce with coquelicot diamonds and made him look like Harlequin.

"Where the *devil* did you get that?" he demanded.

"It's Nugee, old chap! Do you like it?"

"No."

"Oh." A bruised, hurt expression replaced Colin's perennial grin, making Henry feel like he'd just swatted an ebullient puppy with a newspaper.

He relented. "It is certainly... unusual." That was the best he could do. The truth was that Colin looked exactly like the fool he was with his ludicrously high collar points and fussy neckcloth on top of the appalling waistcoat.

Let him have his fun. It will all be over in a few weeks.

For once, Henry listened to the voice without arguing.

"Drink?" Henry asked Colin, who was back to staring at his reflection in the mirror, his brow deeply furrowed.

He couldn't turn his head, so he shifted his entire torso toward Henry. "Hmm?"

Henry held up a decanter.

Colin's face lightened, his troubles sliding away like water off a duck's back. "Ah yes, jolly good. Whatever you're having."

"So," Henry said as he poured, "How was your visit home?" Henry had insisted that Colin pay a visit to his family today. They lived only an hour outside London, yet the man had not gone to see them even though he'd been away almost five years.

Colin strutted toward him and took his glass, causing Henry to notice the enormous cuffs jutting from the skin-tight sleeves of his coat.

He bit his tongue. After all, what could he do? Send him up to his room to change? Likely he would come down in something even worse—although what could be worse boggled the imagination. The bloody tailor who'd done this to him deserved to be horse-whipped. Henry had half a mind to march over to the man's shop tomorrow and call him out.

"All is well back at the vicarage," Colin said, employing a pompous tone that set Henry's teeth on edge. "My youngest sister married the local quack and none too soon, as there will be a brat before you know it. My elder sister still keeps house for my father, who has it in mind to step down after this year."

"And what does a vicar do when he is no longer a vicar?"

"He'll no doubt spend his time surrounded by piles of moldering old tomes."

"Your father is a man of letters?" Henry asked, unable to mask his surprise. The poor bastard must look at Colin and wonder what had gone wrong.

"Can't think how I missed out on his brains," Colin said, unknowingly echoing Henry's thoughts. "I'd blame my mother's rackety ways if I didn't look so much like old pater."

Henry could only stare in wonder and not a little awe: the man had absolutely no filter between his brain and mouth.

"So, when did you get back?"

"Oh, just past three."

"You went and came back by *three o'clock?*"

Colin shrugged, turning one foot side from side-to-side in front of him, admiring his shoe.

"Why did you bolt back here so bloody fast?" Henry narrowed his eyes. "You haven't been back to Whites, have you?" Henry had been livid when he'd learned Colin was on the brink of putting him up for membership at the Tory gentleman's club.

"Er, no, I got back in time to go to that rout at Lady—" he stopped, a frown marring his handsome features. "Well, damn me if I can recall what lady it was other than to say she wore the most hideous chartreuse turban."

Henry didn't think Colin had much room to talk when it came to hideous fashion. He opened his mouth to chide the other man about going to *any* gathering without Henry in attendance but decided he couldn't be bothered.

"I remember she lived in a gray or white house," Colin added, describing half the houses in London. "Or maybe it was red brick?" He shrugged and dragged his cuff over his glass of whiskey.

Henry opened his mouth to warn him to have a care, but he was too late.

The Language of Love

Colin glanced down. "Oh, I say!" His eyebrows plunged, and he raised his soaking amber cuff to his mouth and proceeded to nurse on it.

"Come," Henry said grimly. "Let us go to dinner. I'll get Flitwick to send up a bib."

***

Once they'd dined and Colin had changed his shirt, they were an hour later to the ball than expected.

Baron Penistone and his lady waited outside a ballroom twice as large as that at Rotherhithe House, and the baron greeted Colin as if the two men were old friends.

"Dashing, old man, dashing!" Penistone said, himself sporting a revolting waistcoat of lime green and lavender.

Lady Penistone wore a long-suffering look that spoke of decades of patience—and hideous waistcoats.

Henry followed Colin into the welter of sound, heat, and light and they took glasses of champagne from a harried-looking menial garbed in atrocious yellow livery, and then paused to catch their breath.

The massive room was packed wall-to-wall with the crème de la crème of London society. Those attempting to dance were so crowded by onlookers they may as well not have bothered. The heat was stifling and a miasma of perfume, perspiration, and desperation hung over the cavernous room. Desperation because there were a mere nineteen days remaining before most of the beau monde abandoned the city in droves for their country homes. If a person wasn't betrothed by the end of the Season, it would likely be another nine or ten months before they got another chance.

Since Henry was taller than most of the other guests, he could see over the assembled heads toward the French doors that made up one wall of the ballroom. They'd been flung open to the night, but it was an exceptionally close evening and the air refused to circulate.

"Oh, look! There are Miss Bowman and Miss Susanna Bowman."

Henry glanced to where Colin was—rudely—pointing, hoping to spy a third Miss Bowman, but Annis's distinctive blond head was nowhere to be seen.

Colin waved at the sisters, bouncing up and down on the balls of his feet and grinning fatuously—all habits that even Lady Sedgwick had not been able to break him of.

Henry couldn't understand how Colin could bear the two sisters and their domineering mother—whom Henry collectively referred to as the Three Witches in the privacy of his head.

"I say, doesn't Miss Susanna look *smashing*?" Colin demanded. When Henry forbore to answer, Colin continued. "She looks so—so—dash it, Parker, I just can't think of the proper words to describe her."

Henry could think of a few, but he doubted they were the same ones eluding his bacon-brained employee. The most civil thing Henry could say about the rapacious woman was that she was lovely—as long as one didn't look too closely into her beautiful eyes, which were sharper than a moneylender's, or listen to the acid words pouring from her shapely lips.

Henry had just opened his mouth to issue a few cautionary words about not disappearing *any*where with *any* female when an older woman bear-leading a pallid young chit pushed up beside Colin.

"Good evening, my lord. I was—"

"Ah, yes," Colin said vaguely, thrusting his empty glass into the woman's hands without looking down. "I'd love another. Much obliged," he murmured, shooting his flamboyant cuffs and then strutting like a magpie toward the object of his attention.

The stunned woman held the empty glass in limp fingers as she stared after Colin, her jaw hanging.

Henry took the glass from her unresisting hand and she swiveled slowly toward him, only then noticing his presence.

He smiled down at her shocked face. "I'm afraid you'll have to excuse his lordship for not hearing you, ma'am as he is rather deaf on that side."

Her pale silver brows shot up. "Is he?"

"Yes, I'm afraid so."

"No! And such a *young* man." Both she and her companion looked over to where Colin was now chatting with Miss Susanna Bowman.

Colin was using his hands to describe something to her. One of his waving arms shot directly into the path of a footman carrying a tray laden with glasses of champagne.

The servant hastily stepped back to avoid the flailing limb, an action which caused him to bump into a ferocious-looking woman wearing the better part of a peacock on her head.

The Language of Love

Henry and the women beside him gasped as the peacock careened sideways into a red-faced young buck who was dancing the reel as if it were a Highland Fling.

The dancer staggered back to avoid crushing his partner. In the process, he slammed into the man on his other side, knocking *him* into a throng of spectators hard enough to send several sprawling to the parquet floor.

Somebody inside the writhing mob must have jostled the same unfortunate footman with the glasses—who had somehow recovered his footing without spilling a drop—and the sound of feminine screams and breaking crystal could be heard even over the determined sawing of the orchestra.

"My goodness," the woman beside Henry murmured, her hand raised to her mouth, her wide eyes riveted to the pandemonium.

Colin, majestically unaware of the chaotic series of dominoes he'd unknowingly set off, led Susanna Bowman toward the French doors.

Bloody hell!

What had Henry said—a hundred times at least—about *not* leaving the ballroom with any woman?

Henry handed both his and Colin's empty champagne glasses to the woman still standing beside him, ignoring her indignant gasp as he darted toward his disappearing employee.

Precious minutes ticked by as he shoved his way through the crowd, his elbows and knees earning him lifetime enemies.

Harried and sweating, he reached the other side of the ballroom to find that Colin had stopped just inside the French doors and was displaying his new waistcoat to a clutch of admiring young tulips.

Miss Bowman stood to one side of Colin, arms crossed and tapping her toe, her eyes narrowed with displeasure.

Henry hovered close enough to keep an eye on them, but not too close to be noticed.

Thankfully, two more young men joined the group, and it was clear—to both Henry and Miss Susanna Bowman—that prying Colin from his admiring horde and luring him out into the gardens was now unlikely.

Henry sighed with relief, but the feeling was fleeting. He might have stopped Colin from doing something foolish tonight, but what about tomorrow night? And all the nights after?

He pushed the annoying subject from his mind, and turned his thoughts to another matter, entirely: Annis Bowman.

"Just where the devil are you hiding yourself, Annis?" he muttered under his breath as he swept the ballroom with his eyes.

He made not one, but three sweeps of the ballroom, but did not see his quarry.

It was, Henry decided with a grim smile, time to quit waiting for Annis to come to him.

Tomorrow he would go to *her*.

Chapter 8

The morning after the Penistone ball, Annis found herself at liberty for the first time in weeks.

Her cousins and aunt had risen exceptionally late and then gone off to an alfresco party at Lady Sissington's.

Although Annis's name had been included on the invitation, her aunt said they would be too crushed in the carriage if she were to join them.

Aunt Agnes had been making similar excuses to exclude Annis from events ever since the Tinley ball. Her aunt and cousins had been relentless in their berating in the days that followed that event.

"How *could* you dance with that man? Throwing yourself at a mere clerk in that shameless way?" they'd demanded. "I heard the Company sacked him from his job in India. I heard his mother was a scullery maid and his father a costermonger. Have you no dignity? If not for yourself, at least consider *our* feelings on the matter," they'd accused.

They'd raked her so incessantly that Annis had been grateful to be left behind today, even if it had meant that she'd become a drudge to the seamstress and had worked her fingers to the bone hemming gowns all morning.

But this afternoon she was free!

Annis seized the opportunity to take a walk before the seamstress found her again. Today her destination was Hookham's, the one extravagance she could not do without.

She was past ready to return the *Memoirs of Madame de Hausset,* who'd been a lady's maid to Madame de Pompadour. Annis had found the woman's commentary on the antics of the French court far more tiresome than titillating.

While her uncle's library was rich with a certain kind of book—improving tracts, for instance—biographies and novels were not abundant. After her evening at the Tinley ball—more specifically, after the lively time she'd had with *Henry*—she needed some fluffy reading to distract herself from thoughts of him.

Annis told herself that she should be grateful that she hadn't been able to dance with him or talk to him again. After all, why torment herself by spending more time with him when a poor clerk was simply not in her future?

Not that their brief acquaintance in *any* way suggested that Henry had viewed Annis as a marriage prospect.

But her brain was a willful organ and she still couldn't stop thinking about him. She'd even begun *dreaming* of him; dreams that made her blush and squirm just to remember them.

Annis's first and only beau was Mr. Leech. Although Mr. Leech had treated her vilely—criminally, in fact—he had done one thing that she couldn't make herself regret: he'd made love to her, not once, but several times.

Annis adored that phrase: making love.

It was unfortunate that the phrase was so much more impressive than the deed had been.

But if the experience hadn't been all that she'd hoped for— indeed, their handful of *interludes* had been uncomfortable, quick, and awkward—Annis consoled herself that at least she wouldn't go to her grave without ever knowing physical love.

As brief and unfulfilling as the episodes had been, they *had* released something inside her—some sort of… awareness of the pleasure her body was capable of, even if she'd not experienced it with Mr. Leech.

Of course, there was a considerable cost for that discovery; now she would need to confess her impure state to Mr. Norburg on her wedding night.

You'd do it beforehand if you weren't so completely bereft of scruples.

Annis couldn't argue with that accusation. But there was no point in worrying about her wedding night before Mr. Norburg made the offer. So her mind, like a willful horse, shied away from the unpleasant thought and wandered back to Henry.

In her wicked dreams it had been Henry, instead of Mr. Leech, doing those things to her. She imagined that *making love* with Henry would be a far different experience than it had with Mr. Leech.

You'd better enjoy your fantasies, my dear, because that is all you'll ever get to enjoy of him.

Yes, that was true enough. Painfully true.

The Language of Love

Annis had just turned onto Duke Street when a carriage rolled up beside her. She looked up to see Henry smiling down at her, as if she'd summoned him with her wicked thoughts.

"Mr. Parker," she said rather stupidly.

He tipped his hat. "I thought we'd agreed you'd call me Henry."

"You are out for a ride?" Yet another stupid question since he was looking down at her from a phaeton that appeared twice as high as usual.

Rather than point out the obviousness of her words, he smiled. "I hope you'll forgive me for not getting down, but this frisky pair would be half-way to Newcastle if given a chance."

"Are you headed to the Park? If so, you are going the wrong way."

He flicked a gaze up and down the street. "Am I? Perhaps you might come with me—just to show me the way."

"Come with you?"

"I asked you for a ride in the park at the Tinley ball, but you disappeared without giving an answer."

He was kindly ignoring the reason for her abrupt disappearance that night: her wretched cousin's demand that Annis go fetch her reticule. Immediately after *that* pointless errand, her aunt had needed something, and then Miriam, until finally the night was over without her seeing Henry again.

"I'm sorry I had to leave supper so abruptly that night."

"I was sorry, too. I was hoping to make the offer again when his lordship and I called at your aunt's house—twice—but I've not seen hide nor hair of you since."

Annis perked up at the idiom and then saw his lips twitch into a smile.

"You did that on purpose, didn't you, Mr. Parker?"

He grinned. "Yes, guilty as charged. And call me Henry. If you come ride with me, you can tell me the origin of that fascinating phrase."

"I thought his lordship was going to the alfresco party today?" Annis asked.

"Yes, we both were."

Panic seized her. "And it is already over?" Her aunt would be livid to find her gone.

"His lordship is still at the party. It is only I who left early—you needn't worry, your aunt and cousins should be there for hours yet." He extended a big hand, clad in black leather. "Come, let me give you a hand up."

Annis stared up into his changeable eyes, which were darker today—a fascinating blend of amber, gold, and brown—and were quickly losing their good humor the longer she made him wait.

But still she hesitated, her aunt's stricture—that she do nothing to alienate the affections of Mr. Norburg—running through her head.

But surely Mr. Norburg would never learn about a ride in the park?

Henry's hand wavered, and his expression hardened even more. Annis feared he saw her hesitation as evidence that she would be ashamed to be seen with him, as her cousins had told her she should be.

She shoved aside her qualms and reached up.

"That's a girl," he said. "Put your foot on that step and I'll help you up."

When she did as he bade, he pulled her up with no more effort than he would a doll.

"Here, settle in beside me—there's plenty of room."

Annis had never been in a phaeton before; it was like viewing the world from a cloud. The narrow seat was cushioned and soft, covered in diamond-tucked black leather with an insubstantial back and side rail that made her feel as if she would topple out.

He shifted slightly, his muscular thigh rubbing against her much smaller leg as he attempted to make more space for her.

"Comfortable?" he asked.

His face was very close, and she could see the ring of antique gold around his changeable irises. He was very large and masculine—far more so than Mr. Leech, who'd been handsome, but slender and fine-boned—and something about his chiseled jaw and full, firm lips made her entire body thrum with excitement. A reaction she'd never experienced with Mr. Leech. Or Mr. Norburg.

She blinked up at him, powerful sensations swirling in her belly. He smelled so good and the bergamot teased her nostrils. His hard, warm person pressed up against her and—

"Annis?" His eyes crinkled with a mix of concern and amusement. "Are you comfortable?"

"It is a long way down."

The Language of Love

His beautiful lips pulled up into a rakish smile. "It is. But I shan't tip us over."

She nodded, realizing suddenly that she trusted him—not that she was any superb judge of men, if the mistake she'd made with Mr. Leech was anything to go by.

He made a soft clucking sound, and the horses surged forward.

Annis gripped the low railing on her right side and leaned closer to Henry, clutching her reticule in her lap. For once, she was grateful that her bonnet ribbon was snarled in its habitual knot beneath her ear; her hat would go nowhere.

"Where were you headed just now?" he asked.

She could feel the vibration of his voice through her side, which was pressed up against his. He was so *large* and warm.

"Annis?"

"Er, I was going to Hookham's."

"And what were you going to borrow?"

"A novel." She looked up at him. "Do you enjoy reading?"

His eyes were on the road ahead, which was far busier than the side street. It was the fashionable hour at Hyde Park. Oh, how her aunt would howl when she heard of this little outing. And she *would* hear of it, eventually.

"I enjoy reading," he said. "A lot of manufacturing and scientific articles, by necessity, but also novels when they come my way."

"Was manufacturing something you were involved with for the Company?"

"Er, not exactly, but I read on a wide variety of subjects." A nerve jumped in his jaw as he navigated a wagon loaded with barrels which had stopped in the middle of the street, the dray horse blocking most of the thoroughfare.

Henry's magnificent chestnuts, or his lordship's more likely, were so closely matched as to be identical. They strained against the ribbons and Annis saw the muscles bunch and flex beneath the sleeve of his coat as he held them in check. He did not jerk or pull on the horses' tender mouths, but the subtle pressure was enough to quiet the high-spirited animals and ease them through the bottleneck.

Something about his calm control made Annis clench her thighs together.

Try not to drool on him, my dear.

She jerked her gaze away from his powerful, leather-clad hands, and stared at the horses instead.

The traffic moved in a steady, slow stream as they turned into the park.

Annis adjusted her bonnet brim and tried to sink down a little lower.

"Is aught amiss?" he asked, when she turned away from an oncoming carriage which carried Priscilla Foster, a bosom beau of Miriam's.

She looked up to find that same, tight look around his mouth; he was incredibly sensitive to snubs and slights, which made her think he must have been the recipient of many. "I am not supposed to be riding in the park."

Rather than reassure him, his dark brows pulled down over his regal nose. "Nor attending alfresco parties, or balls, or the theater?"

He noticed my absence.

For a moment she worried she'd spoken out loud, and she flushed under his piercing examination.

Her heart sang; he had noticed her absence! Could anything be more lovely?

"Why aren't you allowed to attend parties or take rides in the park, Annis?"

"My aunt, not unreasonably, believes I should help with various domestic matters in exchange for my upkeep and their kindness."

His sharp gaze flickered over her walking costume; a dress she'd possessed so long it had turned from forest green to mint green.

Annis experienced a sharp pang of regret as he examined her person. She knew she was not pretty and her shabby gown made her look dowdy. Such things hadn't bothered her when she'd walked out with Mr. Leech, but it bothered her now even though Henry didn't wear expensive garments.

But what he lacked in fine clothing he made up for in sheer presence. While Annis was a mere dab of a female, a description she'd heard more than once and knew to be true. Even if she was wearing beautiful clothing, she would never be a suitable companion for such a magnificent man.

"Why are you frowning?" he asked.

The Language of Love

Annis shook herself; she could dwell on her miserable status and frumpy clothing later. Right now, she was sitting right beside Henry and the day was beautiful.

"This is a very fine carriage," she said.

He stared so hard that, for a moment, she believed he might pursue the matter. But finally, he faced forward, taking away the not inconsiderable pressure of his gaze. "It is Lord Rotherhithe's carriage."

Oncoming drivers and passengers eyed him with open curiosity, a few with recognition and disdain.

Annis struggled for something to say, some way to distract him from their rude stares. "You are not much like his lordship."

That got his attention. "In looks, you mean?"

"Oh, well, yes, in looks of course, but I meant, er, in disposition and turn of mind."

A smile softened his severe expression. "No, his lordship does not have a serious turn of mind."

"And yet he has amassed a substantial fortune."

"His father was in India many years ago and acquired a favorable parcel of land as well as establishing his interests in textiles at the right time." He cut her a quick smile. "So, although his lordship worked hard, he had lots to work with."

"And you, Mr. Parker, what drew you to India?"

He cocked one eyebrow at her. "Mr. Parker?"

"Henry."

"I was born in India—in Dacca, as a matter of fact. But I returned to England when my parents died in a typhus outbreak. I moved back to India five years ago to take a Company position in Dacca."

"Your story is like Lord Rotherhithe's."

"Yes, a bit." His lips twitched. "Although my tale is markedly without wealth or a title."

"Were you sad to leave India?"

"There are things I will miss about India." He looked down at her, his expression thoughtful. "It is a huge and beautiful country with a rich history. But the tension between the English and native population is always simmering and each expansion by the British is a loss for people who have ruled themselves for thousands of years." His lips pulled into a frown, and he looked like he was going to say something else but shook his head. "Let us not talk of politics." He smiled down at her. "You asked the first time we met if his lordship spoke Urdu or Hindi. It just so happens that I do."

"Oh, how marvelous! I understand both are very similar when spoken?"

"Yes, the spoken languages are very much alike, but when it comes to writing or reading, they utilize different alphabets."

"Will you teach me a few words—perhaps even some phrases?"

"I will, although you will not find many people among the *ton* to practice with, I'm afraid."

"But I can practice with you."

"If the past two weeks are anything to go by, that will not happen often." He cocked his head. "Or do you think that will change in the days ahead, Annis?"

Something about the way he said her name made her heart hammer. "Unfortunately, I am not my own mistress."

He gave her a penetrating look.

"Why are you looking at me like that?"

He hesitated and then said, "It is nothing. What words and phrases would you like to know?"

The time slipped past with cruel swiftness as Annis did what she loved most in the world and quizzed him on a language so seductive and foreign that she felt as if she had travelled to a different country by the time he brought the carriage to a standstill sometime later.

She looked around, as if waking from a dream, and saw they were close to Hookham's. "My goodness! I didn't even realize we had left the park."

"I would take that as a compliment to my riveting company, but I suspect it is the language rather than the speaker who held you so entranced."

Annis flushed at his words, which couldn't be more wrong. "I hope my questions weren't bothersome."

"You would make an excellent interrogator."

"I'm sorry," she said, flustered. "I know I'm far too curious."

"I enjoyed the interrogation," he said, his gaze no longer amused.

Annis could not look away and the silence—not uncomfortable but pulsing and oddly *charged*—stretched.

The Language of Love

It was Henry who broke it. "Oh, I almost forgot." He reached into his coat and brought out a small cloth packet. "This is for you."

Annis could smell the contents before the package was halfway to her nose. "Bergamot tea."

"Black tea with a tiny drop of bergamot oil. You said you wanted to try it."

Annis filled her lungs with the intoxicating scent. "How kind of you."

"It is nothing," he said dismissively, appearing almost embarrassed by her thanks. "I would love to come and browse books with you, but I didn't bring a groom along. If you tell me how long you will be, I can tool the horses and then return to collect you."

"Thank you for your kind offer, but if you took me home, it would only cause difficulties. My aunt would learn I have been jauntering about unaccompanied, with a male."

"An *unsuitable* male, at that." He smiled as he said the words, but she could see he wasn't amused.

"Thank you, Henry, you have given me a day that I will long remember."

"I would like to give you another unforgettable day. Are you free to meet me tomorrow?"

You know what you must say, Annis.

Annis ignored the voice. "Where?"

"Wherever you like."

Tomorrow, tomorrow, tomorrow… what do I have to do tomorr—

Tomorrow was the day Susannah had her last fitting for a new ball gown. Annis would need to be on hand to help with alterations, so there would be no chance of sneaking away.

"I can't tomorrow," she said unhappily.

"How about the next day?"

She hesitated for only a moment before deciding that she would *make* time for him the day after tomorrow, no matter how unwise it was to accept his attention. "Yes, the next day I can meet you."

"Very well, where?"

Annis could not help but feel flattered that such an intelligent, attractive man appeared driven to seek her company.

"I will come back here. I'm afraid I can't say with exactitude, but between three o'clock and half-past."

"I'll be here at three."

"But I might be later, I should hate it if you had to—"

His beautiful lips curved. "I can always find something to read while I wait."

She climbed down with the aid of one strong hand before looking up. "*Bahut dhanyavaad,* Henry."

"*Hamaare punah milane tak,* Annis."

Annis cocked her head. "You did not teach me that. What does it mean?"

"You can ask me that the day after tomorrow." He smiled. "I have to keep something to lure you back."

He released his horses, leaving her standing and watching, wishing she were still up beside him.

***

"Isn't that true, my dear? Annis?"

Annis's head whipped up. The way both her uncle and Mr. Norburg were staring told her she'd been daydreaming about Henry instead of listening to their conversation.

"I beg your pardon, Uncle."

"You seem distracted this evening," Mr. Norburg observed before her uncle could respond.

Annis met his cold blue gaze and forced a smile. "I'm sorry. I just recalled something my aunt wanted me to do today that I forgot," she lied, her gaze flickering away from his uncomfortable stare.

Her uncle chuckled. "I'm sure whatever it is, it can wait, my dear. Mr. Norburg just asked if you would like to accompany his party to the theater tomorrow evening?"

"Oh," she said, sounding like a breathy nitwit. "I'm sure we would l-love to, if Aunt does not have a prior engagement."

"Mrs. Bowman would not accompany us, Miss Bowman," Mr. Norburg said, once again heading off the older man. "This would be some of my particular friends—people I should like you to get to know."

She swallowed, feeling rather like a rodent staring into the eyes of one of the naja najas that Henry had told her about that afternoon. There was something mesmerizing about Mr. Norburg's eyes and handsome, but austere, face. "I would be honored," she said when she realized the pause had gone on too long.

He gave her a thin smile and turned back to the bloody roast beef on his plate.

The Language of Love

Annis's shoulders sagged with relief as the two men resumed the business-related chatter they'd engaged in through most of dinner.

Even a henwit like Annis understood what this meal was all about: Mrs. Bowman wanted Annis married and out of the way—literally and figuratively. And if she married a banker, she would slip into that nether class between cits and the beau monde.

Mr. Harold Norburg, with his slender, elegant features and perfect manners, was undeniably a gentleman. But he was not the sort of man that her aunt wished to seat at her dinner table. If Annis were to marry Mr. Norburg, they would socialize only infrequently.

Annis would have a new circle of acquaintances, likely the people he was planning to introduce her to at the theater.

She unobtrusively studied the man her aunt—and uncle, to a lesser extent—were strongly urging her to marry.

Although he was twenty years her senior, he was still a very handsome man—if one did not look too closely into his eyes, which were a beautiful pale blue, but so very, very cold.

Annis didn't think that it was her imagination that they seemed to chill even more when they looked at her. It worried her he had not married before. Why now? Why her?

Oh, she wasn't naïve—a marriage between the two of them would considerably elevate Mr. Norburg's social status. While they, as a couple, could hardly expect invitations to *haute ton* functions, his connection to the family of an earl would increase his status. Some might say that an exchange of his money for her connections was a very good bargain for him, even though she was well past her bloom.

A footman came to remove her plate, and she nodded her thanks before glancing at the men. Mr. Norburg was watching her while her uncle spoke to his butler. For a moment—a split second, really—there was an expression in his opaque gaze.

Annis could not identify it, but it sent a shiver down her spine.

***

It did not surprise Annis when her uncle called her to the library to discuss Mr. Norburg the following morning.

The two men had spent an hour closeted together after their port before joining Annis in the drawing room. Although Mr. Norburg had said nothing in particular to her—indeed, he'd barely spoken to her at all—he'd had the self-satisfied look of a man who'd ticked a chore off a list and was ready to move on to more important matters.

When she'd excused herself at eleven o'clock, the two men had retired to her uncle's office to discuss business. Or perhaps her. Or perhaps she *was* business.

"Have a seat, Annis." Her uncle gestured to a chair in front of his desk.

Her Uncle Thomas reminded Annis of her father in a lot of ways, but without her father's spark. Just like Benjamin Bowman, her uncle was tall, with a shock of white hair that would have once been pale blond. Annis supposed he would have been handsome when he was a younger man, but his shoulders were stooped, a natural enough process that had no doubt been expedited by years laboring under the yoke of an abrasive and brittle wife.

Uncle Thomas spent most of his time either at his club or with his mistress. Annis was not supposed to know about her uncle's long-time mistress, but the servants were so accustomed to her presence that they hardly noticed when she was in the kitchen or laundry or stables for some errand or other.

And so she heard all kinds of fascinating tidbits.

After what Annis had done with Mr. Leech—or rather what he'd done to her, since she'd been so inexperienced that she'd simply laid there—she found it difficult to imagine her staid uncle doing any of *that* with her Aunt Agnes. But he must have done *that* at least three times because there was Percy, Sus—

"*Annis?*"

Her face heated as she looked up from her scandalous musings. "Yes, Uncle?"

"As you might have guessed, Mr. Norburg has asked my permission to court you." Her uncle smiled at her; it was the vaguely embarrassed smile of a man who knew he'd abdicated his duty regarding his niece to his wife but could not stir himself to remedy the situation.

Annis looked down at her hands, which lay palm up in her lap, like the bellies of two dead fish.

"Annis?"

She met his apologetic gaze. "Please tell Mr. Norburg that I look with favor on his courtship." It was a hideous lie, but what other choice did she have?

Henry's face sprang up in her mind and she instantly shoved it away. Henry was a clerk—hardly the sort of man to have almost twelve-thousand pounds to spare. Even if he did like her enough to offer her marriage, how could she choose her own happiness over her grandmother's safety and future? Besides, one ride in the park did not equal courtship.

No, her decision was excruciating, but clear: Mr. Norburg was the man she would have to marry.

She looked up to find her Uncle Thomas's concerned eyes on her.

"You will see him this evening, of course, but he asked that you reserve the day after tomorrow for him. He'd like to take you for a ride in Hyde Park."

Thank God he didn't want tomorrow!

"Of course, Uncle."

"Well then," he said, clearly ready to be finished. "I shan't be at dinner tonight, so I will wish you an excellent evening at the theater."

Annis felt sick inside, but she managed a slight smile. "Thank you, Uncle."

Chapter 9

"I'm sorry—but you think Henry is *who?*" Annis demanded, goggling at her friend.

"Shhh," Freddie said, glancing around at the other shoppers.

They were looking for fabric for a new dress for Freddie and the shop was crowded.

Annis sidled closer to her friend. "Why in the world would you think Mr. Parker was really the Earl of Rotherhithe?"

Freddie gestured to a bolt of fabric. "Let me purchase this and then we can talk at the tea shop down the street—that's if you have time?"

Annis didn't, but she'd *make* time. It had thrilled her when Freddie had called on her early that morning and invited her along on her errand. As luck would have it, she'd been at liberty since her aunt and cousins were still abed and wouldn't get up until it was time to get ready for their late-afternoon function.

Annis hoped to be back at the house before they climbed from their beds, but a stop for tea would make that a tricky proposition. Still, this was some news worth getting in trouble for.

She stood off to one side of the shop as her friend handled her transaction, her mind spinning.

Henry the Earl of Rotherhithe?

After her initial surprise, it made far too much sense. The earl—or the man everyone believed was earl—was sweet, but he had no more brains than one of the bolts of fabric piled up on the tables.

And then there was their too-similar histories. And the fact that *her* Parker went by the Christian name of Henry, too—not that Annis had told Freddie about either of those things.

Why would he masquerade as a servant? She'd seen the way people treated him. Did he want to be mistreated?

Annis frowned and plucked at a loose thread on her glove, grimacing when she pulled out a row of stitches. "Well, bother," she muttered. These were her best pair of gloves; now she'd have to mend them. Again.

"Ready?" Freddie was standing in front of her, holding a large brown package.

Once they were out on the street, Annis could no longer check her curiosity. "How did you find out?"

"Only by chance. Colonel Oliver and his wife—do you know them?"

"Is that the sweet old couple who—"

"Don't always remember who they are or where they are?" Freddie finished. "Yes, the same. Did you know they lived in India for years?"

"Yes, I've heard my cousins complain about being bored by the Colonel's stories."

Freddie gave an unladylike scowl. "They *would* complain about such a sweet couple. It was the Olivers who exposed our dear Lord Rotherhithe's deception at the Simpson rout and—"

"The Simpson rout? But that was *weeks* ago."

"Yes, it was." Freddie frowned. "Why?"

"Well, I just—why didn't you tell me until now?"

"Is there some reason that I should have told you?" Before Annis could answer, she added, "Besides, I have not talked privately with you for weeks, thanks to that dreadful aunt of yours."

Annis felt a pang of guilt at her friend's words. She could hardly admit that she'd made time for Henry while ignoring her friends, could she?

"Now, shall I continue my fascinating tale?" Freddie teased.

"Yes, please do."

"So, at the Simpson rout Mrs. Oliver greeted Mr. Parker as Rotherhithe. Of course, Mrs. Simpson corrected her, but Mrs. Oliver was adamant. Nobody believed her and people later made a joke of it. I made a point of sitting next to the Olivers that evening and brought up the subject again."

They entered the tea shop and Annis had to wait on tenterhooks until after they ordered before Freddie would continue.

"Go on," Annis urged, leaning across the table. "What did Mrs. Oliver say?"

"She grew up in the same area in Yorkshire as the Earls of Rotherhithe and she said that the man going by the name Colin Parker was the spitting image of not the last two earls, but the one before—his grandfather."

"But that's so long ago. And can you trust her memory?"

"Perhaps not, but when I combined what *she* said with what her husband contributed, I believe so."

"What did he say?"

"He said there was a portrait of the earl's grandfather hanging in White's and that he looks so much like Colin Parker they could be twins."

"I don't understand. Why would his portrait be at White's?"

"Apparently there are several group paintings of members— some quite old—gracing the walls of that all-male enclave." Freddie thanked their waiter when he set down the pot of tea and plate of scones.

"Yes?" Annis urged.

"Miles says Mr. Parker really could be the man in the painting's twin—"

"Wait—*Miles* knows about this?"

"I could hardly swan into White's and demand a look around, could I?"

Annis laughed at the thought. "So, you enlisted Miles to help?"

"Yes, and he said they are shockingly similar, although his grandfather was not nearly as big. But they share the same deep-set eyes, powerful jaw, and that smirking smile."

The smile that Annis adored so much.

"But... *why*, Freddie? Why would he do such a thing?"

"I suspect he is doing it to evade matchmaking mamas, but still have a look at what the beau monde has to offer." Freddie pulled a face. "I can't blame him if that is his reason. It's positively gruesome the way young women and their mothers are fighting over the man they believe to be Rotherhithe."

Annis nodded thoughtfully. "This way he could take part in the Season without being *consumed* by it." She hesitated, and then asked, "What did Miles think?"

"He thinks Rotherhithe has an ax to grind with everything English—especially the members of the beau monde—and would like to make fools of us all." Freddie chuckled grimly. "Not that we need any help."

"If that's true, then it's a manipulative and unpleasant game he's playing."

"Indeed. I believe he has brought out the very worst of the *ton*. You've not been at many functions lately, but the competition for the wealthy, handsome Lord Rotherhithe has become almost bloody."

The Language of Love

"Oh, I've witnessed plenty of brutal competition between Miriam and Susanna," Annis assured her. "Well, what are you going to do about it?"

"What can I do? At this point I'm either going to be pilloried for concealing the truth and making fools of people, or I'll be a laughingstock for my own ignorance." She shrugged. "I might as well let him keep on with his deception and continue to get paid for it."

"Is this going to cause you trouble, Freddie?"

"It depends how people decide to view his little charade. You know how fickle the *ton* can be. This might be the end of me or it could put me in a position to pick and choose my clients next Season." Freddie slid Annis's teacup toward her. "But enough about Lord Rotherhithe. What have you been up to these past few weeks since I saw you last?"

Annis did *not* want to tell Freddie about her impending betrothal to Mr. Norburg. She already knew her friend would believe that her aunt and uncle were forcing Annis to marry him.

It was either let Freddie believe *that* or confess the truth: that it was Annis's own idiocy that was forcing her to marry.

And given her current situation with Mr. Norburg, she didn't feel right telling her friend about Henry, either—not that she had much to tell other than the innocent carriage ride. She suspected Freddie would be very disappointed to hear she'd been encouraging an offer of betrothal from one man while having clandestine meetings with another.

"What has been keeping you so busy that you have no time to visit, Annis?"

"Oh, just the usual."

"You mean slaving for your cousins?" Freddie's beautiful face hardened. "I really wish you'd put aside your pride and come live with me. You can contribute to the household expenses when you get a job."

Shame flooded her. Here she was lying to her friend, and Freddie was offering her shelter and support.

And still Annis couldn't make herself tell the other woman the truth.

***

Annis arrived at her uncle's house just as her aunt and cousins were finishing their late breakfast. Thankfully, none of the servants must

101

have told them she'd gone out, so they merely assumed she'd woken up late as well.

The last thing Annis wanted to do was sit down to breakfast with her cousins and aunt, but she still hadn't asked about getting a few hours to herself today, and time was running out.

"You're terribly late," her aunt scolded when Annis entered the breakfast room. "Don't expect Coombs to bring you anything else—he's already taken away most of the food."

"Of course not, Aunt. I'll just have a cup of coffee," she said, pouring herself a cup and then taking a seat to wait for a break in the conversation, which was all about the upcoming ball at Lady Jersey's.

While her cousins were bickering about a ball gown, her aunt turned to Annis. "I hope you remember that we've been invited to Lady Monmouth's house today."

"Yes, aunt."

"Your name was not on the invitation, I'm afraid," her aunt said, as if she'd have allowed Annis to go even if she *had* been included.

And then her aunt shocked her, "You may have the rest of the day to yourself as a special treat, Annis."

"Thank you so much, Aunt."

"You are welcome."

The instant Aunt Agnes turned her indulgent gaze on her two daughters, Annis scuttled out of the room as quickly as a mouse, not wishing to linger and draw unwanted attention.

Rather than risk getting dragooned into some chore or other, Annis left immediately for Hookham's, even if that meant she'd arrive hours early. After all, she could always read while she waited.

But when Annis walked into the lending library a quarter of an hour later, it was to find Henry already there, sitting in a chair facing the door with a book in his hands. His eyes met hers and the loveliest smile she'd ever seen spread across his face.

No, not just a smile, but the slow, lazy grin that transformed him from a severe, slightly menacing stranger into a mischievous co-conspirator.

Annis watched with breathless anticipation as Henry unfolded his tall body from his chair and came toward her, his long-legged stride so elegant and masculine.

How could she have believed he was a clerk? He moved with such confidence and command that he was an aristocrat from the top of his dark, curly head to the tips of his well-worn, but highly polished Hessians.

He opened the door, waiting until they were outside to speak. "I'm glad you came early."

Annis was too tongue-tied to do anything but smile—probably fatuously.

A notch formed between his eyebrows. "Is aught amiss?"

"No? Why would it be?" she blurted.

"No reason—you just look a bit unsettled."

"No, nothing's wrong. I'm just glad I could get away," she said, which wasn't a lie.

"I'm glad, too."

His smile did disruptive things to her heart and lungs.

"Do you feel like a carriage ride?"

"You brought the phaeton?" She glanced around.

"Yes, the groom has been—ah, here he comes now." Henry raised a hand, and the servant slowed the carriage, pulling up beside them. "Let me help you in," Henry said, lowering the small step and offering his arm.

Once she was settled, he walked to the horses' heads and held them while the groom climbed down. Annis couldn't help noticing the servant's supercilious expression when he switched places with Henry.

Goodness! Even his servants must believe he was Colin Parker.

"How much time do you have?" Henry asked as he climbed up beside her.

"I have the rest of the day."

"Excellent. Then why don't we take a trip out of the city? A gentleman I recently met told me I should avail myself of his property in Kensington, which sounds like it has some lovely gardens and even a bit of countryside still surrounds it."

Annis tried not to show her relief that they weren't going anywhere near Rotten Row. "That sounds lovely."

Henry turned the carriage off Bond and onto a side street, and then headed in the opposite direction from Hyde Park.

"You are quiet today, Annis. Am I getting you into trouble inviting you on these jaunts?" he asked a few minutes later, cutting her a quick glance.

"Oh no, nothing like that. It's just that I thought it would be too distracting to ask questions while you're navigating these busy streets."

"This isn't busy," he said. "Calcutta and Bombay—now *they* are busy."

"You mean they are more hectic than London?"

"At least twice as hectic."

"That's difficult for me to imagine. I think London is as busy a place as I ever wish to visit."

"You would not want to live here?" he asked.

"No, not at all."

"Ah, so you are a country lass, then?"

"Well, hardly a lass anymore."

That drew a curious glance from him. "You look no more than eighteen."

"I know," she said gloomily.

He laughed. "Why does that bother you?"

"People treat me like a child because I look like one."

His eyelids were lowered halfway when he turned to her. Annis might have very little experience in life, but even she knew what desire looked like on a man's face. Not that any man had ever turned such an expression on *her* before, but she'd seen the way her friends' husbands looked at their wives.

It was an effort to breathe under such a brooding, heated look.

"You don't look like a child to me," he said, and then turned to watch the road.

"Oh. Well. That's good," she said in a silly, breathless voice, suddenly uncomfortably hot beneath her lightweight spencer.

"So, how old are you, Annis?"

"I just turned twenty-six. How old are *you*?"

"Thirty-seven."

"That's the same age as Lord Rotherhithe, isn't it?"

He cut her a narrow-eyed look. "How do you know his lordship's age?"

"My cousins were talking about it."

"Oh."

Annis weighed her next words carefully. It was dangerous to poke the bear, but she couldn't resist. "You certainly have a lot in common with his lordship, don't you?"

104

The Language of Love

"I suppose there are superficial similarities," he said dismissively.

Annis bit her lip to hide her smile. How often had instances like this come up before and she had not noticed?

"Will you tell me about your time teaching?" he asked, clearly eager to move the subject away from himself.

"It's not very interesting."

"Perhaps not to you, but I am very interested."

"Very well. I taught at the Stefani Academy for Young Ladies."

"Is that the same Stefani as Ivo?"

"They named the school after him, but he left not long after it opened and his wife, Portia Stefani, operated the academy until it closed."

"Avington said she married Eustace Harrington, the Earl of Broughton?"

"Oh, have you seen Miles lately?"

"Not for some weeks. Why?"

"No reason." It warmed Annis to think of Henry and Miles talking together and becoming friends. She wished she'd thought to ask Freddie if Miles was going to confront Henry about his identity. Would the men still be friends after the truth came out?

"You like Miles, don't you?" she asked.

"He seems a good sort."

"He's the *best* sort," Annis corrected. "As handsome as he is, he's even lovelier on the inside." She felt him looking at her, but stared straight ahead, her cheeks burning.

After a moment, he asked, "You two grew close when you worked together?"

"Oh yes, all of us grew quite close. Poor Portia—" Annis chewed her lip.

"Poor Portia?" he prodded.

"Well, I suppose it doesn't matter if I share what happened now that she is very happily remarried. Ivo left her with debts and she had to close the school and find work elsewhere."

"The rest of you had to find new jobs?"

"Well, most of us. Honoria Keyes, who taught painting—you haven't met her—did not have to find a job as her father left her an income and the house that Lady Sedgwick now lives in. Serena Lombard, who taught art history and botany, used to live with Freddie and Honey but she married one of her clients not too long ago."

"So those are all the teachers you worked with?"

"And Lorelei Fontenot, who was the literature teacher."

"Has she married, too?"

Annis laughed. "Lorie will never marry—she doesn't believe in marriage."

Henry turned to her. "She doesn't *believe* in it?"

"What I mean is that she doesn't believe it is a good decision for women."

"Why not?"

"Because women become the property of men once they marry."

Rather than scoff, as she'd thought he'd do, he was silent.

"What are you thinking?" she asked.

"I'm thinking about what your friend believes."

"I suppose you think it is bosh?"

"No, I think she has a good point. Unfortunately, if women aren't the property of their husbands, they are usually at the mercy of their male relatives."

Annis couldn't argue with that.

"Where does she work now?" he asked.

"She has not been fortunate enough to find another teaching position. Since the school closed, she's lived with her brother and his family in Cornwall." Annis sighed. "So yes, she is dependent on a man, after all." And Lorie *hated* it.

"You are not," Henry said. "You could leave your uncle's home any time you wished, could you not?"

"Yes, I could." It wasn't strictly a lie, but it certainly wasn't the truth.

"You sound and look so grim at the thought, Annis. Was life with your grandmother really so terrible?"

"Oh, not at all. And I didn't mean to look grim," she added. "It's just that it makes me sad to think about her because I miss her so much."

"I'm surprised you don't live with Lady Sedgwick if she has two empty rooms in her house."

"I cannot afford to share the upkeep of the house."

If Annis had known two years ago that she would meet Leech and throw away both her and her grandmother's futures, she would have swallowed her pride and moved in with Freddie, even if it meant that she'd have been living off her friend.

The Language of Love

Annis felt a suspicious burning sensation behind her eyes. She needed to change the subject before she sobbed and confessed the muddle she'd made of her life. Annis could just imagine his reaction. He had probably gone into hiding to avoid fortune hunting females, only to discover one right beside him.

She shivered at the thought.

"Are you cold?"

"No, just a goose walking over my grave."

"Ah, an interesting saying. We used to say that meant you had an important secret."

"Really?" Annis had no desire to talk about her secrets, important or otherwise. "I've never heard that interpretation. Tell me about this place we are visiting today. Where did you meet the owner?"

"At one of the interminable balls or parties I've attended these past weeks."

Annis smiled. "It sounds like you dislike the Season, Henry."

"I *despise* it."

The leashed loathing in his voice startled her. "Why do you do it? Surely his lordship doesn't force you?"

"No, he doesn't force me. But I feel like I should accompany him."

"You worry about him, don't you?"

"What do you mean?"

"I can tell that you are protective of him." *In case he does something foolish; something that ends in an unsuspecting woman's betrothal to a false peer and a meeting at dawn for you.*

Of course, Annis didn't say that.

"Can you?" he asked, genuinely curious.

"Yes, I can't blame you. He's rather like a child, isn't he?"

Henry gave a bark of laugher. "Yes, very much so."

"What do you dislike about the Season most?"

"Why do you want to know?"

"No particular reason." Yet another lie; she wanted to know everything about him. It frightened her how curious she was about him—even before she'd known his identity.

He grunted and turned back to the road, his jaws flexing as if he were chewing over his words. "I dislike the superficiality and pretension."

Well, that pretty much summed up the beau monde.

Before she could think of a response, he went on. "Take his lordship, for example."

"Lord Rotherhithe?"

"Yes. Women are mad for him—even before they exchange a single word with him." He snorted softly. "All that matters to most of them is that he has money and connections—he could be a blithering idiot or a man who kicks puppies. Or worse."

"*Is* there anything worse than a man who kicks puppies?" she teased.

His lips flexed briefly into a smile, but it did not divert him from his point. "None of that matters to the women who want to marry him."

"What you say is true," she conceded, "But isn't it true for the rest of society, too? Not just the beau monde? If his lordship were a wealthy merchant and not a peer, wouldn't other merchants be jostling to get close to him—to introduce him to their daughters, become his friend? Wouldn't the same be true if he were, say, a respected servant with a secure, well-paying position? Wouldn't unwed female servants flock to him? Doesn't success always attract attention from men and women?"

"Yes, you make an excellent point." He turned to her, his eyes hard, cold, and greener than usual. "I should have been more precise in what I said, which is that I despise people who use others for their money or status, no matter the social stratum. And I reserve my greatest scorn for those who *marry* for money."

Annis could only nod and stare at the oncoming drivers. She had nothing to say to that, since that was exactly what she was planning to do.

***

They spent hours exploring the overgrown gardens and large wilderness at the back of the property.

Henry couldn't recall having spent such a companionable afternoon with a woman—something that shamed him to admit as much as it surprised him. Had he really grown into such an emotionally stunted man over the years? He didn't think that he'd always been so... inaccessible. After all, he recalled being friends with a couple of young female servants when he was growing up in Yorkshire.

Had Julia really damaged him so badly that he'd not allowed any other woman to matter to him or become important in his life?

The Language of Love

Henry shook the disturbing thought away as he watched Annis take pleasure in the property, which actually belonged to Henry. He'd purchased it only the week before, as an investment. He hadn't really *looked* at how charming it was until today, when he'd seen it through her eyes.

It was a pleasure to see her take such enjoyment from this little slice of country. Indeed, he'd *gorged* himself on watching her, treasuring each moment in a way that left him more than a little uneasy.

They ended their tour of the estate in the bit of woods that separated the property from its neighbor. Annis tilted her head back and turned in a circle, holding out her arms and smiling as she gazed up at the huge elms that surrounded them. "I feel like I'm in a magical forest. It's so *quiet* that you'd never know that only a short distance away there are thousands of people."

It amused Henry how much she resembled a magical fairy creature—Titania, the queen of the fairies, in her natural milieu.

And how do you fit into this story, Henry? You are no fair Oberon, no king to her queen. Are you her 'rude mechanical,' Henry? Her mortal lover, Nick Bottom?

Henry scowled at the mental taunting, annoyed with himself for his flights of fancy.

You know you're smitten when you spout Shakespearian nonsense, old man.

Ha! Smitten.

But the truth was that Henry couldn't pull his gaze from her.

Her ancient walking costume—the same one she'd worn the last time—appeared almost magical as the light from the trees filtered down from far overhead, dappling her with sunlight.

She dropped her arms and turned to him, a look of regret on her expressive face. "I'm sorry, Henry, but I probably need to go back now."

He nodded, even though he didn't *want* to take her back yet. He wasn't sure he wanted to take her back, ever.

The uncharacteristic thought sent a bolt of terror straight to his core. He *hated* wanting to be around another person so much. Only a fool put their happiness in somebody else's hands, where they could rend and shred and destroy so easily.

Henry gritted his teeth against his desire, but he couldn't stop wanting her. He found Annis utterly and completely enchanting. Yes—that was the word for it: she had enchanted him.

They walked to where he'd unhitched the horses to let them graze. "I'm sorry we didn't get to see the folly," she said.

"We should come back."

"The owner wouldn't mind?"

Henry smiled. "No, he told me to make myself at home."

"Who does it belong to?" she asked as he harnessed the frisky pair.

"He's just a commoner, I doubt you'd know him."

"I do not choose the people I like based on their lineage or bank account, Henry."

"Obviously, or you wouldn't be here today."

Her face flushed a becoming rosy pink, and she lowered her eyes in a shy, almost submissive, fashion that sent a pulse of heat to his groin.

Henry took her hand. "Up you go," he said, turning his body so that she couldn't see the increasingly obvious evidence of his arousal. "I'm going to hand you the reins, Annis—can you hold them while I get in?"

"Oh, yes. I used to drive our gig into town."

Henry smirked at her comparison of an old nag and gig with his phaeton and high-steppers.

As she took the ribbons in her small hands, he couldn't help noticing that her gloves were as threadbare and worn as the rest of her clothing. There was a tiny hole in the right palm she must have mended. It was skillfully stitched but visible, all the same.

Something about her careful mending made him so angry that his vision blurred. How dare her shrew of an aunt and neglectful uncle dress themselves like kings and queens and keep her in rags?

His own fury rocked him to his foundation. Why the devil did he care so much?

Henry struggled to gain control of the emotions roiling in his gut, wrenching his gaze up from her old glove and meeting her glorious blue eyes.

"Is anything wrong, Henry?"

He forced a smile. "No, nothing is wrong."

Her own smile was uncertain, telling him how poorly he was hiding his inner turmoil.

They were both quiet as they rode back to town.

The Language of Love

Henry didn't know what kept her mind occupied, but he couldn't stop thinking about Annis Bowman and his unprecedented feelings for her.

Feelings.

Christ. Even the word made him want to smash things.

Annis's soft voice shook him from his pointless mental dithering. "You can just drop me here, Henry."

They were only a few streets away from her uncle's house. It was a respectable enough area and the foot traffic was mostly menials or clerks hurrying to do their employer's bidding before the workday was over.

Still, he did not like it.

"Are you sure?" he asked.

"I'm sure. If my aunt and uncle knew what I've been doing—"

"I understand," he said. Although he suspected the Bowmans wouldn't be so eager to scold their niece if they knew it was a wealthy, eligible earl she was spending her days with.

She cocked her head at him, her eyes imploring. "It's not you personally, Henry, it's my aunt, she—"

"Doesn't like you to have any pleasure in your life?"

"Oh, she's not so bad as that," Annis demurred, but not with any conviction.

And so, Henry deposited her on a street corner, feeling like the world's biggest cad as he looked down on her waifish form.

"I suppose I shan't see you for another two weeks?" He said the words lightly, but he didn't like to think of the days ahead if they didn't contain her.

"Actually," she said, grinning at him in a way that made it very difficult not to lift her back up into the carriage and kiss her breathless, "I believe I can get away the day after tomorrow."

"Why, *Miss Bowman*," he teased. "You mean you can slip the leash three times in almost as many days?"

"Events have, for once, conspired in our favor, *Mr. Parker*. My aunt and cousins are going with some friends to Richmond and will be gone all day."

Henry, too, had accepted an invitation to go along on that jaunt. Well, now it seemed like poor Lord Rotherhithe was about to develop a sudden summer cold and have to bow out. And his loyal friend and employee would have to stay home to keep him company…

An answering smile curved his lips. "What time?"

"I could meet you at the same place—earlier, if you wish?"

"I'll take as much of your time as you'll give me, Annis."

"Ten o'clock?"

"Excellent. I shall bring a picnic and we can explore the rest of that charming property at our leisure."

"Oh, lovely!" Her eyes, which were always breathtaking, glowed with anticipation. "I shall see you tomorrow."

He waited where he was and watched her walk away. Before she rounded the corner, she turned and gave him a slight, shy wave, and then she disappeared.

The churning sensation in his gut was more than unpleasant—it was painful.

Henry wasn't sure how many more times he could watch her walk away from him.

Chapter 10

By the time Annis had lived through an evening at the theater with Mr. Norburg's friends and his friends' wives, and another drive in the park the following day, the only thing keeping her from falling into despair was the thought of seeing Henry today.

It wasn't that the banker or his friends had been awful, but just that they'd just been so very… staid. The only topics of conversation were money, banking, servants—how lazy they were—country houses and how the wives all desperately wanted one, clothing and the best shops, the best being any shop that was expensive and frequented by peeresses.

Truly, it was no worse than an evening at a *ton* party, both of which were the sort of hollow, materialistic existence she had always avoided in the past.

Annis dreaded the thought of a future filled with such banal evenings, but Mr. Norburg was the only man interested in marrying her and beggars could not be choosers.

She smiled to herself at the idiom as she approached what she now thought of as *their* meeting place.

As if on cue, she heard carriage wheels slowing behind her and turned.

Rather than the phaeton he'd driven before, today Henry was in a dashing curricle.

Now that she knew who he really was, it made sense that he was so comfortable handling the expensive equipages and costly horses. After a few drives with Mr. Norburg, she realized just how skilled Henry was with the ribbons.

Annis smiled up at Henry as the curricle came to a halt.

"Hello, Annis. Have you been waiting long?"

"Not at all, I only arrived a few seconds before you."

"What do you think of this day that I have ordered up for your pleasure?"

"You have excellent taste, sir: it is glorious."

Henry kicked down the single step and held out a hand.

113

"No yellow bounder today?" she asked.

"No, I thought I'd impress you with my serious, sober side."

Annis laughed. "Yes, because this vehicle is *so* serious and sober."

His eyes glinted with genuine pleasure as he smiled down at her. "That is a very pretty hat you're wearing," he said, as she settled her skirts. The bench in this carriage was, unfortunately, much wider, giving Annis no reason to squash her body against his.

"Thank you, I trimmed it myself last night."

"In honor of today?"

"Yes," she admitted. Why lie? This was the most exciting thing that had happened to her since... well, *ever*.

"It suits you," he said, his changeable eyes darker today, more brown than green.

Annis faced forward and caught her lower lip with her teeth, so excited to be spending a whole day with him that she was afraid of *what* might tumble out of her mouth.

"I brought a picnic lunch prepared at the Clarendon."

"Oh, how extravagant! What are we celebrating?"

"How about your new hat?"

She laughed. "I don't think that merits a picnic."

"Why don't we celebrate a full day of leisure together?"

"Excellent idea," she agreed. "I plan to do nothing but lounge and feast on the delicacies you've brought."

"And I suppose it is *I* who will do the laboring and serve you?"

"Naturally—I am a lady of leisure, after all!"

"Do they work you hard at your aunt's?" he asked, the tightness around his mouth telling her how he felt about that.

"Oh, please let's not speak of my cousins today," she begged, even though to say so wasn't kind to her family. She also wanted to forget that she'd be spending yet another afternoon with Mr. Norburg tomorrow—a thought that was even more unkind. But Annis knew there would be more and more occasions with the cold, slightly unnerving banker now that they were formally courting.

"I can agree with that," Henry said. "What *would* you like to talk about, ma'am?" He skillfully eased the curricle into the flow of traffic.

"Tell me about yourself, Henry." Would he lie to her? Or slide some of the truth in among the lies?

"What do you wish to know?"

"Tell me about your childhood."

His jaw moved from side-to-side, the muscles flexing beneath the skin.

"Not if you don't wish to," she hastily amended, wondering what had given him such a bitter frown

"I was raised in a lord's house, in the servant quarters."

Whose past was this? The real Colin's? Or his own? Now that Annis reflected on it, she'd heard very little about the Earl of Rotherhithe's past. Not even Susanna seemed to know much.

"You've probably heard rumors about me—haven't you?" His eyes were keen—as if he could see inside her mind and would know if she lied.

Annis desperately hoped that was not the case.

"I've heard your mother was a servant and your father a sailor."

He barked a laugh. "A sailor? That's a new one." His mouth twisted into a sardonic smile and he took a corner at a clipping pace that made her clutch the railing.

There was no humor in his brief laugh, and she wished that she'd not broached the subject. But now that she'd opened Pandora's Box, she couldn't think of a way to close it again. Annis smiled; that had been one of her father's favorite idioms

"Why are you smiling?" he asked.

"I was just thinking about my father."

"What about your father?" he asked, probably grateful for an opportunity to move the conversation away from himself.

"He was an Oxford don, which his family considered a shocking downward step. If that wasn't bad enough, he married an actress and cast himself well beyond the pale." She cut him a quick look, but he was staring straight ahead. "Before he married my mother, there were invitations to spend holidays with his cousin, the Earl of Denbeigh, and the rest of my grandmother's family. After his marriage… well, let's just say I've met no one on that side of the family."

"Is that the same grandmother you lived with?"

"Yes, she threw her lot in with her son, which put *her* beyond the pale, too."

"Even I know that one," he said proudly, whatever bitterness he'd been feeling no longer evident. "It comes from the *pale* pieces of wood the Norman invaders used to make fences and protect themselves from the Irish."

"It sounds like you've been cramming for a test," she teased.

"I'm set on becoming the teacher's pet."

Annis laughed.

"But, to get back to your father and grandmother's story," he said. "They were cast out of paradise."

"Some people would agree with that assessment," Annis said. "But then it isn't really paradise, is it?"

"What? You mean you don't aspire to be part of the *haute ton*?" His tone was mocking.

"I've met a lot of miserable peers. I don't believe moving in *tonnish* circles will bring happiness in and of itself."

"Your cousins wouldn't agree. They both seem determined to land Rotherhithe."

Annis did not demur—how could she? But it felt too disloyal to say so, even though they'd done precious little to earn her loyalty.

She couldn't resist another peek inside Pandora's Box. "You said you were born in India—but you grew up in a lord's house in England?"

"Yes, after my parents both died in Calcutta, I was sent back to my family. My aunt was the housekeeper in a lord's house and she took me in."

"How old were you when you were orphaned?"

"Five."

"And you came half-way around the world—alone?"

He nodded, his expression closed and distant. "Are your parents still alive?"

"No, my father died ten years ago and my mother seven."

"Were you close to them?"

"I was close to my father, but not my mother. She was… different."

"Different how?"

"Beautiful, stylish, sought after. She knew how to dress and behave in a way that drew people to her. She…" Annis stopped and shook her head.

"She what?" he urged.

"She did not like books, reading, or language. She was so different from my father that I often wonder how they ever—" Annis realized where her conversation had led her and stopped.

"Made you?"

Annis saw, out of the corner of her eye, that he was smiling. "He was so bookish, and she was so… not. I rarely saw her after my father's death and she remarried a year later and had a new life."

"You have half-brothers and sisters?"

"No, the man she married already had a grown family and did not want another. Neither did my mother. To be honest, I don't think she wanted her *first* family." She bit her lip. "I shouldn't have said that."

"Why not?"

"Because it is unkind."

"Was it the truth?"

"Yes, but—"

"I would rather you always tell me the truth, Annis."

Coming from him, that was an ironic request.

"Always?" she asked, giving him an arch look.

"Yes."

"But sometimes the truth can be so… uncomfortable," she said, staring into his eyes and hoping for something. His confidence?

His mouth twisted into a strange smile. And… was he blushing?

"Yes," he agreed. "It can be uncomfortable."

Well, he would know, wouldn't he?

***

You bloody bounder. What a hypocrite you are asking her to always tell the truth when you're living a lie.

Henry ignored the accusation.

Instead, he unstrapped the heavy picnic basket from the back of the curricle and carried it to the spot Annis had picked out.

She'd stopped in the shade of an immense tree. "This looks lovely—right here, I think."

"As my lady commands."

She laughed, "I'm being bossy, aren't I?"

"Terribly." He dropped to his haunches and unbuckled the leather strap that held the blanket to the wicker basket. "Where, exactly, would you like it?" He stood and unfurled the blanket with a snap.

She assumed an exaggerated pose of consideration and pointed to a spot with all the dignity of a queen. "Right there."

Grinning, he went to spread out the blanket.

117

"No, wait. *There*." She pointed to a spot that was only a few inches away from the first, and then she gave a happy, adorable laugh. "I am only playing. Anywhere here is fine."

"Tyrant," he muttered, making her laugh again. "As I am your servant, I will lay out our feast, too." He dropped to his knees on the edge of the blanket and opened the basket.

"I'll help." She lowered herself beside him, bringing a whiff of her clean, soapy scent with her—and a slight hint of another fragrance, one he easily recognized: bergamot. The smell of his favorite botanical mixed with her feminine scent sent his blood surging. He'd already been half-hard sitting beside her in the curricle. The feel of her slender body against his gave him an erection so quickly it was embarrassing.

No doubt that was his body's way of telling him it had been far too long since he'd had a woman. Not that he hadn't had ample opportunities these past few weeks. The fine ladies of the *ton* didn't want to dance with an earl's poor friend, but more than a few lusty widows had looked at his oversized body and rough-hewn features with a hungry gleam in their eyes. He knew what they wanted: a bit of rough trade, a touch of danger; a proper fucking from a man who worked for a living.

And Henry could have given it to them, too, but he'd simply not felt the desire.

At least not for other women.

But he ached so badly for Annis that it was driving him to distraction.

Being alone with her sent erotic thoughts thundering through his brain, not to mention the rest of his body. But she wasn't like his usual women—experienced widows and bored Company wives—who engaged in sexual encounters without a care.

Annis was an innocent—a virgin—nothing at all like the lovers he was accustomed to bedding.

Unfortunately, that fact didn't matter to his body, which urged Henry to grab her and kiss her into next week—and do other, far less innocent things.

But he wasn't an animal; he could control his impulses, even though such control meant he'd been fisting himself raw several times a night to keep a clear head during these afternoons.

"Henry?"

"Hmm?" He turned and found her staring up at him, mere inches away.

The Language of Love

Her eyes were like the shifting blue depths of the ocean, her skin as porcelain. This close to her, he could see the pale thickets of lashes that fringed her eyes.

"Yes?" he said.

She licked her lips, the nervous but sensual gesture chipping away at his already tenuous self-control. "You went so still," she said. "Is something wrong?"

"I smell bergamot." His voice was raspy with lust and Henry hoped to God that she wouldn't recognize it.

"Y-yes, I hope you don't mind, but I put some of the tea in little cloth bags in my cupboard, like sachets."

"Why would I mind?"

"Well, it was for tea, not to be used in drawers with my un— er, with my garments."

He wanted to tease her and get her to say the word she'd clumsily avoided—undergarments—but she was already blushing so wildly he restrained his mischievous impulse.

Instead, he said, "It was a gift, Annis, to be used any way you liked."

"I *did* make myself a pot of tea with a few precious spoonsful."

"Did you like it?"

Her eyelids fluttered in an expression of bliss that was pure torment for his constricted, throbbing cock. "It was delicious."

Don't do it, Henry!

But he couldn't stop himself. He slid his hand beneath her jaw until the tips of his fingers were resting in the silky-smooth hair at the nape of her neck. "*You* look delicious, Annis. Are you?"

Her lips parted and her already uneven breathing roughened even more. "W-what?"

"I'm going to kiss you." Henry paused, giving her a chance to back away or slap him or call him a cad.

But she leaned into his touch and raised her lips to his.

***

A light, warm breath brushed her lips before he touched her.

Oh.

Her brain uttered that one syllable and then stopped churning as abruptly as a wheel with a spoke jammed through it.

His lips were soft, *so* incredibly soft—and warm—and they pressed against hers with a tenderness that made her body turn to water.

His big hand slid around the back of her neck. "Steady," he murmured.

Annis swayed beneath his gentle hold while his mouth moved over hers with teasing, phantom touches, until she felt dizzy and had to set her hands on his massive shoulders to keep from pitching backwards.

"Open for me," he whispered.

Open?

Annis forced her eyes open and encountered his, hot and black and liquid.

His lips curved into that slow, lazy smile that obliterated her wits. "Your *mouth*, darling."

She startled at the endearment, her lips parting.

"Mmmm." He traced her lower lip with his tongue. And then again, and again, each time delving a little deeper into her mouth.

Mr. Leech had kissed her, of course, but his kisses had been closed-mouthed pecks. Even those four times when they'd done a lot more than kiss, he had behaved staidly and hastily—at least compared to *this*.

This was… well, this was unlike anything she'd imagined in the dead of the night when she'd slipped her fingers between her thighs to drive away the nagging ache.

Her mind seemed to fracture, until there were three, maybe more, distinct Annis's. One reveled in the sheer sensuality flowing through her body, one scolded and warned, and one stared in open-mouthed shock.

And then there was the fourth Annis, a greedy, demanding one that gradually subdued the others, growing larger, braver, more insistent.

A guttural sound slid from between her lips; she wanted—*needed*—to be closer.

Annis skimmed her hands from his shoulders to his neck, pressing herself against him, thrusting her fingers into his thick hair, desperately wishing that she'd taken off her gloves.

He groaned and the world tilted as he wrapped one muscular arm around her waist and lifted her as easily as if she were a child before carefully laying her out on the blanket and then stretching out beside her.

Annis reached for him, not caring how bold her behavior might appear.

The Language of Love

Henry reached for her, too, his powerful arms encircling her and pulling her snug against the length of his long, hard body.

They might have kissed for a minute or ten or an hour; she lost track of time. At first, she was content to savor his commanding, confident touches. But slowly, before she knew what he was doing, he'd lured her deeper until she noticed—with a shock—that she was exploring his mouth with her tongue, her strokes less skilled than his, but pleasing him, if his moans were anything to go by.

"You feel so good," Henry murmured against her jaw, which he was nibbling and licking.

She blinked up at him through lust-hazed eyes. When had they stopped kissing? When had she rolled onto her back?

His lips moved down and down, tracing the modest neckline of her gown.

This is wrong, Annis.

She vanquished the chiding voice with a single thought: *I don't care.*

Henry's slick, hot tongue darted beneath the worn cotton of her bodice, caressing the top of one breast. Her body arched beneath his, her fingers digging into his granite shoulders.

Annis had never been intoxicated before, but it must feel just like *this*. Who would have believed that kissing could bring such full-body pleasure? Each caress of his lips and tongue sent honeyed fingers of delight to every part of her—especially the part that throbbed, ached, and *demanded*—

She startled when his hand settled gently over her pelvis, the combined span of his fingers and palm easily encompassing her from hip to hip.

"You're so small—so dainty," he said, his voice marveling, his touch feather-light.

And then he caressed her, softly, at first, but with increasing boldness.

Annis's response was almost primal, her body undulating and rocking against each rhythmic stroke.

"God, Annis." A shudder racked his enormous frame, and he pushed his fingers between her clenched thighs, cupping her sex firmly over the thin fabric of her gown. "I want to touch you here—to give you pleasure. Tell me to stop."

Annis opened her eyes and found him staring hungrily, desire pulsing in his swollen, bottomless pupils, his lips slick and reddened.

She snaked a hand around his neck and pulled him down, claiming his mouth with a savagery that stunned her. Although she was clumsy and their teeth clicked together, his chest rumbled with low, encouraging sounds, and he opened wider, inviting her to explore.

Through the fog of sensory bliss, she became aware that he was lightly caressing the seam of her lower lips, the tip of his finger teasing the sensitive bud—but never quite hard enough—until she was grinding herself against his hand, greedily chasing her own pleasure

Suddenly, both his mouth and hand disappeared.

Annis whined. "Henry."

"Shhh, darling," he murmured. "Part your thighs for me."

Scorching, incinerating heat licked over her skin at his wicked command—a command her body jerked to obey even as her mind pulsed with shame at her behavior.

Her body won the struggle with embarrassing ease and Annis opened for him, her hips pressing up with a wantonness that made his chest rumble with an approving purr.

Cool air caressed her calves as he lifted her skirt and petticoats, his fingers grazing lightly over her thick stockings, up over her knee, lingering where inexpensive cotton met bare flesh, skimming her inner thigh with slightly calloused fingers.

"Annis," he whispered. The word sounded almost like a prayer as he delved into the damp curls at the apex of her thighs. He stroked her swollen lips with his thumb, not exerting enough pressure to part her folds, not touching that part of her that throbbed with need.

Desperate with desire and stripped of all pride, she opened wider for him, until her hips ached.

"So eager." His voice was harsh and smug and his thumb tormented her, his too-insubstantial caresses *forcing* her to behave like a harlot, until she was bucking and thrusting against his hand.

He gave a low, wicked laugh and claimed her mouth again, his kisses rougher and deeper as he pressed a thick finger between her swollen folds.

Annis moaned into his mouth when he circled the engorged, sensitive nub with his thumb while another finger stroked her slippery sex, lingering over the entrance to her body.

He broke their kiss, his breathing ragged. "You're so wet for me, Annis."

122

The Language of Love

His words sent a lightning bolt of desire straight to her core, and she abandoned the vestiges of self-control and pushed against him, gripping his shoulders to get better leverage as she rode his hand.

His blunt finger prodded boldly at her opening, entering her with one thrust.

A mortifying mewl slipped out, and she bit her lip hard enough to flood her mouth with the metallic tang of blood, her hips helplessly jerking to the rhythm of his pumping.

"Yes, such a good girl, Annis," he praised.

Just when she'd adjusted to the thickness inside her, he murmured against her skin. "Can you take more?" A second finger teased and stroked her slick skin, not breeching her until she nodded.

They both moaned as he eased in alongside the first. "So bloody tight."

Annis teetered between discomfort and desire; the pleasure was too acute—overwhelming—she needed—needed—

"That's right, take what you want—use me, Annis."

His words were a catalyst and a shocking cry tore from her throat as every muscle in her body clenched and the tight knot that had been building and building in her sex exploded.

Annis lost track of herself as wave after wave of bliss buffeted her.

She was only vaguely aware of his labored breathing, soft caresses, and quietly murmured words as she floated slowly back to earth.

"Once more," he whispered, as the waves of pleasure receded. His wicked thumb resumed its skilled dance, driving her toward oblivion much faster this time.

"Yes, that's it," he urged as she clenched and shook. "Come for me once more, Annis."

Come? Come where?

But the thought was born away like a leaf on a gust of wind as the second wave of pleasure consumed her.

"Shhh, sweetheart." Henry's voice was low and rough against her temple as she moaned and thrashed in his arms. "It's alright, darling."

His soothing words brought her back to herself, and the warmth that had enveloped her ebbed away.

Cold, humiliating reality took its place.

You've been rubbing yourself against his hand like some sort of animal.

Annis cringed at the embarrassing picture that lodged itself in her mind's eye, an image of her writhing like a strumpet.

"Annis?"

She pressed her face into his shoulder, like a child believing that what she couldn't see didn't really exist.

But powerful hands took her shoulders. "Sweetheart, look at me."

She squeezed her eyes shut tighter. Maybe if she refused to answer him, he would simply disappear.

Annis felt, rather than heard, the low, gentle laugh that vibrated his body. "I'm not going away just because you refuse to look at me." He eased her a few inches away as he spoke, the loss of his heat and nearness almost physically painful.

"Open your eyes, Annis."

She exhaled a long, shuddering breath, and then she obeyed.

Chapter 11

Good Lord, her eyes were the loveliest things that Henry had ever seen, more beautiful than an endless blue Bengali sky or a priceless sapphire. Cerulean and limpid and bottomless.

And right now, mortified and pained.

Christ, but he was a bastard to have taken advantage of her!

Henry knew he should feel ashamed, but he couldn't—watching her come apart, not once, but twice, had been too damned delicious. Besides, on the scale of reprehensible behavior, he'd not done too badly, only fingering her when what he'd really wanted to do involved his mouth and cock.

Annis must have seen the desire in his eyes because she made an endearing squeaking noise and scooted away from him.

"Please don't feel embarrassed," he said, masking his lust with a—hopefully—reassuring smile.

She looked at him as if he were crazy. "How can I not be ashamed after the way I behaved?" She frantically brushed at the skirts he'd already lowered, as if to erase all evidence of the beautiful events of the last few minutes.

"You weren't alone in your behavior," he reminded her.

"You weren't the one writhing and grinding and—*ugh*! I behaved like a—like a *beast*." She covered her face with both hands and moaned, the sound heavy with self-loathing. "I don't know what got into me."

Henry had to bite back a smile. He suspected that her linguistic appreciation of double entendres wouldn't extend to this particular situation. "Give me your hand."

She peeked over her fingers; her forehead wrinkled. "Why? Just let me be. What else could—"

Henry took her wrist and set her palm against the front of his pantaloons, hissing at her touch. "Do you know what that is?" he asked through clenched teeth.

She scowled. "I'm inexperienced, not an idiot, Henry. It is your breeding organ." She paused, her expression becoming thoughtful. "And it is ready to breed."

He gave a breathless laugh. "Yes, it is. So, if you think you were the only one behaving like a *beast,* then you are wrong."

She looked down to where her hand rested on him. "I did not know they could be so prodigious."

And then she squeezed him.

Henry yelped and yanked her hand away.

"Does it hurt to squeeze it?" she asked, still staring at the front of his obscenely distended pantaloons.

"No, it does not hurt to squeeze it." He could not believe he was having this conversation. "My point in showing it to you was not for squeezing, but to explain that I was every bit as aroused as you were. I want you. Badly. While I'd love nothing more than to lift your skirts and mount you right here on this blanket—"

She gasped and turned a delightful shade of pink.

"—that sort of behavior can have... repercussions," he finished, laying his hand on her shoulder, relieved when she didn't jerk away from his touch. "But what we did together is not wrong or evil, Annis. It is normal and healthy. And it doesn't make either of us bad people." He was desperate that she not hate herself for her wonderfully sensual nature. "I know you don't believe it, but the sort of, er, affectionate behavior"—his face heated at the ridiculous euphemism—"that we just engaged in does not mean that you're no longer a virgin."

"I *know* that," she hissed, her throat and chest still mottled with the aftereffects of her orgasm. And she *had* climaxed—at least twice.

It had been the most erotic event of his life, and he was still fully clothed. Never had he needed to impose such rigid control over his body. He was still shaking with need.

She might be small and slender, but she was wiry and strong and she had ridden his hand like some fierce nymph out of mythology, using him for her own pleasure.

It was an image he'd never forget.

But right now, she needed a moment to pull herself together, so Henry busied himself with their forgotten picnic.

"Are you angry with me?" he asked a few minutes later when she began to help him.

She shook her head but wouldn't look at him.

"Annis?" Henry waited until she looked up. "Do you want me to take you home?" He didn't want to, but he owed her that much, at least.

"No." She spoke without hesitation. "No, I don't want to go. And I'm not angry. I'm just—"

"Embarrassed?"

"Terribly."

"Please, if you can do one thing for me—*don't* be embarrassed. It gave me a great deal of pleasure." Almost too bloody much, another ten or fifteen seconds and he would have spent in his pantaloons.

Her face, which had just been coming back to its normal color, turned crimson again.

She gave an abrupt nod.

"I don't know about you," he said, forcing himself to sound jovial, which wasn't easy with his cock still as stiff as a barge pole, "but I'm famished."

***

Annis wouldn't have believed that she could ever again look Henry in the eye.

But he went about setting out their food, and then serving her a plate in such a matter-of-fact fashion that she was soon wondering if she'd imagined the prior twenty minutes.

"Mm, this is delicious," he said, drawing her attention away from her own plate, which she'd been staring at unseeingly

He smiled at her, a chunk of juicy ham on the tines of his fork. Instead of putting it in his mouth, he held it out to Annis. "Try some."

Her lips had already parted in shock at the oddly intimate offer, so it was easy enough to lean forward and take the savory bit from the fork.

His nostrils flared and his eyelids drooped, his gaze on her mouth as she chewed, the desire emanating off him making her feel as if she were the most attractive woman in the world, rather than a scrawny, long-in-the-tooth nymphomaniac who'd just made the two-backed beast with his hand.

"Good?" he asked.

She swallowed again and nodded.

"I brought plenty—so eat up. Because after lunch we're going to do what you wanted to do and explore the folly and every inch of the grounds."

Annis forced herself to eat while Henry kept up a stream of light, amusing conversation about the Season, sharing anecdotes about the faux earl and making her smile.

127

By the time they'd finished lunch three-quarters of an hour later—when he began to put away the dishes and pack up the remaining food—she could finally contribute something. "I'll clean up, it's the least I can do."

"I was supposed to be your servant today, and you a lady of leisure."

"I want to."

"Are you sure?"

"Yes."

"Hmm." He gave an enormous yawn, and then his darkly tanned cheeks reddened. "I'm sorry, that was extremely rude—and absolutely no reflection on the company. I'm afraid it's difficult to get a decent night's sleep these days."

"Why is that?"

"Rotherhithe House is as cold as a tomb and all the furniture and bedding is ancient, hard as rocks, and moldering."

"His lordship has no plans to make the house more livable?" she asked, not looking at him as she re-wrapped the thick slices of ham that were left over.

"I believe it is his intention to sell it after this year."

"That's unfortunate."

"Why do you say that?"

"Well, it has belonged to his family for hundreds of years. There is probably much of their history wrapped up in it. It seems sad that it will pass out of his hands." It was difficult to remember that *he* was the one selling his family's property.

Henry merely grunted, not looking convinced. Annis couldn't help noticing that his eyelids were drooping, and not with passion this time.

"Why don't you take a nap?"

His eyes flew open. "I'm not tired." He ruined that assertion by smothering another yawn.

"I can see that," she said dryly.

"You must think I'm horribly rude?"

"No, just tired."

He cocked an eyebrow. "What will you do?"

Annis gestured to the satchel she'd brought along. "I have a book and a sketchpad to keep me busy."

"Well, if you're sure?"

"I'm sure. Nap." She could use the time to collect her still scattered wits.

One of his slow, lazy smiles spread across his face. "If that's an order…"

"It is."

He reached for the buttons on his coat and then paused. "Will you excuse my shirtsleeves?"

Annis choked on a laugh. Considering that she'd just been rubbing her sex against his hand…

"Make yourself comfortable," she said, digging through her bag but watching from the corner of her eye as he unbuttoned his coat, folded it into a neat square, and then placed it on the ground to use as a pillow. Within moments, he'd positioned himself on his back, his powerful arms crossed over his chest, his enormous body laid out before her like a masculine buffet.

The urge to climb on top of him and feast was so strong it left her light-headed.

Get control of yourself!

That was excellent advice. She took out a sketchpad and pretended to search for a clean page while stealing glances at him. She might as well just have openly gawked since he was breathing evenly and deeply within less than a minute.

With her sketchpad in hand, she positioned herself at such an angle that she could see all of him, intending to take advantage of the rare opportunity to capture him for posterity in her sketchbook. The only way that she'd ever be able to have him.

But instead of sketching, she just stared, her mind combing over the events of the day, her brain naturally lingering on the part where she'd used him for her sexual pleasure.

If she were a decent, upstanding woman, she would burn with shame at the memory.

But, after those first few mortifying moments, she'd felt startlingly shame-free.

Why should her lack of morality surprise her? After all, she'd lain repeatedly with a man who'd robbed both her and her beloved grandmother.

But you were not almost betrothed to another man when you rolled around in the grass with Mr. Leech.

That was true.

Still, she didn't feel shame.

Today with Henry was an experience that she would likely never have again. Maybe she was doing Mr. Norburg a terrible injustice, but she had not seen even a glimmer of interest—not to mention passion—in his gaze when he looked at her. Annis was a business acquisition to him—and not even a very exciting one. She'd seen more passion on his face when he'd spoken of his bank.

Henry, however, had looked at her as if he'd wanted to *consume* her.

Annis wasn't entirely naïve; she knew it wasn't love he felt for her. If it was, he'd tell her the truth about his identity and end this foolish façade.

No, all Henry felt for her was physical attraction—although why he felt even that, she could not understand. She had never been the sort of woman to elicit male interest, not even when she was young and dewy.

Now Henry, on the other hand... It was easy to understand her almost suffocating physical attraction to him: he was a gorgeous, fascinating man. If she wasn't careful, she'd end up infatuated.

My dear Annis! You're not falling in love with Henry; you've already fallen.

The sketchpad slid from Annis's limp fingers as the accusation echoed in her mind.

But I don't want *to love him*, she wailed silently.

But you do.

A heated denial leapt to her lips, but she couldn't make herself utter the words.

Because it was true: she had fallen in love with Henry.

He looked like a slumbering warrior, his sculpted cheekbones and powerful jaw even more masculine in repose. His lips looked so much shapelier, the lower one especially sensual, almost pouty in its fullness. He was far too rugged to ever be called classically handsome. But to Annis, he epitomized male beauty.

What are you going to do? Tell him you love him and would he please give you twelve thousand pounds right away? He will think you are after him for his money because you are *after money.*

"I *know* that," she hissed under her breath. "What should I do?"

As usual, the voice had no answers.

***

The day had been delightful.

The Language of Love

Henry's only wish was that he'd not slept away so much of it. When he'd woken from his nap, it had stunned him to discover he'd slept for almost two hours.

"You should have woken me," he'd said, astounded and embarrassed in equal measures. "I'm terribly sorry, what a disastrous host I am."

She was leaning against the trunk of the tree, holding a book. "I relaxed and enjoyed myself. I never get to read for as long as I like. Besides, you looked like you needed the rest."

His story about the uncomfortable bed and freezing house were only partly true. He'd slept poorly ever since he'd begun seeing Annis. He suspected part of his inability to sleep was because of guilt.

You mean because you've been lying to her with every breath you take?

His dishonesty had been bothering him, and he'd spent hours thinking about telling her the truth.

Well, now he had no choice; he had to tell her. A man didn't do what he'd done with her today and *not* offer marriage.

Strangely, he couldn't say the notion was unappealing.

In fact, what he'd like to do was take her directly to her uncle's house and declare his intentions, as well as the truth about himself, and arrange their marriage without delay.

But he could hardly start shouting the truth all over town without first telling Colin and Lady Sedgwick. He owed the two of them that, at least.

He would tell her tomorrow—just one more day—and then he would ask for her hand in marriage.

Henry experienced an almost breathless relief—followed immediately by a sharp pang of worry.

She'll hate you when she learns you've been making a mockery of her and lying to her for weeks. They'll all hate you.

Henry knew that was a distinct possibility. But then hadn't he been the one to say to Colin—no, to proudly *crow*—that he wanted the *ton*'s hatred?

He shoved aside the distasteful memory. He could worry about all that later; right now they had a bit of time left together and he didn't want to waste it fretting.

"Ready to explore?" he asked, standing, and holding out a hand to help her up.

"Is there still time?" she asked, setting her small hand in his.

He lifted her to her feet and then reluctantly released her and looked at his watch. "I'd say we have an hour before we need to go. "

They spent the next hour exploring the overgrown path that circled the tiny, lily-pad covered pond.

"This is like paradise. I feel a bit like I do when I'm in Hyde Park—amazed that I am still in a city," she said as Henry escorted her toward the carriage.

"Well, technically you're *not* in the city, although it is certainly encroaching fast enough."

"I can't believe the gentleman who owns it doesn't want to live here."

He just smiled, not wanting to tell any more lies than he had to.

On the drive back, Annis seemed pensive, no doubt still mortified by her earlier behavior.

For Henry's part, thoughts of his impending confession consumed him. Tomorrow—it would happen tomorrow. He'd tell Colin tonight and Lady Sedgwick tomorrow morning. The countess could counsel Henry about how to proceed. And then he would pay a call on Annis and her uncle and—

"Will you drop me off in the same place?" Annis asked, pulling him from his thoughts.

He experienced a pang of irritation at the thought of leaving her on a street corner. But today would be the last time he'd need to practice such deception, so he shoved aside his annoyance.

He'd just brought the curricle to a halt when a town coach rolled to a stop beside them, coming so close that their wheels were almost rubbing. The coach window slid down with a decisive *clunk*, and an older man glared at them through the opening.

Henry was about to ask what the hell the man wanted when Annis gasped.

"Uncle Thomas! What—"

"Not now, Annis," Bowman snapped, his gaze sliding to Henry. "Please follow my carriage, Parker."

Henry's eyebrows rose at Bowman's rude tone. "Where are we going?" He gave the older man the half-smirk that he knew other people—especially men—found exceedingly provoking.

Judging by Bowman's scowl, he was one of those men. "To my house."

"May I ask what for?"

The Language of Love

"I think you know exactly why," Bowman retorted. "I intend to send a message to your employer requesting his presence. Immediately."

Henry amused himself by imagining Colin's frantic reaction to such a hostile summons.

"Is this because I took your niece out for a few carriage rides?"

"Yes, it is about the *clandestine* meetings you've been having. It is also about the fact that you *ruined* her today."

Henry blinked at that, his eyes briefly meeting Annis's—which were as round as saucers—before saying to her uncle. "I'll be right behind you, sir."

Chapter 12

"What do you think he means?" Annis asked in a tremulous voice as the curricle began to move.

"It sounds like he might have had you followed today."

"Oh God." Annis squeezed her eyes shut, feeling faint. She felt a large hand cover hers.

"Don't worry, Annis."

What if Uncle Thomas saw me today?

It was all she could do to keep breathing as her fertile imagination created incident after incident, each more horrid than the last. What if her aunt, uncle, *and* her cousins had seen her today?

The curricle rolled to a gentle stop, and Annis opened her eyes. They were already in front of her uncle's house.

While Uncle Thomas's carriage was nowhere in sight, a servant was waiting outside the front door and another servant came scurrying from the direction of the mews.

Henry tossed the groom the reins and jumped down, coming around to her side of the carriage and helping her.

"Don't worry," he said again, more softly this time. "Everything will be fine. I promise."

He looked and sounded so certain that she was almost convinced. Almost.

In the foyer, Annis struggled with the ribbon on her bonnet, making the knot worse.

Henry wordlessly took the ribbon from her shaking fingers and made quick work of it. She was just removing her cloak when her Uncle Thomas entered the foyer with Coombs on his heels.

"Coombs will dispatch a messenger to Lord Rotherhithe immediately. You, Annis, may wait in the—"

"You needn't bother with the message. I am Lord Rotherhithe, Mr. Bowman."

Her uncle's jaw sagged and her aunt—who'd entered the hall just in time to catch his announcement—made a very undignified squawking sound.

The Language of Love

"You most certainly are *not*." Mrs. Bowman stormed up to her husband, placing her tall form between Henry and Uncle Thomas as if to protect him. "I don't know what this—this *person* has told you, but he is most emphatically not the Earl of Rotherhithe. He is a clerk—a servant."

Henry ignored her. "Could we step out of the foyer to discuss this, Mr. Bowman?" He cast significant glances at the butler and two footmen hovering with their eyes as round as coins.

Aunt Agnes gasped at his condescending tone. "Thomas, I don't know what—"

"Come, my dear," Uncle Thomas said. "This gentleman—whoever he is—is right about this not being the place to discuss anything. Don't send anyone until I sort this out," he told Coombs. And then his gaze—colder than Annis had ever seen—settled on her. "The fewer people who know about *this* particular subject, the better." He took his wife's elbow and gently, but firmly, guided her up the stairs. "Come along, Annis," he barked over his shoulder when she paused and turned to Henry.

Henry frowned at the older man and Annis feared he was about to say something—likely combative—so she hurried up the stairs behind them.

Coombs had barely closed the door behind him when her aunt turned to Henry, her demeanor that of an attacking dog. "Just what do you think you are doing? Who do—"

Uncle Thomas raised one hand. To Annis's surprise, her aunt closed her mouth.

Her uncle turned to Henry, who was lowering himself into a chair with no invitation.

"There seems to be some confusion about who you really are, *sir*. I demand an explanation."

Henry casually stretched out his long, muscular legs, the very picture of a man at ease. "I'm ashamed to admit that any confusion is entirely my fault."

He didn't look or sound ashamed. In fact, Annis thought he was quite proud.

The door to the study exploded inward, slamming hard enough against the wall to make the windows rattle.

Her cousin Percy stood in the doorway, Miriam and Susanna flanking him. The women hung back while Percy strode into the room, staring at Henry as if he were Beelzebub incarnate.

"Just what the devil is going on here?" Percy demanded. "Coombs said something about Parker claiming to be Rotherhithe?"

"Now Percy—" Uncle Thomas began.

"This *person* says he is Lord Rotherhithe." Aunt Agnes looked and sounded far more like herself now that she was surrounded by her children.

Gasps and exclamations filled the room.

Percy marched up to Henry's chair and glared down at him, an ugly sneer on his face. "I daresay I'll have to teach you it's not wise to go about aping your betters."

Annis gasped at his condescending threat, but Henry just smiled.

Her aunt grabbed Percy's arm and tried to lead him away, but he would not budge.

"Please, step away from him, Percy. There is no need to sully yourself." She turned to her husband when her son refused to listen. "Mr. Bowman, I think you should summon the constable. Or the magistrate. Or—"

"Before you summon anyone, perhaps you might want to speak with the gentleman on this card. He can attest to my identity." Henry extracted a slim silver case set with a single, *enormous* emerald. His movements were languid and relaxed, and Annis knew, without a doubt, that he was who he claimed to be. How had everyone failed to recognize his assertive confidence? His aura of command?

Percy snatched the card from his hand and squinted at it before uttering a derisive, "Ha! Anyone can print one of these."

"Percy." Once again, Thomas Bowman used a tone that demanded instant authority. He took the card from his son, looked at it, and quickly glanced up, his eyebrows disappearing beneath a thatch of white hair. "Sidmouth?"

Henry gave a lazy shrug. "We Henrys hang together."

Annis had to stare, too. Viscount Sidmouth—or Henry Addington—was the Home Secretary.

Until that moment, Annis had still maintained a few niggling doubts. She'd not truly believed that Henry was who Freddie had claimed he was. After all, people often bore uncanny resemblances to strangers—there was even a word for it in German: doppelgänger.

But surely Henry would not bandy about Sidmouth's name if he wasn't telling the truth? Such a thing would be easy enough to disprove and only a fool would attempt to lie about it.

He must really be Rotherhithe.

She could see by her uncle's expression that he was thinking the same thing.

"Sit down, Percy."

"But Father, surely you—"

"Be *quiet,* Percy."

For a moment, Annis thought the young hothead might say something. She could see that her aunt *thought* he should and looked disappointed when Percy took a seat far away from Henry.

"Sidmouth has been out of the country," Henry said. "But he returned two days ago." He smirked. "I know that because he invited me to dinner to discuss the possibility of leasing a few of my ships. If you like, you can send your footman to *his* house and summon *him* to discipline me."

Uncle Thomas cleared his throat and swallowed, still staring at the card he held. "I am going to assume you are who you claim to be."

Henry smiled.

Thomas Bowman looked toward the door, to where his daughters still hovered. "You must leave—you too, Percy."

The room erupted in pandemonium as her uncle argued with his offspring.

"I don't understand, Father. How could this happen?" Susanna's voice rose above the fracas and Annis couldn't help feeling sorry for her cousin, who'd just discovered she'd been fawning over the very man—a lowly clerk—that she'd scolded Annis for dancing with.

"This is *outrageous* behavior, sir!" her aunt shouted, glaring at Henry.

"Yes, it is. And I apologize." Henry's lips twitched slightly. "Although I assure you that the real Colin Parker—my employee—is unmarried and the son of an eminently respectable country vicar."

Annis winced at Susanna's wail.

Percy's face twisted into a snarl at Henry's confident—almost arrogant—tone. "You find my sister's pain amusing?"

Henry merely stared at him.

"This is all *your* fault."

"Yes, it is," Henry admitted, flicking a piece of lint from his cuff.

Percy lunged toward him.

Rather than take him by surprise, Henry flowed up from his chair as effortlessly as smoke rising from a chimney, looming over the other man, his muscular torso twice as broad. "You should think very carefully about what you are about to do, Bowman."

"*Percy!*" both his parents shouted.

Aunt Agnes abandoned her sobbing daughter and grabbed her son's arm to stop him—easy to do since Percy had wisely backed away the instant Henry had uncoiled himself from his chair.

"Please, Percy—come away from him."

Thomas Bowman leaned over his desk, propping himself up on his fists, his pale blue eyes positively lethal. "If you speak even one foolish word about duels or challenges, Percy, I shall thrash you myself. Now, all of you leave us—except Annis."

"Surely you are not including me in that order?" his wife said.

Her uncle hesitated, cast a quick glance at Annis, and firmed his jaw. "Yes, you too, my dear."

"Why is Annis staying?" Aunt Agnes's wild eyes slid to Henry. "Good God, Thomas, surely you cannot mean to—"

"*Please* control yourself, Mrs. Bowman," her husband snapped. "Now, all of you—*please leave.*"

It took longer than it should have for the four Bowmans to vacate the room, but finally the door shut behind them.

Uncle Thomas turned to Henry. "Please, my lord, will you sit?"

"Your son is correct, Mr. Bowman." Henry crossed one elegant, pantaloon-clad leg over the other. "It is because of me that your daughter has become enamored of a pauper."

"My daughters are both generously dowered, my lord. If Susanna truly wishes to marry the man, I will not withhold support to show my displeasure."

Annis could see her uncle's words surprised Henry, who murmured, "How very democratic of you."

Her uncle clenched his jaws but ignored the comment. "It is *you* and your behavior with my niece I wish to address." He pulled his gaze away from Henry and turned it on Annis. "I am profoundly disappointed in you, Annis."

She swallowed but refused to look away.

"There is no need to punish her for a few carriage—"

"My footman followed you today, *my lord.*" Uncle Thomas forced the words through clenched teeth. "What he saw her doing is the reason I don't want my wife or daughters in this room right now." His eyes slid to Annis. "I'd say I was ashamed to speak of such matters in front of my niece, but as she is a wanton—"

The Language of Love

"That's enough," Henry said. For the second time in as many minutes, he stood. This time, it was her uncle he loomed over. "Are you telling me you had one of your servants *spy* on your niece?"

"That is exactly what I am saying, sir!"

Annis covered her mouth with her hand. Good God. Somebody had seen what she'd done today.

Henry seemed to expand to twice his already intimidating size. "How dare you send a man to—"

Her uncle leapt to his feet, startling both Annis and Henry. "I *dare* because she is all but betrothed to another man! A man to whom I gave my word."

Henry staggered back as if her uncle had struck him. "What?"

Both men turned to Annis, who felt as though somebody had lowered a building onto her chest. "Er—"

"He doesn't know, does he?" Uncle Thomas asked.

"Is this true, Annis?" Henry demanded.

They spoke at the same time, but it was Henry's question she forced herself to answer.

"I—it was never my intention—" She bit her lip, looked directly into his horrified gaze, and said, "Yes, it is true."

***

Henry knew his mouth was hanging open, but he couldn't find the strength to shut it. "Who?" was all he could manage.

It was her uncle who answered, "Mr. Harold Norburg."

"Norburg the banker?" Henry asked, wrenching his gaze away from Annis's guilty, miserable face.

"Yes." Bowman's mouth shriveled up like a prune. "He might not be a peer, my lord, but he is an extremely wealthy, influential man, and one to be reckoned with." The way Bowman had gone gray told Henry he must have some dealings with the savvy banker, a man Henry had heard about, but didn't know personally.

Bowman's jaws flexed, as if he were exerting a massive amount of will to control himself. "It was Norburg who told me of my niece's afternoon jaunts after seeing the two of you together. He was most displeased and was prepared to sever their relationship. But I assured him that what she was doing was harmless." He narrowed his eyes at his niece. "Then today—"

"So, you had her followed," Henry said. "And what about Norburg—did *he* send somebody to follow her?"

"I sincerely hope not," Bowman retorted.

139

So did Henry, but probably not for the same reasons. Just thinking about another man watching Annis—be it a footman or a rich banker—made him want to destroy something.

On the heels of that thought was another that was even more infuriating: he was *jealous*—surely the lowest of human emotions—of a woman who'd been plotting and planning to marry another man. A very wealthy man.

Bowman's voice yanked Henry from his spiraling anger. "So, this poses a significant problem, my lord."

They both turned to look at his niece.

To her credit, Annis didn't flinch away from Henry's glare.

Another man had courted her while she was meeting him. She was all but betrothed while she'd writhed beneath his hand today?

He looked into her crystalline blue eyes and shook his head; how easily she had fooled him into believing she was an innocent.

Henry's head throbbed with anger, jealousy, and betrayal.

Get hold of yourself, Henry. Yes, she was betrothed, but you don't know the full story—what if her aunt and uncle were forcing her? After all, it makes little sense that she would have done what she'd done today with a mere clerk if she didn't have feelings for you?

The thought stopped his anger in its tracks, the effect on him so sudden it gave him a sort of emotional whiplash.

That last part was true. No woman in her right mind would do what Annis had done today with a poor man if she was genuinely angling to marry a rich one.

Henry realized that both uncle and niece were waiting for him to speak.

He shoved away the tangle of emotions, which he would have the rest of the day—hell, the rest of his life—to sort out, and turned to his host.

"May I have a few moments alone with your niece, Mr. Bowman?"

***

Annis's face scalded as Ford, her aunt's maid, trooped into the library with her needlework basket over her arm.

It was ridiculous that her uncle insisted on her having a chaperon at this point. Annis could see by Henry's expression that he was more amused than annoyed by what was, now, a hollow propriety. All it did was ensure that they could have no honest or direct conversation.

The Language of Love

That was probably just as well; Annis was hardly in a hurry to explain to Henry why she'd behaved like a wanton while she was all but engaged to another man.

Once Ford had settled in a window seat—within earshot—with her stitchery, Henry turned to her.

"What I am about to say will be uncomfortable for you but needs saying. Do you care for Mr. Norburg? Because if you do," he went on, before she could answer, "this,"—he waved his hand to encompass the two of them— "can be resolved in a way that will allow your betrothal to him to go forward." He flashed his teeth in a grim smile. "I will personally ensure that. If you wish to marry Norburg, you must let me know right now."

Annis hesitated, not because she didn't know what she wanted—she wanted *Henry*—but because he'd couched the question in the worst possible way.

If she said *no,* then that begged the question of why she'd allowed Norburg's courtship to begin with.

If she said *yes,* then it made her look like the sort of woman who kept two men on a string, as if they were interchangeable.

I was going to marry another man because he is wealthy, even though I'm in love with you.

No, that didn't sound good, either.

"Do you need more time, Miss Bowman?" His tone was ominous, his eyes hard green stones.

And that was another thing: this Henry—earl Henry—was *nothing* like clerk Henry, the man she had grown to love.

This Henry was commanding, stern, and terrifying.

His eyes narrowed more the longer she dithered.

"No," she hastily assured him. "I don't need more time. I don't wish to marry Mr. Norburg." In her peripheral vision, she saw Ford jolt.

"Will you do me the honor of becoming my wife, Miss Bowman?"

Ford jolted again.

Henry looked… irked, not like a suitor, but like a man of business whose meeting had taken an unexpected turn and was exceeding its allotted time. In fact, he looked so cold and detached that he reminded her of Mr. Norburg.

Annis wanted to explain what she had been doing, but her explanation wouldn't exculpate her.

141

But Ford's presence, combined with Henry's visible—and justifiable—anger, was making Annis's brain seize like a hinge that had rusted shut. If she tried to explain now, she'd sound like a blithering imbecile and—

Just answer the man and explain later!

"I would be honored to marry you."

Rather than looking pleased, his lips thinned into a straight line. "Do you want a large wedding?"

She blinked at the unexpected question. "Er, no—not at all." That, at least, was true.

"Then I think a quick, small ceremony would be best. Would one week suffice?"

Her mind boggled at the thought of becoming this man's wife in a week's time, but she nodded when she saw he looked impatient.

"I shall speak to your uncle and let him know what we have decided. If he is amendable, I will come back tomorrow to discuss the marriage contract. Is there anything else?"

Annis hesitated.

You __must__ ask him now, Annis, regardless of Ford's presence. You can't agree to marriage without asking about the money.

"Yes?" he prodded, a vee of annoyance forming between his brows.

Her eyes slid to Ford.

Henry was quick to understand. "You there," he said.

Ford's head jerked up. "Me, sir?"

"Leave us."

"But Mr. Bowman—"

"Will this take longer than five minutes?" Henry asked Annis.

She shook her head.

"Give us five minutes and then return," he ordered. "Go!" he barked when Ford hesitated.

At any other time, Annis would have smiled to see the normally regal maid bolt like a rabbit. But when she looked at Henry's face, all laughter drained away.

"We have five minutes," he reminded her.

"What I did with you today, while encouraging Mr. Norburg's suit, was wrong and unkind—to both of you."

He merely raised one brow.

"There is nothing I can say that will excuse it. However, I may be able to explain part of my, er, motivation."

"Oh?"

She looked away, unable to bear the weight of his harsh gaze. "I accepted Mr. Norburg's suit because he is r-rich." She swallowed convulsively. "I know it is morally reprehensible, but—" Annis chewed her lip, wishing she were anywhere else in the world right then.

"But?"

She forced herself to look at him. "I needed money to pay a rather large, urgent debt."

Surprise flickered across his face. "What sort of debt?"

"It is a—well, actually, it is a private matter, my lord."

Both his eyebrows shot up.

Her face boiled with shame as she imagined how her request must sound.

Annis took a deep breath and said, "I know this is irregular, my lord, and I also know you did not know of the debt until now. I will release you from our betrothal." She laced her hands in her lap and waited.

"Is that what you want? To be released?"

"No, my lord. That is not what I want." She had to bite her lip to keep from spilling the entire sordid, pathetic story to him.

"So that is why you were going to marry Norburg, to get money to pay a debt?"

She nodded.

"Did he know about the debt?"

She shook her head miserably. "Not yet."

He stared at her; his expression unreadable. Annis wanted to crawl under the settee, but she held his gaze.

"How much?"

"I'm s-sorry?"

"How much do you need?"

"Eleven-thousand-one hundred-and-seventy-two pounds."

When he didn't speak, she said, "I know that is an enormous amount and I don't—"

"I will give you the money."

Annis blinked. "You will?"

"Yes, of course," he sounded almost annoyed that she would doubt him.

"Thank you. That is *very* kind—"

"I can have a bank draft for you by tomorrow. Is that soon enough?"

"That would be lovely. I am so grateful, my lord. I am also sor—"

"You do not need to thank me, nor do you need to apologize."

She had once thought he bore a resemblance to Alexander the Great. Right then he looked at her the way she imagined that long-dead king might have looked at a vanquished and despised enemy.

Annis nodded.

"Is there anything else I should know?" he asked.

"No."

"Very well. I shall see you tomorrow." He stood and took her hand, bowing over it. "You have made me very happy, Miss Bowman."

If that was true, then Annis wondered why he looked like a man who was going to the gallows.

Chapter 13

Henry wanted to head directly to Rotherhithe House and barricade himself in the library with a bottle of whiskey.

No, strike that. He actually wanted to check himself into a suite at the Clarendon, not his draughty pile of bricks. He wanted to eat a decent meal, drink the better part of a bottle of wine, and sleep in a warm, comfortable bed until he could forget what he had just heard: that the first woman in years that he'd felt even a *twinge* of interest in had allowed another man to court her while they'd been spending the last three afternoons together.

Henry gave a snort of disbelief; soon he would be joined for life to a woman who would roll around on a blanket with one man while she was promised to another.

Instead of heading home or to the Clarendon, he turned his curricle toward Lady Sedgwick's town house. He needed to talk to the countess before news of his identity became common knowledge.

His mind whirled while the curricle crawled along through the heavy late-afternoon traffic.

Strangely, it was not Annis whom he loathed—although such a money-grubbing and conniving female was one reason that he'd launched this deception to begin with. No, it was himself that he despised. He was an idiot who deserved his fate. He'd been a fool to conceive of this masquerade to begin with and had ended up hoist by his own petard.

He smiled at the archaic saying. When he saw Annis again, he would have to ask her where the saying orig—

Henry scowled and stopped the pleasant thought dead in its tracks. It would be a long time—if ever—before he could imagine having amusing conversations about idioms with such a lying, scheming woman.

He was *such* an idiot. Here he'd been mocking Colin for chasing after a mercenary woman when he'd succumbed without so much as a struggle.

How many times in his life would he allow himself to be drawn to a woman before he learned his lesson?

Not many more since you'll soon be married, Henry.

He barked a laugh, making his poor horses jolt. "Sorry, lads," he murmured.

Henry needed to get his temper in check, because he would soon have to confess his little deception to Lady Sedgwick and deal with her well-deserved wrath. The countess was, unfortunately, an unintended casualty of his deception, and he was ashamed that he'd used her. Her living depended on her reputation among the beau monde, and Henry had probably damaged that reputation.

Regardless of how much guilt and dread he was feeling about confessing the truth to Lady Sedgwick, an image kept wending its way into his mind's eye like a serpent bearing an apple. An image of Annis on the picnic blanket that afternoon.

His cock, which had lost interest in the day the moment Henry had learned about Annis's banker beau, speedily reanimated at the memory of her supple body squirming and thrashing beneath his hand and—

Henry gritted his teeth against the provocative memory. He didn't want to be thinking good thoughts about her because he was furious with her.

Why had she done it—any of it? Not just their amorous tussle on the blanket, but sneaking away on carriage rides with him when she was trying to snare the rich banker?

Because of his distraction, Henry found himself standing in front of Lady Sedgwick's door far sooner than he would have liked. Indeed, the cowardly part of him—which had grown larger the closer he came to the countess's townhouse—silently prayed that she wasn't home.

"Colin Parker to see Lady Sedgwick," he said, telling his lie for one last time to the domestic who answered the door.

Before the woman could answer him, the countess herself floated gracefully down the stairs.

"Ah, Mr. Parker," Lady Sedgwick said, her shapely lips curving into the feline smile that always made him feel like she *knew* things. She glanced behind him. "Are you alone today?"

"Yes. I wondered if I might have a moment of your time?"

"Of course. Please come up." She turned to her servant. "Will you send up tea, please?"

The last thing Henry wanted was another watery beverage, but he might actually need some tea today.

The Language of Love

Once they'd both settled into chairs in her parlor, she said, "How may I help you, Mr. Parker."

Henry hated to be dramatic, but…

"I'm not Colin Parker. I'm Henry Singleton. Parker—the man who you think is the earl—is actually my employee."

"I know."

Henry blinked. "I'm sorry, but did you say—"

"I have known who you are for some time, my lord."

"How?"

"An acquaintance recognized your resemblance to your late grandfather."

Henry had seen portraits of his paternal grandfather when he'd lived at Stoke. The resemblance had always astounded him.

"When?" he finally asked.

"Weeks ago."

"Why didn't you tell me?"

"I am not entirely sure," she confessed, sounding bemused. "Why did you do it, my lord?"

"Partly a whim and partly to get a look at the *ton* from a different angle. By paying Parker to be me, I could observe without being observed."

"That is almost word-for-word what Miss Annis Bowman said when I told her who you really were."

Her words made the hair on the back of his neck stand up, like an electrical charge from a storm. "I'm sorry—but… what?"

"I aired my suspicions about you to Annis—don't worry, she is discreet and will tell no one—and she said almost exactly the same thing you just did." Lady Sedgwick frowned when Henry remained mute. "Is something wrong, my lord?"

"Who else knows about me?"

"Only Miss Bowman and the Earl of Avington."

Annis knew.

Annis knew.

"—soon, my lord? *My lord?*"

Henry's head jerked up. "I'm sorry, I missed that, my lady."

"I asked if you were now planning to let the truth be known?"

"Yes. Yes, of course," he said distractedly.

"Is something wrong, Lord Rotherhithe?"

"No, I'm sorry. I just recalled something I'd forgotten."

"Do you need to leave?"

"Not right now." He cleared his throat. "In fact, I hoped you weren't too angry with me to take on another commission."

She laughed softly.

"I know," he said, although she'd not spoken. "I don't deserve your help, but—"

"It's not help if you are paying me," she pointed out.

He couldn't help smiling at that. "No, you're correct. If you're willing, I'd like to engage you to help me get through the next week."

She opened her mouth and then hesitated.

"What is it, my lady?"

"Are you asking for help with your, er, employee and the expectations he might have raised with Miss Susanna Bowman?"

"No, that has all been taken care of."

It was her turn to look startled. "It has?"

"Yes, I spoke to Mr. Bowman, and he now knows exactly who Mr. Colin Parker really is. The matter I wish to engage you for is my betrothal."

Her elegant brows arched. "Indeed? And who, may I ask, is the fortunate lady?"

Henry stared at her, looking for some sign that she was lying—that she knew it was her friend. That the two of them had planned this and set a trap to catch him. But she looked genuinely mystified.

"It is one of the Misses Bowman."

Her lovely gray eyes bulged. "You are betrothed to one of the *Bowman* sisters."

"Not one of the sisters. I am betrothed to Miss Annis Bowman."

***

Henry was exhausted by the time he left Lady Sedgwick's house an hour later.

She hadn't raised her voice or hectored or even given him the dirty looks he deserved.

No, she was far more subtle and clever with her punishment.

By the time he'd left her, he had agreed to not only stay in London for eight more days, but to re-join the social whirl, this time with his betrothed at his side, rather than Colin.

"You *must* stay and make amends, my lord. Surely you understand that?"

"I don't, actually."

The Language of Love

That had almost flustered the unflappable countess. "Because you *must* ensure that Annis will be welcome when she returns to London."

"And why the devil would she—or we—do *that*?"

"I assume that part of the reason for marriage is children. If that is so," she'd gone on, not waiting for an answer, "then you will not want them to be outcasts among their own people, will you?"

Well, what could Henry say to that? He, a man who'd spent his formative years cast out not only from the *ton,* but from his own family.

As angry as he was with Annis just now, Henry didn't want to hurt her or make her unhappy—he wasn't that much of a bastard—nor did he want to ruin the futures of his unborn children.

And so—after only a token struggle—he had capitulated: they would stay in town for eight days.

The best thing to have come out of the excruciating meeting was that Lady Sedgwick had agreed to plan their wedding.

The worst part, at least in Henry's mind, was that it wouldn't be a small or quick affair.

"A hasty ceremony would be impossible," Lady Sedgwick had assured him. "You are in London and so is the entire beau monde. There is no reason to have a hole-and-corner affair and it will reflect poorly on you both and be long remembered. Besides, Annis will wish her grandmother to attend, so you can hardly marry tomorrow. Even eight days from now is shockingly quick, but it will have to serve. If you see to the special license, I shall make all the other arrangements."

"I can't believe that anyone other than Annis's grandmother will want to come to our wedding," he'd said.

Her eyes had narrowed. "You may indeed have an empty church, my lord. But you must at least attempt to make amends."

"Annis may wish to be involved in the planning," he'd pointed out.

"Naturally I will consult her first."

Henry had all but sprinted from her house after that—afraid she'd come up with more ideas, such as court presentations or his attendance at one of the Regent's levees.

When he pulled up outside his house a quarter of an hour later, he had to wait for a servant.

Several minutes later, he was still waiting.

Cursing beneath his breath, he did something he'd not done since he was a lad. He put his thumb and forefinger in his mouth and issued an ear-splitting whistle.

The door flew open almost instantly and Owen, the slovenliest and least respectful of his servants, hovered in the opening.

"Take the curricle around back," Henry snapped, his sharp tone galvanizing the man into action.

Flitwick appeared in the opening before Owen slouched his way over. "I heard a—"

"Is Lord Rotherhithe here?" Henry interrupted, tossing the reins to Owen without looking at him and striding toward the foyer.

"Yes, Mr. Parker. He is in his—"

"Tell him I want to see him in the library. Immediately," Henry ordered, stripping off his gloves.

Rather than look surprised, the older man merely nodded. "Of course, sir."

Henry paused and narrowed his eyes. "How long have you known?"

"I had the honor of serving your grandfather, my lord."

Henry barked a laugh. "So, you've known all along."

"Yes, my lord." Flitwick hesitated and then said, "May I tell the others the truth, sir?"

"You mean they don't already know?"

"Only Mrs. Flitwick, sir."

"Yes, make the announcement. And I'll want you to make any necessary changes to the servants." Henry gave the older man a meaningful look.

He wouldn't tell Flitwick to sack any of them, but he hoped the butler would discharge Owen, at least. The man wasn't just insolent, he was also lazy and rude.

"Of course, sir."

"I want you to engage two grooms, two footmen, and a valet who will not mind traveling to accompany me and my new wife to Yorkshire."

Flitwick's eyebrows rose a fraction of an inch. "Congratulations, my lord. And will the auspicious event take place soon?"

"Yes, in eight days. I shall give you more information when I get it."

"Very good, sir."

The Language of Love

With Annis's earlier words still echoing in his head—the ones about Rotherhithe House—Henry eyed the older man and said, "I have also decided to make some changes to the house. I'm authorizing you to implement whatever repairs you deem necessary and hire the staff you need to run the place. Forward the bills to Yorkshire to my steward at Stoke." He hesitated and then added, "I hope you and Mrs. Flitwick will keep your positions for as long as I own Rotherhithe House."

Flitwick's normally slitted eyes widened. "Very good, sir. Thank you so much, my lord," he said, his tone almost tremulous.

Henry fled before the older man dropped to his knees and offered to kiss his ring.

He'd just poured himself a glass of whiskey when the door to the library flew open and Parker came charging in, his eyes wide. "Flitwick said you needed to see me immediately. Is ought—"

"It is over, Colin. The deception is at an end," he clarified when the other man stared at him in perplexity.

"Oh."

Henry handed Colin the glass he'd just poured for himself since the poor bastard looked like he needed it more.

"Thank you, my lord." Colin's hand shook as he took the glass and tossed back the contents.

Henry re-filled it without being asked and poured one for himself.

When he raised his glass in a toast, he saw that Colin's chin was wobbling dangerously and his eyes were glassy. Like Flitwick, he looked on the verge of weeping, but, unlike the older man, he wouldn't be crying with joy.

"What is the matter, now?" Henry snapped, and then felt even worse when Colin jolted. "Is it the damned Bowman chit?"

"I—I love her, my lord. And now she'll never—"

"She will," Henry assured him, not bothering to add the words, *if she really cares for you.* He threw back his whiskey, eyed the bottle, and then decided against a second glass.

"But—but I've no money, no connections, no—"

"The girl has a generous dowry and Mr. Bowman said he will not stand in your way." He grimaced. "I can't say the same about the mother."

Colin winced. "Yes, Mrs. Bowman is rather—"

"Yes, yes, we are agreed on that," Henry hastened to say, not wanting to talk about the abrasive woman.

They sat in silence for a long moment.

It was Colin who broke it. "What are you going to do now? Should I pack and—"

"You are welcome to stay here." Henry pulled a face. "Although why you'd wish to, I do not know."

"Thank you, my lord."

Colin looked so bloody grateful that Henry felt like an ogre.

"I'll speak to somebody at Leadenhall Street on your behalf," Henry assured him.

But Colin looked less than overjoyed by the prospect of a new job. Henry couldn't blame him—the man was not clerk-material. To be honest, the only job that really suited Colin was the one he'd had for the past weeks: that of a feckless, lazy peer.

"I've authorized Flitwick to make any necessary repairs and hire more staff," he added, hoping to cheer the other man out of his gloom. "That means new furnishings, a functioning kitchen, and even a cook."

To his surprise, Colin smiled. "You're going to fix up the old girl?"

"Yes, I guess I am." Henry took a deep breath. "You should know that I am betrothed to Miss Annis Bowman."

Colin goggled. "No... Are you really?"

"Yes, Colin. Really."

His mobile features shifted into a huge grin. "Well, well, well. I never even guessed. Congratulations, you sly dog, you!" He must have recalled to whom he was speaking. "Oh, I say! I didn't mean—"

"Thank you for your felicitations," Henry said, firmly shutting off the flow of groveling.

A boasting Colin was bad enough. An obsequious Colin would be unbearable.

"I'll be staying in London for the next ten days so you might as well finish out what remains of the Season, too," Henry said, and then immediately wanted to bash his head against the marble mantelpiece for making such an absurd suggestion.

"*Really?*" Colin all but bounced up and down in his chair. The mournful puppy was gone and the exuberant puppy was back.

"I shouldn't look so happy if I were you," Henry warned. "It's likely there won't *be* much of a Season for either of us."

Colin's face fell. "Oh. You think people will be angry with us?"

"I daresay you'll be safe enough from too much reprisal. As for me? Well, I shall soon find out." Henry took out his watch and was annoyed to learn there was still plenty of time for his next errand. He replaced the watch and stood.

"Where are you going, my lord?"

"To make amends," he said grimly. "You might as well come with me."

Chapter 14

Annis got less than two hours of sleep that night and woke up with a woolly head and sore, gritty eyes.

After leaving her uncle's office, her aunt had sent a dinner tray up to her room, making her feelings on Annis's betrothal perfectly clear.

Eating dinner in her room should have meant that she could go to bed early, but she'd tossed and turned so badly that her sheets had wrapped into a tight corkscrew by the time she finally dropped off at seven o'clock that morning.

As a result, she was only getting dressed at noon.

Well, Annis thought as she plaited her hair and wound it into the crown-like hairstyle she favored, if her aunt had hoped to hurt her feelings by excluding her from another fractious family dinner, she'd missed the mark entirely.

Missed the mark.

She paused her plaiting, smiling at the ancient, biblical idiom.

Sharing the joy of language was something she'd only done with her father. Until Henry. He'd not only taught her a few phrases in Urdu each time they were together, but he loved teasing her by dropping idioms into their conversations.

After the way he'd looked at her yesterday, Annis would be fortunate if he spoke to her at all—in any language.

"Ugh," she muttered, glaring at her reflection.

There was a knock on her door.

"Come in," she said.

It was Coombes. "Your uncle wishes to see you, Miss Annis."

"Right now?"

"Yes, Miss Annis."

She sighed and then followed the stately butler down the stairs, marveling that he'd lowered himself to deliver a message to her. Apparently, word of her betrothal to a lord was out, and she had risen up the ranks.

Her uncle stood when she entered the library. "Have a seat, my dear."

The Language of Love

Annis sat.

"I understand why you didn't join us for dinner last night, Annis—yesterday was terribly exhausting—but I hope you didn't avoid the meal because you worried that we'd mistreat you. Please join us for the evenings that remain."

It was an olive branch, so she didn't tell him it had been his wife, rather than her own inclination, that had kept her in her room. "Thank you, Uncle."

"His lordship was here earlier this morning and he and I came to a swift agreement on your marriage settlement. He was, er, very generous and you will want for nothing."

Annis didn't want to hear that—especially not after she'd already taken a fortune from the man. She merely nodded.

"His lordship has asked that he be allowed to explain the pertinent details of the wedding contract and his plans for your wedding." He glanced at the long-case clock. "He will be here shortly. I trust you have no difficulty speaking to him on such matters?"

"No, Uncle." Not after yesterday—when she'd had to admit to being an immoral money-grubber willing to marry a man she didn't love, and then, immediately after, had begged him for twelve thousand pounds.

No, she had no trouble speaking to him about anything now.

In fact, she welcomed the opportunity, no matter that it would be uncomfortable. She did not like having her uncle handle her business for her. She would much rather handle her own affairs, no matter that she had bungled things so badly for herself and her grandmother.

Besides, her uncle's help had not exactly inspired confidence in the past.

"I know I have not been the most staunch advocate for your interests in the past," he said, as if she'd spoken out loud. "But I want you to know that you do not need to do anything you do not wish to do."

She lifted her eyebrows at this surprising statement.

"What I mean to say is, you don't need to accept either man's proposal." His pale skin became almost dangerously red. "I know you've already accepted Lord Rotherhithe, but it is not too late to change your mind. He is wealthy and—I daresay—physically appealing, but he will not be an easy man to live with, I think."

Her uncle could not have surprised Annis more if he had broken into a sea shanty.

Before she could generate a response to this uncharacteristic show of affection, the door opened.

"His lordship, the Earl of Rotherhithe."

Thomas Bowman sprang to his feet and approached his guest. "Good afternoon, my lord."

Henry gave him a slight nod. "Bowman."

Uncle Thomas stiffened at the cool greeting and turned back to Annis. "Annis, did you have anything else to say to me?"

She knew what he meant. "No, Uncle. But thank you for the offer."

He nodded. "Then I shall give you some privacy." He paused. "I won't summon Ford, but I ask that you keep your meeting brief."

"Yes, Uncle."

The door shut behind the older man and Henry took the chair nearest to her.

He looked even more impressive than usual, and she supposed he could now dress in a manner befitting a man of his status.

He wore buff pantaloons that molded to his muscular hips, thighs, and calves in a way that left Annis breathless. His dark green coat and gold and green waistcoat gave his hazel eyes a verdant tint. His Hessians glowed the color of rich, polished mahogany, and his linen was as blinding as fresh frost.

He was utterly gorgeous.

Annis wore yet another hand-me-down day dress, this one a less unflattering color—a pale rose that put some pink into her cheeks—but just as poorly cut.

"Do you wish me to explain the marriage contract to you?" he asked coolly.

"That won't be necessary," she said, and then hesitated.

"Yes?"

Was it her imagination, or did he look even more hostile than yesterday?

"I—well, there is something I wish to say."

"Oh?" The smile on his face was not particularly pleasant.

Well, whose fault was that? No doubt he was wondering what *other* surprises she had for him.

"I knew you were Rotherhithe before yesterday."

"I know."

"W-what?"

"I went to see Lady Sedgwick after I left here, and she told me the truth." He put a not-so-subtle emphasis on the words *she* and *truth*.

Oh God.

"You—er, I—" Annis coughed; her throat was too dry to form the words. She swallowed and tried again. "You must wonder why I said nothing."

"Must I?"

Annis cringed at his scathing tone and glance. She opened her mouth to apologize for yet another lie, but he wasn't finished.

"I wondered," he admitted. "Indeed, I spent most of yesterday evening wondering. But then I realized that I hardly have the moral high ground when it comes to telling the truth, do I?"

Annis decided that was a rhetorical question. "Are—are you furious at me for not telling you yesterday?"

"Being angry about something that has already happened is pointless."

Still, he did not look happy, and she couldn't blame him. "May I explain my reasoning—or at least try?"

He inclined his head.

"I assumed you had gone to so much trouble because you didn't want to be the target of fortune or title hunters."

"Yes, I was hoping to see people for who they really were. And it seems I have."

Annis's face flamed at his cold, assessing look, but she pressed onward. "I was wrong to see you when I was already being courted by Mr. Norburg—I knew that. I considered telling you about him, but I believed that you'd be—"

"Disgusted with you for marrying him for his money?"

It was a brutal way to put it, but no less true. "Yes."

"I daresay I would have been," he admitted.

His words caused a lump to form in her throat.

Annis swallowed it down. "And I also worried that if I told you the truth—that I needed money—*you* would think—" She bit her lip, unable to go on.

"I would think that you were angling for *me* to help you?"

Annis nodded. "Yes. It just seemed like nothing I said or did would have made things better." She pulled a face. "Well, other than not agreeing to see you in the first place, of course. But—but I—" Annis couldn't go on, and he didn't ask her to.

"I mentioned a few minutes ago that there is absolutely nothing to be gained by regretting the past, and I meant it." He leaned closer to her, his gaze intensifying, his face hard and stern. "But these will be the last lies we tell each other. Today we begin afresh. Agreed?" He paused, and she nodded. "So, with that in mind, is there anything else you need to tell me?"

Tell him about Leech!

That is in the past and it has nothing to do with what happened yesterday or this past week. I'm sure Henry didn't intend for me to divulge every shameful secret in my life.

"Annis?" Henry asked.

"No." She shook her head. "No, there is nothing more." And there wouldn't be after Annis replaced the money Leech had stolen. That would be the end of that sordid chapter in her life.

"Very well," he said. "I will procure a special license this afternoon. I'd hoped to have a small ceremony, but Lady Sedgwick convinced me it would be a poor way to begin our marriage."

Annis knew Freddie was probably right. "What does she suggest?"

"A proper wedding with lots of guests."

She grimaced. "Yes, I suspect that is what should happen. When?"

"I had thought of marrying in eight days. Is that acceptable?"

"The sooner the better."

"Is your family making things uncomfortable for you here?"

She shivered at the hint of menace in his voice. "No, but I doubt my aunt and cousins will be pleased once the truth is out and the invitations cease to arrive."

To her amazement, he laughed.

"I'm sorry," he said at her startled look. "I'm not laughing at the situation—well, actually, I suppose I am."

"What do you mean?"

"After speaking to Lady Sedgwick, and then Colin, I went to White's to beard the lion in its den." He paused, his lips curving into the slightest of smiles. "Well?"

Annis's throat itched, and she had to swallow back her tears, gratitude all but swamping her at this tiny show of affection—or at least a small peace offering. "It's a Latin proverb based on the Bible—Samuel."

He nodded. "Ah, yes. I should have guessed. In any case, I thought I'd begin untangling the mess I'd made, starting with the male half of the *ton*. Before I could confess, however, I learned the truth was already out."

"It was? But how? Who could have—" she gasped. "Percy! Oh, he didn't!"

"It seems young Percy headed directly from here to White's yesterday. I daresay he was hoping to take me out before I could even fire a shot." His smile grew into a fierce, feral grin. "But his plan backfired—badly. Somebody he told went to the weekly Beefsteak Club dinner—you've heard of it?"

"It's that silly men's club. But why should that matter?"

"You know the Regent is a member?"

"I didn't know that, but I'm not surprised."

"He was there last night and heard the story."

Annis groaned. "Oh no! Why would Percy do that? My aunt and uncle will need to move to another country."

"I don't think so. You see, Prinny was quoted as laughing hugely and calling the entire affair a *jolly lark*. This morning I received a letter inviting both me and Colin to Carlton House for the Regent's last dinner party of the Season."

Annis covered her mouth with both hands.

"So, it is my guess that the invitations will begin *flooding* in today." He smiled as she laughed. "I stopped by Lady Sedgwick's before coming here—hoping to put her mind at rest that at least she wasn't to be blackballed."

"Was she happy?"

"Indeed. It was the countess who assured me that the Prince Regent's approval on such a matter will make not only Colin and me the most sought-after guests for the rest of the Season, but the prestige will probably extend to you and your family, as well."

Annis chortled. "I daresay Freddie is correct. The Regent—for all that he is often the butt of jokes—sets the tone in such matters. What else did Freddie have to say to you?"

"She is adamant that we take advantage of this social windfall and show our faces at every rout, ball, dinner, and party until the wedding."

She grimaced. "But you *hate* such things."

"Yes, well, she convinced me it was for the best."

Annis wanted to ask why, but he didn't give her a chance.

159

"I hope you don't mind that I've enlisted Lady Sedgwick's help to plan the wedding?"

"I am thrilled to hear it. I'm afraid you will discover that I have little experience in—well, in anything except teaching languages."

"You will have your hands full assembling a wardrobe. There is not much time; you will need to have clothing made quickly." His eyes flickered over her person, his lips twisting with displeasure at the ill-fitting castoff she wore. "As of this morning, your uncle provided you with a clothing allowance, but you may keep that for pin money. I shall provide the material for your new garments from my warehouses."

"Warehouses?"

"Yes, I've accumulated a goodly amount of fabric in trade over the years, as well as a great deal of muslin from the factory my partner now owns. It is all the finest quality, much of it unavailable here."

Annis's head was spinning too much to argue with him about his generosity. Besides, he was probably doing it for himself as much as her; he'd hardly want to be seen in her company if she looked like a ragamuffin

"I will take you to a modiste tomorrow."

"*You* will take me?"

"Yes. Is that acceptable to you?"

Something about his confident, *lordly* behavior suddenly irked her. "What if it is *not* acceptable?"

"Then you must tell me what you prefer, and it shall be done," he answered mildly.

Annis ground her teeth. Oh, he knew how to take any satisfaction from defiance!

"Fine. I will accompany you."

"You seem perturbed by the notion. Is it so unusual?"

"I believe it is."

"Well, *I* am unusual," he said, as if she didn't already know that. "Surely it cannot be too scandalous if your maid accompanies us."

"I don't have a maid."

Annis could see by his pinched nostrils he did not like that information one bit. "I shall ask Lady Sedgwick to come along—I've engaged her services right up to the wedding, after all."

"That would be lovely," Annis said, pleased to think of being with her friend while Freddie was earning money for it.

"I will engage a maidservant for you, as well," he said.

The Language of Love

"That is probably unusual, too. Most men do *not* engage servants for their betrothed."

"Do you care?" He sounded genuinely curious.

Did she care if he bought her clothing and engaged a servant for her before they were married? For some reason, it seemed naughty, like something a man would do with his mistress.

It would mortify and infuriate her aunt.

Annis smiled at the thought. "I would be grateful for your offer with my clothing. As to your offer of a maid, Grace, one of my uncle's chambermaids, is hoping to find work as lady's maid. She has occasionally waited on my cousins and has done an admirable job. I will ask her if she is interested."

He nodded. "So, to sum up our battle plan, we shall marry eight days hence. Until that time, we will attend whatever *ton* functions Lady Sedgwick stipulates. After our wedding we shall stay one night at the Clarendon—Rotherhithe House is hardly habitable—and shall depart for Stoke the following day. Do you have questions or requests before we meet again tomorrow?"

A hundred questions bounced around in her skull, but none of them made their way into words. "No, there is nothing I can think of."

Henry reached into his impeccably cut coat and drew out a slender envelope. "This document entitles the bearer to draw the amount you requested from my bank." He handed it to her.

"Thank you." Annis took the letter, breathless at the ease with which he had just saved her grandmother's future. Her face burned with shame as she stared down at the money he'd given without question.

Thankfully, the door opened, and a servant entered, bearing a tray. Behind the maid was Ford with her needlework.

Henry stood.

"You are not staying for tea?"

"I have an appointment I cannot miss." He took her hand and bowed over it. "I will come for you at noon tomorrow."

He smiled down at her, but, unlike in the past, the expression never reached his eyes.

***

Henry didn't have to sit outside Thomas Bowman's house for long before Annis emerged—without a maid or a footman, of course—walking briskly.

"She's the one I should follow, guv?" the hackney driver asked.

"Yes. Do try to be inconspicuous."

The driver laughed. "For what you're payin' me, I can be bleedin' invisible.

"She's hailing a hackney," Henry pointed out, wishing the man would stop yapping and keep his eyes on Annis.

"I see 'er, guv."

Henry sat back and watched the streets flicker past. Did he feel like a bit of a rat following her?

Perhaps. But then she had lied to him immediately after promising there would be no more secrets between them. Truly, the woman was the world's worst liar. He hated it when people lied to him almost as much as he hated when people kept secrets from him.

Not that any of that excused what he was doing.

Henry sighed; it wasn't yet two o'clock, and he'd already had a busy day. It had been damned uncomfortable, too. His second meeting with Lady Sedgwick—which he hadn't believed could be more uncomfortable than the first—was not an hour of his life that he'd care to repeat.

If he'd believed that Prinny's stamp of approval would make the woman forgive and forget his deception, he'd been sorely mistaken.

"Thanks to our Regent, you will encounter nothing but red carpets wherever you go, my lord. I hope you realize how fortunate you are. In the future, if you do not care for society's blessing for yourself, at least think of your wife and children."

Yes, Lady Sedgwick knew how to shame a man while plying him with tea and biscuits.

But she was right; Henry had behaved like an ass, and it was his duty to clean up the mess. Thanks to the Prince Regent—the nominal leader of Great Britain—and his juvenile sense of humor, sorting out the mess would be considerably less unpleasant than it could have been.

His penance would be more misery of the kind he'd endured for weeks: vapid social functions. But as angry as he still was with her—so he'd lied to her about not being angry. What of it? —he would enjoy watching her take part in at least a few events of the Season while well-dressed.

Henry's feelings toward her seemed to change every five minutes. Just when he'd think that she deserved pretty things and the homage of her peers, he'd recall how she'd kept both him and Mr. Norburg on her string.

The Language of Love

Lurching from adoration to anger about things in the past was not comfortable. He was a man on the far side of thirty, not a child, and he knew it behooved him to look beyond his displeasure. Soon, they would be married and would live together until one of them died. He'd been enjoying her company a great deal before he'd discovered that she was planning to marry for money. Now he could enjoy her company for the rest of his life.

The carriage slowed, and he saw they'd gone all the way to the financial district.

"She's gettin' out ahead, guv," the driver said, leaning to the side so Henry could see the road ahead of them, where Annis was paying the driver.

"Pull up closer," Henry said.

Once they'd come to a halt, Henry watched her enter a building that had several brass plaques beside the door. It was some sort of office for solicitors or men of business, judging by the look of the place and the location.

Once she'd disappeared into the building, Henry hopped out. "Wait for me," he said to the driver, tossing him a coin that made the man smile.

It only took him a few minutes to discern the office she'd gone into belonged to Norman Pears, Solicitor and Man of Affairs.

Henry returned to the hackney and climbed inside

"What next?" the driver asked him.

"Now we wait," Henry said.

If Annis insisted on withholding the truth from him, perhaps Mr. Norman Pears could be convinced to clear matters up.

Chapter 15

Annis goggled like a bumpkin at the bolts of fabric that filled a good half of Madame Jenette's stylish Oxford Street shop.

"My goodness!" Freddie's beautiful eyes glowed as she took in the almost magical sight.

"You took the words from my mouth," Annis murmured.

They had arrived at the establishment of Henry's choosing to discover that he'd hired the modiste's shop for the entire day.

"She is *very* exclusive," Freddie whispered. "I've never had a client who has managed to get their toe in the door. Usually, she is quite insufferable," Freddie added.

They watched with some amusement as Henry directed the woman as if she were one of his servants.

As haughty as the Frenchwoman looked, she was behaving with almost comical obsequiousness—whether because of his rank, appearance, or the vast amount of fabric that he'd delivered to her shop, Annis could not have said.

Madame, in turn, ordered her employees about like a general deploying troops, making sure all the finery was properly displayed.

Henry hadn't just brought bolts of fabric, there were also ells of exquisite lace, colorful feathers, beaded trims, silken fringe, and dozens of other luxuries that Annis had never dreamed of buying in the past.

Once he'd given his directions to the modiste, he turned to Annis. "These are the fabrics and colors I thought might suit you best," he explained. "Anything you don't want I've offered to sell to Madame Jenette." His lips twisted into a wry smile. "For an exceptionally low price."

The colors and materials were vibrant and gorgeous and *perfect*; it was as if he'd stepped into Annis's head and selected all her favorites: periwinkle blue, spring greens, a dozen shades of pink, and—most remarkably—a vivid red silk.

Freddie raised the scarlet silk to Annis's face, nodding slowly. "I never would have considered such a color, but it is extraordinary

164

with your fair complexion." She turned to Henry, a gleam of respect in her pale gray eyes. "Aren't you a man of hidden talents, my lord?"

Henry merely smiled. "In addition to the material you see here, I've delivered fine lawns and muslins to a woman Madame Jenette suggested. She will pass along your measurements for custom garments, but you will need to purchase several ready-made items to see you through the next few days."

Annis blushed; he meant undergarments.

Henry gestured to a rack of gowns that two shop clerks brought out from the back room. "Madam selected a number of gowns that can be quickly altered to fit you. You should choose enough to last you at least the next three days until she can deliver some of the new garments."

The loveliest rose-pink muslin snagged Annis's gaze. She reached out to finger the fine fabric.

"Yes," Henry said, his gaze assessing as he looked at her. "I thought of you as soon as I saw that color."

Annis swallowed, suddenly uncomfortably hot. He'd thought of her?

Freddie lightly cleared her throat, shattering the taut silence. "I made a list of what you'll need, Annis."

"As have I," Henry said, handing Freddie a folded piece of parchment, his brooding eyes still scorching Annis.

While the two compared their lists, Annis escaped to the rack of clothing, not really seeing the garments that she was looking at as guilt and shame ate at her. Henry had done all this for her?

He must still like her? At least a little?

And yet his reserve toward her had not lessened.

Annis turned away from both the lovely garments and the unhappy thought. She smiled slightly at the sight of her dearest friend and betrothed pouring over a stack of pattern books and discussing what would best suit her.

She couldn't have imagined such a delightful turn of events and she wanted to enjoy this day—what woman wouldn't be thrilled to have everything she'd ever wanted? At least everything material.

But her throat became uncomfortably thick as she looked at Henry's massive shoulders and the vulnerable nape of his neck as he and Freddie put their heads together. As lovely as this all was, it was still superficial and material. Was this what Henry thought *she* wanted from him? Is this what he believed she was marrying him for? Fine garments and comfortable carriages?

Yesterday he had said there was no point in dwelling on what had happened in the past.

But did that necessarily mean that he looked forward to a future with her?

***

Annis stared at her reflection.

And stared.

Behind her, her new maid's smile turned to a worried frown. "Don't you like it, Miss Annis?"

The *it* in question was the new hairstyle that Grace had insisted upon implementing first thing.

"You have the most beautiful hair I've ever seen, Miss Annis. My fingers have itched to do something with it ever since the first time I saw you."

Annis had laughed at that. "Now is your chance, Grace. You are in charge of my appearance. You must do as you see fit."

Grace had squealed with delight.

And now, as Annis looked at her image in the glass, she could not regret that decision to allow Grace to trim her hair.

"You have done a *lovely* job," Annis said softly.

Grace clasped her hands together and grinned. "Oh, thank you, miss."

She'd tidied it up, claiming it was too beautiful to cut short. "I've never seen hair like this on a grown woman—only children. Beggin' your pardon, miss," she'd added when she'd seen Annis's wry look.

"Oh, you've not insulted me," Annis had assured her. "I'm long past the age of being embarrassed by such a shocking shade."

"*Embarrassed!* But why?"

"Because it *is* a child's color."

But she had to admit the elegant style her new maid had chosen made her look almost pretty.

Of course, a lot of that was because of the ball gown she was wearing, the first that wasn't secondhand.

"It is an excellent color on you," Henry's gaze had slid critically over the gorgeous periwinkle blue silk, which had been one of the handful of readymade garments. "The cut and design are exquisite, but I wish the quality of the material was better."

The Language of Love

To Annis's shock, Freddie had laughed—perhaps one of the most uninhibited sounds she'd ever heard her elegant friend make.

"What is so amusing?" Henry had asked, raising one imperious brow.

"It is some of the nicest silk I've seen until what you brought today. You are spoiled, my lord."

His lips had quirked into a faint smile. "Perhaps."

Annis saw her maid frown as she looked at the beautiful gown. "What is it, Grace?"

"With that neckline you need something around your neck, miss."

Annis thought unhappily about her grandmother's pearls. Yet another thing Mr. Leech had stolen from her.

"Well, I shall have to do as I am." She picked up the matching reticule Freddie had insisted on.

There was a knock on the door.

"Yes?" she called out

Coombs's head appeared in the doorway. "His lordship is here, Miss Annis. He is waiting for you in the library."

"Goodness. Is it time already?"

"Don't forget your wrap, Miss Annis." Grace held out yards and yards of delicately spangled netting and draped it with infinite care around Annis's shoulders.

"There, miss. You look perfect."

"Thank you, Grace."

Her legs felt wobbly as she made her way to the library. She'd been with Henry most of the day—he'd already seen her in this dress, for pity's sake! —and yet she felt like a girl going to her first ball.

"Idiot," she muttered as entered the library.

"Ah, here you are, my dear." Her uncle smiled as if he were genuinely pleased to see her.

Henry, who'd been sitting in the chair across from her uncle, stood.

Annis caught her breath. She'd seen him in evening blacks before, of course, but never in any that were so perfectly fitted to his body.

His eyes flickered over her briefly before he met her gaze.

The icy layer of fear that had closed around her two days before melted at the look in his eyes—not cold but pleased.

"You look beautiful." The compliment was as sensual as a caress.

"His lordship brought something for you, Annis." Her uncle's voice shook her out of her pleasurable reverie. "I told him that giving jewelry before you are wed is most irregular." His pale cheeks darkened. "But then I realized that I—who should have made sure you had at least a decent set of pearls to wear—have left you without—"

"That doesn't matter, Uncle," she interrupted, not wanting to watch him flagellate himself—no matter how merited it might be.

Henry gestured to a large velvet case on the corner of her uncle's desk. "I believe this will go well with your gown."

She opened the box with shaking fingers and gasped when she saw what lay on the white satin inside. The set comprised a necklace, bracelet, and earbobs. The silver setting was simple, but elegant, and the large blue stones were unlike anything she'd ever seen.

Her uncle came to look. "Goodness. That is quite—"

"Exquisite," Annis said, turning to Henry. "Thank you."

"They are sapphires from Ceylon, which are known for the pale blue." His jaw flexed as he looked from the stones to Annis. "They reminded me of your eyes."

Annis was having too much difficulty breathing to answer him.

He lifted the necklace from the box and stepped behind her, lowering it around her throat. His large, warm fingers barely touched her as he hooked the lobster clasp.

"Give me your arm," he ordered quietly.

Annis complied, sneaking a look at his bowed head as he fastened the matching bracelet around her wrist. Once he'd finished, his eyes wandered over her, a slight, possessive smile curving his lips. "Put on the earrings, Annis."

As if in a trance, she lifted the last of the jewels from the box.

"You are going to the Burton ball tonight?" her uncle asked, clearly determined to be polite.

"Yes."

Her uncle reddened at Henry's curt answer. "Her maid should accomp—"

"Lady Sedgwick is awaiting us in my coach."

"Oh," Uncle Thomas said, visibly nonplussed. "You should have brought her in."

Henry's lips flexed into a brief smile, and Annis knew he was probably remembering Freddie's words from earlier today: *I shall wait for you in his lordship's carriage, Annis, but I'm afraid I couldn't bring myself to speak civilly to anyone in that family just now.*

Henry held out his arm to Annis. "Are you ready to slay the dragon, Annis?"

Her lips parted, and she gave a soft huff of laughter. "Why, I think you might have bested me with that one, my lord. I have no idea where it came from."

"Ah." He gave her the first genuine smile she'd seen on his face all day. And, as she looked up into his eyes, Annis flattered herself that there was at least a little affection in his gaze.

Chapter 16

By the morning of the wedding, Henry wished that he'd grabbed Annis and run for the border.

He'd believed that the social whirl would be as draining as it had been before, when he'd been mere Colin Parker.

He could not have been more mistaken. It had been *twice* as exhausting as a peer.

Now that he was an earl—and the current favorite of the Regent, a man who almost made Colin appear wise by comparison—the hordes had descended on him the same way they'd descended on Colin. Except Henry, unlike his employee, didn't have himself to keep all the hangers-on at bay.

He'd hoped that having Annis beside him would have eased the irritation of socializing.

Again, he'd been wrong.

Although he'd attended social engagements with Annis every single day and night, they'd had no time alone—not even five minutes.

Part of that was because Lady Sedgwick accompanied them everywhere.

But even at the dozens of balls and other functions, there was only one dance per night, no more. And he wasn't allowed to monopolize her company when they weren't dancing.

"You have barely a week to be seen," Lady Sedgwick reminded him when he'd complained about the fact that they went to two or three social occasions every day.

"Annis needs this week, and you owe it to her to do everything you can to establish her place in society."

Henry hadn't argued because he'd agreed with the countess.

As a result, the days before the wedding were so hectic and draining that Henry hadn't had a moment's peace.

But the hectic pace was almost behind him now.

The rector's voice echoed through the cold, cavernous nave, pulling Henry back to the present.

"*If any man can show just cause why they may not lawfully joined together, let him now speak.*"

The Language of Love

For a tense moment, he wondered if somebody—he didn't know who—might leap out of the shadows and stop the ceremony.

Naturally, that didn't happen.

As Henry stood in the church before a small collection of guests—mostly hers—and looked down into Annis's face, he could not be sorry for his choice of bride. Even if she did not love him, she would be an amusing companion and life with her would never be boring.

Now that she'd been kitted out properly, she no longer looked like a wild pixie or fairy, but like a surpassingly lovely young woman, dainty and ethereal. Her corn silk hair—her glorious crowning glory—had been styled in a way that no longer overwhelmed her small face but heightened her delicate beauty. Her sky-blue eyes looked larger than ever, and her complexion was as velvety as a white rose. The only hint of color in her cheeks was that reflected from the rosy-pink silk of her wedding gown.

She looked beautiful.

She also looked terrified.

Henry would have believed she was terrified of what was happening right then—their marriage ceremony—if he had not seen a similar expression on her face often during the past eight days; something was worrying her.

He wished she'd share her burdens with him, but they'd started off this marriage wrong-footed, and life had been too chaotic to come to a meeting of the minds over the last week.

Once they were married and could get away from London and its superficial distractions, he would assure her he was prepared to do everything in his power to make a success of the marriage.

"*—so long as ye both shall live?*"

The words shook Henry from his reverie.

Annis met his gaze directly. "I will."

The vicar turned to Henry.

"*Wilt thou have this woman to thy wedded wife, to live together after God's ordinance in the holy estate of Matrimony? Wilt thou love her, comfort her, honor, and keep her, in sickness and in health; and, forsaking all other, keep thee only unto her, so long as ye both shall live?*"

"I will."

When he took Annis's hands in his, he could feel they were ice cold, even through two layers of gloves. He rubbed his thumb over her clenched knuckles and smiled down at her.

Her eyes widened and some of the tension eased from her body.

He must have lost himself in her blue gaze for a moment, because the next thing Henry knew, he was escorting her from the church and walking toward the friends and family who'd gathered to shake his hand and embrace Henry's new wife.

***

They were married.

Annis was his wife.

She looked down the long table toward her husband, her stomach churning at the word.

Husband.

Uncle Thomas had insisted the wedding breakfast be at North Audley Street and Annis knew it would be churlish to suggest some place else, even though her aunt's stiffness toward her had not abated in the week since the betrothal.

If anything, her family had grown chillier, as if displeased by her good fortune.

But the morning had gone off well, and this breakfast was a festive occasion with some of Annis's dearest friends and her grandmother in attendance.

Henry's offer to send his traveling chaise for Lady Cecily had spurred her uncle out from beneath the cat's paw and he'd sent his own carriage for his mother, bringing her in two very easy stages to London and putting her in a lovely suite of rooms in his house. In the past, her uncle had allowed Aunt Agnes to force Grandmama to travel in a crowded coach and then shunt her into the smallest guest room.

"See how you have raised my status already, my dear?" her grandmother had laughingly whispered upon arriving in London.

When Annis looked at her grandmother—so happy and safe now—she could not regret the lying and scheming she had done to arrive at this point.

Lady Cecily would have a life of comfort and Annis could also buy her grandmother additional luxuries with the ridiculously generous pin allowance Henry had granted her.

Thinking of the pin money reminded Annis of her last private conversation with Henry when she had asked him to keep part of her quarterly allowance back as repayment for the loan.

It was the first time Annis had seen him truly angry.

172

The Language of Love

"Do you really believe that I would dun my own wife for a loan like some back-alley moneylender? Let us not speak of this matter again, ma'am."

His fury about the money had left her speechless.

And tonight, Annis would pay for that money.

Fear and dread coursed through her as she pondered the evening ahead.

Oh, it wasn't the thought of physical love she feared. Indeed, just *thinking* about tonight had woken her up repeatedly over the past week. Each time she'd been flushed, hot, and aroused. Each time she'd taken her pleasure from her body, using her hand the way Henry had done.

No, it wasn't the marriage bed that terrified her.

It was her dread of the moment when he realized that she'd lied to him, again. That he'd married a ruined woman.

Annis struggled to swallow down the lump in her throat as she cut a furtive glance down the table to where Henry was engaged in conversation with Lorelei. Whatever Henry was saying to Annis's usually prickly friend—at least where men were concerned—was making Lorie laugh.

Lorie had arrived unexpectedly only two days before—her appearance such a delightful surprise that Annis had cried. She loved all her friends, of course, but she had known Lorie the longest.

Lorie was even poorer than Annis, so a trip from Cornwall to London would have been a significant expenditure.

But when Annis had offered to pay for her fare back home, Lorie had surprised her yet again. "I will stay in London for a while."

"Did you find work?"

"Of a sort," Lorie said, her cheeks darkening. "I sold one of my stories to the Minerva Press and they want more. So, I shall be able to afford to share expenses with Freddie."

Annis hadn't been sure whether to congratulate her on the sale, or not. "That's good, isn't it? I mean, about them wanting more?"

"Yes, it is good. Don't worry, Annis, I haven't stopped working on my *real* novel."

Lorie was a brilliant writer, but the sort of stories she enjoyed writing were not the sort that publishers wanted from female authors.

"I'm so glad you'll be here with Freddie," Annis had said. "She will need you, Lorie."

At the time, they'd been in Freddie's sitting room. Their friend had been out on the small terrace reading a letter from Miles, her beautiful face pale and stricken.

Both Annis and Lorie had known what that meant: Miles had finally become betrothed. Or at least he soon would be.

Tears prickled Annis's eyes at the memory of Freddie's shattered expression and Annis felt guilty that she had been fortunate enough to marry the man she loved—even if Henry didn't love her—but poor Freddie and Miles could never be together.

"Is aught amiss, Annis?" Portia—now the Countess of Broughton—was rudely leaning across her gorgeous husband, Stacy.

"No, of course not," Annis assured her.

"You are so quiet, my dear. It is unlike you."

"I am just enjoying having my friends together."

Portia dropped her voice to a whisper. "You are worried about tonight, aren't you?"

Annis gave a nervous laugh and glanced at Lord Broughton. She could feel his gaze on her even if she couldn't see his eyes, which were hidden behind the dark spectacles he was never without.

Although both his coloring and the classical perfection of his features made him look like a marble statue, his lips curved into a warm, human smile. "Portia, my love, I believe you are embarrassing your friend."

His irrepressible wife shrugged off the earl's gentle chiding. "Nonsense, Stacy. Annis is far too practical to be missish about physical love. But it is natural to be a little nervous."

Annis's face was on fire. "No, Portia, I am not nervous."

"Making love can be a very beautiful thing," Portia went on, cutting her husband a quick but scorching look. "Would you like me to explain what happens?"

"No!" she squeaked. "At least, not now," Annis hastened to say. "Perhaps we might have a quick word before we leave?"

Portian nodded. "*Bene. Io parlo con te più tardi.*"

It was easier to accept her friend's offer of a quick, after-breakfast conversation about coitus than to tell her the truth—that she was already familiar with the process.

Although perhaps she could practice confessing the truth to Portia?

Somehow, Annis suspected that confessing to a friend wouldn't be the same as telling her brand-new husband.

The Language of Love

Annis grimaced. A man expected his bride to come to his bed unsullied, and yet she had deceived him. And she had done so after promising him there would be no more lies between them.

She took a deep breath and exhaled it slowly; there was no point in worrying now. She couldn't do anything about it. Besides, there was nothing Henry could do if he was displeased with her.

Well, he could beat her or starve her now that she was his property under the law, but Annis knew he would never hurt her—at least not physically. She even believed that he still liked her. At least a little.

She could only hope that this next confession would not kill off the delicate sprout of affection that remained between them.

Annis sighed. Tonight, she could finally stop living a lie. And if he hated her for it, well, she would deal with that tomorrow. And for the rest of her life.

***

They were leaving London first thing in the morning, so they were saying goodbye to their friends right after the wedding breakfast—a meal that was actually a cross between nuncheon and dinner.

Henry thanked Mr. and Mrs. Bowman for hosting the meal, but, other than that, he didn't have a soul to bid goodbye to.

Well, other than Colin.

But his erstwhile employee was so busy gazing longingly at Susanna Bowman that Henry doubted he would even hear him.

Colin had done his best over the past week to court the younger Bowman sister, but he was no match for Mrs. Bowman, who had made sure that Colin never had a dance or conversation with Susanna.

"I'm at wit's end, my lord," Colin had whined just two days ago. "And so is Susanna. Her last message to me suggested Gretna Green."

Henry was pleasantly surprised that the object of Colin's affections reciprocated his regard, but he had cringed at Colin's pronouncement.

"You may take her wherever you like, Parker. But you will wait at least a week after I've left London before you do anything. I don't want to give your prospective mother-in-law reason to hate me any more than she does. You also might want to consider whether Miss Bowman will agree to live at Rotherhithe House with you." It was the gentlest way he could think of to remind the man that he had neither a job nor a home at this point.

"She said that she'd live in a mud hut as long as she was with me. Can you credit that, my lord?"

No, Henry couldn't. But he'd kept that to himself. He'd also kept to himself any skepticism he felt at the thought of Miss Susanna Bowman living in Rotherhithe House while it was undergoing restoration.

But Henry had developed a soft spot for the man, so he'd given Colin permission to live in the house as long as he liked, with or without a wife—although he'd asked Flitwick first.

"But my lord… it is your house. You may do whatever you wish," his startled butler had assured him.

"You shall have to put up with him," Henry had pointed out. "And I daresay Mrs. Flitwick shall have to care for him like a baby chick, so let me know whether you wish me to chuck him out before I leave."

Flitwick had looked so horrified at the suggestion that Henry realized the old servant was yet another person who Colin had effortlessly wrapped around his little finger. Henry wouldn't have really chucked him out, but it had been amusing to tease the unexpectedly soft-hearted Flitwick.

As much as Henry liked Colin, he was glad that he no longer had to spend all his days and nights with the man.

While Henry couldn't wait to get away from his only wedding guest, Annis was visibly heartbroken to say goodbye to her friends.

Not only Lady Sedgwick and Lord Avington but also the two who'd unexpectedly made the trip to London at the last moment, Miss Lorelei Fontenot and Lady Broughton, who'd come with her husband, the Earl of Broughton.

Henry had been surprised to discover that he'd done business with Broughton in the past, but knew him as Eustace Harrington, owner of a sizeable shipping company based in Bristol, which he'd built himself, before inheriting his title.

He'd not had much of a chance to speak to Broughton, but what he'd learned about him—that he was practical and not high-in-the-instep—he liked.

"Hello, Rotherhithe."

Henry turned to find Avington standing beside him. The man's words were friendly enough, but his gaze was cool.

"Hello, Avington," Henry said, just as coolly.

Miles had only spoken to Henry once this past week, even though the two of them had crossed paths frequently. Their single conversation had taken place at the Asquith ball and had been hostile and to the point.

"Ah, Rotherhithe, just the man I've been looking for," Avington had said.

Henry had taken one look into Avington's cold, flat eyes and had guessed what was coming. "Well, here I am, my lord."

"Perhaps we might step onto the terrace for a moment?" He had turned without waiting for an answer.

Avington had led Henry out through the French doors, onto the terrace, waiting until they were well away from the house before speaking. "If your asinine masquerade makes any problems for Lady Sedgwick, you'll be answering to me, *my lord*."

That had *not* been what Henry had expected the other man to say, and he'd been momentarily speechless before replying. "I've already told the countess to inform me if she encounters any difficulties."

"If only it were as simple as that, Rotherhithe, but the *ton* doesn't always show its disapproval in overt ways."

Henry knew that was true. As unfair as it was, the Prince Regent's vocal approval of Henry's masquerade had not only absolved him of any wrongdoing, but it had brought him into fashion.

The same was not true for the Countess of Sedgwick. His thoughtless behavior *had* jeopardized Lady Sedgwick's credibility and threatened her livelihood.

He deeply regretted that, but he'd done all he could to help her. He wasn't about to grovel. Especially not to the Earl of Avington.

And that was exactly what he'd told the other man before he'd walked off and left Miles seething on the Asquith terrace.

"I haven't yet wished you happy," Avington said now, a mocking smirk sitting oddly on his angelic features.

"Thank you, my lord." Henry gave him a smirk of his own and couldn't help adding, "I understand you might be celebrating your own nuptials soon."

Avington recoiled. "What are you talking about?"

"I'm talking about Miss Mary Barnett—she of Barnett Iron fame." Henry gave him an innocent look. "Or is there some other heiress that you are almost betrothed to?"

Displeasure emanated from the other man like heat from a forge. "Who told you that?"

"The beau monde does not have a monopoly on gossip, Avington. We cits have our own grapevine, you know."

"It is disingenuous of you to claim the designation of cit, Rotherhithe. Your title is ancient, your blood far bluer than mine." He stepped closer until they were barely an inch apart. "I've noticed that Annis has not been her usual ebullient self this past week. I hope nothing is amiss between you?"

The smile slid from Henry's mouth. "You needn't concern yourself with my *wife*, Avington."

"Annis is very dear to me, Rotherhithe, and I would take it personally if she were to be made unhappy." Avington's normally friendly blue eyes were like ice.

Henry closed the bit of distance that remained between them, bumping the other man's chest hard enough to drive him back a step. "You gave up any right to feel *personally* about my wife when you forsook her for money, my lord."

Avington's brow furrowed. "What in the world are you talking about?"

"Please don't insult my intelligence by pretending you're not in love with her. I've seen the way you look at her."

"Me and… Annis?"

"There is no *you* and Annis," Henry hissed, his raging jealousy slipping its leash like a savage dog. "You had your chance with her and made your choice. If you know what is good for you, my lord, you will stay away from my wife."

Avington blinked. "You want me to stay away from Annis?"

"That's right."

Avington stared at him for a long moment.

And then the bastard *laughed*.

"What is so bloody amusing?" Henry demanded.

The earl grinned and shook his head, still chuckling as he sauntered back toward his clutch of friends.

A low growl slipped from between Henry's clenched jaws as he watched Avington lean down and kiss Annis's cheek.

She reached up and cupped his face in her hands, her eyes glassy as she gazed up at the godlike Avington, her expression one of deep sadness.

The Language of Love

"Bloody hell," Henry muttered, turning away from the affecting scene. Would she ever get over Avington? Or was her love for another man something that Henry would need to contend with for the rest of his life?

He felt a light touch on his arm and turned to find Annis beside him.

"I'm ready to go," she whispered.

He guided her out of the foyer to where his town carriage waited to take them away to their new life. Once he'd settled her inside, he took the seat across from her, watching as she smiled and waved at the small clutch of guests who'd followed them outside to see them off.

She waved until she couldn't see them any longer and then turned to Henry, the cheerful expression she'd worn only moments earlier—with her friends and grandmother—nowhere in evidence. In the bright afternoon light, he could see the dark smudges beneath her jewel-like eyes

Avington had been right about one thing: she didn't look happy.

He'd believed the Earl of Avington had been a fool for throwing away her love. Had Henry been a fool for marrying a woman who loved another man? Was she so in love with Avington that she would never be happy without him?

Neither of them said a word until they reached the Clarendon, where Henry had engaged the largest connecting suites.

Once the porter had shown them to their rooms—where both their servants were already busy settling in—Henry stopped in the doorway between their adjoining chambers.

"I thought you might wish for some rest, so I ordered a private supper for you in your room. I will come to you at nine o'clock."

She startled, as if his words surprised her. Had she believed that he would forego bedding her?

If so, then she'd been sorely mistaken on that score.

Henry might not possess her heart, but her body belonged to *him*, bought and paid for.

Nice, Henry. That's an excellent way to think of your new wife, as your possession.

"Thank you, my lord." She nodded stiffly and shut the door, leaving Henry standing on the other side.

Chapter 17

When Henry rapped on their connecting door and entered his wife's room at nine that night, the maid had gone, but Annis was still seated at her dressing table brushing her hair.

She set down the brush, stood, and turned to him when he entered her room.

Henry struggled to look at all of her at once. Her froth of pale blond curls fell all the way to her waist and his fingers twitched to feel the thick, silken waves.

Rather than wearing one of the lacy confections that he'd ordered made for her, she'd donned the primmest white lawn nightgown that he'd ever seen. He wanted to be angry that she'd not worn the clothing he'd chosen for her, but the puritanical night-rail was somehow more erotic than even the flimsiest lace gown.

Not that he needed any help with arousal.

He'd been half-hard since that damned day on the blanket. It had become worse with each night that passed. Right now, he ached so badly that the mere brush of his robe over his rigid shaft was agony.

"God, you are so beautiful," he said in a voice he didn't recognize.

She gave a breathy, nervous laugh. "Thank you."

Henry set down the bottle and glasses. He'd never been with a virgin before, but he suspected she'd have some anxiety about tonight and a bit of alcohol might help relax her.

"Would you like a glass?"

"Please."

"Did you get any rest?" he asked, opening the bottle.

"No." Any color that had been in her cheeks at his earlier comment drained away.

Henry poured two glasses and handed her one.

"To our new life together," he said, raising his glass.

She lifted her glass, but before she took a drink, her face crumpled and a tear slid down one cheek.

The Language of Love

Henry cursed beneath his breath and snatched the wine from her shaking fingers before it fell. He set both glasses down on the dressing table and turned back to her.

She was staring at her feet, her shoulders shaking.

"Don't cry, Annis," he begged, awkwardly patting her on the shoulder.

She jolted at his touch, but when he dropped his hand to his side, she threw herself against him; her face buried in his chest.

Good God, this was a nightmare. Why the devil did men ever want virgins?

"It will be fine, Annis," he soothed. "I promise I will be gentle. It's my understanding it only hurts the first time—for a little while. If you are too tired, we could wait until—"

"No!"

He recoiled at her sharp retort.

"I'm so sorry, Henry," she mumbled against the thick satin of his robe.

"Look at me, darling." He took her heart-shaped face in both hands, gently wiping at the tears with his thumbs. "Everything will be fine. I know I've been awkward with you since all this happened, but I'm not angry with you and I shall never—"

"No, it's not that. I have something to tell you, Henry."

Unease wormed its way through him. *Bloody hell. What now?*

"Yes?" he asked, steeling himself for the worst.

"I'm not a v-virgin."

It was not the confession he'd been dreading—that she was too in love with another man to allow Henry to touch her—and Henry was too surprised to have a quick response.

Objectively, he knew he should feel angry. After all, men wanted to marry virgins. That was no secret.

"Henry? Are you horribly disappointed?"

"Er… disappointed?" Was he? He wasn't sure what he felt.

Henry didn't like the thought of her lying with another man, but that was jealousy rather than disappointment. He wanted to ask who it was but didn't really want to hear the answer. Because if it was Avington, a man she loved, Henry could never compare.

He opened his mouth to reassure her that he wasn't angry or disappointed, but she spoke first.

"You're probably thinking that I'm a—a—shameless hussy."

He gave a startled laugh. "I'm sorry," he said when she looked hurt. "I'm laughing because that was not what I was thinking." He could hardly tell her he was hoping it wasn't Avington who'd been her lover.

So, instead, he said, "You needn't be upset, Annis. I don't blame you for doing something I've done, myself." Pretty much every week since he'd been sixteen.

She stared at the lapels of his robe, restlessly stroking his hip and buttock, smoothing the fabric over his hot, sensitive skin again and again. Henry suspected she didn't realize just what she was doing—or how it was affecting him.

"But that's different. Men aren't considered spoiled if they— well, you know. But men expect a maiden on their wedding night. Especially—" she broke off, chewing that delicious lip of hers again.

"I hope you weren't going to say *especially wealthy men*?" But her expression told him that was exactly what she was about to say.

Henry sighed. "First off, you aren't *spoiled*. Second, I didn't buy you, Annis. And I certainly didn't buy your maidenhead." His mouth flexed into a moue of distaste. "To be honest, I don't understand the male preoccupation with virginity." He carefully teased out a strand of hair that was tangled in her eyelashes and tucked it behind her ear. "I'll admit I don't enjoy thinking of you with another man, but I don't think any less of you. Understand?"

She nodded but kept chewing her lower lip.

"Is this what has been making you look so miserable all week?"

"Yes."

"Well, you can stop worrying now. We're married, Annis. Let's try to forget about our awkward betrothal, shall we? Let's go back to that day on the picnic blanket—but instead of stopping, we can explore each other fully all night long."

"I can't believe you're not angry."

"Believe it." He slid his arms around her slender body and brought her up onto her toes, but he still needed to bend almost in half to kiss her.

Her arms twined like sturdy vines around his neck and drew him down while he plundered her mouth.

His Annis was not shy and plundered him in return, albeit clumsily and adorably. It didn't take him long to lure her tongue into his mouth, and he closed his lips around her and suckled.

She jolted and gasped.

The Language of Love

"Didn't you like that?" he asked, trailing soft kisses from her mouth up to her ear and nibbling gently on her velvety lobe.

"I liked it," she said in a breathy voice, "But you surprised me. I wouldn't have guessed it would feel so good to do that."

Henry slid his hands beneath her surprisingly generous bottom and lifted her up as he straightened his back. "Wrap your legs around me."

"But—aren't I too heavy?"

"No. And it's far easier on my spine than bending is."

She opened her slim legs and Henry grunted when she pressed her spread sex against his hard shaft.

"God, you feel good," he muttered, rolling his hips to notch himself in her soft cleft.

"Henry," she gasped, shifting to give him better access.

He ground against her like a horny lad. "You like that?" he asked when she gave a low moan, her breathing ragged, her lips parted.

Her only answer was an inarticulate growl.

Henry walked her over to her bed, where he laid her out on the mattress and then pulled away.

"Henry?" She stared up at him with eyes that were black with desire.

"*Tsk, tsk,* so impatient," he teased, unbuttoning the short line of buttons on her prim white nightgown.

She pushed his hands away. "I can do it faster. I want to see you. Please."

Her eagerness for him was an aphrodisiac, not that he needed one on top of everything else, and he pulled the sash on his robe and let it slide to the carpet, watching her face as he bared himself.

"Oh, goodness," she whispered, her lips parting in a way that gave him all sorts of ideas.

He gritted his teeth and wrapped his hand around the base of his cock, squeezing hard.

She pushed up on to her elbows, her gaze riveted to his hand. "What are you doing, Henry?"

"I'm trying to make our evening last a bit longer," he said, his voice taut with both arousal and discomfort.

"How does that work?"

He gave a strangled chuckle. "You like to know things, don't you?"

"Especially things like this," she agreed.

183

"I don't exactly know how it works, but if I squeeze hard enough, I can delay my climax. Remove your nightgown," he ordered.

She scrambled to obey, not taking her eyes from him.

Any progress he'd made slowing his arousal went out the window when she flung away the muslin gown and exposed herself to his hungry eyes.

"Lord, but you're lovely," he said, his gaze skimming slowly over her small, pert breasts with their tiny, pebbled nipples, down to her flat stomach, and settling on the triangle of wheat-colored curls at the top of her slim legs.

"I'm too scrawny," she demurred, her gaze still on his cock.

"No, you're delicate—like a fairy."

She cut him a quick, startled glance before dropping her gaze again.

He wanted to worship every inch of her with his lips and tongue, but he'd not last thirty seconds. Instead, he climbed up onto the bed.

"Lie back," he ordered gruffly. "I had plans to take things slow our first time, but we'll have to leave that for later. Right now, love, I need to be inside you."

She continued to stare at his cock, her lips parted, her expression odd.

"Annis? Is something wrong?"

***

Annis couldn't stop looking at his membrum virile.

"Annis? Is something wrong?"

She could hear the concern in his voice and wrenched her gaze away before shaking her head.

"You look frightened."

"No—no, not frightened. Just, er, concerned." Her willful eyes dropped down again.

Yes, it was still as large.

"You said you've done this before," he said, sounding confused.

"Yes."

He paused for a second. "So…?"

"He was not so, er, prodigious."

He laughed, and she tore her eyes from the fascinating flexing of his muscular stomach to look at his face. "Thank you," he said.

The Language of Love

"It is not a compliment; it is a statement of fact," she assured him, entranced by the thick vein that ran up the front of his shaft. She tilted her head so she could look at the place where it joined his body, the root, she supposed it was called. Below the thick root were his testicles, a fleshy, lightly furred sac that hung heavily between his muscular thighs.

Annis's brain struggled with what she was looking at. She had seen anatomical drawings aplenty since her friend Lorie was practically obsessed with educating women about their own bodies and men's.

And of course, she'd actually had intercourse more than once, but she'd never seen a naked man.

"Annis? Are you going to say something?"

She'd forgotten that Henry was still in the room. "I suppose it makes sense."

"What does?" he asked, his voice rich with amusement.

"You are very large all around. But I just thought… Never mind."

"No, tell me what you thought." He smiled down at her, seemingly unaware of how godlike he looked towering over her, his powerful body on display.

"I guess I thought they were all the same size."

"Ah."

"But not all noses or mouths or ears are the same, so why would I have believed such a thing?" she asked.

"I couldn't say."

Something else occurred to her. "So then, women—are they, er…"

"Different sizes inside?"

She nodded.

"Yes."

Annis struggled to absorb that information. "But—"

"Annis darling?" His voice sounded strained.

"Hmm?"

"Could we discuss human physiology *after*?" He was staring at her with a certain urgency.

"Oh," she said, blushing. "Of course."

He lowered himself over her with a sigh of contentment, his knees between her thighs, nudging her open as he supported his weight on his forearms. He pressed his mouth to her throat and began to lick and kiss and suck. "You taste delicious," he murmured, his knees pushing her legs wider, until his hips lowered and—

She jerked as his hot, hard length slid over her lower belly.

"Sh, love," he whispered, holding himself up on one arm while he cupped her breast.

Annis moaned and her back arched as his hot palm rubbed over her nipple. She made a series of mortifying noises as he pinched the pebbled tip between two fingers while the blunt head of his penis stroked against the soft flesh of her belly, his mouth hot and wet on her throat, sucking and biting until her skin was on fire.

But inside her body, she felt achingly empty.

"Please," she begged.

When his hand disappeared from her breast, she whimpered at the loss of him.

"Relax, sweetheart," he soothed in between kisses. He snaked a hand down over her belly and then long, thick fingers penetrated her private curls.

Annis cried out when he brushed that part of her that was engorged with need.

He flicked the exquisite spot again, far too briefly, and she bucked up, chasing his touch. Annis tossed her head in frustration as he stroked her but kept missing the place that begged for him. Didn't he know? Couldn't he tell? Why didn't—

"Ah!" she cried as he brushed against the source of her desire. She dug her fingers into his hips and tried to pull him lower.

But he just chuckled, as unmovable as a boulder, while his thumb circled her with teasing, taunting touches.

Without pausing his torment, another finger pressed at the opening to her body.

"Henry," she groaned, as he caressed her there, her thighs spreading wider as she opened herself—begging him with her body.

This time he gave her what she demanded and pushed a thick finger into her, sliding through her wetness, stretching her.

He grunted as he pushed all the way inside, his thumb stroking her harder now, the way she needed.

Annis thrust her hips higher, straining to take him deeper.

He chuckled, the sound low and oddly filthy. "So eager for me—so wet and tight."

Embarrassment and desire battled inside her at his smug confidence. Annis was stunned and aroused by the effect his words had on her, his praise ratcheting the taut, quivering muscles in her body even tighter.

He fell into a smooth rhythm of stroking and pumping, meeting her thrust for thrust, easing a second finger into her, the stretch bordering on pain but the pleasure building and building until—

Annis's back arched off the bed. "Henry!"

"Yes, come for me darling," he murmured, his fingers buried to the knuckles, the fullness intensifying the pleasure each time her inner muscles convulsed around him. Bliss consumed her, wave after wave of intense sensation pummeled her. She floated on pleasure, only vaguely aware of him shifting, until something thick and hard pressed against her entrance and Annis came back to herself.

"Are you ready to take me?"

She grabbed his hips, digging her fingers into the impossible hardness of his muscles. "Now," she begged, "do it now."

He filled her with a long, hard thrust that made her cry out.

"Shh, love," he murmured.

Annis squirmed as he held her stretched and full; this felt nothing like his finger—not even like two. And *nothing* like Richard.

He supported his weight on his elbows, but his pelvis was snug against hers, pinning her to the bed like a butterfly on a board.

"Are you in pain?"

She shook her head, even though it *had* hurt and was still uncomfortable. But already the pain was changing to something else—something unspeakably erotic.

Annis hissed out a breath as he withdrew and then reentered her with exquisite slowness, making her feel every inch. And there seemed to be a lot of them.

His eyes were black and bottomless as he worked her in deep, measured strokes while she struggled to adjust to his length and girth.

"I've thought of doing this with you for weeks," he said, his voice tense with suppressed need while his hips pumped harder. "You surpass even my fantasies, Annis."

Annis feared her heart would explode with love for him. She couldn't express what she felt with words, so she opened herself to him, tilting her hips to invite him deeper.

He gave a grunt of approval and plunged deeper.

Annis hooked her legs around his hips and clung to him as his thrusts became wild and savage, until he hilted himself almost painfully deep and threw back his head with a shout, his shaft flexing and thickening as he filled her with heat.

After a long moment, he shuddered, sighed, and then lowered his body onto hers, engulfing her and crushing her.

It was a struggle to breathe but being surrounded by him was worth the effort.

You surpass even my fantasies, Annis.

She shivered as the beautiful words wended their way through her exhaustion. Had anyone ever said such a lovely thing to her before? If they had, she couldn't recall it.

Annis pressed her lips against the damp, faintly salty skin of his throat and reveled in her happiness.

All too soon, he came back to himself. "Crushing you," he mumbled. "Sorry."

Before she could deny it, he turned both their bodies, so she was lying on top of him, his softening shaft still inside her.

He pulled the blankets up over them, covering her before sliding his arms around her and holding her tight.

"Good?" he asked, an enormous yawn stretching the word. "Good."

One big hand cupped her bottom and gave her a gentle squeeze before his breathing deepened and his body relaxed.

You surpass even my fantasies, Annis.

Annis was smiling as she drifted into a half-doze, the lovely, lovely words echoing in her head.

Chapter 18

It was still dark when Henry woke, the only light in the room a few guttering flickers from some candles across the large bedchamber.

He had always slept lightly and woke frequently during the night.

But tonight was different.

Tonight, he had a small body on top of his; tonight, his hard, pulsing shaft wasn't cradled in his fist, but inside his new wife.

Henry experienced a moment of pure, undiluted happiness as he stared up into the gloom.

Calm down Henry, it's only been one night—not even, just a few hours.

He knew it was only one night, but it had gone far better than he'd hoped. Their marriage might have been born of lies, but they were both attracted to each other physically. They liked each other—at least she seemed to like him—and marriages were often built on far less, so perhaps they had a chance?

He certainly adored her body and the way she looked at him, curiosity and intelligence and desire brimming in her magnificent eyes.

Henry settled his hands on her lush bottom, cupping one cheek in each palm, and then flexed his hips, sheathing himself more deeply in her tight, wet heat.

She made a soft snuffling sound against his neck, where her warm breath had dampened his skin. "Henry?"

"Yes, it is your husband." He smiled foolishly at his words. "Are you too sore to take me again?"

She gave a sleepy gurgle of laughter. "I think I'm *already* taking you again." And then she answered his question by tightening her inner muscles around him.

He hissed in a sharp breath as he withdrew slowly and then re-entered her with a powerful thrust.

She moaned, and her body squeezed him like a fist.

"That feels so good," he murmured.

He felt her lips curve into a smile against his skin. "I've been practicing."

Her words startled a laugh out of him. "Have you?"

189

She nodded, her silky hair gently abrading his sensitive skin. "Yes, if I do it enough, er…" She shoved her face into his neck, as if she could burrow into him, and Henry knew she'd spoken without thought—one of his favorite attributes of hers.

"If you do it enough, you can give yourself an orgasm?" he guessed.

She nodded.

"Such a wicked, wicked girl," he praised, and then groaned when she clenched in response to his words. He smiled to himself, working her with slow, steady thrusts that penetrated her deeply each time.

She shivered and then sighed, the sound one of profound contentment.

Henry caressed from her arse to her thighs, picturing what she looked like from behind, open and exposed, while his thick shaft tunneled in and out of her tight passage.

He groaned at the mental image and slid a hand between their bodies, wanting to feel the place where they were joined.

"Mmm, I like this," he said, exploring their slick, hot flesh with the tips of his fingers.

When he brushed her bud, she squirmed and ground against him, using him for her pleasure. Together, they easily worked a climax from her responsive body.

"Bloody hell, that feels divine," he ground out as he stilled inside her, his body shaking with need as she convulsed around him, wave after wave of her orgasm rocking them both.

"Sit up," he coaxed when her contractions ebbed. "I want to see you."

She obeyed without hesitation and Henry's lips parted with a gasp as he took in the sheer wonder of her wild tangle of hair, heavy-lidded blue eyes, and the gentle curves of her slender body.

His broad, sun-darkened hands looked huge and brutish as they covered her delicate breasts. "You're so perfect."

She shivered under his touch, pressing into his palms.

He teased her pebbled nipples, tweaking and pinching them until she became wild. "Ride me, Annis. Make me come," he ordered, thrusting up into her hard enough that his buttocks lifted off the bed.

Her glorious eyes widened at his vulgar words, and then the most delicious, wicked smile curved her lips.

The Language of Love

"Just like a horse," she said, leaning forward until her hands were on his chest.

He moaned when her fingers grazed one of his nipples.

"Do you like that, too?" she asked, staring down at the puckered brown nub in wonder.

He muttered something incomprehensible as she imitated the tweaking and pinching he'd used on her body earlier.

Annis smiled, looking very pleased with herself.

Henry seized her hips, pulling her down while he thrust up into her. He'd have to teach her about riding him some other day—right now, she was having far too much fun torturing him.

It took a shameful five or six more thrusts before he emptied his aching balls inside her and placed his hands over hers, stilling her nimble fingers while his body spasmed.

When he opened his eyes a few moments later, she was staring down with an expression of triumph.

He smiled lazily. "Look who is pleased with herself."

She grinned, the expression robbing him of breath. "It's a beautiful view from up here," she said. "Like sitting atop a mountain."

Henry shook with laughter.

"Or a volcano that is about to erupt," she amended.

"This volcano has had its last eruption for a few hours," he said, rolling her off him and onto her side, until they lay face-to-face.

He tucked a lock of hair behind her ear. "Will it take ages to untangle?" he asked, dropping his hand to rest on her hip.

"It will take a while," she admitted. "But it will be easier with two of us to tame it. Grace is very skilled and patient."

"Good. Because I love seeing it down."

"Freddie thought I should cut it, but Miles said you would like it long."

Henry's hand clenched on her hip, and she frowned.

"Did I do wrong? Would you like me to cut it?" she asked, misunderstanding his jealous spasm—thankfully.

"No, I like this way," he said, pleased that he didn't sound as irritated as he felt.

Was it Avington that she'd given her virginity to?

Thinking about that will not make you a happy man, Henry.

He knew that, but that didn't mean he could stop himself.

She traced light patterns on his palm before raising his hand to her lips and kissing the tips of his fingers.

Although Henry had just ejaculated for the second time in only a few hours, a bolt of desire shot straight from his fingers to his empty balls.

"Tell me about Stoke, Henry—what is it like? How long shall it take to get there?"

Henry rolled onto his back, relieved to change the subject, even though the topic was almost as unpleasant as his wife's love for another man.

"Stoke was a shambles when I last saw it twenty years ago. I daresay it is far worse now."

"Your cousin was poor?"

"The family was not rich," he admitted, "but a good part of that was because of mismanagement. My uncle could never bring himself to make improvements to either Stoke or the tenant farms, and his son was much the same, I fear. A few years of doing without hunters or riding with the Quorn would have left enough money to make much-needed repairs, but he wasn't willing to sacrifice such pleasures." He turned to her and pulled a face. "You will see when we get there that everything in the area has suffered because of my family's neglect."

She reached up and cupped his jaw with one of her small, warm hands. "But you will fix all that."

Her tender gesture touched him more deeply than was comfortable. "*We* will fix it together, Annis. Stoke needs a good mistress, too."

"Was your cousin not married?"

Henry felt his face twist into a sneer. "Oh yes, he was married. But if Julia is anything like she was back then, she will have joined my cousin in syphoning money off to fund her own pleasure."

Annis lowered her hand, an expression of concern in her blue eyes. "You dislike the countess?" She paused. "Well, I suppose she is the dowager countess now that we are married."

"I'd not thought about that." Henry smiled; Julia would not care for that at all. He caught Annis's hand and kissed the back of it. "As to whether I like her? Let's just say there was no love lost between us by the time I left."

"But she makes her home there? Won't your dislike make living together... uncomfortable?"

"Don't look so worried, darling, we shan't have to live with her for long. She has the Dower House." Not that she could live in it without the expenditure of thousands of pounds, if the letters from the Stoke steward could be trusted. Well, now that he was married, he'd spend the money to fix the bloody house just to keep her away from him.

"Will you tell me about your childhood, Henry? I never knew how much was really true and what you made up."

"I stuck close to the truth in essentials," he said. "It wasn't a happy childhood, although I was fed and clothed well enough," he admitted. "I grew up in the servant quarters at my uncle's house."

Her lips parted in horror. "But *why* would he do such a thing?"

That was the *last* thing he wished to get into.

Henry shrugged. "It doesn't matter," he lied. "Suffice it to say that everyone in the area took their cues from my uncle when it came to how to treat me. In fact, he showed his displeasure to anyone who had the audacity to be kind to me."

Annis gasped. "Did nobody show you any kindness at all?"

Henry felt a strange tightness in his throat and rolled back onto his back. "Mrs. Jenkins, the housekeeper, wasn't so bad," he said gruffly.

She was still there. Henry knew that because he'd seen her name on the list of employees that he'd requested from the Stoke steward, Stephen Milner. The first letter he'd written to Milner had included a substantial raise in pay for Mrs. Jenkins.

"I'm sorry you had a miserable childhood."

Henry snorted, feeling like a whiny infant. "I was fed, housed, and cared for," he said. "That's a lot more than many people can claim."

She kissed his arm and then laid her silky, fragrant head on his shoulder. "You've got me to love and care for you now, Henry."

Henry's heart pounded painfully in his chest at her words, and he opened his mouth to say—say what?

Besides, she hadn't meant that she *loved* him. It was just a figure of speech.

So, instead of responding, Henry closed his mouth and said nothing at all.

Chapter 19

As they rolled along in the well-sprung, leather-lined splendor of Henry's traveling coach Annis reflected on the delicious evening before, an evening that had lasted all the way until first light, when Henry had woken her with loving one last time before they'd begun their first full day as man and wife.

The best part of the night hadn't been all the physical pleasure he'd given her, or the wonder of sharing a bed for the first time. Rather, it had been the way she'd been able to give pleasure back to Henry.

Each time they'd come together, he had worked tirelessly to ensure her own satisfaction before taking his own. Watching him come apart in his passion had been the most erotic experience of her life. The sense of power she'd felt that she—hen-witted Annis Bowman—could bring this awe-inspiring man to his knees had been intoxicating.

"What are you looking so smug about, Lady Rotherhithe?"

Her head whipped up. Her new husband was watching her, the open book in his lap ignored.

"I was just thinking it was a lovely day." That wasn't entirely a lie. It *was* lovely.

His smirk told her he didn't believe her for a minute.

While their relationship was still stiffer than it had been before that fateful day, he seemed to thaw more with every hour that passed. Annis had high hopes for their future happiness.

"What are you reading?" she asked.

He lifted the book, and she saw it was about farming methods.

"Is there a great deal of land?"

"Not as much as there used to be—thirty-thousand acres, I believe."

"Was it entailed?"

"Yes, everything except the London house was entailed. The only reason they didn't sell that is because it is so encumbered and dilapidated that only a fool would buy it. If I ever sold it, the new owner would probably demolish it to build a new house."

"That would be a tragedy."

The Language of Love

He met her gaze with a sardonic look. "I should have taken you on a tour before we left London. It's draughty, leaky, and it was last improved during the reign of George I."

"You don't want a house in London?"

"I have three—if you want to keep one, you can take your pick. If you like Rotherhithe best, we'll keep it."

"*Three?*"

"Yes. In fact, the one where we spent those lovely afternoons is one of mine."

"*You're* the gentleman who owns it?"

He gave her a raffish smile. "I know calling me a gentleman is a stretch."

"Why did you buy it?"

"I sold a great deal of property in India and needed to invest some of the money, as I don't care to have it sitting idle. I added several new ships to my fleet, but property is an excellent investment in the current economic climate."

Annis could only nod.

He smirked. "See? Your husband *isn't* a gentleman. He's a businessman."

"Can't a man be both?"

"Not according to your beau monde."

"They're not *my* beau monde."

"They are now, if you want them. I didn't get to spend much time with you the last week, but you seemed to have a full dance card and I understand from Lady Sedgwick that you had plenty of callers."

"Yes, that is all true. It astounded me how quickly I became *somebody*."

He gave a bark of laughter. "Just remember that it can disappear just as quickly."

"Will we be going to London often?"

"I'll leave that up to you."

"You will?" she asked, not bothering to hide her disbelief.

"Why not? If you want to go to town, I could probably answer the next writ of summons rather than ignore it."

She gasped. "You didn't!"

"Did."

After a long moment, she asked, "Don't you want to belong, Henry?"

"It has never been a priority. Do you?"

"I want to belong with people of my choosing, but not with strangers or people who judge me based on my money or connections."

"You mean your friends from the academy?"

"Yes, they are friends for life. If they go to London, then I would like to spend part of the year in town. But, in general, I prefer the country."

"What do you do in the country?"

"I suppose the sort of thing I did at my grandmother's will differ greatly from what I'll do at Stoke. When I lived with her, we supplemented her income with a garden, a few hens, and I tutored private students."

"You won't have to do any of that," he agreed. "Not unless you like." His mouth flexed into a frown. "I know the home farm was a disaster when I lived at Stoke. The succession houses were in disrepair, and the earl saw very little fruit. All that's to say that if you have any interest in horticulture or botany or whatever it's called, there will be plenty of opportunity to do something."

Annis felt a frisson of excitement at his words. "Gardening is actually one of the few things I do well."

"I suspect you do a lot of things well. I can think of several, myself." He gave her a brooding, wicked smirk.

"Tell me about the house," she said, flustered. "I know it is ancient and I've heard about the Stoke relics, but that is all I really know."

"The original structure is a castle, but that isn't really used for daily living. It's rather cramped, cold, and uncomfortable. The part built during the 1500s constitutes the *modern* hall and the two wings off that are newer, yet. I think the intention was an Elizabethan 'E' shape, but it had to accommodate the original structure, so it's more of a 'G'."

Annis laughed. "It sounds fascinating."

"It was a wonderful place to explore as a boy. So much of the older parts of the building are closed off and hazardous from rot and decay, so those were perfect places for a boy to roam and pretend."

"And you grew up there with your cousin?"

His jaw flexed, an action she was beginning to recognize as a sign of displeasure.

"Two cousins, Charles and Edmund, and my uncle's ward Lady Julia Tybald."

The Language of Love

By the time he'd finished listing the names, his mouth had twisted into a sneer.

So, not good memories of those three.

He continued, "Charles, of course, inherited the earldom. Edmund, my heir presumptive, still lives at Stoke. And Julia I already mentioned."

"You did?"

"She is the dowager countess."

"Ah, so you've known her all your life."

"Something like that."

Annis wasn't sure what to say about that. Of the four children who'd grown up together, three would soon live in the same house. And her new husband did not look especially pleased about that.

***

The journey to Stoke would take them six days.

"We could do it far quicker," Henry had replied when Annis asked. "But there is no need to wear ourselves out. Since I'm cheating you out of a wedding trip, I thought I'd put a little effort into making this journey more enjoyable."

He'd offered to take her on a wedding journey—to anywhere she wished to go—but Annis wanted to see the place that would be her home first.

For his part, Henry was in no hurry to get to Stoke. The more he thought of his prior plans—to make Julia suffer by depriving her of money—the less it appealed to him.

As he'd said to Annis a scant two weeks before, that was all in the past. What was the point in taking out his grievances on a person who now depended on him? Where was the sport in that?

Intellectually, Henry could understand that argument. But emotionally, he was still that sixteen-year-old boy who'd been cast out of Stoke like a piece of rubbish.

He wanted revenge or at least redress—some sort of compensation, although he knew not what. Unfortunately for Julia—and Edmund, to a lesser degree—they were the only ones remaining on whom he could vent his spleen.

***

That night Grace dressed Annis in one of the nightgowns that Henry had selected for her.

She'd been too worried last night to don any of the elegant, sensual garments, fearing that he would storm from their bedchamber upon learning the truth.

"Oh, you look lovely, my lady," Grace cooed as she brushed out Annis's hair.

"This is a beautiful gown," she agreed.

"It's not just that, my lady—it's that color. I think nothing suits you better."

Annis studied her reflection and couldn't help smiling; it was true that periwinkle blue made her eyes appear larger and almost lavender.

The nightgown itself was the most scandalous scrap of lace. Fortunately, Henry had purchased a far less revealing dressing gown in the same color, so she wasn't bright red as her maid brushed her hair.

Annis smiled as she thought back on their evening. They'd had a delightful dinner and a game of chess.

"I've not played for ages," she admitted as they set up the board.

"Did you play with your father?" Henry asked.

"Yes, but more recently I played with Miles."

"Ah."

Annis had the strangest feeling that Henry no longer liked Miles, even though the two of them had seemed so friendly back when Henry had first moved to London.

Grace set down the brush and Annis nodded at the younger woman. "Thank you, Grace, that will be all for tonight."

The door had barely closed behind Grace when the connecting door to Henry's room opened.

Annis wondered if she'd ever stop feeling that spark of pleasure that hit her each time she saw him anew; she hoped not.

"Stand up and let me look at you," he said, his eyes hot as they flickered over her.

Annis swallowed her nervousness and stood, her body taut as he prowled around her in a circle, coming to a halt in front of her.

"You are exquisite, wife." His lips quirked into the lazy smile she loved.

"Your turn, *husband*," Annis ordered, stepping back and crossing her arms.

His eyebrows leapt. "Ah, a tyrant in the bedchamber." He turned for her, slowly, holding out his arms as he did so.

The Language of Love

Tonight, he was wearing a dark green silk banyan that had gold dragons embroidered up both sides of the front and a remarkably detailed scene on the back that included mythical creatures and an elegant building with a hip-and-gable roof.

"The robe is beautiful," she said, not to mention the large body it covered.

"Thank you. I found the fabric on one of my trips to China."

"Was China wonderful?"

"It is a place like no other." He grinned suddenly. "Please don't ask if I speak Mandarin or Cantonese. I'm afraid I can barely say *hello* and *thank you* without starting a war."

"Tonal languages are hard for English speakers to learn."

His eyebrow lifted. "Do you speak Chinese?"

"My father was learning Mandarin from a man he met in Oxford. He'd planned to teach me after he knew enough, but he died before that could happen."

Henry cocked his head. "You miss him greatly."

It wasn't a question, but Annis nodded.

She shook away the sudden sadness that had descended over her and ran her hands up the dragons on his robe. "I don't want to be sad right now."

"Me neither." He stepped closer to her, his big fingers going to the fastenings of her dressing gown. "I have been fantasizing about this gown on you."

His words made her legs turn to water; Annis looked up and up to meet his gaze. "Thank you for choosing it."

"I enjoy dressing you—imagining the clothing I select against your skin." His eyes were hooded. "There is something unspeakably intimate about dressing a woman for one's pleasure."

Annis thought she might melt into a puddle before he got the robe off her.

He reached the bottom belt and slid his hands beneath the fine silk, gently pushing it off her shoulders.

He sucked in a harsh breath when he saw the lacy gown beneath. "God. Annis." His chest rose and fell faster, his throat moving as he swallowed. And then swallowed again. When he raised his hands and cupped her breasts, it was her turn to swallow.

He caressed the sensitive mounds, tormenting her nipples, which had been puckered and needy since slipping on the wicked gown earlier.

"Look at you," he whispered in a rough voice. "This makes you look more naked than if you were naked," he marveled, pulling his eyes briefly away from her chest to meet her gaze, his lips curling into a delighted smile. "You'll forgive me if I take a moment to pat myself on the back for such an inspired choice of nightgown."

Emboldened by his desire for her, she reached for the sash that held his robe closed, an action she'd never have imagined she was capable of taking.

"You've done well for yourself, too," she teased. "This robe suits you. But I want it off." Her face flamed and her fingers fumbled as she untied his sash, and the gorgeous robe fell open to reveal an even more gorgeous body.

He *was* naked. And erect. She reached for him without thinking and then jerked her hand back, shocked by her audacity.

"Touch me," he murmured, taking the hand that had been reaching for him and setting it on his engorged shaft.

He moaned when she closed her fingers around him and her eyes jumped up to his face.

His expression was unguarded, and, for a fraction of a second, she saw raw, unbridled lust before he schooled his features into a more civilized mask.

"You make me feel so good with your hands," Annis said. "I want to make you feel that good."

"Let's take off your gown."

The gown was loosely fitted, so he could push the fine lace off her shoulders and down over her narrow hips. It puddled on the floor along with the robe, and Annis felt a pang of guilt at treating the lovely garments so badly.

But when she reached for the beautiful silk, he growled, "Later."

He shed his own robe with a graceful shrug while walking her backward to the bed.

He was so big—a wall of man—that she should have felt oppressed by his size. Instead, she felt protected and safe as he took her by the waist and lifted her onto the bed, positioning her as if she were a doll.

"Lie down," he ordered.

Annis fell back onto her elbows, too excited to do anything but watch.

The Language of Love

As he'd done the night before, he knelt above her, affording her a magnificent view of his body as he wrapped his huge hands around her thighs and opened her legs wide.

When she realized what he was staring at, she tried to close her thighs.

She might as well have been a fly as she struggled in his firm, unbreakable grasp.

"Quit fighting me, Annis. I will make it good for you," he promised, his heavy-lidded eyes flickering to hers before dropping back to her exposed sex. "So good."

Annis's heart pounded so hard she could feel her pulse beating beneath the sensitive skin at the base of her throat.

He released her legs and the taut muscles in her thighs twitched to pull together and protect that most private part of her against his intense stare. But she did as he bade her and left herself open.

She tensed when he reached for her, stroking her mound lightly but firmly.

"Sh," he murmured, pushing his thumb between her swollen lips and grazing the source of her pleasure.

Annis bit her lip to keep from begging, her gaze darting from his stroking hand to his hard, stern face.

He caressed the thin skin of her inner thigh with his other hand. "So soft," he said, his wicked thumb already at work.

Annis squirmed from pleasure rather than embarrassment this time, and his lips twitched into that sensual, arrogant smirk she loved so much.

His hands barely paused their erotic motions as he lowered himself between her legs, his broad shoulders spreading her wider.

Annis pushed up onto her elbows to watch, and he cut her a quick look. "Has anyone kissed you down here before?"

It wasn't what she'd expected him to say. "*Kiss* me?"

Henry looked pleased. "I guess that's my answer."

She watched in shocked anticipation as he parted her lower lips with his thick but nimble fingers.

"God, Annis." He gave an almost pained grunt at whatever he saw; his lips parted, and his breathing roughed. "You're so perfect and pink and wet."

Annis's entire body blushed.

He licked his bottom lip, the gesture so carnal that her inner muscles clenched.

It was Annis's turn to grunt when he lowered his mouth over her, the soft heat of his mouth enveloping her.

And then his lips closed around the sensitive bud, and he sucked.

"Henry!"

She felt the curve of his mouth against her lower lips before he destroyed her ability to think.

He used not only his tongue and lips, but even his teeth. Annis watched his dark head between her thighs until the pleasure overwhelmed her strength and she flopped onto her back, her climax swift and intense.

He made an approving sound against her swollen flesh and then pushed a finger into her clenching and bucking body. She was vaguely aware that she'd lifted her hips higher to grind against his mouth and that her fingers had tangled in his thick, silky hair as she tugged his head lower, using him for her pleasure.

Time passed in a blur as he worked her toward release after release, relentlessly driving her body until she was a bundle of quivering nerves.

"Too much," she mumbled, yanking on his hair.

He chuckled and then pushed up on to his knees.

Annis stared up at him through lust-slitted eyes, shivering at what she saw. His lips and chin were red and slick, his eyes black.

His mouth curved into a wicked smile when their eyes met, and he slid a hand around his engorged penis and gave himself a slow, hard pump. "See what you've done to me, Annis?"

She stared, mesmerized, as he stroked himself. His crown was slick with moisture and each caress of his hand made more, until the thick, ruddy shaft glistened in the flickering candlelight.

"Roll over," he said, his voice raspy.

Annis heard him speak but couldn't pull her eyes away from the erotic sight before her.

"R-roll over?" she repeated, unable to recall exactly what the words meant at that moment.

He chuckled, released himself, and flipped her onto her belly before she knew what was happening.

The Language of Love

"Hands and knees," he ordered. This time, he didn't wait for her to obey, but took her hips in both hands and lifted her up onto her knees.

Annis struggled up onto her hands and then turned to look at him over her shoulder.

He met her gaze, his face stern and unsmiling as he caressed the curve of her bottom and then pushed a finger into her.

She gave a startled cry at the sudden penetration, which was so different—more intense—at this angle.

Annis's head fell forward, and she closed her eyes as he used both hands on her, spreading, stroking, thrusting, invading her with two, and then three fingers, until she was whimpering like an animal and pushing back against him for more, deeper, harder.

He withdrew his fingers, but before she could miss them, a now-familiar blunt heat pressed against her entrance.

Annis groaned as he entered her, not stopping until his groin pressed against her bottom.

He paused, keeping her filled while he caressed her back and hips. "Feel good?"

She made a noise and hoped he understood it was assent.

He chuckled, flexing his shaft inside her, making it dance. "Feels deeper, doesn't it?" he asked, withdrawing almost all the way before thrusting back in.

"Henry," was all she could manage.

He worked her with deep, lazy thrusts. "I wish you could see the way you look taking me." He eased out until only the fat crown of him still penetrated her and then pulsed, gently stretching her opening.

Annis shoved herself back at him—or at least tried to—but his hands held her hips immobile.

She growled.

Henry laughed, the sound so self-satisfied that she wanted to hit him. "Poor darling," he teased. "Do you need something?"

Annis refused to beg.

He gave her three deep, savage thrusts. And then stopped.

"What was that?" he asked when a frustrated moan slipped out of her.

Annis bit her lip.

He did more pulsing, teasing, and tormenting, his shallow thrusts stoking the flames of her lust higher and higher without ever quenching her desire.

When he stopped, she gritted her teeth.

He chuckled, even though she'd not made so much as a peep.

This time, it wasn't three or four lazy pumps, but a dizzying flurry of fierce, powerful thrusts.

A different, deeper tension built inside her and Annis rocked back against him, meeting each thrust. She was close—so close—

And then he stopped.

"Henry!"

"Henry what?" His voice was thick with the smug, arrogant amusement that drove her to distraction. "Did you want something?"

"You know what I want," she whined, appalled by her need, but too desperate to care.

"I do." His shaft flexed inside her, but still he didn't move. "Beg for it, Annis."

Her body clenched at his shocking command, but her mouth was already forming the words. "Please, Henry. Please make me… come." The last word was barely a whisper, but—thankfully—it was enough.

He gave a triumphant bark of laughter and lowered his body over hers, covering her back with his chest, his arms caging hers, his hips drumming into her hard and fast.

He took her chin in his fingers and turned her head. "Look, Annis."

There was a three-part mirror on the small dressing table. Annis gasped. The mirror showed them from the shoulders down, Henry's huge body enveloping hers, his muscular thighs and buttocks flexing with each powerful thrust.

The dominant position was primitive and raw; it was also the most erotic sight she'd ever seen.

He supported his weight with one arm and slid the other beneath her body.

Annis cried out and clenched around him as he worked her engorged bud, his hips pounding into her, his sac slapping against her sex, his finger caressing.

"I want you to come with me, Annis." His words were hot and harsh against her temple. "I want to feel your tight little pussy squeeze me. I want you to milk me dry."

The shocking words were all she needed to shove her over the edge.

The Language of Love

His pumping became wild and irregular before he drove himself home with a savage thrust, his arm like a band of iron around her waist while his body jerked, hot jets of seed lashing her deep inside.

***

"Did I use you too roughly?" Henry asked once he'd come back to himself a short time later.

"Mmm, no."

He smiled at her thickly mumbled answer. His own body was pleasantly sore, so he knew she would likely feel the effect of their intense lovemaking tomorrow. He would need to restrain himself for a few days.

"Are you comfortable in this position?" he asked her a few moments later.

But she didn't reply, her breathing already deep and regular.

They were lying on their sides, like two spoons, her much smaller body curled against his chest, his cock nestled in the cleft of her arse against the tight little rosette that he'd been sorely tempted to play with more than once while he'd fucked her.

But that was something for later. He was already using her far harder than a man should use a bride of only two days.

He was beyond fortunate that new wife was an adventurous, curious, and sensual little thing. Henry had just about spent in her fist when she'd asked him to show her how to pleasure him.

So, it doesn't really matter that she is a liar, then?

Henry scowled into the darkness. *Where have you been? Never mind. Go back there.*

Mocking laughter echoed in his head, dimming the glow of happiness. He tried to hang on, to grab back the joy—like a child clutching at a favorite toy—but the contentment he'd been feeling ebbed away.

Are you happy now?

But his imaginary friend had sown doubt and fled.

Annis shifted in his arms, her slender body going stiff, her breathing suddenly harsh and rasping. "No, Richard… please, don't tell. I can't—I can't…"

The rest of what she said was too garbled, but her voice pulsed with raw terror, and it sounded as if she was forcing them through clenched jaws.

Henry frowned. *Richard? Can't what?*

She moaned and thrashed in his arms.

"Annis?" he whispered, pulling her closer. "You're having a nightmare."

She struggled against him for half a heartbeat and then went boneless in his arms.

"Annis?"

But she slept on, her breathing slowly returning to normal.

What was that all about? What, exactly, had Richard done to her?

She made a soft whimpering noise and burrowed back against him, her bottom grinding against him in a way that ensured Henry didn't sleep anytime soon.

Chapter 20

By the time they rolled down the pitted, bumpy driveway that led to Stoke Castle, Annis was more than ready to get out of the carriage. As well-sprung and luxurious as it was, her bones were sore, and she was thoroughly sick of sitting for almost six solid days.

Fortunately, the last leg of the journey was such a short one that they would arrive at her new home while it was still daylight.

"The old place looks impressive—at least from a distance," Henry had explained. "So, it's worth getting your first look at it in the daylight."

Henry had done small, considerate things like that throughout their journey—from assuring that she had the foods she liked best, to putting her in the nicest of the rooms that he'd secured at the inns, he'd done everything in his power to make her comfortable. Never before had anyone taken such care of her.

And then there were their evenings.

Although their journey had been more leisurely than most, she'd still been so tired after a day in the carriage that she could barely move.

Henry, whose strength and energy seemed boundless, had sent an outrider ahead to ensure a hot bath and tea tray awaited her at their nightly stops.

Later, after she'd rested and eaten dinner, he came to her bed and pleasured her into unconsciousness.

If their nights had been filled with dreamlike pleasure, their afternoons had been down-to-earth and delightful. They'd either conversed on a wide range of subjects, read, or played cards or chess—both of which Annis was a disaster at, but Henry didn't seem to mind.

For the last few afternoons, she'd read to him from her current book, *Waverley*.

"I could become accustomed to this," he'd said earlier that day, when she'd paused to rest her voice. "I hope you will continue to read to me when we are at Stoke."

It had delighted Annis to hear he'd enjoyed her reading. As much as he read, it was always scientific journals or newspapers. She looked forward to initiating him into the world of fiction, which they could explore together.

"Only a few more minutes now."

Annis looked up at the sound of Henry's voice. He smiled at her. "You will get the best view on this side." He gestured to the righthand window.

Annis put away her book and scooted closer to the window. "Oh, there is a village ahead."

"Yes, it is Stokely, which actually sits on Rotherhithe land."

The carriage slowed as they entered the tiny but picturesque village on the banks of a river.

"Oh, look, Henry!"

People were coming out of the shops and houses that bordered what Annis had assumed was the driveway to Stoke but must actually be the main road.

"They've come out to welcome us, Henry." Annis waved at a woman who was holding a little girl in her arms, the child was waving so enthusiastically that her mother's nose was in danger.

She looked at Henry when he didn't answer. He was staring out the window with a mocking smirk—this one far more supercilious than any expression she'd ever seen on his face.

Annis lowered her hand. "Henry?"

He turned to her slowly, his eyes so cold they didn't even look like his. "These people despised me even more than my relatives did. But now, it seems, all is forgotten. At least by them."

Annis couldn't bear his dead stare. She turned and looked out the window, instead, smiling and waving at the people—Henry's people—although all the joy had gone out of the day.

***

Henry knew his words had shocked her.

He'd shocked even himself with his fury. But it felt like hardly a day had passed since he'd been here last. The Singleton Bastard people had called him. Or just the Bastard.

There had been a certain glee in the way the townsfolk had gone about tormenting him. Henry knew a large part of their enjoyment was because it was an opportunity to pick on one of the earl's family without incurring any wrath.

And the villagers had taken advantage of that opportunity even more often than his cousins had. Even the adults had mocked and taunted him, and gangs of village boys had caught him more than once.

The Language of Love

Henry watched his wife as she gazed at the people and village. When Annis sat back in her seat, she was no longer smiling, and her eyes were creased with concern.

"Don't worry, my dear. I won't take out my anger on them. I've already instructed my steward to inspect the various tenant farms, as well as the buildings in the village that I own and lease—which is most of them. The people of Stokely will find me a beneficent lord."

If he thought his snide assurance would ease her frown, he was sorely mistaken.

"What happened to you here, Henry?"

Henry set his elbows on his thighs and leaned toward her, suddenly furious at being back in this place that made him feel so small and powerless—even though it was *his* decision to return. "What happened?" He snorted. "I'm not sure where to start the litany of offenses, my lady. But language fascinates you—have you ever heard of *lingchi*, or death by a thousand cuts?"

She shook her head.

"It is a form of torture used in China. The victim is strapped to a wooden frame, placed in a public square, and cut dozens, if not hundreds, of times. Each cut, by itself, is never enough to kill. It is a punishment that is saved for the most heinous crimes, a slow, lingering torment that continues even after the victim is dead. *That* is what the villagers and my family engaged in for eleven years. Slight cuts administered as publicly as possible. If I had remained, I'm sure I would still be alive, crippled and beaten down but too much of an entertainment to ever be allowed the relief of death."

She stared at him with eyes shimmering with tears. For him, he assumed.

Henry smiled and caught her hand. "Don't waste tears on the past, Annis."

"Will you ever be able to forgive the people in the village and your family?"

"I will use my money and power to ensure that life is happier and healthier for all who rely on me, Annis. Is my forgiveness really necessary?"

"Hate and anger and resentment are so… corrosive." She laid her free hand over their joined ones. "Forgive them for *you*, Henry—it would be a kindness to yourself."

Henry sat back on his bench, and their hands slid apart. He turned to look out the window just as they passed through the gates that led to Stoke. When he'd been a boy, the gatehouse had been occupied. Now the small, quaint stone house was shuttered and lifeless, yet another casualty of his uncle and cousin's mismanagement.

"Look," he said, as they crested the slight rise.

She opened her mouth as if she might say something more, but then sighed and turned to look where he directed.

"Oh, my goodness, Henry. It is beautiful!" She was close enough to the glass that her breath fogged the window.

"Yes," Henry agreed, looking at his kind, lovely wife rather than the building where he'd spent the worst years of his life. "Very beautiful."

***

It was like a castle out of a fairytale—or so Annis believed until they came closer. Then it was impossible to ignore the neglect and decay: crumbling or missing chunks of stone and mortar, windows filled with brick or boards rather than glass, cracked and missing roof slates, and—most remarkably—what looked to be a small tree sprouting from one section of a moss-covered turret.

"Ah."

She looked up at Henry's soft exhalation and followed his line of vision.

Ah, indeed. While she had been looking at the structure, she'd missed the double line of servants that stretched out from the rather incongruous portico that had been built—unadvisedly, in her opinion—onto the original structure, probably in the last hundred years.

A woman emerged from beneath the portico. Annis was vaguely aware there was a man beside her, but she could not look away from the most beautiful female she had ever seen. She was tall and had an hourglass shape, with a headful of honey-blond hair with flashes of auburn glinting in the sun. She moved with a sinuous, sensual grace and her plain gray gown was a perfect foil for her almost shocking beauty.

Annis darted a look at Henry as the footman put down the steps and opened the door. Her husband was staring out at the pair who approached them, his smile sardonic, the unnerving, stony expression back in his eyes.

He opened the door and hopped out before the footman could assist them, helping Annis down before they both turned to face the approaching duo.

The Language of Love

"Henry! How lovely to see you after so long," the woman said, her hands held out in front of her in welcome, her dark blue eyes glittering with amusement, full ruby lips curved into a smile that looked almost… gleeful.

Henry ignored her hands, instead turning to Annis. "Annis, my dear—this is Julia, the Dowager Countess of Rotherhithe and my cousin Edmund Singleton." His smile shifted into a faint sneer before he added, "also known as Viscount Singleton, my heir." He nodded at the couple. "Julia, Edmund, this is my wife, Lady Rotherhithe."

Without so much as a flicker of surprise, hurt, or annoyance, the dowager offered her hands to Annis, who was so mortified by Henry's snub that she warmly took the other woman's hands in her own.

"What a *delight* to meet you, my lady. And welcome to Stoke." The dowager smiled down at her, making Annis aware of what a little dab of a female she must appear beside such an exquisite specimen.

"Thank you, my lady," Annis murmured, a bit overwhelmed by the woman's enthusiastic greeting and stunning looks.

The slender, dark-haired gentleman beside her was a smaller, less distinct version of Henry—like a piece of stone that had been tumbled and eroded until all the sharp edges had worn away.

"It is a pleasure to have a new cousin—and a new mistress of Stoke." The viscount cut the dowager a quick, sly look and turned to Henry, his pleasant smile slipping only slightly. "Henry, it has been many years."

"Indeed." Henry turned to Annis and missed the other man's flush at his frosty, dismissive greeting. "Will you inspect the servants, my love? Or are you too fatigued after our journey?"

She jolted slightly at the *my love*, searching his face for any sign that he meant his words.

But his face was a mask, his eyes shuttering his thoughts.

Annis smiled. "I should be delighted to meet everyone."

For such an enormous house, there were far too-few servants—only thirty for both inside and out—and most of those were either quite old or very young.

"This is Mrs. Jenkins," Henry said, his voice warming slightly as he introduced Annis to a woman who looked to be in her early sixties and dressed in the sober attire of a housekeeper.

Annis recalled Henry had mentioned the name once—that she'd stood as a sort of parent to him while growing up.

"My lord, my lady," the older woman said, dropping a graceful curtsey, her large brown eyes pulsing with some powerful emotion and never leaving Henry's face.

"How have you been, Mrs. Jenkins?" Henry asked, some of the frost melting as he faced the gaunt, strangely rapt servant.

So, here, at least, was one person at Stoke he didn't loathe.

"I have been well, my lord." She hesitated and then added in a rush, "I am pleased that you have returned home."

He stared at her for a long, uncomfortable moment and her pale cheeks darkened.

And then he turned to the short line of male servants who were mainly dressed for outdoor work, along with two aged footmen in faded, moth-eaten livery.

"Where is Cooper?" Henry asked Mrs. Jenkins.

"He died last year. I'm afraid we have not yet engaged a new butler," Lady Rotherhithe said, her soft voice startling Annis, who'd not known she was right behind them. She turned her glorious midnight blue eyes on Annis. "May I escort you to your chambers? I've—"

"Jenkins will show us," Henry said, his tone curt and cold.

Lady Rotherhithe inclined her head, a faint, tight smile on her lips. "As you wish."

"We shall want tea in half an hour," he said to Mrs. Jenkins. "The Red Salon?"

Again, it was the dowager who answered. "I'm afraid there was a fire in there three years ago and it has not been refurbished. We have been using the smallest of the sitting rooms—just down the corridor from the Red Salon."

"Lead on, Mrs. Jenkins," Henry said, as if the dowager hadn't spoken.

"Thank you, my lady," Annis added hastily before following Henry and the housekeeper.

Mrs. Jenkins led them into a truly magnificent, but freezing, stone entry hall. The walls were festooned with ancient weapons and two suits of armor were on display in front of exquisite wooden screens that had obviously been installed more recently.

Annis knew she was gawping like a rustic but couldn't help herself.

"Next we will pass through the lower gallery, which is—"

The words blurred together and her head whipped from side to side as she tried to take in everything.

The Language of Love

"You are going to give yourself a neck ache, Annis," Henry teased. "You needn't see it all at once—you will have plenty of time to acquaint yourself," he said as they climbed a set of ancient-looking stone stairs.

After a bewildering series of turns and two more sets of stairs, they passed through a stylized arch with double doors.

"Goodness," she whispered as they entered another world. Instead of frigid stone and slitted windows, the broad corridor was filled with warm wainscotting and carpeted wooden floors.

Although the carpet was threadbare and the silk hangings on the wall dulled by age, everything was polished, meticulously clean, and smelled of beeswax and turpentine.

Mrs. Jenkins stopped beside a door and turned to Henry, a notch of apprehension between her brown eyes. "The master and mistress's chambers have not been occupied since your uncle's death and are somewhat, er, old-fashioned, but I thought you would wish for them as both suites are the most spacious and afford the best views."

"My cousin and his wife didn't occupy the rooms?" Henry asked.

"No, my lord. They kept their original rooms."

Henry's eyebrows shot up at that.

Mrs. Jenkins opened the door and Annis felt as if she'd stepped back in time.

The chambers were undoubtedly feminine, decorated in deep rose and antique gold, both colors from a more opulent age. The bed was a baroque monstrosity covered in rose velvet with a gold satin canopy suspended from a ceiling, complete with clouds, cherubs, and angels. The floors were a beautiful, burnished wood layered with carpets composed of rose, cream, and gold.

And every single stick of furniture in the room had been lavished with gilt.

She stared up at the ceiling, her mouth opened.

"A room fit for a queen," Henry said beside her, his voice heavy with amusement.

Annis gave a breathless laugh.

"The dressing rooms connect your rooms with his lordship's." Mrs. Jenkins led Annis and Henry through a capacious dressing room toward a white and gilt door.

On the other side was the masculine counterpart to Annis's chambers, complete with velvet and gilt, but in blood red.

The door opened, and a very young maid entered.

"Ah, here is your hot water. Put it on the dresser, Agnes," Mrs. Jenkins directed before turning to Henry. "Will there be anything else, my lord?"

"No, thank you, Mrs. Jenkins," Henry said. "I'm sure preparing these rooms in the brief time you had was a challenge. Everything looks meticulously clean and comfortable."

The housekeeper blushed at his praise and then curtsied before soundlessly leaving the room.

Henry turned to Annis, a rueful expression on his face. "It is a bit—" he broke off, shrugged, and chuckled.

"Yes, it *is* a bit," she agreed wryly.

"Perhaps these two rooms might be the first ones that will require your attention."

Annis quailed at the thought of redecorating such magnificent rooms—or such a magnificent house; she'd never had enough money to decorate so much as a cupboard before.

The door to Henry's room opened and his new valet, Norwich, entered, bearing a large valise.

Annis turned to Henry. "I suppose I'd better get ready."

Henry opened the door for her. "I shall knock for you in half an hour, if that is agreeable?"

"Yes, thank you."

The door closed and Annis took a deep breath and exhaled, struggling to calm the thumping in her chest at the thought of the challenge that faced her.

Well, there was no point in worrying about it. All she had to do *now* was freshen up.

And drink tea with your new husband's family. Whom he appears to hate.

Annis grimaced and shoved aside the thought.

After she'd washed off the travel grime, Grace tidied her hair and helped her into a lovely gown of moss-green velvet. Annis had believed the dress would be too warm for this time of year, but it would be perfect for her new home, which was damp and draughty.

She was ready with a few minutes to spare and went to look out the windows that faced west. There was a snaky glitter that must be the small river that ran alongside Stokely. She could see the roof of a largish house not too far from a little wooded area. It seemed too close to be a neighbor, so perhaps this was one of the tenants that Henry had mentioned.

She heard the door open and turned to find Henry. "Are you ready, Annis?"

His hair was damp, and he looked fresh in a clean shirt and new cravat. He smelled delicious, which meant his valet must have shaved him with his special soap.

"Yes, I'm ready."

He held out his arm.

Annis tried to pay attention to the way they were going, but again, she lost her way after three or four turns.

Henry smiled down at her. "Will I have to draw you a map to help you find your way?"

"Probably. I have a dreadful sense of direction. Miles always said I should carry a pocketful of bread, so I could leave a trail of crumbs."

He didn't respond and when she glanced at him, he was staring straight ahead, his jaw tight.

Annis sighed, saddened that he was jealous because she had a male friend. She set her own jaw; she refused to give up her friends just because her new husband was jealous.

"Here we are," he said, interrupting her unhappy thoughts and stopping in front of a wooden door with a prominent raised cross. "You will find these doors all over the house. Many were installed by the ancestor who brought back either the second or third relic. I can't recall which one right now."

"Are the relics kept here?" she asked, more than a little curious to see the famous objects.

"There is a special reliquary that is kept in the vault and brought out once a year on St. Oswald's Day."

"I've not heard of that celebration before."

Henry chuckled. "I'd be astounded if you had—as far as I know, we are the only ones in Britain to celebrate it. You won't have to wait until August fifth, however. I shall show you the relics whenever you like." He opened the door to a charming, sun-filled room with two occupants.

Viscount Singleton and Lady Rotherhithe looked to have been sitting in silence, separated by several chairs and settees. They both smiled and stood, like automatons that had only been animated by Annis and Henry's entrance into the room.

While the four of them waited for the tea tray, they exchanged awkward, empty conversation about the weather.

Well, it would be more accurate to say that Annis and the two others conversed while Henry watched.

"And how do you like your chambers?" the dowager asked. "Mrs. Jenkins and the maids worked day and night to get the rooms ready. I'm afraid that nobody has occupied those rooms since my husband's mother was alive—almost forty years ago now."

Annis smiled. "They are lovely, my lady."

"I beg you will not stand on ceremony; you must call me Julia."

"And please call me Edmund," the viscount chimed in with false-sounding heartiness.

Annis smiled. "Thank you. You both must call me Annis."

After a long, awkward silence, Henry said, "You two may call me Lord Rotherhithe or my lord."

Edmund and Julia stared for a moment, and then Edmund laughed. After a moment, Annis and Julia joined in.

Still chortling, Edmund said, "You always did have a sharp sense of humor, Henry."

Henry didn't reply to his cousin.

Annis did not think her husband had been jesting.

***

Annis was already in bed—and had been for several hours—and was wondering if Henry would join her when the connecting door opened and he entered her room, still wearing his dinner clothes.

He looked... tense.

Annis put aside her book as he strode toward her bed. "Henry? Is ought—"

He slid his arms around her, his broad palm cradling her head as he lowered his mouth and claimed her in an open-mouthed, urgent kiss.

Annis melted into his embrace and carded her fingers into his hair, her body pliant against his.

He groaned as she tugged his hair in the rough way she'd learned he liked. She was dizzy and breathless when he pulled away.

"Open my fall and take me out," he ordered gruffly.

Annis's hands fumbled to obey. His thick shaft was thrusting against the fine material of his evening breeches and sprang free when she opened the last button.

The Language of Love

He raised her nightgown up to her hips and lifted her off the bed with disconcerting ease, cupping her bottom with both hands as he lined himself up with her entrance and then entered her with a savage thrust.

Annis cried out in a mixture of pleasure and surprise, her legs hooking over his narrow hips.

His arms were like iron bands as he raised and lowered her body to meet his driving thrusts, each stroke deep and hard. It couldn't have been more than a minute or two before he gave a hoarse shout, hilted himself, and spent deep inside her.

It was the first time that Henry had ever taken her without seeing to Annis's pleasure first. He'd seemed almost crazed in his need. While she enjoyed his passion—even without climaxing—his behavior caused uneasiness to coil in her stomach.

He held her tightly and she couldn't see his face, but she could feel when his arms slackened and he came back from the fugue of pleasure.

As quickly as he'd taken her, he set her on the bed, staring down at her as if he didn't know who she was. His skin was flushed and slicked with sweat from the effort of the past few minutes. His glistening shaft stood upright, a shockingly carnal sight when contrasted with the civilized elegance of his evening clothes.

"Henry?" She reached out to him, but he took a step back.

"I'm sorry," he said, giving his head a slight shake. "That was—"

"Don't apologize."

"Did I hurt you?" he asked, his hands absently closing the elegant satin breeches he'd worn for the first time in her presence. Usually he wore pantaloons, even to most formal events. But tonight, he'd looked every inch the aristocrat he was.

"No, of course you didn't," she said. "But what is wrong?"

"Nothing," he muttered, shoving a hand through his hair in an uncharacteristically weary gesture. His dark eyes flickered around the room before settling on her, a tired smile curving his lips. "I'm sorry for being a selfish lover."

She made an exasperated noise. "I think I can survive one night without the surfeit of pleasure you usually give. What is the matter?"

His sudden grin startled her. "I don't want you to just *survive*, my lady. I want you to be a slave to my body."

Annis rolled her eyes. "You have already achieved that objective. But why do I suspect that telling me what is bothering you will not be something you will do for me?"

"I don't have specific words for what is bothering me," he said, pacing restlessly about her room and studying the appointments in a vague sort of way.

"Where did you go after dinner? I waited for you, but you didn't come to the library after you and Edmund had port."

"I'm sorry, darling—that was rude. I didn't have port with Edmund; I left him to it." He snorted. "Although judging by all the red lines on his cheeks and nose, that wasn't the first time he'd indulged today. I won't leave you alone with them—or her—again."

"It was fine, Henry. Julia told me a bit about the house, the servants, and the local gentry." She smiled. "She has been planning a party for us—a combination welcome home party for you and a wedding celebration."

"Has she? Well, don't let her do anything you don't wish, Annis."

"She has been most kind, Henry. Why don't—"

He raised a hand, and she stopped speaking from sheer surprise. "I would rather we *never* speak of Julia. Especially not in either of our bedchambers."

"Won't you tell me what happened? Please? I can feel the tension between the three of you, it is like—"

"It would take me days—weeks—to explain what happened to me in this house, Annis."

"But we have to *live* with them, surely—"

"I will see to the Dower House as soon as possible and get her out from under our roof. As for Edmund, he has a home of his own, but he's leased the place or he'd be gone tomorrow." He resumed his pacing; his powerful shoulders so tense she could feel it in her own body.

"Won't you come to bed, Henry?"

"I'm not ready for bed, Annis. I'd just keep you awake."

"I don't mind. In fact, I sleep better when you are near. You won't dist—"

"I'm going down to the library. I doubt I'll be ready for sleep anytime soon." He spoke sharply, but then frowned, coming toward the bed. "I'm sorry," he said for the third or fourth time. His eyes flickered over her disheveled person. She was still above the covers, her nightgown rucked up to her thighs. His eyelids lowered. "Let me give you something to help you sleep," he murmured.

He ignored her—admittedly weak—protests and spread her thighs wide before lowering his mouth over her sex, his lips and tongue working their magic.

Annis groaned. "Don't think I'm not aware that you are distracting me."

His lips curved into a smile against her sensitive folds.

"I shan't forget this convers—Ah!" A shudder rocked her body as he sucked her aching bud into his hot mouth.

"We need to talk," she mumbled, sounding unconvincing to her own ears. "After," she added.

His answer was to shove her legs wider, plunge two thick fingers into her, and drive her toward bliss.

Chapter 21

Henry knew he was behaving like a man unhinged, but he couldn't seem to stop himself.

Every night before he went to bed—usually far closer to dawn than dusk—he swore the next day would be better. That *he* would be better.

But today was his sixth morning at Stoke and he was tenser than he'd been the first morning.

He was determined to spend some time with Annis today. He'd neglected her shamefully since coming to Stoke, leaving her alone in the decaying pile of bricks with Julia and Edmund most days while he'd toured the various farms, horrified by the repairs and maintenance that had been deferred for decades.

Both he and his steward, a sturdy, phlegmatic middle-aged man named Milner, had worked sunup to sundown, hiring everyone they could find in the building trades to tackle the most important tasks first. Like roofing, for example. Every single tenant farmhouse had ancient, leaking roofs.

By the time Henry returned home in the evening, he barely had enough energy to bathe, shave, eat dinner, and then he was at it again, reading everything and anything he could find on farming, a subject on which he was woefully ignorant.

He'd also made time to inspect the Dower House and had arranged for a crew of roofers to start work on the house the following week, after they'd fixed one of the tenant roofs, which had a hole the size of a coach wheel.

For the first few nights he'd gone to Annis, made love to her less selfishly than he had the first night, and then tossed and turned in her bed until dawn. He would have gone to his own room, but he knew she liked to have him nearby.

Her courses began four nights ago, so he'd gone to his bed on those nights, usually not sleeping until an hour or two before the sun rose.

She had asked him, more than once, what was wrong.

The Language of Love

How could he tell her if he didn't know? All he could say was that he felt... frantic, as if he were working against a clock that he couldn't see.

The only thing that made him feel better was to keep moving. Whenever he had too much time to think, he felt like his skin would crawl right off his body.

Today was the first day he would work from Stoke, rather than ride around the estate with Milner. Just being in the castle with Julia and Edmund nearby was enough to make him feel violent but Stoke was *his* house and he could scarcely avoid it forever.

He entered the breakfast room a little later than usual, at six-thirty. His first morning at Stoke, he'd come down to eat at six and found a cold fireplace, no food, and no servants.

He had summoned Mrs. Jenkins to ask where he might find breakfast.

"Viscount Singleton and Lady Rotherhithe usually eat in their rooms, my lord."

That wouldn't do, not at all. There were hardly enough servants to keep the house running. The last thing they needed to be doing was serving breakfasts to people in their rooms.

"Everyone except my wife will eat breakfast in the breakfast room from now on," he'd decreed. "The countess may eat whenever she wishes, wherever she wishes."

By *everyone,* he meant Julia and Edmund.

All the ancient great aunts and uncles who'd littered Stoke when he'd been a boy had died off. To a one, they had been dismissive and obnoxious to him. He now knew that most of their behavior had been his uncle's fault—anyone who was kind to Henry had risked censure from the earl.

In any event, the breakfast room was now the only place for his two remaining hangers on to eat.

He arrived in the small, sunny room to find a series of chafing dishes on the rather gothic sideboard. As usual, Mrs. Jenkins was on hand to see that Henry's coffee arrived scalding hot.

"Good morning, my lord," she said, dispensing the black, viscous brew from a steaming silver pot.

"Good morning, Mrs. Jenkins."

"Your coddled eggs will be here shortly, my lord."

Henry nodded, not wanting to look at her and encounter the worshipful gaze she seemed to reserve just for him.

"And here is the post… my lord." She hovered just to the right of his chair.

Henry sighed and looked up to find her staring down at him like a proud headmaster with his prime student. He couldn't help being amused by how many times she'd said *my lord* in the past five minutes.

The master and servant dynamic between them made Henry more than a little uncomfortable. For all intents and purposes, Jenkins had been his mother *and* his father when he'd been growing up. While she'd never been affectionate—at least not in words—she had treated him with kindness, making sure that he had a gift to open on Christmas morning, something special on his birthday, and that he was decently, if not expensively, clothed. Given his uncle's clutch-fisted ways, Henry suspected that Mrs. Jenkins had spent her own money on him.

"I shall be at Stoke all day," he said, taking a sip of coffee and almost groaning in pleasure at the black, oily brew. "I want to speak to you about the servant situation."

"Her ladyship meets with me at eleven, but I have nothing after that, my lord."

"Her ladyship? You mean my wife?"

"Yes, my lord."

Hmm, interesting. Annis hadn't mentioned that to him. But then he'd hardly seen her other than to bed her or eat dinner with her.

"Come to my study at noon and bring a list of what we need."

"Her ladyship and I have been conducting an inventory, my lord. I shall be ready."

It pleased him that Annis was taking matters in hand.

"You may go," Henry said, knowing she was content to stand and stare if he allowed it. He turned to the pile of mail, not really relaxing until he heard the door close behind her. The way she looked at him—so worshipful and needy—made him anxious. How should he respond?

He'd spoken with her his third morning at Stoke and offered to pension her off and she'd looked stricken.

"But… I wish to stay here and work, my lord. Please, don't send me away," she'd begged.

Henry had felt like a bloody ogre at her response and had allowed the matter to drop. But he felt strange every time he had to give her an order, something he had to do often as she was his housekeeper.

The Language of Love

He sighed and turned his attention to his mail, most of which was business-related, either having to do with his shipping company or the many properties he'd acquired over the last two years.

The only private correspondence that came was for Annis. Today there was a letter from Lady Sedgwick. Henry smiled at her copperplate handwriting, so proper and lovely, just like the woman herself.

There was another letter for Annis and he had to squint at the messy frank in the corner to decipher it.

He scowled; it was from Avington. Wasn't it unusual for men to write to women who were not related to them? Henry glared at the envelope, as if it would give him answers.

He knew Avington held a special place for the female teachers from the Stefani school. He'd seen first-hand how at least four of them—Annis, Lady Sedgwick, the Countess of Broughton, and that little termagant Lorelei Fontenot—had all treated Avington as if he were a special pet.

To say that Henry was annoyed that Avington was writing to his wife was an understatement. Henry *seethed* with jealousy.

His first reaction was to send the man an angry letter demanding that he stop corresponding with his wife—and also to forbid Annis to write back to him.

Not only was he disgusted by his primitive impulse, but he was wise enough to know it would be exceedingly ill-advised. Yes, she was his wife and legally bound to obey him. Henry could use every method short of murder to discipline her. But the thought of making her unhappy was viscerally repugnant to him. She was his wife, dammit, not his serf.

Henry scowled at the letter; he would say and do nothing. She could exchange letters with whomever she bloody well chose.

The door opened, and Henry looked up. He must have been glaring because Harold, the young footman, froze in the doorway, clutching a tray of food to his chest like a shield.

"Come in," Henry barked, not helping the lad's composure.

He tossed Avington's letter onto the pile for Annis and turned back to his meal, shoving Miles Bloody Ingram from his mind.

An hour later he'd gone through all his mail and was just finishing his second pot of coffee—and also the *Times*, which he had delivered along with several other newspapers—when Edmund drifted into the room.

Drifted. That was an excellent word to describe his cousin. And heir.

"Henry—haven't seen you about this early." Edmund's face was wrinkled and red, as if he'd hastily packed it into a too-small box the night before.

Henry glanced pointedly at his watch: it was after eight. He rarely lingered so late in the breakfast room, but since he would spend the day at Stoke, he'd decided to take his time.

"I would like you to come to the library at nine." It was too bloody early to cock up his day by having to speak to his cousin, but he might as well get it over with.

Edmund hesitated, the milk pitcher paused above his tea, which he was systematically destroying with both milk and sugar. "Is aught amiss?"

Henry allowed himself a very unpleasant smile, which grew even larger when his cousin blanched. "That is what we shall talk about in three-quarters of an hour." He tossed his frayed linen napkin onto the table and stood.

Unfortunately, the door opened before he left and Julia entered.

Her face lit up when she saw him. For a moment, it transported him back twenty years and his heart lurched uncomfortably in his chest. How many hours had he spent dreaming about her smiling at him like that? Several days' worth of mooning if you added it all up.

Now her smile just made him want to hurt her—not physically. No, he wanted to crush her spirit and humiliate her. He wanted to see her weeping and humbled, cast out and terrified for her future, as he had been all those years ago.

He wanted retribution.

It was not a gentlemanly feeling, but he didn't give a damn.

"Henry, I'd begun to suspect that you only materialized long enough to eat your dinner every night." Her laughter was melodic enough to make angels weep.

"Suspect no longer, Julia. Here I am." He smiled and her own smile dimmed at whatever she saw on his face.

"I wanted to speak to you, when you have a moment, Henry."

"How serendipitous, Julia. I wish to speak to *you*." He stepped closer to her than was polite.

Julia, no shrinking violet, did not step away. Indeed, she blossomed, like some rare variety of flower that only bloomed when exposed to male attention. "Serendipitous, indeed," she purred, her eyes all but caressing his body as they flickered over him.

He smirked at the lustful expression she'd so easily conjured. "I shall be in my study. You may pick your time—nine and noon are already taken."

"You didn't let *me* pick my time," Edmund said.

Henry ignored him, not taking his attention from the beautiful viper before him.

"I am meant to be at the vicarage this afternoon," she said. "Would tomorrow be too late?"

"Tomorrow is fine." In fact, it would be better; Henry didn't want to have the two of them on the same day. He might not be able to control his punitive impulses.

"One o'clock?" she asked.

"One o'clock it is." He sketched a bow and left the two of them to whatever it was they were plotting and scheming. And he knew they were up to something, although what, he couldn't say. All he knew for certain was that it would involve money.

Edmund had received a small bequest in his cousin's will, but there wasn't enough money left to fulfill it—at least not without help from Henry. And Julia's jointure was entirely funded from Henry's pocket. It wasn't his legal duty to support either of them—and he'd not planned to do so. But now that he was married, he'd changed his position. He would pay ten times as much to get them out of his house.

Henry worked his way through not only today's correspondence, but all the other business that he'd allowed to pile up over the last week.

He was deep in a letter from the captain of his newest ship when Edmund knocked and entered.

"Are you too busy?" he asked, hopefully eyeing Henry's disaster of a desk.

"Not too busy for you, cousin. Please, have a seat."

Henry took off the spectacles he needed to read and leaned back in his chair. A quick glance at the nearby long-case clock said his cousin was twenty minutes late. So, Edmund was showing a bit of teeth, was he?

He smiled; Edmund's puny rebellion would make breaking him to bridle more enjoyable.

"I shan't beat about the bush, Edmund." Henry made a mental note to ask Annis about that idiom later. "Why are you here?"

225

Edmund blinked. "But you asked me to come."

"No, not in my library. Why are you living in my house?"

"The family has always lived at Stoke."

"Spinster aunts and relatives too old to care for themselves have always had a place at Stoke. But you have your own estate."

"Falcrest is—"

"Leased. Yes, I know." Henry cocked his head. "Tell me about this lease."

"But… why?"

"Because I would like to help you break it, Edmund. I would like to help you go back to your own home."

Edmund's eyes narrowed and the mask he'd been wearing for the last six days fell away like feathers from a molting bird. "You want to toss me out, Henry. Why not just say it?"

"I want to toss you out, Edmund."

His cousin sat back, as if Henry had slapped him.

"The lease is a seven year one and there are still two years left. To break it would be… prohibitive," Edmund said, his face sullen.

"I will pay you the two years and I will also compensate the lessees for their inconvenience."

Edmund's jaw sagged in a way that was not attractive but still managed to be very satisfying. "But—that will be several hundred pounds, perhaps as much as a thousand."

"Yes, I daresay it will."

"You will pay all that money just to get me out of Stoke."

"Yes."

Edmund gave a laugh of disbelief. "You must dislike me a great deal."

"There is no need to go into that, Edmund." Henry smiled. "Besides, I should think my actions speak louder than words."

Edmund's face reddened. "This will take some time."

"You have until St. Oswald's Day. That seems fitting, doesn't it?"

Edmund ignored his question. "You don't understand. First, I shall have to—"

"I don't need to hear the gory details, Edmund. I just want you to make it so."

"What if I don't have the money to *make it so*, Henry?"

"You lack money?"

The Language of Love

"You know I do! Without the money I get leasing Falcrest I have nothing."

Henry took his keys out of his pocket and unlocked the top drawer of his desk. He pulled out a wad of paper and threw it across the desk; the chits flew like confetti. "Those are yours."

Edmund picked up one piece that had fluttered and landed beside his expensively booted foot. He looked at it and gasped. "Where did you get this?"

"That doesn't matter." Henry leaned across his desk. "Here is what matters: You say you don't have money and yet you've lost a fortune at the tables. I will pay these debts you've accumulated."

"You w-will?" Edmund's eyes were as round as marbles.

"Yes. Every one of them, which is no insignificant amount, is it?"

Edmund swallowed and shook his head.

"Once I've paid them off, that is all the money you will ever see from me. Even if I predecease you without a son and you inherit Stoke, you will not get my fortune."

Edmund shook his head, as if he couldn't believe what he was hearing. "This is because of that one night, isn't? I had *nothing* to do with that. It was all Julia's idea. I don't think even Charles knew what—"

Henry gave a genuine laugh. "It isn't because of *one night*, you pusillanimous little reptile."

Edmund gave a henlike squawk of surprise. "But—"

"You were a complete bastard to me for eleven years, Edmund. You were never the leader, but you danced to both Julia and Charles's tunes readily enough. And now, as they say, the pigeons have come home to roost."

Yet another idiom for Annis.

"That was twenty years ago! We were children, Henry," Edmund whined. "It was just a prank."

"Yes, we *were* children. And out of the four of us, only one of us was cast out into the world thanks to your little *prank*. Only one of us had to feed and take care of himself. Something you have yet to learn to do even though you are fast approaching forty, Edmund." Henry took out his watch. "Now, I have a rather busy morning. So, if there is nothing else?"

Edmund lunged to his feet. "The head of the family is supposed to care for its members, Henry, not exact revenge. You're doing an appalling job thus far."

"I can live with that, Edmund."

"You... *bastard*."

The word had once stung like nettles. Now Henry just smiled.

Edmund stalked from the room and slammed the door behind him.

Henry sighed and slumped in his chair, drained but relieved to have begun the process of claiming Stoke as his own.

Unfortunately, Edmund had only been the dress rehearsal.

Julia would be the actual performance.

Chapter 22

For once, Annis would have Henry all to herself at dinner.

She didn't know where Edmund had gone, but Julia was dining at the local squire's house.

Sharing their meals with two people her husband loathed had not made for relaxing evenings, and Annis was thrilled at the chance to be alone with Henry.

She wore a misty green silk gown that Henry had chosen. The bodice was lower than she would normally wear and there was only one insubstantial petticoat.

Grace had needed to lace her stays extra tight so she could fit into the gown and, for once, Annis actually had a figure.

Today marked the end of her courses and she wanted to make it clear to Henry that he was not only welcome but wanted in her bed.

When she arrived in the dining room, he was already there, pouring a glass of wine from a decanter.

His eyes traveled from head-to-toe-to-head again. Although he didn't smile, she could see he was pleased. "You look lovely."

"Thank you. And thank you for selecting the fabric for me. And the design." She laughed. "All I have to do is wear it."

"Which you do excessively well." He pulled out her chair and then filled her glass with wine.

"Mrs. Jenkins said she was to have a meeting with you today," Annis said after she'd taken a sip.

"Yes, it was most profitable. And thank you for assembling that impressive inventory. I will go to York in a few days to visit my bank, so I shall drop off her letter at the hiring agency and place the various orders she gave me."

"You are going to York? May I come along? I've always wished to see the Minster."

He hesitated, but then smiled and said, "I would enjoy your company and the Minster is well worth seeing."

The door opened, and the servants brought in the first course.

Annis waited until they were alone to say, "Julia says the date for the party is the end of the month."

Henry lowered his spoon. "And is that convenient for you?"

"I have no preference."

He didn't look entirely convinced but resumed eating.

"How is the work progressing on the tenant farms?" she asked when he remained quiet.

"There is a lot to be done and too few workers to do it, but I believe the worst of the roofs shall be patched by the end of summer."

"I would like to visit the farms with you the next time you go," she said.

"Of course. I was just speaking to Squire Benson about a mare he is selling. I think she might be suitable for you."

"I love riding, but I'm not much of an equestrienne," she warned. "I've not ridden in years."

"You shall have plenty of opportunity here."

Although their conversation seemed easy enough on the surface, Annis sensed that something else was bothering him.

When they finished eating, she said, "I shall leave you to your port."

"I don't wish for port tonight. I thought I'd do a little more work in the study, if you cared to join me?"

"That would be lovely."

But it wasn't lovely, not quite.

While they sat in companionable silence, it *was* silence. Henry appeared quite involved in whatever he was working on and scarcely looked up.

Annis sat in front of the fire and did needlework for an hour, but she was making even more of a hash of her project—a cushion cover—than usual. So, she set aside her tambour and sat down at the small secretary desk that she'd been using for her correspondence.

She'd received letters from Lorie, Portia, Serena, Freddie, and Miles over the past few days.

The first four had been easy to answer. The one from Miles, which had come only that morning, was far more difficult.

"Dearest Annis:

I write you this letter in the strictest confidence. I don't know if Henry told you, but I am betrothed to Miss Mary Barnett."

Henry *hadn't* told her, and Annis was curious beyond bearing how he knew such a thing.

She glanced up at him through her lashes. He was wearing the spectacles he needed to read. Was something wrong with her that she found the sight of such a powerful man wearing glasses wildly attractive?

His brow was furrowed in concentration and the brackets around his mouth were deeply graven. He looked unapproachable, to say the least.

She suspected that tonight would not be a good time to ask him such a question.

Annis turned back to the letter.

"It was Freddie who introduced me to my wife-to-be."

Annis bit her lower lip, her eyes prickling. Of course, it was Freddie. She would have known that if she'd hadn't helped Miles, he would have married the first heiress who angled for him.

All their friends knew the story of how Miles's father had tried to force him into marriage years earlier. Miles had joined the army and gone to war rather than marry for money.

Now he had no such refuge.

"I know you use the same man of business as Freddie," Miles wrote.

Indeed, it was Annis who'd introduced Freddie to Mr. Pears, who'd worked for Annis's father for years and had been happy to take charge of Freddie's meager savings.

Because Freddie had no family, she had made Annis a co-signatory. Annis thanked God that Freddie's paperwork had been with Mr. Pears and not at her grandmother's house or Mr. Leech would have stolen it, too.

"I know you are a signatory for Freddie. I want you to give Mr. Pears the money left over from selling my commission. I want him to add it to Freddie's annuity. Of course, she cannot know the money is from me."

"Is something wrong?"

Annis's head jerked up at the sound of Henry's voice. He was staring at her with some concern.

"No? Why would you ask?"

"You just made a whimpering sound."

"No, nothing wrong."

His gaze dropped to the letter in her hand. "Something upsetting in your letter?"

She forced a smile. "I was laughing. Maybe that's what you heard," she lied. "Freddie has several amusing stories about your former employee," at least that was the truth. "I shall give it to you to read when I've finished replying to it."

Today's letter from Freddie was the third she'd received. Annis had shared the previous two—which had detailed Colin's antics in his pursuit of Susanna—with Henry.

"I see you received a letter from Avington."

"Yes, I did."

"What does he have to say?"

"He is betrothed. But he says that you already knew that."

"That is true. I have a shipping contract with Barnett Iron. I met Miss Barnett in London recently."

Annis was confused. "And *she* told you of her betrothal?"

"No. I found out about that from somebody else."

She waited for him to share his source, but he merely stared at her.

Her face heated under his fixed look. "Why are you looking at me that way?"

"What way?"

"I don't know how to describe it, exactly." She didn't want to say she thought it was suspicion she saw on his face.

"Are you going to share Avington's letter with me, as well as Lady Sedgwick's?"

As questions went, it wasn't only startling; it was also unfortunate.

Annis swallowed, stalling for time. "I, er, I'm afraid I can't. It is private."

His eyebrows rose, and he gave her the smile she'd seen him bestow on Edmund and Julia. A smile he gave to people he didn't like, in other words.

And then he put on his glasses and turned back to his papers.

Annis stared down at the letter in her hands, not seeing it.

She hated the answer she'd given Henry and she wouldn't have liked to receive the same answer from him if a woman friend had written to him. Annis liked to treat people the way she liked to be treated, and she'd just done the opposite with her husband of barely two weeks.

But Miles's letter bound her to secrecy.

Hopefully she could make up for hurting him in bed tonight. They had their best, most honest conversations after they'd made love.

But for now, she needed to draft a response to Miles. And to be honest, she wasn't quite sure what to say.

The Language of Love

On the one hand, the extra money would give Freddie a cushion against difficult times. On the other, Annis would be lying to her friend if she helped Miles do what he wanted. Freddie was a proud woman and she would not want Miles's money. Especially not if he was going to marry another woman. A rich woman.

Annis massaged her aching temples. No matter what she did, she would hurt or disappoint one of them.

She couldn't think straight to answer the letter, so she returned the paper to the drawer and turned to find Henry watching her again.

She forced a smile. "You mentioned earlier that you might show me the relics. Would it be possible to see them?"

***

Henry hesitated a moment before answering.

What he really wanted was to be left alone. But he'd been the one who'd brought up showing her the religious icons, so he smiled and stood.

"Of course. Come see the vault that was specially built for the reliquary. It is quite lovely in its own way."

"How long have they been in your family?" she asked as she followed him.

"The fragment of the One True Cross was the first, but it is unclear exactly when that came into the family's possession. We believe that an ancestor who'd joined one of the later Crusades brought it back."

Henry took the key from his pocket and showed it to her. "This is the only copy at Stoke, but we keep a second one in the private vault in a bank in York."

"Is that where you're planning to go on your trip?" she asked.

"That's one errand."

Paying a visit to the bank and inspecting the contents of the safe was on a long list of chores to take care of over the next few weeks. Henry doubted there was anything of value in the bank safe as his cousin and uncle before him, had sold off everything they could sell years ago.

"Has anyone ever tried to steal the relics?" she asked.

"Oh yes, there have been three attempts that the family is aware of, the last one a mere seventy-five years ago. Apparently, the steward at the time took the idea into his head. He got as far as Bristol when he was apprehended, and the relics recovered. I believe that was the most successful attempt. The other robberies were foiled before the items could be taken from the vault."

"Are you sure you should carry the key on you? What if somebody were to steal them again? Wouldn't they attack you?"

Henry pulled back the painting that hid the vault. "According to the terms of the will, I'm supposed to carry the key on my person at all times." He smiled at her. "Don't tell anyone, but I usually keep it in a hollowed-out space beneath one of those andirons." He gestured to the wrought iron dogs in the enormous fireplace.

Annis gave a nervous laugh. "I wish you'd not told me, Henry."

"Why? Are you not to be trusted?"

"Yes, but I'd still rather not have such information."

Henry inserted the key and turned it until there was a dull *clunk* and pulled open the heavy door.

Annis cooed softly when she caught sight of the reliquary. "It's beautiful."

Henry reached in with both hands and lifted the gem-encrusted box with a grunt.

"Is it solid gold?"

"I wouldn't be able to lift it if it were, but there is enough of it," he said, setting it down carefully on a sturdy trestle table that was there for that purpose. He lifted the lid off and set it aside.

Annis stood close beside him, like a girl on Christmas morning. "You're right; the reliquary itself is a work of art."

He handed her the beveled glass box.

She took it in careful fingers, staring at the splinter inside in awe. "Why, it looks just like a regular splinter of wood."

Henry laughed. "Indeed. A person has no way of knowing whether it was from the cross Jesus Christ carried up Golgotha or from one of the many rotten beams that riddle Stoke Castle."

She stared at it in silence, and Henry knew what she'd say before she said it. "If it is genuine, then it is a piece of wood that was touched by the son of God."

"Do you want to touch it?"

"No!" She cut him a horrified look. "Have you?"

"No. It didn't seem right," he admitted.

She handed him back the glass box, her hands shaking slightly.

He gave her the gold goblet next. "This is said to be the Diocletian chalice of St. George—allegedly a cup the saint drank from before he rode off and slayed whatever it was that he is alleged to have slayed."

"It's heavy." She hefted it in her hands and examined the sapphires and diamonds set in the soft gold.

Next was a ruby-encrusted cross. "This is the only one of the four relics that is well-documented. It was acquired during the Crusade led by Richard of Cornwall." He gave her a wry look. "My guess is that it wasn't given freely to my ancestor."

The last item he handed her was a small gold-framed painting. "This is St. Oswald."

She held the small wooden portrait in both hands. "It is very heavy. Is it gold, too?"

"Yes, and those are rubies, not garnets."

"And you cannot sell any of these?" she asked, handing back the portrait.

"Doing so would invoke a clause that would cause Stoke to revert to the church."

It was ironic that even one relic would have been enough to not only repair Stoke but pay off the crushing encumbrances that both his uncle and cousin had accumulated.

"Why keep them here?" she asked when he reassembled the reliquary and returned it to its resting place.

"That is an excellent question," Henry said, closing the vault and returning the portrait to its proper place. "After this year's St. Oswald Day, I will have them taken to the bank. One letter I found in the pile of documents that have accumulated since my cousin's death is from York Minster. The bishop has, apparently, requested to host the relics for years."

"You would consider that?" she asked as they walked back to where she'd been sitting.

"I think people should be allowed to see them more than once a year."

She smiled up at him.

"What?" he asked.

"I like that you would do that."

Henry ignored the frisson of pleasure he experienced at her praise.

She glanced at the clock. "It is late. I believe I will go up," she said, gathering her things. Henry opened the door for her, but she paused beside him, rather than go through. "Will I see you this evening?"

It was her way of letting him know that her courses had finished. Her face was flushed and Henry knew it embarrassed her to be so bold.

Naturally, his cock was delighted by the offer. "I shall be up in half an hour."

He shut the door behind her and then poured himself a glass of whiskey.

Was it wise to go to her? Although he'd subdued his anger at the letter from Avington, it was still simmering beneath the surface.

And yet, if he didn't go to her tonight, then when? When she no longer loved Avington? What if that never happened? Would he live his life without the pleasure of a woman in his bed?

Henry was furious with himself; he'd married a woman in love with another man and he didn't see their situation changing soon.

He'd hoped that Avington would have had the grace to leave Annis alone, but clearly that was not to be. Not even Henry's warning had mattered. If anything, he'd seen a gleam of mischief in Avington's far-too-perfect blue gaze that day. Clearly, *Miles* considered the women from the Stefani Academy to be his purview. He probably wrote letters to all of them.

Damn it, but such thoughts grated on him. Jealousy grated on him.

He threw back the rest of his whiskey, snuffed the candles, and went to his chambers. Norwich, who didn't appear to sleep, was fussing around in his dressing room.

"I'll have a shave," Henry said.

His valet must have expected as much, because there was already a steaming pitcher of water.

Throughout undressing and being shaved, his temper ebbed and flowed. First, he'd tell himself that Annis had a right to correspond with whomever she wanted. Hell, she didn't look at *his* letters or ask to read them.

Henry would almost convince himself, but then he'd remember the tragic, longing expression he'd seen her cast in the handsome lord's direction more than once and jealousy would flare in his belly, threatening to choke him.

The Language of Love

Did she simply tolerate Henry's touches and his presence in her bed? After all, how could she like what he did to her body when she loved another man?

Henry couldn't believe his touches disgusted her—unless she was a superlative actress.

Thank God he'd not allowed himself to develop any deep feelings for her. Loving somebody who loved another would be… unfortunate.

He might not love her, but he did like her a great deal. Too much, in fact.

It would be wise to put some distance between them. He would continue to go to her, of course—he needed an heir, after all—but he would no longer sleep all night with her. The closeness that had been developing between them would only lead to expectations on his part. And pain.

Ten minutes later—less conflicted, although no less unhappy—Henry entered his wife's room to find her reading in bed.

She was wearing one of the nightgowns he'd ordered for her, a creamy white silk that was almost the same shade as her pale skin.

Henry could see the shadows of her nipples through the lace.

She smiled and set aside her book, welcoming him to her bed even though she loved another man.

Somehow knowing that she made the best of her situation soured, rather than pleased, him.

For once, he didn't want to look at her while he took her. Instead, he snuffed the candles on his way to the bed, until only the lamp she'd been reading by remained. He reached beneath the glass shade and trimmed the wick, casting the room into darkness.

Once he'd slipped off his robe, he slid beneath the blanket. Rather than remove her nightgown, as he usually did, he lifted the hem until he'd bared her hips. And then he lowered his mouth over her sex and took his fill of her.

Henry adored the taste of her and reveled in the way her body responded to his touches. He made sure she experienced at least two orgasms before he got to his knees, pushed her thighs wide, and entered her slowly, relishing the sweet sensation of stretching her, making her feel every inch of his cock.

He was in no hurry for his pleasure and took his time, making it good for her by angling his hips in such a way that he brought her to climax once more before he increased the power and speed of thrusts, riding her hard before he surrendered to his need and emptied himself deep inside her.

He allowed himself to rest a moment, to gather his strength, and then withdrew from her body and rolled onto his back.

The only sound in the room was their heavy breathing.

When he finally pushed himself up and swung his feet to the floor, she said, "Where are you going?"

"I'm going to sleep in my chambers." He felt about for his robe on the floor and slipped it on in the darkness.

"Are you displeased with me, Henry?"

"No," he lied. "I just haven't been sleeping well." That was true enough. "I shall get more rest in my bed." Yet another lie.

"Oh. I see." She sounded so small and so... forlorn that he almost relented. But then he remembered she was in love with Avington.

No, this would be best. For both of them.

He could see the faintest outline of her as the moonlight poured over her bed. He leaned over and kissed her temple. "Thank you, Annis. Sleep well."

Not until Henry was slipping off his robe and getting between the icy sheets did he realize that she'd never responded.

Chapter 23

Henry was expecting Julia to flex her muscles the only way she knew how: by making him wait.

But she showed up exactly on time.

He stood up as she entered. "Please have a seat, Julia."

It was difficult not to look at her, even though he despised her. Objectively, she was still the most beautiful woman he'd ever seen. She might be even more lovely at thirty-six than she'd been at sixteen. Her body was voluptuous, and the few lines around her eyes added a certain texture to her perfect face.

But, unlike twenty years ago, when she'd made him as hard as a poker just by existing, she now left him cold.

Now he liked eyes that were a paler shade of blue, hair that was like corn silk rather than spun gold. And a smile that was genuine rather than one that mocked and teased and taunted.

She opened her mouth—no doubt to utter something either confusing, obfuscating, or ensnaring.

Henry cut her off before she could get started. "The first matter I'd like to discuss is the party you've undertaken to arrange."

Only a flicker of irritation, as swift as—well, a swift—flew across her face. "I spoke with Annis yesterday and told her July twenty-seventh would be best. Will that serve?" Her expression said her question was a mere formality.

"No."

She frowned. "Why not?"

"We can have the party on August fifth and roll it into the usual celebration."

"You wish to host a St. Oswald celebration this year?" She appeared more than annoyed. She looked… worried?

Henry watched her more closely, his senses tingling. "You sound unhappy with that idea."

"No, no, not at all," she said hastily. "It's just that we've not done so for the past two years, nor have you mentioned it since your return. I thought you'd dispensed with the somewhat fatiguing ritual."

"It would have been difficult to host a party since Charles's death considering you didn't have an Earl of Rotherhithe—nor a key for the relics." He smiled. "As for the event being fatiguing? Well, fortunately for *you*, my wife will be here this year, so you shan't need to fatigue yourself."

"Yes, quite," she said tightly. "So, you will also host a viewing, then?"

"Naturally. It is the duty of the current earl to share the bounty of the Lord with his people, after all."

For the first time ever, Julia looked uncertain. "I did not think you were especially religious."

"But then you don't know me, do you?"

She smiled and lowered her eyelashes in a way that would have charmed him, once. "I used to know you quite well indeed, Henry."

It was a struggle not to laugh at that. "You knew a sixteen-year-old boy, Julia."

Her lips curved into a condescending, superior smile. "Ah, I can see you still bear a grudge."

"You think this is me bearing a grudge?" Henry did laugh this time. "Oh, darling, trust me—when I bear a grudge, you will feel it most keenly."

"Thank you for the warning, dear Henry. But don't you think we should bring the subject of that night—your last night at Stoke and the trick we played on you—into the light and have done with the matter?"

Henry stared into her perfect blue eyes and saw no shame and no regret. He knew with certainty that she'd rarely, if ever, thought about his last night at Stoke. Indeed, he doubted that she'd thought about him at all. At least not until her husband died without an heir and Henry arrived back in her life, rich and in control of her future. He suspected that for the last two years, she'd thought about him a great deal.

For Henry, that last night was a wound that had never healed; it was a sore he prodded and poked and kept raw, year after year. And she wanted to bring that subject *out into the light and be done with it?*

The last thing he intended was to expose a raw wound to the woman across from him. The only thing such a conversation would do was afford her amusement.

"I have no intention of discussing that evening now, or ever, my dear Julia."

The Language of Love

She chuckled. "Poor Edmund is right, then."

"Oh?"

"Yes, he is certain that you bear a grudge and that you mean to dispossess us both and see us destroyed."

"Edmund is not as stupid as I thought."

Her smile hardened. "The solicitors were kind enough to let me know that any money I receive would come from *you*. Are you saying that you will make my life difficult, Henry?"

"Goodness, no. In fact, I've already arranged to have men work on the Dower House next week. If things go well, you should be able to move in before Michaelmas. As for the annuity, I funded it immediately after Charles's death and the money shall continue to be paid out for the rest of your life."

He didn't expect any thanks from her, and she didn't disappoint him.

"I'm sure it will be amusing to watch me try to survive on such a meager amount."

Henry smiled.

She sighed. "I know you are under no obligation to fix the house or give me any money."

"You are correct—there is no legal obligation, but there is a moral one."

"I daresay I should thank you."

"Please save your thanks, Julia."

"I don't suppose you would consider allowing me to live in the London house, rather than at the Dower House?" she had the effrontery to ask.

"I'm afraid not. A friend of mine is living at Rotherhithe House for the foreseeable future."

Her lips twisted into a bitter smile. "You know it would be better if I did not live right on your doorstep."

"Better for whom?"

"For both of us," she snapped. Her mask slipped, and she allowed her eyes to blaze with the loathing she felt for him. "Surely you're not such an ignorant peasant that you can't see that?"

Henry grinned, beginning to enjoy himself. "What can you expect from a servant's get, my dear?"

Julia gave a harsh bark of laughter. "Oh, how you must be enjoying yourself at this moment."

241

Henry didn't argue with her. "So, you believe I should buy you a place to live elsewhere when there is a perfectly good house here?"

She got to her feet, skewering him with a look of disdain. "I refuse to squirm for your amusement. If that was all you wished to say, may I go?"

"Let me get the door for you."

"Don't bother." She strode from the room with unladylike haste, slamming the door almost as loudly as Edmund had done the day before.

Henry waited for some feeling of satisfaction to flood him, but he felt nothing except for a vague sense of embarrassment that he had bullied a woman with absolutely no power.

That is what he'd become: a bully.

***

The weeks flew by in a busy, hectic blur, which was just as well since Annis did not want to have too much time on her hands to ponder what had happened to her briefly happy marriage.

Not that her life was unpleasant. In fact, other than Henry sleeping in his own bed at night, they rubbed along fine.

Indeed, they had spent not one, but two lovely days together in York. On both occasions Henry had taken time from his busy schedule to explore the town and visit the Minster with her.

He came to her every night and gave her as much physical joy as he ever had, teaching her new and exciting ways of pleasuring each other.

While they spent very little time together during the day, that was the result of exigency rather than any desire to avoid each other's company.

Henry was working hard to get the house and estate in order before winter was upon them. For Annis, there was the refurbishment of Stoke, repairing the succession houses, and the seemingly unending preparations for the Feast of St. Oswald.

So, yes, they were both terribly busy.

And if there was perhaps a little more reserve in Henry's attitude toward her than during those first few days of their marriage, that was understandable, as he was living among people he deeply disliked.

Julia and Edmund, also, had changed in their behavior. Both had cast aside their polite veneers, and neither made any effort to mask their loathing of Henry.

The Language of Love

It overjoyed Annis that the Dower House would be ready for occupation right after the celebration feast, barely a week hence. While Annis got along well with Julia, she did not like the effect the other woman's presence had on Henry.

Not that Julia planned to inhabit her new house for long.

"I shall join a school friend in Paris who has kindly invited me to visit for as long as I like," Julia announced at dinner a few nights before.

"Funny that you've never mentioned this friend before, dear Julia," Edmund had sniped.

And that was another thing. Edmund and Julia fought with each other just as much as both of them *tried* to fight with Henry.

Annis had been relieved to hear that Julia was going on an extended trip. Why Henry insisted on setting her up so close to Stoke, she did not know. By now, she'd discovered that his wealth was far beyond what she had expected. Like his distant forbearers, his shipping empire was one of the largest in Britain. He could easily afford to house Julia in York—or even London—somewhere she would have been far happier and out of their way.

Unfortunately, Annis did not feel that she had the right to interfere in his family business, so she kept her tongue behind her teeth.

And then there was Edmund.

Annis had initially believed that forcing Edmund to truncate the lease on his property was both unkind and unnecessary. But three weeks spent in proximity to her husband's heir had convinced her that a life of leisure was deleterious for Edmund.

Running his own estate would give him a reason to get up in the morning—not at two or three o'clock in the afternoon. He drank copiously at dinner and Annis knew, from talking to Grace, that he went to the village most nights to carouse in the tiny pub.

Each day Edmund became more belligerent toward Henry.

Each day Henry became colder, more supercilious, and more detached.

Each day the atmosphere of simmering violence left her feeling more anxious.

The sooner Edmund was gone, the better.

"Quit thinking about them," Annis muttered under her breath as she hurried toward the vicarage. Henry preferred that she took either the gig or ride the fine little mare he'd bought for her, but Annis loved walking and missed the long jaunts she'd had in London.

As for bringing a servant with her, she did not like to be bothered with waiting while Grace dawdled or worrying about making a footman wait if she dawdled.

Truth be told, Annis needed a little time on her own. She had never lived with so many people—most of whom were there to serve her—as she did now. It oppressed her to keep so many servants busy and directed, so she enjoyed these half-hour walks by herself.

The vicar and his wife, Mrs. Townshend, behaved as if Annis were royalty when they saw her.

"Would you like tea, my lady?" Mrs. Townshend fluttered around in a way that made Annis feel anxious and guilty for causing such a fuss.

"I'm afraid I can't stay. I just stopped to deliver your invitation to the St. Oswald dinner."

Mrs. Townshend did more fluttering. "Oh goodness, personal delivery! What an honor."

And so forth.

Annis could only leave with the excuse that she needed to get to the mercantile before it closed. Even then, it wasn't easy.

"Why, Mrs. Coleman would be happy to open up for you if she is closed," the vicar said.

"She shan't need to, I hope," Annis said, hastily taking her leave.

But Annis soon feared that she would not get to the store in time, as every single person in Stokely stopped her to say something or thank her for something.

Annis never saw Henry with the villagers, so she didn't know how they behaved around him, but they treated Annis as if she walked on water. She suspected that was because she had personally visited most of them.

She had been surprised to learn that Julia had visited no tenants in decades. Apparently, she had embraced none of the duties that went along with her position.

The more Annis learned about Julia and her dead husband, the more she understood that their marriage had been a profoundly unhappy one. Neither the earl nor Julia had appeared to care for much beyond their own pleasure.

Because of Annis's popularity, she had less than ten minutes to purchase the few things she needed when she finally reached the mercantile.

The Language of Love

Another fifteen minutes to exchange more pleasantries with Mrs. Coleman, the owner of the shop, and several other people on her way out of the village and soon it was close to six o'clock, and she had to hurry, or she would be late for dinner.

She took the shortcut through the woods, which led her past the Dower House.

Annis paused when she reached the house, curious to see what work they had done since the last time she'd come by, a week earlier. The new roof was already on, and they had replaced the broken panes of glass. The front door had been freshly painted and—

The door in question opened, and two women and a man stepped out. One was Julia, but she didn't recognize the other woman.

Then Annis looked at the man and the ground seemed to fall out from beneath her.

"Good afternoon, Annis," Julia said, apparently unaware that the earth had just tilted wildly on its axis. "This is Mr. Gates and his sister, Miss Gates. Mr. Gates is enjoying a holiday in the Dales before he takes up his curacy in Kent. They were searching for the wishing well but got lost and found me, instead."

All three chuckled.

"Mr. and Miss Gates, this is my dear cousin, Lady Rotherhithe."

Like a ghost or a nightmare, Richard Leech came toward Annis, his warm brown eyes glinting with amusement. "It's a pleasure to meet you, my lady," he said, bowing when she failed to offer her hand.

Annis could only stare.

"Good afternoon, my lady," Miss Gates said, dropping a graceful curtsey.

"Annis? Is aught amiss? You look so pale." Julia's beautiful face creased with concern.

Pull yourself together. Now!

"No, I'm just a little breathless from hurrying from the village," she said, her voice raspy.

Julia peered at the little watch she kept pinned to her bodice and grimaced. "Goodness! It's so late. We'd better hurry, my dear, or we shall be late for dinner." She turned to Richard—or whatever his name was—and the woman. "If you take a left at the mile marker, instead of a right, you'll find the path that leads to the old well."

"It was a pleasure to meet you, Lady Rotherhithe." Richard bowed, smirked, and then the two headed back down the path.

It was all Annis could do not to break into a run.

"My," Julia said from beside her. "You *are* in a hurry."

Annis had forgotten all about the other woman. "I'm sorry." She slowed her breakneck pace.

"Is Henry that much of a tyrant that he punishes you if you're late for dinner." Julia chuckled, but Annis heard the bitterness in her voice.

She ignored the comment.

"What a nice brother and sister Mr. and Miss Gates are," Julia said. "It is a shame they are only here for a holiday. I love Reverend Thompson, but he *is* getting on in years. It would be nice to have a young vicar who is full of vim and vigor like Mr. Gates. Don't you think?"

Annis had to swallow down hysterical laughter. She made a noncommittal noise, rather than risk opening her mouth.

The ten-minute walk passed in a blur, with Julia chattering away. Annis probably didn't say five words, but Julia didn't appear to notice.

When Annis reached her room, she shut the door and collapsed against it.

How had this happened? Was it merely a coincidence? After all, Mr. Leech had said he was taking up a curacy in Yorkshire. Obviously, he had lied about the curate part, but perhaps he'd intended to come to Yorkshire all along?

But Yorkshire was a big county—the largest in Britain—what were the chances that he'd end up on Annis's doorstep?

She felt the door move behind her and realized somebody was trying to come in. She stepped away, her legs as wobbly as a newborn colt's.

"Oh, I didn't see you come in, my lady," Grace said. "I went down to look for you, but his lordship hadn't seen you."

"No, I just arrived."

"I don't think you'll have time to bathe before dinner, my lady. I laid out the blue and silver, like you wanted."

Annis felt like she was going mad, getting dressed as usual and answering mundane questions about baths and clothes while the man who'd almost wrecked her life—and that of her grandmother—was mere minutes away.

This had to be a bad dream. Surely this could not be happening.

But it was.

Oh God. What was she going to do?

Chapter 24

"Are you sure you're feeling up to it?" Henry asked when Annis invited him to her chambers

He was more than a little concerned about his wife. She'd looked dreadful at dinner. And afterward she'd sat in his study with a book in her hands, never turning a page.

"Yes, I'm well enough," she assured him, her smile more of a rictus.

"Then I shall be up in half an hour."

After she left, Henry turned to the message that had been waiting for him after dinner.

It was terse, but then Jonathan Green was a man of few words, one reason that Henry had hired him in London.

I arrived just a few hours ago. I didn't contact you immediately as I was busy following our quarry. I am staying at the Crown under the name of Ned Bowen. I have a significant amount of information to impart. Please advise when and where we might meet.

Henry quickly jotted out an equally brief reply and rang for a servant.

A footman opened the door a few moments later. "Please give this to Haskell and tell him to deliver it to the Crown right away." Haskell was one of the new grooms he'd hired before leaving London. Jonathan Green had recommended the man, and Henry trusted him implicitly.

Once the servant had gone, Henry threw Green's message into the fire and snuffed the candles before leaving. Just as he was closing the door to his study, he saw a flash of royal blue out of the corner of his eye, the same color as one of Julia's cloaks.

Henry frowned. It was almost midnight; what the hell was she doing?

He barely hesitated before heading down the stairs after her.

But when he got to the ground floor, only a few seconds behind Julia, he did not see any sign of her. How the devil had she disappeared so quickly?

The Language of Love

He investigated the rooms up and down the corridor, but they were all empty. Just as he closed the last door, a maid came from the hallway that led to the foyer.

"Did Lady Rotherhithe pass you?"

Fear suffused the girl's features, as if Henry might eat her. "The countess, my lord?"

"The dowager," he clarified, not for the first time wishing there was a less confusing title for Julia.

"No, my lord. I passed nobody."

Which made Henry wonder why she'd needed clarification about the women, but he left it alone and headed back up the stairs. Whatever Julia was up to, he didn't have time to follow her; he would already be late getting to Annis.

As he made the not insignificant journey to their chambers, he thought about how she'd looked at dinner: frightened.

Henry desperately wished that she would confide in him, but he'd given her several opportunities to clear the air and she'd told him nothing. He could hardly badger her to tell him the truth when she'd already claimed to do so.

Perhaps you don't need to badger her, but just show her some kindness.

I'm never cruel to her.

Cruel, no, but you've been reserved and distant since that letter from Avington, and you know it. So does she.

The accusation, which had more than a grain of truth, annoyed Henry. He *had* kept her at a distance these past weeks. Not to punish her for her attachment to Avington—or so he told himself—but to keep himself from developing… expectations.

Perhaps you might confess what _you_ know instead of waiting for her to come to you.

But Henry couldn't. He simply couldn't.

By the time his valet finished shaving him, he was fifteen minutes late and Annis startled when he entered her room. For once, she was not reading, just staring blankly at the opposite wall.

"I'm sorry I'm late." Rather than snuff the candles, as he'd been doing for weeks when he came to her bed, he left them burning. He needed to see her.

"I thought you weren't coming." She was pleating the sheet, her movements jerky and anxious.

Tell me. Tell me. Tell me, he begged silently.

Instead, she dimmed the lamp beside her bed, leaving only the candles behind Henry burning.

Shadows danced on her pale face as Henry sat down on the bed. "Annis, are you—"

She pushed out from beneath the bedding and launched herself onto his lap, straddling his thighs and covering his throat with hot, frantic kisses as she ground her soft cleft against his aching shaft.

Henry groaned and pulsed his hips, stroking himself against the silky fabric of his dressing gown, which was all that separated her sweet little pussy from his cock.

"I need to see you." He easily put her at arm's length, even though she resisted.

"No," she whimpered. "I wasn't finished with you."

He ignored her complaining and squirming and dropped his gaze to where her gossamer-fine nightgown had rucked up around her bare hips, exposing the golden triangle of curls to his hungry gaze.

Christ, she was beautiful. Henry had come to her in darkness these past few weeks to restrain his impulses. Lord, but he'd missed the sight of her.

He slid a finger between her pouting lips and lightly flicked her clitoris, smiling at the sounds she made as he teased her swollen bud.

Her hand closed over his wrist. "Please," she begged in a husky voice. "You never let me give you pleasure."

Henry could have easily broken free from her grasp, but he was curious what she would do, so he nodded and released her.

She leaned forward and clamped her hot mouth over his nipple.

Henry hissed as she suckled him, bucking up against her and rolling his hips, the motion stroking his cock, which was still trapped beneath his bloody dressing gown. She met him thrust for thrust and they fell into an erotic rhythm that satisfied them both if the purring sound she was making was anything to go by.

When her movements became jerky, Henry reached between her thighs, intending to bring her to climax.

But Annis released his nipple with a damp, sucking *pop* and sat back, her delicate hands splayed over his chest. "No. You always take care of me. I want to take care of *you*." She stared down at him with eyes that glittered like sapphires beneath their heavy lids. "Teach me."

He took her wrist and moved her hand toward the flap of his dressing gown.

The Language of Love

"No," she said again, her eyelids drooping even more, twin spots of bright red blooming in her cheeks. "With my mouth."

His balls, already full and aching, tightened at her words.

She parted her lips and then deliberately swiped her tongue over the lower one.

Henry growled and lifted her off his lap before standing. He shrugged out of his robe, smirking at the way her breathing stuttered when she looked at the evidence of his desire for her.

"Pull off your gown and then sit on the bed with your legs crossed," he ordered.

She quickly complied, baring her body to his greedy eyes.

Henry tore his gaze away long enough to locate the small set of steps that he never used, moving them until they were in front of her. When he stepped onto the first riser, it brought his body to the right level.

It would have been easier to have her kneel on the floor, but the carpets were old and thin, and he didn't want her to be any more uncomfortable than she needed to be this first time. Already he worried that his thick shaft wouldn't fit into her small rosebud of a mouth.

He took her hand and closed her fingers around him, just below the crown. "Use my foreskin to stroke me. Like so." He moved her hand in a pumping gesture, exposing the ruddy head and weeping slit and slicking her palm before pushing her hand back down.

"Yes," he said gruffly, as her grip tightened. "The crown has the most feeling, especially just below the ridge. Use your tongue and lips there. Just make sure you don't use your teeth."

She smiled at that, her eager expression making him throb for her.

Watching her take him was every bit as erotic as the silky heat of her mouth. Her lips stretched and stretched to accommodate his girth, until they were thin, pale pink lines.

Henry groaned at the sight and prudently closed a hand around the base of his shaft and squeezed as she used her lips and tongue to explore him, taking him a little deeper.

"Don't try to take too much," he cautioned in a strained voice. "Mmm, like that," he praised as she bobbed her head. "Now suck me."

She shivered at his raw command, her eyes black with passion as they held his gaze, tongue stroking and cheeks hollowing as she tried to coordinate sucking, licking, and pumping.

"Yes," he hissed. "You're making me feel so good, Annis." He used one finger to trace where her slick lips wrapped around his shaft. "So beautiful."

She scraped him a little, but Henry didn't care. His Annis was a quick learner and once she forgot to be embarrassed about the wet, sucking sounds such an endeavor created, her motions became more confident.

He carded his fingers through her thick mass of curls, struggling to keep his touch light when what he really wanted was to ride her sweet mouth like a demon.

Instead, he pulsed his hips in a barely perceptible motion, reveling in the sight of his length sliding in and out of her mouth.

He wanted to make it last and last, but all too soon, he had to stop her. Henry didn't want to spend in her mouth and disgust her. He adored how much she wanted to please him. The last thing he wanted was to destroy her innocent eagerness.

There was another reason he didn't want to empty in her mouth. Because putting a baby in her belly had become a mania with him. Never before had he wanted a child—or a family—and yet now the idea of a little girl who looked just like her, or a boy who had Henry's large body but his mother's fine looks and sunny disposition, had become something he even dreamed about.

There was also the primitive desire to mark her in a way that was plain to the world.

You mean plain to Avington.

Fine, yes! Plain to Avington. He might have Annis's heart, but at least Henry got to live his life with her and have children together.

Henry was getting far too close to the edge of his self-control, so he laid a hand on her shoulder and stilled her motions before carefully removing his cock from heaven.

Annis's lips clung to him, her kitten tongue flicking his slit to lure him back.

"You're not making this easy, darling," he said through gritted teeth, unspeakably aroused by her desire for him.

"Was I bad at it, Henry?"

"You were incredible," he assured her, nudging her onto her back as he climbed up onto the bed and spread her thighs. "But I want to be in here." He pushed a finger between her swollen lips, breaching her tight entrance and fingering her tight channel with deep, vigorous

The Language of Love

strokes until she was writhing and bucking and drenching him with her pleasure.

Once her body was limp and relaxed, he withdrew his slick digit and licked it clean, smirking at her stunned gaze.

"Henry," she whispered, her eyes comically huge, her cheeks a brilliant scarlet. "That's so *wicked.*"

He grinned and positioned himself between her thighs, sliding his hands beneath her buttocks to lift her and line himself up. And then he entered her with one hard, long stroke.

Her back arched off the bed as she took all of him, her tight sheath flexing hard enough to be painful, but oh what an exquisite pain it was.

Henry angled himself in a way that would give them both pleasure and then proceeded to work her harder than he'd ever done in the past, suddenly desperate to be in her as deeply as he could go.

Annis was like a wild thing as he pumped into her. She scored his chest with her nails, her hips bucking to meet his, her cries echoing loudly in the vast bedchamber.

"Henry!"

Henry surrendered to his own need as she came, pounding her with a flurry of savage thrusts before hilting himself and emptying his balls deep inside her. His body jerked with each spasm of his cock and he filled her with jet after jet of seed. Annis held him tightly as her inner contractions milked him until there was nothing left.

Henry began to roll off her, but she wrapped her legs around him, holding him tight to her body. "Stay," she whispered. "Lay on me for a little while. I want it, Henry. Please."

Henry nodded. *Just for a minute, no longer*, he promised himself.

But he must have dozed for longer than a few minutes because his back was cold when he woke.

"I'm crushing you," he mumbled groggily, rolling off her.

"No, you're not," she wheezed.

Henry wanted nothing more than to spoon her to his chest and sleep.

But that would be a mistake—a *grave* mistake.

Before he could sit up, she grabbed his upper arm, her fingers digging into the bulge of muscle, her small hand not coming close to spanning his biceps. "Sleep with me tonight."

The pleading in her eyes did something to his breathing.

"Just for a little while."

Henry knew he'd regret this decision later, but he nodded. "Let me snuff the candles, first."

When he came back to bed, she'd pulled back the blankets for him. He'd hardly laid all the way down before her small body pressed against his, her back to his front.

Henry gave a sigh of contentment and ignored the very faint warning voice in his head.

Tomorrow he could deal with the voice.

Tonight, he would sleep with his wife.

Chapter 25

Annis lived in constant dread of receiving a message from Richard. She wasn't stupid; now that he knew who she was, he would want to take advantage of her connections just as he had the last time.

Even though the days before the St. Oswald's Feast were a mad rush, she didn't step foot out of the house, sending servants on any errands or trips into Stokely. She was behaving like a child, hiding away at Stoke and pretending that he couldn't hurt her if she didn't see him.

But now there was a chore that she could not delegate to a servant.

"It is a tradition for the mistress of Stoke to deliver the St. Oswald baskets," Julia told Annis last night when the two of them had retired to the sitting room after dinner.

It had surprised Annis that the other woman had joined her. She'd also been disappointed since she'd hoped to go to Henry's study and catch up on some correspondence.

But she could hardly beg off when she so rarely saw Julia these days. Besides, the woman would be gone in less than a week; Annis could put up with her until then.

The antipathy between Henry and Julia now ran in both directions. Whatever had transpired between them, Julia avoided Henry as much as he did her.

"I would accompany you to deliver the baskets if I were not so busy," Julia had said when Annis asked if she would come with her.

Julia had only stayed a scant half-hour in the sitting room before retiring to her own quarters, almost as if she'd *only* joined Annis to deliver the news about the baskets.

Perhaps she had. After all, despite Julia's initial claim that *she* wanted to arrange their welcome home/congratulations party the other woman had handed over all aspects of running Stoke and organizing the feast and ball.

Annis had never organized a party in her life.

Thank God for Mrs. Jenkins, who kindly and efficiently guided her through the myriad details involved in such a large undertaking.

"The feast and ball have been much smaller in recent years," the housekeeper confessed as they'd arranged the seating chart for the dinner before the ball, which was only for the local gentry, while the ball itself was open to anyone.

"How many do you usually seat?" Annis asked.

"Twenty at most."

And this year they would have forty.

"Even years ago, when the old earl was still alive, there wasn't such extravagance." Mrs. Jenkins had added. "But his lordship insisted that we invite everyone of any rank to dinner and have enough food and drink to accommodate every single person living in the area. It will be a magnificent way to celebrate his homecoming." A small, but extremely pleased, smile had hovered around her mouth.

It amused Annis how much the rather reserved housekeeper adored Henry. She couldn't help wishing that she felt comfortable enough with her husband to ask him about his relationship with the older woman, but he'd volunteered nothing, so Annis had kept her questions to herself.

In any case, she had quite enjoyed arranging the party with Mrs. Jenkins's help—at least she had until she'd seen Richard Leech.

Since that horrid encounter, Annis could hardly be happy for five minutes before she'd remember he was lurking somewhere nearby. The only time she could truly forget about him was at night, when she was in bed with Henry.

Unfortunately, Annis would need to get through yet another day before she could be in bed with him again.

Even if she delivered all the baskets without seeing Richard today, she knew he could just walk into Stoke on St. Oswald's Day. After all, they invited everyone to the ball.

Tell Henry, Annis. Tell him now before Richard makes any demands. You owe him that much. You owe him—

A knock on her door disturbed the familiar hectoring.

"Come in," Annis called out.

The door opened and Gordon, her favorite footman, stood on the threshold. "The gig is loaded, my lady."

"Thank you, Gordon, I'll be right down." Annis turned to Grace, who was engaging in some last-minute fussing with her bonnet.

"Are we almost done?" she asked. Grace would take all day getting her ready if left unchecked.

The Language of Love

"Yes, my lady." Grace hurried to fetch her cloak from the dressing room while Annis stared sightlessly at her reflection.

Go tell Henry right now.

I'll tell him if Richard makes any demands. He might just be here by coincidence.

The voice hooted uproariously at that.

Annis couldn't blame it.

***

By four o'clock that afternoon, Annis had begun to hope that she might escape unscathed.

They had already dropped off twenty-nine baskets, had twenty-nine awkward visits, and politely turned down twenty-nine offers of tea.

"Only three more baskets to go," Gordon said after climbing onto the gig seat beside her.

"Who is next?"

"Horace Brown. It shouldn't take us more than ten minutes to get to his cottage."

Annis forced herself to relax and enjoy the lovely day, even though her head was pounding. All morning and afternoon her eyes had darted constantly as she'd expected Leech to leap out from behind every bush and tree.

And then, just when she stopped expecting him, she saw him.

For a moment, she believed it was a mirage. But then Gordon said, "Oh, there is the visiting curate, Mr. Gates and his sister."

So, it wasn't a hallucination.

"Good afternoon, my lady," Leech called out, waving at them.

"Shall I stop?" Gordon asked in an under voice.

Annis could hardly order him to *run them down*, so she nodded.

Before the gig had stopped, she said, "Good afternoon, Mr. Gates, Miss Gates. I'm afraid we don't have much time to chat."

Beside her, Gordon flinched at her rudeness.

Leech looked amused rather than offended. "We wouldn't have interrupted your mission of mercy, but poor Laura has strained her ankle while clambering over the stile. Would it be too *terribly* inconvenient to get a ride back to the village?"

"Of course not," she lied. "But I have several more deliveries to make first, so it might be quicker if you walked."

Gordon stared at her; his mouth open.

"I don't mind waiting in your gig," Laura assured her. "Taking my weight off it will feel far better."

Annis ground her teeth. "Fine. But you'll have to sit in the back. Gordon will clear you a space."

"Thank you, kind lady." Richard smirked up at her before helping his *sister* into the back.

Soon they were trundling along again. Thankfully, the gig made too much noise to converse with their passengers. Not that Annis could have talked to either of the *Gateses* without snarling.

The next delivery was a scant few minutes down the road so Annis could escape the pair while she went to the little house. Gordon accompanied her, carrying the huge basket in both arms.

As usual, the lady of the house was overjoyed to see her and begged to give her refreshment.

Annis wanted to move in with the woman rather than go back to the gig.

Instead, she politely declined the tea and went back to suffer through the next hour.

By the time they had delivered the last basket, Annis was as taut as a bowstring.

She had hoped to drop off the pair at the Crown and leave immediately, but she should have known better.

"Oh drat," Miss Gates said as her brother helped her down. "I must have left my reticule at the millinery shop earlier and it is about to close."

"What a goose you are, my dear," Richard chided, his gaze sliding to Gordon. "I don't suppose you'd fetch my sister's reticule while I help her up to her room, kind sir?"

Gordon gave Annis an inquiring look. Annis could see the poor young man worried that—in keeping with her rude behavior—she would deny this simple request for help.

What was the point of dragging this out? She might as well hear what Leech wanted. Not that she couldn't guess.

"Please fetch the lady's bag, Gordon."

The second Gordon was out of earshot, Leech grinned, his eyes glinting maliciously. "Why, dear Annis! What a chore it has been to get a moment with you. Such a grand lady you are."

"Whatever you want, you won't get it," Annis hissed.

Leech gave a mocking chuckle. "Oh, my dear, deluded Annis. Of course, you will give me what I want. Unless you'd like to drag your new husband's name and reputation through the mud."

"Lord Rotherhithe doesn't give a fig what other people think."

The Language of Love

"He will when his wife is facing accusations of theft."

"Telling my husband about me would mean confessing your own crimes, Mr. Leech—or whatever your name is, although Leech certainly suits you—so your threats are hollow."

He shrugged. "If you don't care for your or your husband's reputation, perhaps you might care about your poor grandmother's? I daresay her life would become intolerable if it became known in the intimate village of Cocklesham that she harbored a thief in her bosom. Some people might claim Lady Cecily even *knew* what you were doing and encouraged it. After all, she had so little to live on."

Fear and fury warred inside her. "Thanks to *you,* she had even less to live on, you—you vile, disgusting snake. If you think—"

"Here comes your servant," Richard said quietly, no longer smiling. "Meet me at the Dower House at midnight. If you don't, you won't like the consequences."

"I'm afraid your reticule wasn't at Mrs. Morgan's," Gordon said.

Miss Gates, who'd merely watched Leech and Annis argue with a smile of dark amusement on her face, said, "Oh dear, what a ninny I am! I recall now that it is up in my room. I'm terribly sorry."

Annis barely made it through the protracted goodbyes without screaming.

She kept her jaws clamped tightly shut all the way home, rudely grunting or nodding at anything poor Gordon said.

What in the name of God was she going to do?

***

Henry watched Annis talking to Mr. and Miss Gates—who were really a married couple named Richard and Martha Loring—from Jonathan Green's room at the Crown and Antler Inn.

His wife was glaring at the Lorings with utter loathing.

His footman, Gordon, had run off somewhere, no doubt on a trumped-up errand, leaving Annis and the two thieves alone together.

"Loring has been lurking around your house for the last five days," Green said from beside him. "He and his wife met up with the dowager again last night."

"What about Edmund?" Henry asked. "Has he met with them?"

"The only things Viscount Singleton has met up with are several dozen pints of homebrew down in the taproom."

Henry snorted at the dry assessment. He liked Jonathan Green a great deal and was planning to offer the man permanent employment once this assignment was over. With his wire-rimmed spectacles and slender build, Green looked nothing like the popular perception of a Bow Street Runner. His nondescript appearance was especially useful for investigations like this one, where he was impersonating Ned Bowen, Henry's solicitor from London.

Henry's frequent meetings with Green were causing a great deal of curiosity among the citizens of Stoker.

During his first few weeks back at Stoke, Henry had avoided spending any time in the little village. But that was foolish behavior that couldn't go on. Annis had been right about one thing: it was time to get over the past.

Henry had spent a great deal of time in the village since Green's arrival. As a result, he'd encountered several people who had once tormented him and—to a man—they had all abased themselves. The boys who had beaten and taunted him were now husbands and fathers, some even grandfathers, who were barely scraping by and feeding their families.

And every single one of them relied on Henry for their livelihood in one way or another.

Henry could take no pleasure in making such people grovel.

Indeed, he'd found it best to behave as if he'd never met his former persecutors. Not only did such behavior eliminate unwanted apologies, but it also afforded Henry a bit of amusement to watch their faces when they discovered they had mattered so little to him he didn't even remember them.

One interesting result of behaving like he had no recollection of them was that Henry had begun to forget the past. Forgetting wasn't the forgiveness that Annis had suggested, but it was a step in that direction.

Henry watched Annis drive away with Gordon before turning from the window and saying to Green, "I'm guessing they accosted her today, hoping to pressure her into a meeting."

The Runner nodded, his expression uncomfortable. No doubt he was reticent about saying anything at all when it came to Henry's wife. He was a wise man.

"I'm surprised it has taken them so long to approach her," Henry said. "I suppose he wanted her to stew and suffer a bit, first."

Green cleared his throat but remained silent.

The Language of Love

"Speak freely," Henry said. "Your candor will not anger me."
Well, he'd *try* not to get angry.

"I, too, think he wanted her to stew for a few days," Green said. "I also believe Loring is worried that her ladyship might not be as, er, tractable as he hopes, so the less time he gives her to think once he's approached her, the less time she'll have to change her mind. I believe there might be some difficulty between Loring and the dowager."

"Ah, interesting. You think he's trying to do the job without Julia?"

"I do. Mainly because it is unheard of for Loring to work in partnership with anyone except his wife."

"But he is in the business of selling his forgeries," Henry pointed out.

"Yes, but usually that is an arm's length transaction, and he never meets his clients in person. He either works alone or he sells his counterfeits and leaves his clients to substitute the fakes on their own."

Henry had first learned of Richard Leech's existence from Annis's man of business, Mr. Pears. The older man had become voluble about Leech when he'd learned that Henry was betrothed to Annis.

"Leech forged Miss Bowman's name on several financial documents," Pears had admitted. "And I suspect he did a great deal more that she didn't tell me about. I urged her to tell the authorities, but she became agitated and I did not press her."

Henry knew she would have worried about the effect of a public inquiry on her grandmother. He considered letting the matter go—it really wasn't his affair—but he simply couldn't stomach the thought of Leech getting away with what he'd done.

And so, he'd engaged Jonathan Green and made sure the Bow Street Runner was aware of the sensitive nature of the investigation.

Green had needed only a few weeks of diligent digging to discover that Richard Leech was Richard Loring, a man who'd used dozens of aliases over the years. Most of Loring's clients believed it was only one person who did the counterfeits. In truth, it was a husband-and-wife duo, and they were collectively known by the sobriquet, *The Artist*.

The pair had been operating in Britain for over a decade, stealing jewels and artwork by replacing the originals with skillful fakes.

Many of Green's sources—constables and other Runners—speculated that most of The Artist's thefts went undetected because the forgeries were so good that nobody noticed the originals were even gone.

And *this* was the man—a slimy, clever career criminal—who'd preyed on Annis.

Loring was the reason that she'd been willing to barter herself to Norburg.

He was the reason that she *had* bartered herself to Henry when she was in love with another man—a poor man.

Henry had been furious that she'd kept such a dreadful secret to herself. He'd been deeply offended that she wouldn't trust him to lift the burden from her shoulders. He was her *husband,* for God's sake. It was his duty to protect and care for her.

But then, two days ago, Henry had experienced an epiphany of sorts.

He wasn't the best when it came to putting himself in other peoples' shoes—hell; he was a disgrace at it—but he'd suddenly, *finally,* understood why Annis was too terrified to come to him for help.

The poor woman had been the victim of one of the preeminent swindlers in Britain. Loring and his wife had bilked dozens, if not hundreds, of people over the past decade. The man was a virtuoso at what he did. It was no surprise that she'd been too scared to ask for help.

Lord only knew what Loring was holding over her head to keep her in such a state of fear, but Henry suspected it had something to do with her grandmother, the person she loved most in the world.

She was petrified—and had been for months.

Tonight, Henry would put an end to her suffering.

Chapter 26

Annis's mind seized like a piece of machinery that had undergone so much stress it simply ground to a halt.

"My lady?"

She looked up from the book she'd been blindly staring at to see Grace hovering uncertainly in the doorway of the dressing room.

"Yes?"

"Don't you want to get ready for dinner? It's already—"

There was a brief knock on her door before it opened.

Henry strode into her room. "Ah, here you are. I'm glad I caught you before you changed for dinner." He gave her the warmest smile she'd had from him in weeks—not since those early days when they'd gone for their illicit drives. "I've ordered dinner for us in my chambers tonight. You've been working too hard, my dear, and I think you've earned a leisurely evening." He turned to Grace. "Have a bath sent up to my room immediately. Set up the tub in front of the sitting room fire and make sure it is blazing. Once the bath is prepared, no one is to disturb us until I ring for dinner. After you've done that, you are at liberty for the rest of the evening; Lady Rotherhithe won't need you again tonight."

Grace looked as startled as Annis felt but dropped a curtsey and hurried from the room.

Henry dropped to his haunches beside her chair, giving her such a sweet look that she felt even sicker inside at what she was going to do tonight.

He caressed her jaw with the back of his fingers. "I shall be your body servant and bathe and dress you before we enjoy a relaxing dinner in my chambers."

Annis knew she was gawking but couldn't shut her mouth.

He chuckled. "You look as if you doubt my lady's maid skills?"

"You don't have to do that," she said, feeling worse by the minute.

"I want to," he said, taking one of her feet and removing her slipper. "And I am your lord and master, so you have to submit to my ministrations."

His hands looked bigger than ever on her shoes, which he carefully set aside and then stood, lifting her to her feet.

"Come," he said, leading her to the dressing room, where he proceeded to strip her with an ease and skill that could only have been gained by doing the same thing for many other women over the years. The unwanted thought made her burn with jealousy.

Still, any emotion was more welcome than terror or shame at this point.

"I can't image where you have become so conversant with ladies' stays, my lord," she couldn't resist saying when he got her out of hers both faster and more nimbly than Grace.

"I read about it in a journal."

Annis laughed.

"That's better." He dropped to his knees in front of her.

Annis's breath hitched as she stared down at him. On his knees, he wasn't much shorter than her own five foot one and five-eighth inches.

He took her foot and placed it on his thigh, and then untied her garter, his expression rapt as he slowly stripped her leg.

Annis couldn't resist running her fingers through his thick dark hair, surprised to see a strand or two of gray in among the dark brown.

"Mmm, I like that," he purred.

"How tall are you?" she asked.

"I think perhaps six feet and two inches."

"I'm over a foot shorter than you."

He chuckled. "You're only noticing that now?" He finished rolling down the second stocking, leaving her in nothing but her chemise. And then he stood, towering over her. "Lift your arms."

He'd seen her naked many times, of course, but never with so many candles burning. Still, her body ached for his touch, so she resisted the urge to cross her arms and cover herself. Instead, she did as he bade and closed her eyes as he raised the fine muslin over her head.

There was utter silence for a moment, and then, "You're perfect."

She opened her eyes at the raw need in his voice and saw the same emotion reflected in his darkened eyes. He traced a finger down from her collarbone, over her breastbone, not stopping until it rested just above her pubic bone.

"I don't think your bath will be ready yet," he murmured, parting her curls and giving her already swelling bud a negligent flick.

The Language of Love

"We will have to find some way to entertain ourselves for a few minutes."

***

Henry was so bloody hard that he hurt with his desire for her—but that was nothing unusual.

What was unusual was that he was still fully dressed while she was as naked as the day she was born. He decided he enjoyed that very much.

He also loved the dazed way she was looking at him.

"I think we should make a brief stop at your bed," he declared, and caught her up in his arms.

"You are still dressed."

"Yes," he agreed. "Does it make you feel like a hussy to be naked while I am not?"

She gave one of her adorable gurgles of laughter. "Did you know the word hussy is a contraction of the word *housewife*?"

"No? Is it?" Henry tossed her onto the bed, earning a startled squeak. "Lie on your back, hold your knees with your hands."

Her jaw sagged and he could see that she was visualizing how such a pose would make her look like. "But—"

"Shh." He laid a finger across her lips. "Do as you're told and keep your eyes on me."

The effect of his words was instantaneous: a wild flush mottled her face and chest and the pulse point at the base of her neck beat like a tiny war drum under her skin.

She laid back, her eyes never leaving his as she assumed the position, until she was an erotic butterfly, spread wide for their mutual pleasure.

He'd meant to tease her—to make her beg—but that thought fled the moment he saw her. Instead, he took her in his mouth. The angle was awkward and his clothing and shoes made it more awkward still, but he didn't give a damn.

He was relentless, working her with fingers, lips, and tongue, and pushing her over the edge into bliss over and over, until she sobbed and released her knees, shaking her head from side to side.

"I can't—it's too much." Her body spasmed with the aftershocks of her last orgasm—her third, by his reckoning.

Henry scooped her up in his arms and strode toward his bedchamber, pausing a moment to listen at the door. But all was quiet beyond, so he fumbled for the door handle. Inside his chambers, the fire was blazing. The room was, for the first time, uncomfortably hot, but it would feel good when Annis got out of the bath.

Steam rose from the big brass tub and he lowered her enough that she could dip a toe into the water. "Too hot?" he asked.

"It's perfect."

Henry carefully deposited her in the tub, his cock throbbing when she gave a low, sensual groan of pleasure.

He stripped off his coat and cravat and then rolled up his sleeves before tossing a cushion onto the floor by the side of the tub. He paused to admire her body. The water buoyed her small breasts, the triangle of her sex was shadowy, and her skin was flushed pink and glistening.

"Have you fallen asleep?" he asked, reaching for the washcloth and cake of soap.

"Mmm-hmm."

He smiled and soaped up the cloth before beginning with her hands; he was going to wash every inch of her body.

She sniffed and then smiled. "Oh, goodness—it smells like you, Henry."

"You may have some of my soap, you know," he said, switching to her other arm, his gaze on her breasts, which were making his mouth water, as if he were a beast afflicted with hydrophobia.

She opened her sleepy blue eyes and caught him gawking. Her smile was the lazy and sated expression of a woman who'd just enjoyed multiple climaxes. "Ah, I could get used to this level of service," she teased.

"Me too." He slid a hand into the water between her thighs.

She groaned. "I can't, Henry." But she opened her legs as wide as the tub would allow.

Henry grinned. "Hussy," he said, approvingly. He'd only meant to clean her, but once he felt her slick pearl and silken folds, he couldn't resist stroking another orgasm from her limp body.

"Can a person die from too much pleasure?" she asked a few moments later.

"I shall make sure you don't come to any harm," he assured her.

She chuckled. "Liar."

Henry soaped up his hands and took her breasts in his palms, earning another moan of pleasure.

The Language of Love

He could have played with her all day, but the water was cooling.

Leaving her to soak for a moment, he rang for a servant and ordered dinner.

When he returned to the tub, she smiled and held up her hands. "I'm getting pruny."

He lifted her out and set her on her feet before wrapping her in a fluffy towel and drying every part of her while she remained pliant in his arms, like a doll.

He'd just slipped her arms into a dressing gown when there was a timid knock on the door.

"That will be dinner," he said, tying her sash and leaving her in the chair closest to the fire before opening the door to find Mrs. Jenkins and two maids waiting with trays of food. "Set them on that table, please." He pointed to the long table behind the settee. He would rather organize the dishes himself than have servants faffing about, especially Jenkins. Having her in the room with a wife he'd just repeatedly debauched made his face heat.

"Thank you," he said. "I will ring when I want somebody to clear."

Jenkins bowed her head, a sly smile on her lips as she backed out of the room and closed the door without a sound.

"Mrs. Jenkins adores you."

He turned at the sound of Annis's voice. "I thought you were asleep."

"Won't you tell me about her, Henry?"

He busied himself plating their alfresco-style dinner, using the distraction to consider what she was asking.

She wants to know about your childhood, Henry—it's not like she's a spy who'll be selling your darkest secrets to the French. It's the sort of things married people talk about. It's the sort of things one tells the people close to them.

Henry wanted to argue with his imaginary persecutor, but the truth was he was bloody tired of holding himself apart from her. Maybe if he confided in her, she would trust him and do the same?

There is only one way to know…

Once he'd set up their plates and poured the wine, he could no longer avoid her question.

Henry settled on the chair across from her and began to talk. "My uncle never believed that my parents had married." He took a sip of wine and stared into the glass. "When my father's business partner

Jitesh Chanchani—a middle-aged Indian bachelor who had no idea what to do with a five-year-old boy—sent me to Stoke it didn't occur to him to send a copy of my parents' marriage lines back with me." He stared at his plate, moving the food idly.

"I don't understand," Annis said. "Why would he have needed to send such a thing?"

Henry sighed and looked up. "Because my mother was a chambermaid here at Stoke." His eyes narrowed as he watched for her reaction. "Your husband is the child of a servant and the family black sheep, my dear Annis."

Rather than the disgust that he'd expected, she merely looked concerned, concerned for *him*, he realized, not for her reputation.

"When my uncle—who was the earl by then—learned that my mother was pregnant, he threw her out of the house. He threatened my father with disinheritance if he didn't discard my mother, but my father refused, so my uncle threw *him* out, too. Before giving him the boot, he handed over a deed to some property in India and a small amount of money on the understanding that my father would never return to England.

"So, my mother and father left. They married in London while they waited for the ship that would carry them to India." He gave her a bitter smile. "My uncle could have easily found proof that they'd married, but he didn't want to accept that fact, so he never looked. And when I arrived, he pinned the name *bastard* on me and gave me to Mrs. Jenkins to raise."

Annis raised a hand to her mouth to cover her gasp.

"Jenkins treated me kindly—if distantly. I'd always assumed that any lack of sentimentality on her part was because I was a duty to her." He snorted. "It wasn't until a few weeks ago that I learned differently."

Henry still shied from thinking about that morning ten days earlier, when Jenkins's words had opened a very old wound.

"Jenkins told me that my uncle had threatened her against showing me any *affection*."

"Dear God," Annis whispered, a tear sliding down her cheek.

Henry didn't tell her how Jenkins had wept when she'd confessed the truth to him. Or how she'd dropped to her knees beside his chair, taken his hand, and begged for his forgiveness.

"I was weak and afraid, Henry," she'd cried, her forehead pressed hard against his fingers. "You were just a scared little boy and

268

instead of loving you, I let fear keep me at a distance." She'd sobbed so badly her words were almost unintelligible. "I'd lost my own baby only a few years before taking the job with the earl. My husband and little Tommy both died within a few months of each other. When your uncle gave you to me, it was like my prayers had been answered: a boy of my own to love."

She had looked up at him then, her eyes anguished and red-rimmed. "I don't blame you if you hate me. But... I was so afraid. You see, his lordship t-told me he'd take you away if I coddled you. *He's a bastard, Jenkins—he'll need to learn how to earn his way. Babying him will only make his life harder.*" She'd given a half-hysterical laugh. "You were just a *child*. I should have stolen you away—we could have hidden somewhere; he wouldn't have come for you. I'm sure of that now. But I was weak." Tears had rolled down her cheeks. "Can you ever forgive me... my lord?"

What else could a man do when faced with a kneeling, weeping woman? So, Henry had lied. "There is nothing to forgive, Mrs. Jenkins," he'd said, helping her to her feet. "You did your best in the face of my uncle's vindictiveness. You took care of me and were always kind." That was all true, but Henry feared he would always harbor a certain resentment toward her. Or perhaps resentment was too strong a word. *Reserve* would be better. He wasn't angry with her, but he still felt the echoes of betrayal when he looked at her.

Henry realized Annis was staring at him and shook himself.

"Jenkins did her best to see that I was fed, clothed, and cared for."

"She loves you, Henry. I can see it on her face—in her eyes—when she looks at you."

Henry shrugged off her words and continued, "I have often wondered why my uncle didn't pack me off to a workhouse and can only guess he knew what opprobrium such an action would have brought down on his head. As it was, I rarely saw him. I grew up underfoot in the kitchen. The servants were not cruel to me, but nobody wanted to show me too much kindness and draw the wrath of the master."

He finished his wine and replenished his glass before resuming his tale. "Charles took his cue from his father, and Julia and Edmund followed Charles. The townsfolk and farmers in the area followed my uncle's lead as well.

"I was fortunate to grow large and strong and I learned early on how to fight. But even the largest boy cannot succeed against four or five or more attackers."

He met her horrified expression with a wry smile. "My tormentors were inventive and persistent. I once spent four days trapped in an abandoned mine; another time five boys ambushed me in the woods and I ended up with a broken wrist and collarbone; once they tied me to a tree in a pasture, where I was gored by a bull—that scar I still bear on my leg, and I'm fortunate it was not far worse. Those are the ones I remember well, but there were dozens of other episodes."

"But... *why?*" she asked, utterly stunned by such cruelty.

"I was like a stray dog that was amusing to kick and bait when there was nothing better to do. Bullying, it is well known, is a group sport and there were few who resisted the urge to join in the entertainment."

He swirled the wine in his glass and stared at it. "Life got better when Charles and Edmund, both a year older, went away to school. When they left, even the village boys were less aggressive. And so, for months at a stretch, I could live without the constant fear of violence."

Dark humor glinted in his eyes. "Best of all, when they were gone, Julia would be kind to me. In fact, she would seek me out—because of boredom—and we became... playmates. She, too, had to hide any time we spent together from my uncle."

He gave her a wry smile. "I daresay you can guess what happened next. I was a foolish, lonely boy, and I fell in love with her. She led me a merry dance for a few months, until one night, not long after my cousins came back for the summer break, Julia invited me into her chambers."

"It was a trap," she said in a hoarse whisper.

"Indeed, it was. My cousins raced bravely to the rescue of the damsel in distress, and my uncle accused me of attempted rape. My options were simple: jail or India." He gave a bitter laugh. "History had repeated itself, in a way. Except I left Stoke alone at sixteen, not with a pregnant lover and a property deed in my hand. I was damned fortunate that my father's business partner, Jitesh, is an honorable man. He took me in, taught me the business, and signed over the half that had belonged to my father. If not for Jitesh—well, I don't like to think about it."

The Language of Love

His eyes settled on her finally. "So, you see why there is no love lost."

Her blue eyes were fiery, like the center of a flame. "I wouldn't forgive them either," she bit out, her flaring nostrils making her resemble a tiny, adorable bull.

Henry gave a startled bark of laughter at her fury.

"I am not speaking in jest," she insisted. "What they did to you is a crime. And you see these same people over your dinner table and whenever you go into town. A town that is benefitting from *your* largesse. I would let them all starve!"

A warm rush of pleasure flowed through him at her words. "Ah, my champion," he teased.

But she wasn't smiling. Instead, she was breathing roughly, her chin wobbling, her cheeks darkly flushed.

"Lord, what is wrong, Annis? It was a long, long time ago. You needn't—"

"There is something I need to tell you, Henry."

Ah, was this it?

She cleared her throat, looking everywhere but at him.

"Annis—"

"Please don't be kind to me," she begged. "I can't—just…"

She sprang to her feet. When Henry made to follow suit, she shook her head. "Please, just sit and listen. I need to pace to tell you this story."

Chapter 27

Henry briefly considered sparing her the confession—telling her he'd known about Leech since before he'd left London. But he believed that telling him in her own words would be cathartic.

"A little over a year ago, a man came to the village of Cocklesham. He went by the name Richard Leech and was handsome, kind, and interesting. He was a curate who was taking a last holiday before he moved to his own parish in Yorkshire. And best of all, he was interested in *me*." She gave a mocking laugh. "*Hope springs eternal,* as Mr. Pope said. When Leech paid court to me, I believed he was serious."

She paced restlessly, her hands clutched before her, her eyes in constant motion, as if she were searching for an escape.

"I'll make this pitiful story short. He used his acquaintance with me—a faux courtship—to get him into the local squire's house, among others. Because of his connection to me and my grandmother, they invited him to a dinner party at which he had access to an extremely valuable item. In fact, it was the only thing of value this poor country gentleman had: a small Vermeer that some intrepid ancestor had acquired. Foolishly, the man kept it in his house, in a room all its own. Mr. Leech stole the painting. But the clever thing he did was to replace it with a fake so well-done that nobody has noticed the switch even a year later. That wasn't the only house he robbed. Each time he was invited to social functions, he'd spend some time getting to know the house. He would then come back and help himself to anything of value. Never the same night—he knew that would have drawn attention to him—but a few nights or even weeks later."

Her breathing was ragged now. "I'm telling you all this as if I knew what was happening while he was conducting his thieving—but I didn't know at the time. He only told me the truth after I caught him at it one night. He wasn't ashamed; he *laughed* and told me that if I reported him to the authorities, he would take me to jail along with him—and my grandmother, too. He said he'd tell the authorities that it was my grandmother who'd come up with the idea—that she used her position to get him access to peoples' houses."

The Language of Love

She swallowed convulsively. "He'd been openly courting me, coming to our house almost every single day, eating dinner with us, driving the gig with me—" She broke off and wrung her hands. "I know it was wrong, but I kept my mouth shut and let him go. I thought it would be over when he left, but it wasn't. A few months ago, I received a letter from the man of business I've used for years. He told me that my annuity, my grandmother's cottage, and her savings were all gone. That I'd signed off on the papers."

Annis stopped in front of him, breathing so hard she sounded as if she'd run from the village without stopping. "I know I told you I wasn't holding anything else back. I thought Richard Leech was in my past, that it wouldn't matter. But—but—it matters because—"

"Because he is here."

She blinked. "What?"

"Richard Leech—he is here, in Stokely."

"How—"

Henry held out his hand. "Come sit with me and I'll explain. Let me hold you."

"You won't want to hold me when you learn what he wants from me."

"He wants you to help him steal something from me. My guess is, based on his particular set of skills, that he'd like to steal the relics."

She stared.

"Come and sit with me, Annis."

She came toward him like a sleepwalker. When she would have sat down on the settee, he gently tugged her onto his lap, pulling her small body against his chest and cuddling her.

"I don't want you to look so haunted anymore," he said.

"I have my reasons."

"I know you do. I've known about Leech since the day I gave you the money in London."

"What?"

"Yes, I followed you to Mr. Pears' office. I waited until you left and then I questioned him about you."

Her pale brows drew down in a fierce V. "He shouldn't have told you anything about me!"

"No, he shouldn't have. But I can be very persuasive."

"You threatened him."

"Not physically, but I made him understand it was ill-advised to deny me what I wanted. He also knew the bank draft was from me and that we were betrothed. And he wanted somebody to do something about the man who'd stolen from you."

"Why didn't you say anything until now?"

"I kept hoping that you would tell me the truth."

She dropped her gaze. "I should have, Henry, I know that. But—"

"You believed I would be angry and feel betrayed, and that it would make our already rocky start even worse?" he guessed.

She nodded.

"I'm sorry I didn't speak sooner, Annis. It took me far too long to see matters from your perspective."

"And you know Leech is here?" she asked.

"Yes. His real name is Loring, and he is the preeminent counterfeiter of art and antiquities. If you need a painting copied, Loring is your man."

"And his sister? What does she do?"

"Martha Loring is an artist, as well. She learned her trade from her father, Fritz Doehner, who was a jeweler in some Prussian dukedom until he got greedy and stole from his employer by counterfeiting pieces brought in for repair and sending paste replicas back in their place. He fled to England, where he continued his occupation, but with more success. Eventually, he brought his young daughter into the trade with him. It was Doehner who introduced Martha to her future husband, Richard Loring."

Annis groaned. "He was married to her when he was pretending to court me, wasn't he?"

"Yes, I'm afraid so. But—if it is any consolation—you are not the first woman he tricked and bilked. Not even close. The trail of victims is a long one."

"How did you learn all this?"

"After speaking to Mr. Pears I hired a man to look into the Lorings." He tucked a curly lock of hair behind her ear. "And I also hired him to lure the Lorings here."

"*What?*"

"I knew the appeal of the relics and your presence would be too much for Loring to resist."

"But *why* would you do that?"

"I wanted them to be punished for what they did to you and your grandmother, Annis. But here is the most interesting part, I didn't need to lure the Lorings here, they were *already* coming to Stoke."

The Language of Love

"I don't understand?"

"They'd already been hired to make counterfeits of the Stoke Relics."

She gasped. "Good God, Henry! Who hired them?"

"Somebody close to the relics who could help the thieves enter the house and get into the notoriously difficult-to-rob vault."

"Edmund?"

"That's who I thought it was, but it turns out that I was wrong for a couple of reasons. First, Edmund is far too lazy and drunk most of the time. Second, Edmund still holds out—ever waning—hope of inheriting Stoke. If he sold the relics, he might very well risk losing Stoke if it were ever discovered. No, not Edmund, but one of his conspirators from years gone by, although relations have soured between them in the interim."

"*Julia?*"

"You sound so surprised, my dear."

"That's because I am."

"Why? Do you think women are not capable of thievery?"

"Not at all," she said. "But why would she steal when she has a delightful house and enough money to live comfortably?" She frowned at him. "She *does* have enough to live on?"

"Oh, yes." He didn't tell her that he'd doubled the amount her husband had bequeathed her.

"Then why?"

"Julia doesn't want a life of comfort. She wants one of *luxury*. In addition to getting rich by selling the relics, she could take Stoke away from me—a usurper." He smiled. Judging by the way his wife recoiled, it was not a pleasant expression. "Julia could have just stolen the relics herself, but that would hardly have been any fun. No, it's my guess that she will take the stolen goods, get herself safely away, and then alert the authorities to the fact that the relics in the vault were all forgeries that I was hoping to pass off as real. That way she could yank Stoke from my grubby fingers while branding me a thief at the same time."

"Goodness! Why would she be so vindictive?"

"People hate worst the ones they harm—didn't somebody famous say that?" he teased.

But, for once, she didn't look diverted. "What a hateful person she must be. And she seems so genuine and helpful."

"She is very good at appearing sweet and kind and caring," he agreed grimly. Henry could still remember that night, when he'd truly believed he might end his life on a gibbet, or perhaps be transported to some brutal convict colony.

"What are you going to do, Henry?" she asked.

Henry smiled. "Not me, *we*. We are going to bring them to justice, my dear."

Chapter 28

"You want *me* to steal them for you?" Annis repeated, glaring at the smug husband and wife team. She shook her head and crossed her arms. "No, I won't do it."

Richard chuckled. "I told you she had pluck," he said to his wife.

Martha Loring gave Annis a look filled with loathing. "You also told me that fucking her was like bedding a corpse, Dickie."

Annis flinched at the vile words and hateful look.

Again, Loring laughed. "Now, now, my dear. Let us stick to business." He turned to Annis. "You will do what I ask, or everyone will know the truth about you. And your grandmother."

"I will take that risk rather than become your accomplice." Annis could see that her words startled him. "I'm not a thief, *Dickie*."

Henry had told her it was important that Loring be the one to do the actual thieving if they were to arrest him. "Don't let them talk you around into doing anything, Annis. And don't give them the location of the key too easily—make them work hard for it or they will be suspicious."

Martha Loring lunged toward Annis. "You'll do what Richard says, you little bitch, or he'll—"

Loring grabbed his wife's arm and yanked her back. "Hush, Martha!" He glared briefly at his wife before turning to Annis. "Why are you being so difficult about this? It's not as if your husband could ever sell any of the relics—everyone knows about the conditions. The replacements we made are so good that nobody will ever be the wiser."

"Replacements?" She snorted. "I think the word you want is fakes."

Loring's smile was that of a snake. "Call them whatever you like, my dear. Either you help me exchange them for those in the vault or I will make you *very* sorry."

"You've already used the threat of imprisonment and humiliation. I am a peer's wife, now, so at least half of your threat is without teeth."

He took a step closer to her and whispered in her ear. "You think your status will protect your grandmother? She might not go to jail, but she is a very old lady—they are fragile. They die all the time."

Annis leapt back, bumping into a wing chair that was shrouded in a Holland cover. "Are you threatening to *kill* my grandmother if I don't help?"

He just smiled.

Annis's entire body was suddenly shaking; she dropped her hand to the chair to steady herself.

Richard made a soft clucking sound. "This has become so…
ugly. But it doesn't need to come to that, Annis. I tell you what, my dear, you just get me the key and I'll see to the rest."

"How do I know this will be the last time? Or that you'll not hurt my grandmother?"

"This will be enough for us to live for the rest of our lives. Once we've done this, we're leaving England for good."

"And how do I know that the counterfeits you made won't be discovered?"

Loring nodded at his wife, who lifted the cover off a nearby settee, exposing a black physician's bag.

She took four items from the bag and set them on the sheet-shrouded table.

"Go ahead, Annis. Have a look—I take it you've seen the originals?"

She lifted the dark lantern she'd brought with her and raised the shield to illuminate the items on the table. Her lips parted in shock.

"They are good, are they not?" he asked, his voice self-congratulatory. "Go ahead, pick them up and look closer."

She lifted the cross first. "It's heavy—just like the original."

"Lead coated with gold," Martha said, preening.

Annis picked up the painting next. It, too, was heavy, the gold frame—or lead, she supposed—encrusted with gems that sparkled brightly enough to look real, at least to her. She put it down and picked up the beveled glass case. A splinter rested on the velvet cushion.

"A piece of wood from a wagon spoke," Loring said, his voice thick with glee at his own cleverness.

Annis looked up at him. "How did you know what they looked like?"

The Language of Love

"The Stoke Collection is famous and there are many drawings. In terms of reproducing them, it was not difficult." He grinned. "Certainly not as much of a challenge as that Vermeer."

"You obviously have enough talent as a painter to make money honestly. Why do you do it?"

Martha Loring scowled. "That's none of your—"

Loring waved a staying hand at his wife. "I used to be a portrait painter." A bitter expression flickered across his face. "Wealthy people treated me worse than their servants. They complained if the portraits were too realistic and they wanted Sir Joshua Reynolds for the price of a street sweeper." He shrugged. "So, I went to their homes and painted flattering portraits of their wives and daughters by day and copied and replaced their priceless works of art at night. It was good work while it lasted."

"You got caught?"

"Not quite, but too close for my comfort. And then my darling Martha came up with a new plan. After all, everyone loves a young, handsome man of the cloth, don't they, Annis?"

She ignored the dig. "What do you want me to do?"

"First, where does the earl keep the key to the vault?"

Annis hesitated, but Henry had told her to tell them the truth. Still, it was irksome to just—

"Annis," Richard said, the menace in his voice unmistakable. "If you are thinking of lying, please remember your grandmother."

"It's in the study," she retorted.

Richard's eyebrows shot up, his expression justifiably skeptical. "I thought that was where he kept the vault? He'd never keep the key in the same room."

"He keeps it beneath one of the andirons, there is a hollowed-out place for it."

"Ah, clever—and convenient. I thought you were going to have to sneak it out of his pocket." He turned and looked at his wife. "What do you think, my dear?"

The other woman cut Annis a hate-filled look. "I think now is as good a time as any, Dickie."

***

Henry watched from the woods, Green beside him. Even though the Lorings had never exhibited violence in the past, Henry and Green were both armed with pistols as a precaution.

The windows of the Dower House were covered, but a sliver of light escaped from a gap between the heavy drapes in the downstairs parlor.

"You're sure they'll do it tonight?" Green asked. "My understanding is that they arranged with the dowager to wait until the feast night."

"I'm sure they did," Henry said. "But I somehow doubt they want to split the profits with her now that they have my wife to help them get into the safe."

Green clucked his tongue. "Thieves double crossing each other. What has the world come to?"

Henry chuckled. "Here they come," he whispered, ducking back behind the tree when the servant door opened.

First came Annis, holding the lantern. A moment later, the other two followed, and all three headed toward Stoke.

"I'll be damned," Green murmured. "You're right."

"You go fetch the constable," Henry said. "I'll meet you at the house."

"Aye, my lord—have a care, animals get dangerous when cornered."

Chapter 29

Things were *not* going as planned, Annis thought as she hurried toward Stoke with the Lorings on her heels.

"You want to do it *tonight*?" she'd squeaked.

Richard had chuckled in a way that made Annis want to kick him. "Yes, tonight, my dear. After all, we don't want to give you time to change your mind and do something rash, do we, *my lady*? If you had a day or two to ponder, you might tell your husband. You might even get bold and inform the constable—perhaps even the magistrate."

The humor had drained from Richard's face while she'd deliberated. "We will do it tonight, Annis. *Right now*."

And so, they were trooping through the darkness toward the vast shadow that was Stoke.

Her mind raced far faster than her steps, which she was making as slow as possible, not an easy thing to do given that Richard was breathing down her neck.

"Quit dawdling, Annis."

She stumbled, and he grabbed her arm to keep her from falling. "Have a care," he warned.

"Make up your mind, Richard. Do you want me to hurry, or do you want me to be careful? Because I can't do both."

He chuckled, but there was no mirth in the sound. "When did you grow a backbone, Annis?"

She ignored his taunting, her mind on Henry.

He'd told her he would wait for her in the library. Was he there already? What if Richard got in and out of the house before Henry realized she wasn't coming? What if she ran? What if—

"We'll go around back."

Richard's voice came from so close to her ear that she startled.

"Calm down, Annis. We don't want you expiring from fear, do we?"

"The back?" she repeated stupidly.

"Yes, an entrance beneath the old weapons room."

"I've not heard of that."

281

He laughed softly; the sound so arrogant that Annis *hated* him. If she'd had a pistol, she could have easily shot him.

"Dim your lamp," he ordered as they came out from behind the high hedge.

It was already so dim that she stumbled every few steps, but she trimmed the wick even more.

Richard took the lead, leaving Martha to walk behind Annis. The hairs on her neck stood on end having the hateful woman so close to her back.

Richard led them to a part of the building that she'd never had reason to visit. It was the oldest section of Stoke, and there was a small stone shed attached to the structure, hidden by a clump of shrubs.

The shed was unlocked and once inside, Richard shoved aside ladders and tools to expose a metal door so short that even Annis would have to duck.

Richard yanked hard on the door before it finally opened with an unpleasant screech of metal on stone. "Ladies first," he said, stepping back.

Annis raised her lantern and squinted into the darkness; there was a short hallway with yet another door at the end. It was surprisingly free of cobwebs, so she stepped inside.

"Push on the left side of the door," Richard instructed when she got to the rude slab of wood, which had a metal ring, but no handle.

Unlike the other door, this one didn't make so much as a whisper when she pushed it open and stepped foot into the weapons room, a place she'd only briefly seen the day Mrs. Jenkins had taken her on a tour.

When Richard shut the door, Annis realized why she'd never noticed it. The door itself was disguised by a wooden plinth attached to it, with daggers, battleaxes, and maces on display. Once it was closed, it didn't look like a door at all.

She could only assume that Julia had told them about the entrance. Did Henry know about it, too? If not, he mightn't know that they'd entered the castle.

Fear and dread writhed in her belly at the thought. Should she make a racket to draw attention? Should she—

Richard's voice was a low hiss beside her ear, "Don't do anything foolish, Annis."

Annis swallowed down a yelp.

The Language of Love

"Get going," he ordered.

She prayed they'd pass a servant on their long, winding journey to Henry's study, but at one-thirty in the morning there wasn't a soul about and they reached Henry's study without incident.

"Open the door, Annis."

Annis did as Richard bade her and lifted the lamp shield higher as she entered. The fireplace glowed darkly, the embers a sullen red, telling her it had been hours since Henry had last been in the room. She liked to tease him about his need for fires, even in the summer.

The door clicked shut behind her and there was a flare of light from Martha's lamp.

Richard strode toward the fireplace and grunted as he tilted the andiron off the stone hearth.

"Ha!" he muttered in triumph, taking the key before lowering the heavy firedog. Without hesitating, he went to the portrait covering the vault, and his wife followed.

Annis inched backward, toward the door.

As if she had eyes in her head, Martha swung around. "Not so fast." She lifted the pistol. "Put the lamp on that table and come sit over here where I can keep an eye on you." She gestured to the chair in front of Henry's desk.

Annis did as she was told, and Martha positioned herself so that she could keep both Annis and Richard in her line of sight.

There was a dull metallic *clang* and then Richard's low laughter. "Bloody hell," he murmured. He grunted and stepped back.

When he turned, he had the reliquary in his arms. "This thing must be worth a fortune by itself," he said in a strained voice, setting it on the table with a *thump.*

"It's not solid gold, but it will be thickly plated." Martha craned her neck to get a better look while still keeping Annis in view. "It's a shame we don't have time to remove some of those emeralds."

"We stay with the plan, my dear," Richard said as he lifted the top. He whistled softly at the contents. When Martha took a step closer, he gave her a sharp look. "Keep an eye on her ladyship, Martha."

His wife scowled but stepped back.

Richard opened the doctor's bag he'd brought along with him and took out a bundle of thick felt, laying a piece flat before reaching into the reliquary.

The first thing he took out was the painting. He held it closer to the lamp, turning the religious icon side to side, his grin turning slowly to a frown as he stared.

"What is it, Richard?" Martha asked. "Is something—"

"Well, well, well. What do we have here?" Julia's voice shattered the tense silence.

The way Annis would remember it later, five things happened simultaneously.

She shrieked, Martha shrieked, Richard dropped the painting, a deafening *bang* echoed in the cavernous room, and the silk-covered cushion she was leaning against exploded, filling the air with goose down.

A fraction of a second later, a second shot went off and Richard made a muffled grunting sound before staggering back a step, raising his hand to his chest, his eyes wide. "You shot me," he said, his voice thick with disbelief.

"Richard!" Martha cried out, dropping her still smoking pistol and running to her husband. She caught Richard as he slid to the floor, staggering beneath his weight, and falling down with him.

Annis's head whipped around to where Julia stood, a pistol still in her hand, her lips parted in shock. "I didn't mean to," she said, her face as white as parchment.

"Richard!" Martha wailed.

The door flew open, clipping Julia hard enough in the back that it knocked her forward.

Henry stood in the opening, armed men on either side of him, his gaze frantic until it landed on Annis. He pushed past Julia, who was still frozen in shock.

"Are you hurt?" he demanded, dropping to his haunches, and taking Annis's hand.

"I'm fine," she said, forcing a smile. "Just a bit shaky."

He gave her hand a fervent kiss. "Thank God." He helped her to her feet and slid a steadying arm around her before turning to the other occupants in the room.

"He's *dead*!" Martha sobbed and scrambled to her feet, her wild, murderous gaze on Julia. "You killed him," she screamed, launching herself at the other woman hard enough to knock Julia off her feet.

Henry guided Annis away from the rolling, fighting women.

The Language of Love

"I don't think we'll need the pistols," he told the two men. "Mr. Caldwell, why don't you take the guns and step outside. Please keep the servants from entering the room." He jerked his chin toward the door, where several gaping people stood, wrapped in robes, slippers, and sleeping caps.

Once the door shut behind the constable, Henry turned to the remaining man. "Mr. Green, please separate the ladies."

Jonathan Green glanced at the slapping, scratching women rolling on the floor and hesitated.

"You'd better get in there," Henry advised him, humor in his voice.

While the Runner pried the women apart, Henry turned to Annis. "We were watching and followed you here," he said. "I'm sorry I didn't tell you, but—"

"You wanted my reactions to be genuine?" she guessed tartly.

"Well… yes," he admitted, his lips almost twitching into a smile.

But then the humor slid away, and his arm tightened around her. "I'm *very* sorry they used a gun, Annis. Nothing in their past crimes indicated any propensity for violence and neither I nor Mr. Green anticipated such a thing. I'm afraid I put you in danger."

"I don't think they would have actually hurt me," she said. "Julia startled them, and I think Martha pulled the trigger from fear. I daresay Julia did the same."

Henry stared at the pillow that had taken the first bullet, and he blanched. "Good God, but that was too close, Annis."

"I'm fine," she assured him.

He looked like he wanted to apologize again, but Annis pointed to where the Bow Street Runner was now caught between the fighting women who'd knocked off his spectacles and ripped his coat. "I think Mr. Green might need your help, Henry."

***

Julia was a pale shadow of her usual self, and Henry could not blame her. He had never killed a man before and imagined that it would be years, if ever, before she would get over what she had done.

As for Martha, she was devastated by Loring's death, but a lifetime as a criminal had taught her to adjust quickly. Her husband might be gone, but she still had to live. And she'd been caught in a lord's house with an open safe, a dead husband, and a bag full of counterfeit relics at three in the morning.

285

"What's stopping me from telling the magistrate about your *wife*, my lord?" Martha snarled at Henry when he told her she was going to get in the carriage that was waiting below to take her to Hull.

He smiled unpleasantly. "It is unfortunate for you that *I* am the magistrate in this area, Mrs. Loring."

That shut her mouth with a snap.

"Here is what will happen," he said. "Mr. Green will accompany you to Hull where he will make sure you get on the first packet to Amsterdam. Never come back to England because it will not go so well for you the next time. And one more thing: *never* threaten my wife again." He narrowed his eyes at her. "Do we understand one another?"

She gave him a hate-filled look but nodded. And then she turned her venomous gaze on Julia and spat, "What about her?"

"What about her?" Henry asked.

"She killed my husband and deserves to be punished!" Martha shrieked.

"The gun she was holding accidentally discharged and killed a man who was robbing her house, Mrs. Loring."

"But you know she was—"

Henry jerked his chin at Green, who was standing beside her chair.

The Runner clamped a hand over Martha's mouth and not ungently lifted her to her feet. "We'll be off, my lord," Green said, bowing low while easily holding the squirming thief.

Once the door shut behind them, the only people left were Henry, Annis, and Julia. The constable was still keeping guard outside the door. Henry hadn't sent Caldwell out of the room because he feared his servants would barge in, but because it wouldn't serve to have the man hear any of the conversations taking place inside the study.

"What are you going to do with me?" Julia asked listlessly, staring at her feet.

"You are also going to Europe."

Her head jerked up at that.

"Not on the same ship as Mrs. Loring," Henry assured her. "You will make an extended tour of the Continent—much as you'd planned to do, but without taking the Stoke relics with you."

Rather than look grateful, she scowled. "I won't have the money to do such a thing now."

The Language of Love

"I shall make sure you have ample funds to enjoy a long journey. You were already packed?"

She nodded.

"Remain in your chambers and be prepared to leave as soon as Mr. Green returns from his errand. He will escort you to Dover personally."

She snorted, and her lovely face twisted into a mocking, miserable smile. "I suppose you expect me to thank—"

"Just go, Julia," Henry said. "Go before you make me change my mind."

She huffed and strode from the room in a flurry of skirts.

Once she'd gone, Henry went to the door and opened it again to exchange a few quiet words with the constable regarding the disposal of Loring's body, which had been transported to the village already.

Caldwell looked perplexed by Henry's decision not to charge Mrs. Loring with any crimes, but he nodded. "If that is what you'd like, my lord. I'll see to the burial."

When Henry returned to the room, he saw that Annis had picked up the St. Oswald painting, which had been lying forgotten on the study floor.

"I'm afraid it has been damaged." She showed him where the frame had come loose from the painting.

Henry chuckled. "That doesn't matter."

Annis gave him an affronted look. "Henry, it is a priceless relic—of course it matters."

"It is a fake, my dear."

"*What?*"

Henry took the painting from her hands. "It's a very good fake, but a fake nonetheless."

Annis pointed to the doctor's bag. "No, the fakes are still in there."

"That is yet another set of fakes."

"I don't understand. Where are the genuine relics?"

"In a bank safe in Leeds—exactly where they belong."

He put the damaged painting back in the reliquary, lowered the lid, and replaced it in the vault.

A stitch formed in her brow. "I'm confused."

He straightened the painting that covered the vault and turned back to her. "About?"

"Did you put fakes in the vault because you knew the Lorings were going to steal them?"

"The real reliquary and its contents have been in the bank vault for the last seventy-five years—after the last attempted theft. The set that is shown to the public every year is a fake."

"But… why?"

"After the last robbery attempt, my grandfather decided that keeping such a valuable collection at Stoke was criminally foolish."

"So, all these years people have been admiring fakes?" She snorted. "*I* admired fakes."

"As did I. It wasn't until I went to Leeds with you a few weeks ago to see if there was anything of value in the family vault that I found the originals and a document explaining why they were there."

She frowned. "But I don't understand. Why would Julia have gone to all this trouble to steal fakes?"

"Because she didn't know. The letter—written in 1743—instructed subsequent Earls of Rotherhithe to keep the location of the true relics a secret to protect them."

"But you've just told me."

He slid his arms around her. "That's because I trust you."

"And you don't think your cousin trusted Julia?"

He laughed. "No, Charles was smarter than that. Jenkins told me their marriage was an unhappy one even before it started. Apparently, Charles had fallen in love with the sister of a schoolmate, but my uncle had his heart set on him marrying Julia. Julia did, too, it seems. I gather she tricked Charles into compromising her so he had to marry her." He shrugged. "All these years I believed that he'd taken part in the charade that got me thrown out of Stoke because he loved Julia. But it was just another spiteful prank."

Annis laid her head on his chest. "Thank you for trusting me, Henry."

Henry kissed the top of her blond head. "Thank you for marrying me, Annis."

"Henry?"

"Yes, darling?"

"I really, *really* don't have any other secrets now," she said, her voice muffled by his coat.

Henry laughed. "Me either, love. Me either."

Epilogue

The Night of the St. Oswald Ball

"Oh, my lady! You look like a fairy princess," Grace gushed, her eyes shining as she gazed at Annis.

Annis chuckled. "If any part of me looks like a princess, it is because of your ministrations and my husband's excellent taste in clothing."

Truth be told, Annis couldn't help admiring herself in the mirror, either.

Tonight, for the first time, she was wearing the startling scarlet gown that Henry had chosen for her. The color was not only magnificent, but it looked extremely well on her. She'd worried that such a vibrant shade would make her look insignificant and even paler than usual. Instead, it brought out glints of gold in her hair that she'd never noticed before and made her eyes appear a darker shade of blue.

Grace draped the ruby necklace around Annis's neck and frowned. "It don't look quite right, my lady."

Annis looked at her reflection and had to agree. "The reds clash. But my pearls will be lovely with it." The pearls were yet another gift from Henry, who'd bought them for her on their recent trip to York, where he'd taken her to see the real Stoke relics. It had astonished Annis that the genuine relics had actually looked a bit battered and not nearly as magnificent as either set of fakes.

Grace was fastening the pearls around her neck when the connecting door opened, and Henry entered.

"You might as well take those off again, Grace."

He held up a beautiful inlaid box and grinned at Annis's— likely—embarrassed expression.

"Henry! You shouldn't have. You will spoil me."

"Impossible. Open it," he ordered when she merely stroked the smooth wood.

Annis opened the box, and Grace gasped. "Oh, my goodness!"

Inside the box was a diamond parure—the most spectacular one Annis had ever seen, complete with diadem, necklace, bracelet, brooch, and earbobs.

"Oh, my," she whispered, running her fingers reverently over silver filigree work that was delicate and intricate, her hand trembling as she stroked one of the enormous diamonds.

Annis rapidly blinked before looking up and handing the box to Grace. "Silver is my favorite, my lord. It is beautiful. Thank you."

His eyebrow cocked at the *my lord*, but he smiled. "It is not silver, but platinum, a much harder and more durable metal than silver."

They both looked at her reflection as Grace fastened the necklace.

Henry nodded slowly. "Exquisite."

Of course, she blushed, and Henry chuckled when she raised her hands to her fiery face. "You always do this to me, Henry."

"Because you look even more beautiful with roses in your cheeks. Put the bracelet, diadem, and earbobs on her, Grace. But not the brooch, I think."

Once Grace had finished festooning her with jewels, she dropped a quick curtsey and left them alone together.

Henry came to stand behind her, and their eyes met in the mirror. The top of her head, she saw, didn't reach his chin.

He caressed her upper arms, stroking the place where her skin met the ivory kid leather opera gloves. "You take my breath away, Annis." He dropped a light kiss on her temple.

She swallowed, a dangerously itchy feeling behind her eyes. "Are you trying to make me cry, my lord?"

He grinned. "Are you ready to host your first ball, Lady Rotherhithe?" He leaned low again, this time brushing his lips over her nape.

Annis shivered. "I'm as ready as I'll ever be."

His lips turned up at the corners, his smile sinful and sensual and suggestive of the pleasures they would enjoy later tonight. Looking at the promise in his gaze made Annis wonder why they were having this party at all, when they could be in bed together.

"You're blushing again," he accused. "What naughtiness were you thinking?"

Annis couldn't tell him what she was really thinking, but there *were* two things she needed to say. Well, three, actually.

The Language of Love

"The letter I received from Miles—the one I wouldn't let you read. The reason—"

"You don't need to explain. You are allowed your private correspondence. I shouldn't have—"

"I *want* to explain." Annis turned in his arms, needing to crane her neck to look up at him. She gave an exasperated huff. "You are too tall. Sit here on the bench."

He sat.

"Much better," she said, reveling in the chance to see him at eye-level. She laid a finger across his full, soft lips. "Now, I have several things to say. It will be easier if you let me say them."

He kissed her gloved finger and then nodded.

"Miles wanted to give Freddie what remains of the money he received when he sold his commission. He knows that I'm a signatory on her account and he wanted me to deposit the money without telling her."

Henry frowned, a notch forming between his eyebrows. He opened his mouth, but then shut it.

Annis couldn't help chuckling. "You may speak."

"Why would he give the money to Lady Sedgwick?"

"Because he loves her, Henry. And she loves him."

"*What?*"

"Yes, although neither of them has ever said as much. And I doubt they've ever acted on their feelings—or perhaps they did. Perhaps they would have married if Miles had not inherited, but I somehow doubt it. Something bad must have happened to Freddie during her marriage because she has always said that she will never remarry. By the way," she added, when Henry continued to goggle. "I wrote to Miles and asked his permission to tell you, so I am not speaking out of turn." She narrowed her eyes at him. "Why are you looking at me that way?"

"I thought it was you."

"Me, what?"

"That Avington loved."

Annis laughed. "Miles? Lord, no! I think of him as a brother."

"I thought you loved him."

Annis stopped laughing when she saw the intense, almost pained expression in his beautiful eyes. "Why would you think that?"

Henry inhaled deeply, his enormous chest expanding and expanding, until he finally exhaled in a huff. "Never mind. I was obviously mistaken."

She cupped his jaw. "Have you been thinking I was pining for Miles?"

He shrugged, but the slight flush of color over his cheekbones told her she'd guessed correctly.

"Oh no, Henry," she murmured, brushing a thumb over his lips. "I'm so sorry. Why didn't you say something? Why, you must have thought—"

"Shh," he whispered. "It's my fault, you have nothing to be sorry for."

She snorted. "Well, I *was* allowing another man to court me while seeing you. No doubt you believed me capable of being in love with Miles *and* courting Mr. Norburg *and* marrying you. I made a mull of things, Henry. But I don't love anyone else." She kissed him, a slow, thorough, lingering kiss. When she finally pulled away, she said, "Except you."

His reddened lips parted in shock.

"Why do you look so surprised? Have I not shown you I love you?"

"I thought you were merely putting the best face on things."

She laughed at that. "I'm not that good an actress."

Henry took her face in his hands and kissed her until they were both breathless. *"Main tum sy pyar karta hun."*

"What does that mean?"

"I love you."

Her eyes welled with tears, and one slid down her cheek.

"Good Lord, don't cry, love," he begged.

"I can't help it," she sniffed. "I'm so happy."

He pulled a terrified face and wiped away the tears that wouldn't stop coming. "Maybe next time you're happy, you could just smile or laugh?"

She gave a watery chuckle. "Well, I can't promise that I won't be emotional and weepy for the next eight months."

"Hmm." He kissed her cheek, his tongue flicking out as quick and light as a snake's to lap up a tear. "Salty," he murmured, kissing a trail down her cheek to her jaw. And then he suddenly pulled back. "Eight months?" he repeated, eyes wide. "Do you mean—"

"I think so. Mrs. Jenkins thinks so, too." She cocked her head when he just stared. "Are you happy?"

"I'm so happy that I might start crying, myself." He was smiling, but his voice was rough with emotion.

Annis laughed, and he caught her up in a crushing hug, holding her so tightly that she could barely draw a breath.

"You'll flatten your lovely cravat," she wheezed.

"I love you so much, Annis," he said, the words fierce and hot against her scalp. "I feel like I've waited a lifetime for you." He put her at arm's length as suddenly as he'd embraced her, his gaze hot with more than just desire this time. "But it was worth the wait, darling."

Annis was crying openly now. "Look what you've done to me."

He daubed at her face with his handkerchief. "Lord. Everyone will think I've been beating you."

"You made me forget about the ball," she said, attempting to straighten his crushed cravat.

"I'd *like* to forget about it," he muttered. "I'd *like* to take you back to bed. And I'd *like* to keep you there for a solid week."

She groaned. "We can't."

"No, we can't."

"How will we ever get through the evening, Henry?"

Henry took her hand, gave it a light squeeze, and gave her one last, lingering kiss. "Together, darling. We'll get through it together."

I hope you enjoyed Henry and Annis's story of love!

The next book in *The Academy of Love* series features Miles, the new Earl of Avington, and his marriage of convenience with the scarred and reclusive heiress Mary Barnett.
Check out my website: www.minervaspencer.com to read an excerpt of
DANCING WITH LOVE...

The password to read the free excerpt is: romance
That's all lower case letters.
I hope you enjoy it!

Printed in Great Britain
by Amazon

81357127R00174